PALM TREE PIPE DREAMS

A Novel

by

Maureen Paraventi

Palm Tree Pipe Dreams is a work of fiction. Names, characters, places and incidents are the products of the author's imagination or are used fictitiously. Any resemblance to actual events, locales or persons, living or dead, is entirely coincidental.

Visit the author's website at: www.maureenparaventi.com.

CALIFORNO*

Well I woke up tired in a cheap motel
On the edge of the desert, on the edge of dawn
You were already up and havin' a smoke
Drinkin' gas station coffee, ready to move on.

California's in the rear view mirror
Palm tree pipe dreams, lapping at the shore
The more miles behind us, the more it gets clearer
I wanted you
And you wanted more.

Coyotes howl in the Hollywood Hills
Or was that just another bad dream of yours?
And the mudslides tumble down on Malibu
It's a postcard paradise, but who's keeping score?

How winds blow through the Valley of Dreams
But you wiped my margarita tears away
We got lost on the billboard boulevard
Where the seasons don't change and the players don't play.

Stars in the sidewalk and signs in the hills
Dreams by the ocean are pulling me
underneath the memory of who we were
Your features now just a beautiful blur.

California's in the rear view mirror
Palm tree pipe dreams, lapping at the shore
The more miles behind us, the more it gets clearer
I wanted you
And you wanted more.

Lyrics and music by Maureen Paraventi, ©2009

Download the mp3 of "**Californo**" here:
www.cdbaby.com/cd/themclaughlins6

Table of Contents

PART ONE

PART FOUR

PART ONE

CHAPTER ONE:
BEVERLY HELLS

Ira O'Riley dialed the number of the casting director and tensed, sucking hard on a Mentos, the freshmaker. Adrenaline kicked up the tempo of his heartbeat, producing a delicious tingling sensation throughout the length of his body.

He focused on concocting a mental image of himself as a swimmer crouched on a diving platform high over the glassy azure rectangle of a pool, poised for a demonstration of superb athleticism. Detail by detail he fleshed out the scene. *Think of it like a paint-by-numbers canvas*, the Power to Succeed Workshop instructor had explained. *And when you've filled in every last blank, you'll be ready to act. You'll be powerful.*

He concentrated fiercely, visualizing himself as the diver: broad shoulders rigid and ready, his even breath lifting his ripped chest in a steady rhythm, the rock-hard muscles of his arms and legs in a relaxed but ready state. Like a coiled cobra. No, no. He deleted the cobra image from his mind. Best not to mix metaphors. He was doing so well with the diving scenario that he felt momentarily dizzy, looking down from his imaginary but spectacularly high perch above the imaginary but invitingly blue pool. He could almost feel the sun overhead, baking his skin warm. The diver -- Ira O'Riley, that is, bent his athletic knees and leaned ever so slightly forward, perfectly balanced, while the imaginist Ira O'Riley inserted the final few details into his mental Picture of Personal Power. He could actually see the fine golden hairs on his tanned forearms, the dry brown foothills of the Valley in the distance. He was almost finished and then he could--

No! No, stop! His imaginative powers suddenly abandoned him. Helplessly, he witnessed the arms that were corded with heavy muscles morph into skinny ones, pale and undefined. His real arms. The legs in his mental image stayed long but, in a queasy flash of reality, lost a great deal of their mass, turning from strong to spindly, from tanned to skim milky white. His Herculean chest collapsed into a concave shape. Deprived of its central character, the rest of the imagery swirled away like sudsy water disappearing down a drain. Olympic Diver Ira surveying his watery realm from on high disappeared. Skinny Loser Ira remained, sitting in an office chair at a cluttered desk overlooking the reception area of a successful Beverly Hills talent agency in which he was nothing but a low-level drone.

Damn. Damn damn damn. Sid was waiting for him to place this call. So what, if he couldn't use the techniques learned at the workshop he'd attended last weekend, the latest in a series of workshops, seminars, classes and self-help books and tapes that were supposed to transform him from peon into player? He could still pull this off the way he wanted to, but it would require timing both elegant and ruthless. Also finesse -- he couldn't forget about finesse. He reminded himself that this agency experience was simply practice for what he really wanted to do with his Personal Power: pitch his screenplays to producers. This was all just one long dry run for the day when he'd finally start living his own life, instead of being a wage slave commanded to do menial chores by Sid.

The bitterly sharp morning sunlight swept up chromey glints from the many cars and trucks stuck in Wilshire Boulevard, several stories below, and shifted them through his window at an angle painful to the eye. He stood in his customary slouching posture, cradling the phone against one ear, and subdued the aggressive light by twisting the cord that splayed the Venetian blinds across the window. Sometimes the sunshine was hateful to him. Like so much else in Southern California, it was illusory. As bright and attractive as the day appeared, he knew that if he tried to go outside on his lunch hour he'd end up wheezing and gasping, his eyes stinging, his nose dribbling snot and his asthmatically-shrunken lungs straining from the foul particulates in the gorgeously sunny sky.

Sid hadn't buzzed him yet about the call, so he procrastinated some more. How would he write this as a scene?

INT. HALLWAY -- OFFICE BUILDING -- DAY

TWO YOUNG WOMEN dressed in trendy, semi-casual office attire stride down a hallway, chatting. They pass a door stenciled with the title: MIDWOOD AGENCY.

INT. AGENCY LOBBY -- DAY

IRA O'RILEY, dressed in khakis and a short-sleeved shirt, sits at a desk, holding a phone to his ear. Ira is tall, thin and unhappy-looking.

Ira mentally crossed out the last sentence and instead mentally wrote: IRA O'RILEY leans his long, agile frame back in the chair, a determined expression on his handsome face.

> IRA
> *I don't want to hear it, Palmer.*
> *You get Ruben on the phone*
> *within the next two seconds or I*
> *will personally see to it that*
> *you're out of a job by this*
> *afternoon!*

He waits, listening.

> IRA (CONT.; angrily)
> *I don't care if he's on the line*
> *with Scorcese! He can damn*
> *well call Scorcese back!*

Reenergized, pleased with himself for coming up with bold dialogue (*He can damn well call Scorcese back!*), Ira finally dialed the number. He had mad skills and it was time to use them.

"Ruben Leckner's office," said the petulantly gay, posh London-accented voice of Palmer Lu, Ruben's assistant. Ira despised Palmer, and *not* because he was a total phony: Chinese features topped with platinum hair, an American (Ira was almost sure) who spoke with a snobby British accent. It was a good bet

3

the name Palmer was fake, too. His real name was probably something ordinary, like Dave, or Herb. None of that mattered. Phony was embraced in the entertainment industry. It was Palmer's arrogance that annoyed him. Palmer was a thrall (almost a zero), just as Ira was, but he acted as if he was so much more.

At this moment, as befitting an assistant to a casting director, Palmer was vocally poised to go in one of several directions. If the caller turned out to be a producer wanting to hire Ruben to help cast a new project, Palmer would spin that tone into cotton candy-level sugary sweetness, quickly affecting the warm, deferential tones of a true ass-kisser.

If the caller was an actor, God forbid, some feckless, misguided soul who thought that calling up a casting director was a way to get a role, Palmer's voice would turn chill and pitiless, making that pathetic creature quickly wish he or she was back in Little Rock, Arkansas or Bemidji, Minnesota, still doing community theater and waiting on customers at Denny's.

If the caller proved to be from an important agent's office -- as was the case now -- Palmer would be sleekly professional. Agents -- the right agents, anyway -- were actually *necessary* to casting directors. They served as screeners, sifting through the flotsam of wannabe actors that floated into L.A. on an endless succession of human waves, finding the few worthy ones or more accurately, the few lucky ones that might be castable and referring them to casting directors for the appropriate roles. Agents and casting directors were linked together on the Hollywood food chain.

"Hi, Palmer." Ira's own voice was pitched exactly halfway between assurance and haughtiness. He might be a peon, but he worked for a player. "It's Ira, in Sid Kirschenbaum's office. Sid would like to talk to Ruben."

His breezy delivery was rooted in a subtext of which Palmer was well aware. Before starting his own boutique agency, Sid had been with Bascomb-Lewis, a top-tier talent agency with enough A-list names on its roster to ensure that its agents' calls were taken promptly. As the head of his own boutique agency, Sid was almost more powerful than he'd been at Bascomb-Lewis. He no longer had to battle in-house competition for clients. He also didn't have to handle more clients than he could comfortably cultivate. More was not necessarily merrier in this business -- not if the clients that one did have were good earners. Each actor had to feel as if he or she was the agent's most important client. Without too much effort, Sid could easily manage a small but incredibly profitable list of stars that included talents like Cody Torrance and Gitana Ardon.

Not only that, but Sid had been in the business a long, long time. He had solid relationships with all the top casting directors. That included Ruben Leckner, a 380-lb. aging, balding queen who collected toy trains and Amish quilts and who maintained his grip on the industry, as did so many others, through sheer tenacity.

"Ruben's frightfully busy this morning," Palmer said, sounding bored in that pseudo-British way of his.

Busier than Sid? Is that what Palmer was insinuating? More important than Sid?

"This Rita Webb pilot has him at sixes and sevens. I assume that's why you're ringing us up? To pitch someone for it?"

Of course Sid wanted to pitch someone for the Rita Webb pilot, but Sid wanted to talk to Ruben himself, and Ira was not about to let Palmer outmaneuver him by taking a message as if Sid were just any caller. He tried to remember some tips from the Power to Succeed Workshop, but came up blank.

"Why don't you just go ahead and give me the name? I'll try and pass it along to Ruben."

Did Palmer's accent slip just a little in that last sentence? Ha! His Americanness was threatening to rise up and pierce his facade of precisely modulated audio snobbery. Did Palmer go home at night and look up British slang to use? What a jitbag.

Ira knew the name of the actor Sid meant to pitch, but Sid would be greatly annoyed if he wasn't put through directly to Ruben. The actor wasn't a name yet. She was *fresh* -- a fairly new discovery of Sid's who was not yet familiar to casting directors. Sid would need to sell her a bit in order to get her an audition.

Ira popped another Mentos into his mouth, thinking: timing, finesse and leverage. That's the one he'd been forgetting – leverage.

"Sid didn't say," he lied. "Palmer, he'd *really* like to talk to Ruben himself."

Maybe that was a mistake. It sounded like begging. Palmer was forcing him into the role of supplicant. Where was this cheek coming from? Palmer was definitely getting bolder. He must be sleeping with Ruben. Ira tried not to think about it. Visualizing Ruben Leckner's white whale-like body naked next to Palmer was just too--

"Darling, *everyone* would like to speak with Ruben this morning. There's so much buzz over this pilot, after all. I'm sure you understand."

WTF. It was time to call Palmer's bluff. He didn't need his diving imagery. He could do this without it.

"Palmer," Ira said crisply. "Are you saying that Ruben is refusing to take Sid's call? Is that *really* what you want me to tell Sid?" He allowed a subtle shading of outraged disbelief to creep into his tone. Just enough to let Palmer know he was royally pissed off, but too professional to raise his voice.

"I didn't say that he *wouldn't* take his call," Palmer said quickly. "There's no need to get cheesed off about it." He sounded little whiny and aggrieved. "It's just that Ruben is frightfully busy. He has this pilot and is meeting a producer about a feature film today. Still, I suppose I could have a word with him..."

Don't do me any favors, you little faux accented, faux hair colored prick, seethed Ira inwardly. He wondered irritably if Palmer was even really gay. That could be an act, too. A way to get ahead in a gay-friendly industry.

"Palmer, I've got Sid on the line right now and he doesn't like to be kept waiting." He paused, then struck, resurrecting the coiled cobra image he'd discarded earlier. "Well, if Ruben really is too busy to take Sid's call, I guess Sid could just contact the producer directly. It's Billy Minton, isn't it? Those two go way back. I think they went to high school together…in Brooklyn."

He had no idea if Billy Minton was from Brooklyn, but Minton *sounded* as if he were from New York. It was a safe bet; it seemed like two out of three people in the industry in L.A. were from New York. Fellow Brooklynites or not, Sid *did* have enough clout to call a producer with a casting idea, but just like a nuclear warhead, this was a weapon you hoped you didn't have to use. If Sid went over Ruben's head, he might get his client cast in the project, but Ruben's usefulness to the producer would be diminished. Ruben, consequently, would feel resentful. He might quietly, vengefully freeze Sid's clients out of good roles in the future.

Sid probably wouldn't bypass Ruben, but would Ira's bluff work? Ira waited, feeling pretty good about his Personal Power at this moment.

"I'll get Ruben," Palmer said, his tone sounding like a deflating balloon.

As Ira listened to the "on hold" New Age Peruvian mountain music, he refused to allow himself to revel in the victory. There was still one more challenge ahead, but he felt up to it now. *I have ten hearts, a thousand arms*, he muttered to himself. *I feel too strong to war with mortals. Bring me giants!*

Like Cyrano de Bergerac, he was a man whose gifts were often overlooked. Someday, though, that would change. He'd be an unspeakably successful screenwriter. Hell, he'd be a director/screenwriter. A producer/director/screenwriter. Why not? He'd be sought after by all the top industry players. A-list stars would adore him, begging him to write those challenging, career-transforming roles for them that he wrote so well. Roles that got them Oscar nominations. He'd be invited to their homes...

And when his writing career was flourishing to the extent that he needed an office space in which to write, he'd pick a better color of paint for it than this revolting shade of pink Sid had chosen for *his* office walls. Sid was certain that he knew more about interior decorating than any interior decorator, just as he knew more about basketball than any NBA coach, more about food than any chef or nutritionist and more about cars than any automotive engineer. Like many successful men, Sid assumed that his considerable knowledge in one area meant that he had considerable knowledge in all areas. He was a classic know-it-all.

Ira wouldn't have minded so much if he didn't have to look at this "Pacific Salmon" color every day, for hour upon hour. It made him feel nauseated. It's pink! Ira wanted to scream. Pink, you fool!

Sid felt that "Pacific Salmon" effectively showcased his collection of contemporary art. Ira tried hard to appreciate the gigantic, vaguely angry, vaguely ethnic modern paintings that hung throughout the suite of rooms that comprised the agency. Since he knew that each one cost more than his salary for an entire year (Sid just had to share that information with him), he settled for *not hating them too much*. If he didn't force himself to remain relatively neutral about them, he might just go berserker one day and slash them to shreds with a large knife. It could happen. There were several sharp knives in the kitchenette that would do the job.

Palmer came back on the line, all business. "Ira? I've got Ruben on the line. Put Sid on."

"Will do," Ira said, only he didn't. Palmer clicked off.

Ira waited until he heard Ruben's mournful, slightly sibilant speech: "Hiya, Sid."

"It's Sid's assistant, Mr. Leckner," Ira said. "One moment. I'll put Sid on."

He put Ruben on hold and intercommed Sid. "Ruben's on three."

"OK," Sid said. "Hey, not for nothing, but I think the cleaning crew's been stealing my cigars. Jesus! The Monte Christos! When I'm done with Ruben, get me that building maintenance guy on the line." After eight years in this building, he still didn't know the name of the building maintenance guy. It was William.

Then his voice was gone.

Only when Ira saw line three's blinking light turn to a solid one did he congratulate himself for a connection well made. Ruben Leckner had had to talk -- however briefly -- to a lowly assistant! Ira had bested the smug Palmer. In this power play between the powerless, he, Ira was the victor.

In the very next instant, he realized how pathetic he was. Feeling jubilant about winning a round of telephone roulette reminded him of just how far off track he'd gotten since he'd arrived in L.A. Or, more accurately, of how he'd never managed to get on track. This job was no stepping stone. It was a

8

quicksand pit, trapping him in place like one of those mammoths in the La Brea Tar Pits who'd gotten stuck in one place for so long that they were either eaten by predators or they starved to death, their flesh eventually rotting away, their bones destined to be stared at by tourists in millennia to come. That would be comparable to Ira's fate – unless he made a move, and soon.

When he'd first arrived, he found a job at one of the gazillion or so post-production companies in the Valley, reasoning that *anything* having to do with the entertainment industry would at least get his foot in the door. He found a cheap apartment nearby in North Hollywood. For awhile, the arrangement worked, until he realized that the closest he was getting to making any meaningful contacts within the industry was his daily exchange with the FedEx guy who picked up packages every afternoon that were bound for studios. When the company bookkeeper mentioned a job opening he knew of at an agency in Beverly Hills, Ira jumped at the chance. Beverly Hills! He'd interviewed with Sid – who seemed like a kindly, genial uncle – and had gotten the job. Unfortunately, his landlord refused to let him out of the lease he'd re-signed just a month earlier. Like so many others, Ira found himself sucked into the time-killing vacuum of a long daily commute.

So here he was, in la de da Beverly Hills. Was he making connections? Networking with people in the industry who might recognize his writing talent?

He spent his days getting celebrities on the phone for his boss. Some famous actors -- like Cody Torrance -- even knew his name, greeted him cordially when he called to get him on the phone for Sid. Cody had class. He made an effort to be kind to the little people.

But at the end of the day Ira would get into his 1994 Chevy Cavalier and drive home to his small, stifling apartment in the Valley, to dine cheaply on a bean burrito from a taqueria down the street and work on his latest screenplay into the deep folds of the night. When he couldn't sleep he'd watch late night infomercials for things he didn't need and couldn't afford: devices that sucked fluid out of fruit; stretchy undergarments that flattened out stomach bulges and made back fat less disgusting looking; videos that make your kids smarter; pills that rid you of cellulite, gave you an erection, gave you a longer lasting erection, grew back your hair, gave you thicker eyelashes, put you to sleep or rid your intestines of parasites.

When TV left him restless and his insomnia proved unconquerable, Ira would sit by his living room window with his lights off, watching meth dealers conduct business in the gang-infested park across the street. Business was brisk, even late at night. Especially late at night.

Sometimes he'd solemnly light a candle and spend time staring at the Shrine to the Great Screenwriters that was housed on his bulletin board. The Shrine was a collage of scraps from what he judged to be extraordinary movies. There were copies of title pages from scripts, scrawled bits of lines he wished he'd written. Sometimes there were pictures of the writers themselves, torn from the glossy pages of magazines, but more often it was their work that was represented. *What in heaven's name brought you to Casablanca? My health. I came to Casablanca for the waters. The waters? What waters? We're in the desert. I was misinformed.* There was the cover art for the video of "Alice Doesn't Live Here Anymore," with the incomparable, luminous Ellen Burstyn embracing the wooden-yet-somehow-right-for-that-role Kris Kristofferson. A photo of Sofia Coppola on the set of "Lost in Translation." *Thank God for that. For a moment there I thought we were in trouble* - from Butch Cassidy and the Sundance Kid, written by one of his personal heroes, William Goldman, who also wrote "Marathon Man" and "All the President's Men." He didn't have a picture of David Mamet, but squibs of dialogue from "The Untouchables" and "House of Games" and Frank Galvin's entire summation speech in "The Verdict" was up there. So was Terrence Man's line from "Field of Dreams," about memories being so thick people would have *to brush them away from their faces.* In the center of it all was a small picture of Charlie Kaufman, his personal hero, taken during some interview. So many layers of clippings had accumulated in the Shrine that the montage took on mass, threatening to pull the bulletin board down from the wall that held it. The Shrine probably wouldn't make sense to anyone else. He acknowledged to himself that it was nerdivistic in the laughable extreme. If he ever got a girl to come to his apartment he'd have to hide it or dissemble it, but for now, the Shrine was inspirational. Some guys had porn collections. Ira had the Shrine.

This was his life. Portrait of the Artist as a Thrall.

Sid, on the other hand, would dine at the Ivy or some restaurant like it, first stopping off at Cole-Haan on Rodeo Drive for *another* pair of shoes. Then he'd valet park his Mercedes Benz at his Beverly Hills high-rise condo complex and settle in to watch the Lakers on a TV screen that was as big as a Santa Monica Boulevard billboard. Ira knew it was that big because Sid had told him how big it was, not because he'd ever been invited to Sid's home.

Tall and lanky, blessed with thick salt-and-pepper hair at an age when other men were enduring painful transplants, Sid had a homely face not unlike a rutabaga -- a face that, perversely, put people in this slick, lifted, tucked and surgically sculpted industry at ease. At this stage of his career, Sid enjoyed the ideal work-to-pleasure ratio: a small amount of work and a great deal of pleasure. Sid's workday consisted of making a few telephone calls, scanning the bits of mail Ira deemed worthy of his attention, reading -- or at least skimming -- scripts for his clients, screening an occasional demo video from an actor seeking representation and watching many hours of television. He had a bookkeeper to process the commission checks that poured steadily in from his productive clients, and a financial manager to advise him on how to invest his disposable income, which was a lot.

Some nights Sid had to do a little handholding by going to tapings of the TV shows his clients were in. There used to be movie premieres or casual get-togethers at the Malibu or Pacific Palisades or Brentwood homes of mind blowingly famous actors, but not anymore. With the way traffic was these days, Sid tended to go straight home and let the world come to him.

That was the real measure of success in L.A., Ira thought resentfully: when you didn't have to spend half your life in your car, running errands. When you had the clout or money to have other people do your wheelwork for you.

Ira was the one who made Sid's appointments for him. He knew that the masseuse and acupuncturist and colonic hydrotherapist were only too happy to pack up their heavy folding tables and oils and CDs of soothing, chakra-balancing music and sets of sterilized needles and whatever equipment colonic hydrotherapists used (which he preferred not to think about) and brave the angry traffic to go regularly to Sid's office and Sid's house. It wasn't that Sid was a generous tipper. In fact, he was known to be a tightwad. The battalion of service-providers necessary to maintaining Sid's well-being had other motivations. These people were either aspiring actors hoping for representation or non-actors hoping for referrals. The tailor who altered Sid's designer suits, the florist who delivered enormous and artful arrangements of fresh flowers each week, the agency who provided Sid with illegal Latino housekeepers at cut rate prices all sucked up to Sid so that that he would send his famous clients to them.

Everybody kissed Sid's ass. He accepted it as his due.

This was Sid's life: Portrait of Someone Who Had Exactly the Life He Wanted to Have.

Ira knew that his jealousy was misplaced. Sid must have had to pay his dues at one time, just as Ira was doing now. Taken on a day job, done work he didn't particularly like until he could become a top agent. Hadn't Ira heard all the stories about screenwriters, development people, studio execs, agents or producers who'd begun their careers as humble mailroom clerks or assistants at William Morris or Warner Brothers or TriStar or *wherever* before hitting it big in the industry?

But doubt attached itself to him like the psychic version of a flesh-eating disease, quietly, inexorably attacking his defenses, making him wonder if he had the talent or the nerve to ever break out of this wretchedly low level of Hollywood hell. Had his move out here been foolhardy? Rooted in hubris and self-delusion?

Being an assistant meant you had to suppress every bit of self-esteem you possessed and expend all of your intelligence and abilities on mundane tasks. It was a job that, over time, sucked the soul right out of you. Was it time for him to pack it in and go home, in order to avoid this fate? After nearly two years out here, he'd failed to get the attention of the entertainment industry in any meaningful way.

A screenplay Ira had written that Sid had *sort of* agreed to read sat on a corner of Sid's enormous desk, amid a stack of other screenplays Sid had sort of agreed to read. This was a different pile than the much smaller one situated toward the center of the desk. That one consisted of screenplays Sid actually was going to read, because they were involved in deals he was making for clients. Ira's screenplay was in the "favor" pile. Sid's accountant's wife had written a screenplay: would Sid take a look at it, as a favor? Or, Sid's nephew from New York wrote a wonderful screenplay, according to his mother, who was Sid's sister. Would Sid read it and get it into the hands of some big director? As a favor? Sid apparently felt no hurry about performing these favors. Every day when Ira went into Sid's office with the mail he glanced down at the pile, trying to gauge whether or not it had gotten any smaller. Had Sid read *any* of them? He knew better than to ask Sid if he'd gotten to Ira's screenplay yet.

The novelty of being in glamorous L.A. was dead, buried under the exhaustion of simply trying to survive here. L.A. traffic was now just one massive collection of logjams. Ira got home later each night and had to leave for work earlier each morning, in order to be at his desk by nine. Sid, naturally, lived a mere half mile from work. He could afford to. Still, even Sid was occasionally inconvenienced by the traffic glut. But the difference between the two was striking. Sid lived in Beverly Hills. Ira worked in Beverly Hells.

"I don't care how bad it gets, though. I'll never leave L.A. This weather. Can't stand those New York winters anymore," Sid often said, as if there were only two places in the country that accommodated human habitation.

Should Ira finally concede that working at Midwood Agency was not going to get him anywhere and look for an industry job in the Valley, closer to the lease he was stuck in for another five months? A job that would be no doubt similarly lowly, but might have more potential than this? He hated the thought of starting all over again somewhere new, at the bottom of the pile, trying to get people to think of him as a writer. He couldn't get out of his lease; he'd already tried. "Oh, you don't wanna do that," the building manager told him. "Oh, no. The guy who owns this place? Russian mafia. You don't want to cross him." Was he telling the truth? The Russian mafia. It would sound preposterous anywhere but here. He could believe anything here.

Should he pack it in and go back to Michigan, where he could at least breathe? Who would have thought he'd miss the smell of Detroit? The memory of the foul gray steam rising up out of sewers on bleak winter mornings back home now made him feel...*nostalgic*.

The ever idling vehicles here were making the air worse than ever. The tight, tortuous feeling of captivity in Ira's lungs that used to trouble him on some days was now present every day. And it wasn't just the pulmonarily-challenged like himself who suffered. He heard comments from all around him, from *normal* people who now found themselves straining to breathe, their noses leaking mucous, their throats coated with a slick, bad-tasting slime that no amount of throat-clearing could expel.

The light on line three blinked off. Sid buzzed Ira. "Make an appointment for Brenda Burris to read for that new Rita Webb sitcom. The mother-in-law role. Did you already send over a head shot and resume?"

"Yes, Sid."

"I don't mean did you email them. Ruben is old school. He wants things down on paper. To tell you the truth, he's not that good with computers."

Ira knew all this. "I sent them by messenger yesterday."

"You sure? Because Ruben said he didn't see them."

"I sent head shots and resumes for the four actors whose names you jotted down on the breakdown for that pilot. Brenda Burris was one of them."

"And you put what role he should read her for?"

"Just like I always do."

"You included a letter? On our letterhead? Because Ruben said he didn't see it."

"I've still got a copy of what I sent, saved in the computer."

"Maybe you typed it up but forgot to print it out and send it."

What truly infuriated Ira about this nonversation was that Sid didn't *sound* as if he were berating him. No, Sid was kindness itself when questioning Ira's competence, which was every day. He spoke to Ira deliberately, patiently, as if he were talking to one of those retarded people supermarkets hire to bag groceries. "Put the bread on top," he might have been saying.

Ira wondered if Sid could sense he was seething. Doubtful. Sid didn't spend much time thinking about Ira's mental state. He considered pointing out that he was not responsible for whatever mismanagement went on in Ruben's office. Maybe that phony blonde Chinese prick Palmer took his time about opening mail.

"You there?" Sid was still waiting for a reply.

"I sent it, Sid."

"Well, just to be sure, why don't you send it over again? And bring me the letter before you send it. I want to make sure it's right."

A trained monkey could do it right, raged Ira mentally. The simple form letter (or email) that accompanied submissions to let casting directors know which actors on the agency's roster might be right for which roles -- as described in the daily project breakdowns sent to agents -- went thus: Dear blank. Please consider blankety blank for the role of blank. A photo and resume are enclosed (or attached). Sincerely, blankety blank.

"Yes, Sid," Ira said, dying a little more inside.

"Oh and forget about the maintenance guy. I counted those Monte Christos again and they're all here."

"Yes, Sid," Ira said.

"I bet the cleaning crew would *like* to steal them, though."

CHAPTER TWO:
AMERICAN INGENUITY

Blog entry
iraorileysblog.wordpress.com
August 9

I don't even know if I can explain it to people who are not living here, in the midst of it. An accurate description is going to sound like hyperbole. It's impossible to exaggerate what's going on but I feel that no one's going to listen, because L.A. has been crying "wolf" for so long. "Yeah, the traffic is bad in L.A.," I can hear people in other parts of the country saying. "So what else is new?" After all, it's not an *exciting* news story, is it? No bombs or blood. No celebrity scandals. None of the excitement of those high-speed police-criminal chases for which L.A. used to be known. I almost miss them.

No, it's a whimper, not a bang. No wonder our fellow Americans (you?) are tired of hearing about it. I don't blame you.

And it really doesn't matter if people don't believe what they're hearing. It's not like Congress or the president or the army can fix this mess. I'm not sure anyone can. It's not that kind of a mess.

This is going to be a long post. I've got plenty of time and a lot to say. Right now, I'm trying to get onto the 101 and it's taking forever. There's no alternate route that isn't worse than this. Here's how bad it is: I'm not even in my car at this moment. I'm sitting in the Haughty Latte with my laptop, typing and consuming a highly caffeinated beverage while keeping an eye on my (unmoving) car through the front window. I might as well be comfortable while I wait. When traffic finally gets going, it'll do so slowly and I'll have plenty of time to get back to my ride.

So, think of this malady like an infection. It started out like an angry rash; unsightly and annoying but not serious. Bound to be temporary. Something you put up with in order to live in this fabulous, glamorous place, amid all of these opportunities. (Is my sarcasm coming through?)

We had what we now think of as ordinary gridlock: slow traffic during morning and evening rush hours. Everyone got used to that being the new normal. Sure, it took a long time to get anywhere, but eventually, you did move. Then the rush hours lengthened until they practically met in the middle, and we all got used to that.

Then they met in the middle.

A few months ago the experts were estimating that L.A. motorists lost an average of 90 hours a year due to gridlock. Now that era seems like the good old days. There was talk about expanding Ventura Freeway, building new roads, changing signaling patterns, coming up with more mass transit. Some of it was actually accomplished, although most of L.A. is so congested that there's no room for new roads. Of the measures that *were* taken, nothing much helped. There are just too many damned people here. What did I read the other day? That the number of drivers has doubled over the past 30 years, but the number of roadways has increased by only 29%. What did we expect?

The rash got worse, became something much more serious, popping up on the 101 and Interstate 5 in the San Fernando Valley, quickly spreading to the Hollywood Freeway and the 405 and the 10, from freeways to surface streets, from main arteries and vital intersections to quiet residential cul-de-sacs. There've been outbreaks of it in Northridge and Bellflower and Alhambra, down Pico Boulevard and up into Benedict Canyon. Pasadena is in pain. Westwood is worried. Pacific Palisades and Malibu are practically stranded in splendid, unreachable isolation, or they will be soon. Parts of Reseda and Glendale and Century City are paralyzed; Compton and West Hollywood are stagnant.

The rash has spread down Sunset Strip, over to Venice and Santa Monica to the west, La Canada and Altadena to the north. On the East Side and the West Side, in Chinatown and Koreatown and Little Armenia, MacArthur Park, Echo Park and Hancock Park, the Valley and South L.A., Beverly Hills and Hollywood, people are barely moving. No one is driving down Rodeo Drive. There are no miracles on Miracle Mile.

17

There was a horrible trampling incident last week. Did you hear about it? Two people were killed, at least a dozen injured. It happened because a seething, sweating, stymied crowd was trying to cram all at once onto the Gold Line from downtown to Pasadena. They were worried about not getting on board, and with good reason. The rail system just can't cope with the massive numbers of people seeking an alternative to vehicular travel. I'm betting it won't be the last such incident.

I hate to sound so dramatic. Maybe somebody will come up with a solution, but right now, it feels like there is no escape. Between the sharp spines of the San Gabriel Mountains and the glittering cold blue sweep of the Pacific, this vast congested plain that we call home is suffering. Our collective frustration is great. Cars are moving by inches, like cattle milling about in crowded feedlots.

I'm about done with this iced cappuccino mocha. Trying to decide if I should get another. The guy behind the counter raises an inquiring eyebrow and I hold up my empty cup and nod for another round. Why not? It's a little extravagant, money-wise, but the air conditioning is heavenly. The thousands upon thousands of idling cars spewing their emissions into the air have made breathing even harder for me than it was before. I saw a headline yesterday about the spike in pulmonary deaths, but refused to read the story.

So, back to my topic. If you want to know what it's like here, just picture cars and jeeps, SUVs and minivans and pickup trucks and recreational vehicles, buses and limos and big rigs sitting end to end like jointed metallic snakes, filling every lane of every freeway and boulevard and twisting around corners onto secondary streets. Some motorists get stuck for so long that they run out of gas. There are squadrons of mobile vendors (they seemed to appear out of nowhere) walking between the lines of unmoving cars, Latinos, mostly, selling bottled water and canned energy drinks, high-protein bars, oranges, hot dogs, bags of peanuts. Oh, yes- and gasoline. The cops aren't bothering to stop them or see if they're licensed, and why should they? People need food, fluids and fuel. I saw one enterprising driver who'd been hauling portable toilets on his flatbed set up shop with them, charging fellow stranded motorists a dollar each to climb up on the truck and take a crap. American ingenuity.

I wouldn't be surprised if riots broke out soon.

Ah, here's my drink. Mmmmm. So, some people are simply giving up and abandoning their cars, expecting to reclaim them later – probably from a city impound lot, after paying lots of fines. This, of course, only makes things worse. I was walking yesterday and passed cars that were empty and driverless. I knew that the motorists sitting five or ten vehicles behind them, waiting in grim patience for the chance to move ahead a few feet had no idea that they were doomed to keep waiting.

I didn't walk back and tell them. What would have been the point?

Why am I still here? (You're asking yourself if you're reading this blog.) Why haven't I tucked my tail between my legs and slouched back to Detroit in defeat? My parents keep asking me the same thing. They're up on current events. They know what's going on here and they can't understand why anybody would put up with this. Plus, there's their favorite topic: *my asthma*. How I love hearing them mention that.

Why am I still here?

Fake answer: Because escape wouldn't be easy. By the time I got out of here, the crisis might be over. It would take me months to make my way to the outer perimeter of the mess, or equally long to get to LAX, if I chose to leave my car in California and just take off.

Real answer: Because I keep thinking that as soon as I leave, the traffic problem will get fixed but I'll already have melded back into the gray, unimaginative landscape of the Midwest and will never get the momentum to come back here and become the wildly successful screenwriter that I know I'm meant to be.

Seriously.

Oh, gotta go. I see some movement out there. About time.
TTYL

CHAPTER THREE:
MOSES MULDOON REPRESENTS THE "D"

Moses Muldoon, a big, burly, rough-around-the-edges Detroit cop, busts up a gun-smuggling ring operating between Canada and the U.S. via the Ambassador Bridge. (There's got to be a big scene right up on the bridge, with Muldoon hanging over the side, about to fall wayyyyyy down into the Detroit river while one bad guy tries to throttle him and other bad guys shoot up at him from speedboats.) Hmmmmm, Ira thought. Could he work Mounties in here somewhere? Their uniforms were a lot cooler than border guards' uniforms, which were boring. *The gun-smugglers would turn out to be part of a global criminal ring that funds terrorism. Muldoon, who is (naturally) a renegade within the department, is called into his lieutenant's office for what he thinks is yet another come-to-Jesus meeting (sure, he saved the country, but he broke departmental regulations again!). Instead, he's introduced to an overbearing "suit" from Homeland Security and a suave, English Interpol agent to whom he takes an immediate dislike. The fed reveals that the terrorist-backers arrested in Detroit have their evil tentacles reaching into cities all over Europe. The Interpol agent, Daniel Stowaring, explains that he's been working on the case for some time. Because of Muldoon's familiarity with the bad guys, and because of a certain talent the Detroit cop has, Stowaring has arranged for Muldoon to partner up with him, go to Europe and help him track down the rest of the terrorist organization. Muldoon's lieutenant is only too happy to have his loose cannon of an underling get out of Dodge for a while.*

Muldoon, predictably, is not thrilled about the assignment. (Of course not, thought Ira. He's a renegade. Any normal person would be happy about a free trip to Europe.) *Muldoon's dislike of Stowaring is understandable. The Englishman is openly condescending during their first meeting, plus he dresses rather well. What kind of a cop -- even a Brit – wears nice clothes like that?*

Ira was writing so fast that his hand was cramping, but he was too excited to take a break. He *knew* these people, this story, even before they flowed from his pen onto the page. It was as if he were revealing them, not creating them. He felt feverish. The yellow legal pad on the desk in front of him filled up so rapidly with scribbled script that he feared not being able to read his own handwriting later.

Although Muldoon is of Irish/Jewish parentage, he grew up in a neighborhood in Detroit that became heavily populated by Arab immigrants. Thus, he speaks fluent Arabic. That is the special talent he has. It's what makes him so valuable to Stowaring, despite the urbane Interpol agent's disdain for Muldoon's macho, bull-in-a-china-shop methods. No one expects this non-middle-Eastern-looking guy to understand, much less speak, Arabic. He's a secret weapon.

Muldoon really doesn't want to go and work with Stowaring. Why? Is he afraid to fly? Would that show a vulnerable side? It would be something for the ladies, who like a little contradiction in their steroidal heroes? Or, was it really plausible that a cop who faced down vicious criminals nearly every day would be a big pussy about flying? Couldn't he just nut up, take a tranq like everybody else and get on the damn plane? Or maybe Muldoon really does dislike Stowaring that much? Or is there some dark secret he's keeping? Did he go to Europe years ago and get with some woman who broke his heart, and now he hates all Europeans?

Ira knew he really needed to work out the reason for Muldoon's resistance. Back stories were important. However, these oil-and-water partnerships always started out with one or both members not wanting to work together. Like in Beverly Hills Cop. And Rush Hour. He conceded that his story was somewhat...formulaic, but didn't life itself consist of formulas? What was getting married and having children, if not a formula???

The broken heart angle might be very useful. Muldoon could meet up with this woman in the present. Would sparks fly again? Probably, because she was still going to be hot. Ira knew he was going to have to come up with a love interest for Muldoon, one way or another. *Maybe this hot female Detroit cop who'd been having a thing with Muldoon gets sent over to Britain to help him with the case and finds him doing the nasty with this hot European ex-spy and the two get into a really sexy catfight...*

Wait a minute. Wait a minute. He was getting ahead of himself. It was important to work out the main plot before he developed the subplots. Ira made a mental note to return to that possible subplot *(love interest/catfight)* before returning his focus to his hero.

Ultimately, Muldoon's lieutenant threatens to fire him over all the departmental procedures he's violated unless he goes with Stowaring and helps him with the terrorist case. Muldoon is forced to pack his bags and travel overseas with his new partner.

Not only does he not know how to behave properly on the plane (the polished Stowaring, of course, totally charms the flight attendants), Muldoon is even more out of his element once he lands. The posh Europeans he encounters are appalled by his crude manners, his brusquely straightforward approach to things. His fish-out-of-water status is especially apparent in the ritzy casinos, etc., to which Stowaring takes him. (The evil wealthy people who bankroll the world's armed conflicts hang out in such places, Ira was pretty sure. They always did in the Bond films, after all.) *Muldoon commits some fairly entertaining faux pas.* (Entertaining for us, not for him.) *The rich snobs he encounters are contemptuous but also a little afraid of him. He is a primitive, raw and physical. Stowaring gives him unsolicited advice on how to behave in civilized milieus, making Muldoon hate the Englishman even more.*

He's representing the D! Detroit! Ira thought almost indignantly. He knows how to kick ass and fix cars, not how to use the proper fork! Of course, Ira admitted to himself that he was from the D and did not know how to kick ass, fix cars OR use the proper fork.

He felt that there needed to be a scene where Muldoon is fitted -- under Stowaring's supercilious supervision -- for a tux. *Muldoon resists, finds it uncomfortable, complains, but all the women working in the tux shop stop what they're doing and gravitate toward him, practically drooling, because he looks so damn good in it. He sees their reactions and decides he can tolerate wearing the damn thing, when absolutely necessary.*

Muldoon thinks Stowaring is a tame pencil pusher, a sissified bureaucrat with a badge. Much too genteel for police work. Stowaring thinks that Muldoon is an uneducated, unrefined, hotheaded thug. Much too reckless for police work. Events prove them both wrong about each other. Stowaring is brave and physically formidable. Muldoon turns out to be more sophisticated than he lets on, and quite capable of subtlety and cunning.

Ira paused for a moment, unsure about where to go next. Those events that would illustrate the characters' opposite traits: what would they be, exactly? He tried to think of some specific scenes. Maybe it was too early in the process for that. He just needed to focus on the characters and the story, and let the scenes emerge organically. Wasn't that what he'd learned in that one workshop?

He probably shouldn't even be doing this at work, but it was slow right now and he wasn't neglecting anything. To be on the safe side, he kept his legal pad close to the edge of the desk as he scribbled on it so that he could dump it in his top desk drawer should Sid approach. He'd type all this into his laptop as soon as he got home.

So... Muldoon and Stowaring don't get along. They have jarringly different styles. But they team up and work together to prevent some important government building or landmark from getting blown up by terrorists. The Eiffel Tower? No. Too French. Buckingham Palace? Better. Does the Queen actually live there? He'd have to go online, do a little research on that. Maybe the Parliament building would be better. He relished the image of British lawmakers losing their wigs as they fled from the bomb threat.

At the crucial time, in order to avert catastrophe, Stowaring has to do things Muldoon-style, and Muldoon has to act like Stowaring. They save the Queen, or the Prime Minister, or someone important like that. Maybe the President of the United States is visiting that day, and they save him as well. Or her. Too bad Diana wasn't still alive, and still a princess.

23

The intercom buzzed, startling him and making him jump guiltily in his chair. "Ira?"

CHAPTER FOUR:
A FEW COSMOPOLITANS TO DULL THE PAIN

"Yes, Sid?"

"Get that Lupe in here to cut my hair, would you? This afternoon?"

"Will do." Ira was annoyed and exhilarated. A little aroused, too. Also embarrassed. He was annoyed that Sid couldn't go to the salon where Lupe Sevá worked, which was all of ten minutes away, because he couldn't be bothered. Maybe he didn't want to sit with the common people (Beverly Hills' version of the common people, that is) and wait his turn.

He was exhilarated and aroused because Lupe Sevá was a particular obsession of Ira's. He was more than a little jealous that another man – a man with power and money – could summon someone like Lupe and she would come to him. Lupe was small but perfectly proportioned, not choosing (yet, anyway) to artificially expand her breasts into the oversized globular focal points that so many women in L.A. sported. Ira did look at them when he came across them, of course -- how could he not? He found them to be *intimidating*, though. They seemed to have lives of their own, these breasts, jutting ripely forward ahead of their owners, like tanned, plump bows on ships. As often as the situation arose – and it rose often here – he still never knew where to look or how to act around a woman with such gigantic breasts. Anxiety usually trumped desire whenever he encountered one. Or two, so to speak.

Lupe's pert, toned body was showcased perfectly by the retro wear she favored. The short skirts or mini dresses, boots and vintage prints that she loved might look costumey on someone else but they looked just right on Lupe, Ira thought approvingly. Her hair was contempo, though: sleek black and asymmetrical, curving in a bob on one side of her head and razor cut short and edgy on the other, the ends tipped magenta one day, metallic green or cobalt the next. Her skin looked sunkissed, with the faint blush of natural rose color under her cheekbones. Her eyes were the same deep, rich brown as the cigars soaked in

25

brandy that Sid had Murphy buy for Cody Torrance whenever they signed him to a new contract. She was definitely facebookable.

The embarrassment came from a long-held lust for Lupe and a torrid if unconsummated encounter Ira and Lupe had had at a party in the Valley some four months earlier.

Ira's face flamed red -- he could actually feel the heat in his cheeks -- when he remembered that night. He replayed the scene in his mind, resisting the impulse to mentally rewrite the humiliating parts.

INT. LIVING ROOM -- NIGHT

Casually dressed people cluster in various parts of the room, talking and drinking. IRA is conversing with a MIDDLE-AGED WOMAN.

SHOT: DOOR

Lupe Sevá enters with MIMI, a chunky, stylishly dressed woman in her mid-twenties. Lupe looks around the room, sees Ira and strides unsteadily but enthusiastically toward him just as the middle-aged woman finishes talking with Ira, nods and walks away.

> LUPE
> *Ira! Ira. I didn't know you'd be here. Ira.*

She throws her arms around him. Ira is startled and pleased by the embrace.

> IRA
> *Lupe. Hi. What a nice surprise.*

She is visibly leaning against him, obviously drunk. This leaves Ira and Mimi face-to-face. It's an awkward moment. Mimi extends her hand to Ira.

MIMI
Hi, I'm Mimi. A friend of
Lupe's.

IRA
Ira. Ira O'Riley.

MIMI
You're kidding.

Ira is starting to be uncomfortable with Lupe's apparently never-ending hug.

IRA
Uh...Lupe?

Lupe separates herself with some difficulty but stays close to
him, using him to prop herself up.

LUPE
(to Mimi)
Ira works at Midwood Agency.
(to Ira)
I didn't think Sid ever let you
out of your cage.

IRA
He's not the boss of me.
(beat)
Oh, that's right. He is the boss
of me.

Lupe finds this uproariously funny. She laughs heartily, slaps Ira
on the shoulder. Ira is cautiously gratified at her reaction to his
mild witticism, but he can tell that her zest is alcohol-fueled.

MIMI
I'm going to see if there's any
coffee. She could use some.

She leaves them, threading her way through the crowd.

                    LUPE
                  (to Ira)
          I had no idea you were this
          funny. Why don't you ever let
          this out at the agency? This side
          of you.

                    IRA
          I don't want to show up Sid.

Lupe laughs again then leans in close, lowering her voice.

                    LUPE
          I hate Sid. Ihate cutting his hair.
          He is such a pompous know-it-
          all.
                       (pause)
          But I must.
                       (nodding)
          Cut his hair.
                       (sighing)
          God, I hate him. Your hair looks
          nice, Ira. Where do you get it
          done?

                    IRA
          Budget Hair.

She looks disbelieving. Ira shrugs.

                    IRA
                  (CONT.)
          It's a chain. It's cheap.

Lupe leans toward him. Their faces are very close together.

> LUPE
> *I could do you better. Why don't*
> *you let me do you, Ira?*

They nearly kiss. Instead, Lupe grabs Ira's upper arms and shoves him down a hallway. He does not resist.

INT. BEDROOM - NIGHT

The light is on. Ira's back is against a wall. Lupe is pressed against him, kissing him fervently.

> IRA
> *Lupe, are you--*

Lupe silences him with more kissing, while reaching down and unbuckling his belt. Ira is thrilled with this development. Lupe unzips his pants. She nuzzles his neck, breathing heavily.

SHOT: DOOR

It opens suddenly. Mimi stands in the doorway, glaring at Ira.

> MIMI
> *What a jerk! Taking advantage*
> *of her like this.*

Ira quickly tries to zip his pants up. Lupe, laughing and still kissing him, unzips them again. They struggle. She tries to disrobe him, he tries to stop her.

> IRA
> *(to Mimi)*
> *What? But she--*

> MIMI
> *You can't see that she's an*
> *emotional mess tonight? I mean,*
> *does she look normal to you?*

29

IRA
I can't really tell.

MIMI
(angrily)
Her boyfriend just broke up with
her. He's not--
(gesturing with her fingers)
"into her" anymore. It's time
for them both to
(gesturing again)
"go their separate ways." His
just happens to include some ho
he met while working on a
movie in Vancouver.
(disdainfully)
A low-budget piece of crap
that's bound to go straight to
video.
(beat)
How could you?

Lupe stops kissing Ira. She looks suddenly distraught, starts to
cry.

IRA
I didn't—But she's the one--

MIMI
She usually never drinks
anything stronger than wheat
grass. But the one night she
downs a few Cosmopolitans to
dull the pain, you take
advantage of the situation.
(sarcastically)
Nice. Real nice guy.

Lupe starts crying.

> Lupe
> *(to Mimi)*
> Rob's really not coming back, is
> he?
>> *(crying hard)*
> My God. It really is over.

Mimi takes Lupe by the hand and starts leading her out of the room.

> MIMI
> *(to Ira)*
> You asshole.

They exit the bedroom.

CLOSE ON Ira, standing there in disbelief, his belt still unbuckled.

CHAPTER FIVE:
THE CELEBESPHERE

He'd seen Lupe a number of times since then -- Sid was meticulous about the state of his hair -- but Lupe gave no sign that she recalled the episode. Had she really been so drunk that she didn't remember nearly raping him? Or was she simply putting a bizarre night behind her? Did she try to convince herself that she'd never come on to Ira? Because she had. Oh, yes, she had. A hot chick had wanted to get with him. His lips still tingled when he remembered her kisses until he realized that unlike him, she might be revolted by the memory. She'd almost gotten naked with a gnerd. Done a little gnerdoodling. Was the memory that horrifying? Was that why she acted so *normal* when she saw him afterward? Because she was in denial?

Or maybe Lupe had been intending a pity screw, something she could write off on her karma the way people wrote charitable deductions off on their taxes.

He sighed and picked up the phone, dialing her number. Lupe hated cutting Sid's hair. Sid directed every snip of her scissors personally, as if he'd attended cosmetology school and graduated with honors, yet he was still never completely satisfied with the final result. Ira knew why Lupe kept coming back, though; because Sid sent his clients to her. At first it had been the minor ones, like the girl who played a paramedic on *Trauma Central!* -- the one who rode on the gurney, straddling the blood-spurting patient and shouting out vital signs while being wheeled into the emergency room. Or the wife's eccentric uncle on *Spare the Rod* -- a wry character actor who appeared in every third or fourth episode.

Then it was more important clients. When Gitana Ardon's regular hair stylist got an infection from that procedure everyone was having lately -- the one to shorten her second toes so she would look better in Jimmy Choo sandals -- and she couldn't do Gitana's hair for a movie premiere, Sid had Ira call Lupe. Ira had mixed feelings about offering Lupe the assignment. The volatile star could be especially cruel when she smelled fear, and Lupe was still new enough to the celebrity dimension to be intimidated. Lupe stepped up, though -- saying no to the opportunity would have been unthinkable -- and Gitana had actually been satisfied with the substitute's work.

Some day, a head that Lupe styled might be seen in a feature film, or at the Academy Awards. That would be the payoff. It *should* happen for Lupe, because besides being hot, she had mad skills.

The entertainment industry's parasitic sub-industry -- people who made their living off stars -- relied to a breathtaking degree on name dropping and referrals. As talented as Lupe was, her career would not really take off until she had some "name" clients as regulars. Celebs were like lemmings, following each other from one trendy hair stylist, wardrobe stylist, makeup artist, personal trainer, dog trainer, plastic surgeon, therapist, eyebrow shaper, interior decorator, masseuse, leg and bikini waxer, spirit channeler, ear reflexologist, limousine company, party planner, feng shui consultant or New Age healer to another.

In order to get traction in the celebesphere, Lupe would do what she had to do. She would come to Sid's office when he called, drape him in a cape made out of organic cotton (God forbid synthetic fabric should touch his skin – it might give him an allergic reaction!) and position his full-length floor mirror and his portrait-sized desk mirror just so -- at his instructions -- so that he could see enough to effectively micromanage her work.

Lupe would do Sid's bidding just like William -- the black man who valet parked cars for the building -- would drop everything when Sid decided his car needed washing. Sid didn't trust his detailing to commercial car washes, with their used towels and non-English-speaking workers who couldn't understand him when he specified EXACTLY how he wanted his car cleaned. ("Jesus! It's an $80,000 car! You think I'm gonna trust it to some José?")

Ira did Sid's bidding as well, in ways that went beyond normal administrative assistant duties. When Sid did not feel like going out to lunch, Ira would order Sid a take-out meal from some expensive restaurant or other, feeling more like a fussy spouse than an assistant ("You're sure the mahi mahi is fresh?

He said it smelled a little funny last time.") Ira would order the clothes Sid selected from high-end catalogues, then package them up and schlep them to the post office to be returned ("It's cheaper than UPS, Ira.") when Sid found some flaw in them, which was usually. Ira went to a special art supply store over on Fairfax *on his own time* to buy the particular slender magic markers Sid insisted on using when he signed his name on deal memos, because mere ink pens -- even Montblanc pens -- did not give him sufficient authority to visibly one-up whomever he was doing the deal with. His ink line had to be just a little bit thicker than theirs. In Sid's mind, size really did matter.

"Lupe? It's Ira. At Midwood."

"Is it that time again already?"

"Yes, Lupe, I'm afraid it is. Sid's hair is approximately 1/64th of an inch too long and must be trimmed IMMEDIATELY."

She laughed. It was a pleasing sound.

"How does your afternoon look?" He hated to ask but he had to ask. When Sid wanted something, he wanted it TODAY.

"Oh, God. Let's see. Well. I can move a few things around this afternoon without too much of a backlash. Tell Sid....ah, three o'clock."

Once he'd ended the call, Ira gave in to a brief fantasy in which the night Lupe kissed him had ended much differently, with lots of nakedness and some moaning, panting and whimpering as well. Mimi never made an appearance at all in this version. Oh she tried to, but Ira mentally highlighted the name of Lupe's chunky, hostile friend and hit an imaginary "delete" button with some satisfaction.

But who was he kidding? Why bother cultivating even a wispy filament of hope where Lupe was concerned? She obviously had no desire to repeat their liplockery. What did she see, when she looked at Ira? A peon assistant? A scrawny, asthmatic geek who was perpetually anchored to a desk, phone and computer monitor? Did she guess at the romantic, imaginative depths of him? The complexity? The passion? The sexual adventurer at his core who had not yet been fully or even partially released but could be freed -- by the right woman?

He cursed his Irish-Jewish ethnic composition, which had visibly given him all the wrong features and invisibly given him all the right ones. He had a prominent Semitic nose and a dissolute Irish chin. His brow that was too heavy for his lean face and his watery, blue-grey eyes that his mother insisted were like the sea "on a stormy day" made him look, he thought, as if he'd been up all night either drinking heavily or reading the Torah. He was unattractively pale and lightly freckled. That, he thought resentfully, was probably from the Irish side.

But he also had the verbal dexterity, the fierce love of words and talk and storytelling of both sets of ancestors, along with wit and a creativity that could help him find a way *(many ways)* to make a woman like Lupe Sevá happy.

He was rarely allowed to display any of these attributes at this job. Who could blame Lupe for not seeing the real Ira O'Riley? Ira did not *look* the part of a successful *anything*. In the entertainment industry it was all about packaging, and he knew that his *package* was lacking. It was a great frustration to him. He was smarter, his mind more agile and fertile than a great many of the people he encountered. He knew that. But when an actor or producer (or Lupe) gazed upon him, what they saw was a lowly assistant. He was one of an army of easily replaceable worker bees who helped the industry hum along. A drone.

Ira couldn't afford to do much with his wardrobe, but he did occasionally scour thrift stores, knowing that people like Sid, when they tired of their exquisitely cut Perry Ellis shirts and Ferragama trousers, their sleek Canali ties and Armani Collezioni cotton shirts, would have their assistants bag them up and drop them off at charity-run stores so that the poor had a shot at used chic. It was a magnanimous gesture and a nice tax deduction, too. Ira had made a few good finds, although the clothes never looked as good on him as they probably had on their original owners.

He mixed a revolting green powder guaranteed to make him gain weight into his orange juice every morning and worked out at the Y when he had the time – on those rare days when the ozone and nitrogen dioxide levels were low enough so that exercise, even indoor exercise, didn't provoke a bout of intense wheezing. His physique, however, gave no indication that it was forming into a buff body. "Remember, Dr. Hart said it's better to be lean when you have asthma," his mother reminded him over the phone.

Lean, schmean! He was 26 years old and scrawny like a 16-year-old.

He was foolish for wasting his time thinking that he had a shot with Lupe Sevá. Maybe in an alternate reality he did. Still, he looked forward to seeing her. Three o'clock couldn't come too soon.

CHAPTER SIX:
SACRACORNIA AND LOSANGELENTO

The city council blamed the mayor. The mayor blamed the governor. The governor blamed the state legislators. The state legislators blamed Caltrans. Caltrans blamed the budget.

Governor Jorge Olmstead was indulging in a rich, pleasant fantasy about being a private citizen again, something he did more and more lately -- ever since his fledgling administration became thoroughly mired in this hellish traffic issue. He'd barely been governor long enough to figure out where his office was and get an overview of fiscal problems -- which he'd thought would be his forte -- when everything in the state had ground down to a slow, agonizing crawl. Traffic hadn't even been on his campaign agenda. Traffic jams in California were like the poor in the Bible: they would always be with us. As long as they weren't too bad and didn't last too long, people put up with them. Sure, the state wasn't perfect, but this kind of weather, people were willing to tolerate a lot of inconvenience.

Olmstead interrupted a reverie he was having about a threesome involving his own naked self, his girlfriend Misty and an unidentified fantasy woman, a redhead -- or maybe an Asian woman -- to try and focus on what Macalroy was saying. Everyone else at the long, boat-shaped cherry and mahogany conference table was listening to the Caltrans rep. Olmstead should be, too.

"We've identified the critical points as being here, here, here and here." Macalroy indicated several positions on a map. "One option would be to use helicopters to airlift vehicles from those key junctions."

"Is that possible?" Olmstead asked, feeling stupid. "Can a helicopter pick up something as heavy as a car?" What he was really wondering was: *How many more emergency meetings will we have before a bunch of angry southlanders bearing torches storm this conference room and take us all outside for hanging?* Then he remembered: *They're stuck. They can't get out of Southern California. We're safe -- for now.*

37

"Yes, Governor. Some choppers are used in logging operations, for instance, to move trees that weigh up to ten thousand pounds." Macalroy consulted the map again. "The theory is that freeing up those vital intersections and arteries would get things moving again."

Someone else spoke up: "But this is just a temporary fix, right? Unless we can come up with some way to reduce the overall number of cars on the road, or increase the number of roads *fast*, the whole thing will come to a halt again, and soon."

Olmstead sighed. He'd already given up any hope of a second term. Plus, he was resigned to the fact that he was going to be hated and vilified for the remainder of this one. This mess was happening on his watch, even though its seeds were rooted in decades past. There would be no political future for him. The glorious public career he'd allowed himself to imagine had already vanished in a puff of automobile exhaust. Would he even get a book deal out of it?

There was a strange, liberating sort of comfort in accepting one's fate. Olmstead felt his lips move strangely, felt himself smiling a serene smile. He could tell it was serene by the uneasy expressions on those around him. *They think I'm cracking up*, he observed.

"So," he said, clearly startling several people with the decisiveness, the gubernatorial firmness of his tone. "Let's review our options. Congestion pricing won't work here like in London, because we don't have a central area where traffic is concentrated the most. There are too many activity centers. We could increase the number of toll roads and increase the fees on existing toll roads. Our analysts tell us that would raise revenues, but not necessarily cut down on the number of drivers. With not much room for new roadways -- at least in the most densely populated areas -- we've got several engineering companies investigating the feasibility of double decker roads and freeways: where they could be located, how they'd be integrated with existing systems, how long they'd take, how much they'd cost. Whether or not they'd even be safe in an earthquake-prone area. But that's a long-term solution. We still have to figure out how to get cars off the road, NOW."

Damn, he sounded good. Almost as if he'd read and absorbed the agenda bureaucratise: "Identify and evaluate short term strategies for vehicular reduction and long term strategies for increased traffic capacity." It sounded so easy, when put like that.

"The council still thinks that a random lottery will draw the least heat," said Nolan Huxley, an emissary from the L.A. city council.

Olmstead sighed. "Legal maintains that a random lottery wouldn't hold up in court. People who lose the use of their cars could say that we're preventing them from getting to their jobs, jeopardizing their employment, causing them financial hardship."

"What's interesting," said his aide, Marla Lobello, "is that a coalition of environmentalists and motorists have already filed a lawsuit against the state for not developing a better mass transit system. Those pesky Green Wavers are leading the charge. I think they're wasting their time, though. After all, we built the most expensive subway system in the country. More than a quarter of a million people ride it every day -- although it's true that fare increases had an inverse effect on ridership levels. They're down twenty percent from a couple of decades ago, even though the population is up. What do people expect? We have to pay for the thing somehow." She frowned, looking thoughtful. "The losers of the driving lottery might join the Green Wavers in the lawsuit, I suppose."

"Gee, maybe you could suggest it to them," Olmstead said irritably.

"I'm just trying to anticipate new areas of exposure. I *am* a lawyer, remember? And as a lawyer, it's my professional opinion that whichever way we jump here, we're going to land in a pile of--"

"I know what we're going to land in," Olmstead said, wishing again that he was in bed with Misty and...some redhead...at this moment. "Actually, I think you're a little late with your assessment. We're standing hip-deep in it already."

"We could go with the D.U.I. plan," someone suggested. "The public wouldn't put up too much of a fuss about that. Anyone with more than one conviction loses the right to drive a car in the state of California. For good. It wouldn't be too controversial. No one could argue with the premise that chronic drunk drivers are not people we need cluttering up the roadways."

They all looked at Olmstead, and he knew what they were thinking: that he would block this idea because *he* was a recovering alcoholic who had been arrested three times for driving under the influence (although he'd avoided convictions, thanks to a phalanx of highly-paid attorneys). He'd made his personal history very public during the campaign. Part of his surprising, third-party-candidate victory had been attributed to the honesty and teary remorse he expressed on every talk show that would have him as a guest. The drinking binges, the prolonged cocaine odyssey, the three failed marriages -- all his fault, he confessed. There was the grown daughter who wouldn't speak to him and the son who would, after a grudging reconciliation which just happened to be captured on camera and aired on "L.A. Exposé." The time he accidentally set his own bed on fire and burned down part of his home, resulting in injuries to two firefighters. Minor injuries, but he'd nonetheless sought them out and made amends, giving them each generous contributions toward their children's educational funds. Conveniently, cameras had been on hand then, too. The brawl he started at a subordinate's retirement party. The accounting firm that he destroyed -- after founding it and growing it to a sizeable and successful company -- leaving people who once trusted him without jobs or pensions. The incident in which he groped the breasts of a female cop while she was arresting him for public intoxication. The time he lost his balance and fell onto the table of some fellow diners at a prominent mid-Wilshire restaurant, crushing their paella, sending their martini glasses crashing to the floor, blubbering his apologies.

There'd been many, many financial settlements (thank God for that trust fund from his Caucasian Grandad). Amends made. Apologies tendered. Mea culpa. Mea culpa. Mea culpa.

The Public loved a sincere apology, his campaign manager Ray insisted. The Public would accept a deeply flawed man as their governor, as long as he acknowledged his defects and promised to do better. Everyone wants to believe in second chances.

Ray was absolutely right about that. Olmstead wished Ray were here right now, to advise him on this traffic impasse, even though Ray's expertise was in getting people into office, not on what they should do once they got there. Still, Olmstead intended to give Ray a prominent place in his administration once he got out of sex addiction rehab in Connecticut. After his latest relapse, Ray wanted to get far, far away from California clinics. Too many bridges burned locally.

"Isn't this really Luna's problem?" Who could blame Marla for indulging in a little wishful thinking? "It's a Southland problem, after all. Hey, here in Sacramento, the freeways are only really bad during morning and evening rush hours. The central part of the state is moving O.K., too. Isn't there a way we can sidestep this and let the political fallout fall out on *him*?"

It was tempting, Olmstead thought, to dump this in the lap of Hector Luna, L.A.'s fiery Democratic mayor. Analysts would see it for the dodge that it was, but...

"Is it too late to resurrect that proposal to divide the state, north and south, into two new states? Or three? Maybe it wasn't as crazy as we thought." The suggestion provoked some welcome laughter, softening the tense edges of the meeting.

Olmstead smiled. "Yes, we should have done that when we had the chance. We could be here in Sacracornia, happy and driving free, while our neighbors to the south -- in the state of Losangelento -- crowd their freeways into an inpenetrable logjam. We could watch from a distance, relieved that we avoided their fate."

"Our state motto could be: Drive Free or Die," Marla suggested.

More laughter.

"But back to reality," Olmstead said. "And let's not forget that Sacramento's population is increasing, too. What's happening in the south could easily happen here, if we don't make some serious statewide changes. Ask not for whom the bell tolls. And you think other cities in other states aren't watching closely, to see how we handle this? You know how bad the rush hour has gotten in Philadelphia? New York? It's also terrible in

41

Chicago, Houston and Atlanta. They're all making cracks at our expense, but they know it's only a matter of time before they're in the same boat we are. California needs to lead the way on this issue, as we do on so many others. The rest of the nation looks to us for innovative ideas. Now that D.U.I. plan is worthy of consideration. Have we crunched the numbers? How many drivers would it take off the road? Enough to make a real difference?"

"I can have those figures for you by tomorrow," Marla said briskly.

Numbers. Figures. Math. These were things Olmstead was good at.

"We need to do a comparison before we can make decisions here," he asserted. "We're going to have to defend our actions and it won't be easy. Whatever we do, it's going to cause considerable pain to a great many people. Marla, you'll line up the statistics on how many drivers will be eliminated if we go with two DUIs, and also if we start at three DUIs. In addition, let's open up the field to moving violations in general. Habitual reckless drivers."

"The state's already got a point system, with penalties-," someone interjected.

"Which we may have to supersede," Olmstead pointed out. "This is a crisis, ladies and gentlemen. We can no longer operate on the basis of 'business as usual.' It's a defensible position. Speeders and red light runners are as much a danger to society as drunk drivers."

"And now we're the morality police," someone grumbled.

Olmstead ignored that. "And let's anticipate that this will be a multi-tiered program of permanent vehicle elimination. ('PVE' he thought to himself. Catchy.) Perhaps we should evaluate vehicles on the basis of usage-versus-space required. Buses, for instance, would get a high grade. Even though they take up lots of space, they carry many riders. Limousines would get a low grade."

"You're going to ban limousines?" A transportation expert sitting at the far end of the table was amused. "*In California*? Horrors! The celebrities will riot in the streets. I can already hear the howls of outrage."

"Maybe not ban them outright," Olmstead said slowly, thinking aloud. "Maybe we could hit them with new fees. Make it prohibitively expensive to operate them. Or at least use those funds to help mitigate the traffic problem. After all, limo users can afford it."

"What about recreational vehicles? They're big."

"We can NOT go after seniors. They've got too much clout and they're not afraid to use it. We'll get our heads handed to us."

"Will there be different rules for visitors than for residents? And how will that affect the tourism industry?"

"Maybe we should establish an age limit. For cars. Take all of the old cars off the road. They're polluters and eyesores."

"And then you'll be accused of discriminating against people who can't afford new cars. Latino activists, for instance, will call it thinly disguised racism.

"People will say that if their cars can pass the emissions test, they should be allowed to drive them. And what about classic cars? Would they be exempted from an age limit?"

"Why should they be? Even if they've been lovingly restored, they get lousy mileage."

"Those classic car owners all belong to clubs. They can mobilize against this in a heartbeat. And they've got lots of money to spend on lawyers. It's an expensive hobby."

Olmstead's head throbbed. Oh, to be anonymous and unfettered again. He tried to remember why he had wanted to be governor. He let the others talk on and on while comforting himself with daydreams of Misty giving him a hot oil massage. Even that didn't work. He reached back to his happy childhood, remembered sitting at the dining room table with his family and eating tamales. Yes, that was better. Everything was so simple then. He knew he should be paying attention to this discussion, but what was the point? After a brief spasm of optimism, a resolution was spiraling out of reach. He had a sudden image of the galaxy, rapidly expanding, every object moving further and further away from every other object at unimaginable speeds. Until now, he'd never truly been able to grasp the concept of the expanding galaxy.

Part of him would like to escape California. Simply walk away from his title and public duties and flee to some less vivid part of the country.

But he could never leave this weather.

CHAPTER SEVEN:
CUPFULS OF WATER OVER MY HEAD

Blog entry
iraorileysblog.wordpress.com
August 16

I've taken the last few blog posts off (my favorite topic, that is), but I feel that I must address it again. Are you sick of hearing about it? I know that to those in the outside world, saying that gridlock is a problem here is a lot like saying that it snows in Buffalo. But it really has gotten much worse. Did you see the story on CNN last week? I think it's fair to characterize it as a full-blown crisis at this point.

People are adapting, as they always do. Southern Californians are nothing if not adaptable. They're like Americans are in general, only more so. Everything is extreme here except the weather. The billboards are bigger. The women are prettier. The phonies are phonier. The rich people are richer. The poor are more numerous. The grand ideas are grander than those you'll find anywhere on the planet, and the problem is, some of them actually materialize into fabulous fruition -- enough to keep the rest of us perching precariously on the wicked knife edge that is ambition, our eyes dazzled by the glint of the steel. Eventually, we either give up or get hurt, but until one of those two things happens, we try to keep our balance, as uncomfortable as our lives may be.

Did I just mix metaphors? I try to be careful. I always used to get marked down for that in creative writing class.

But back to the resiliency of the inhabitants in this gloriously delusional metropolis. One example: this, don't forget, is a desert that shouldn't support any sizeable civilization, much less the ginormous throng whose cunning members inhabit every inch of space here, even if they have to prop their mountainside houses up with wooden stilts to do it.

Take me. I can be adaptable. Resourceful, resilient. Yes, I can.

I was sick of being late for work. Actually, I was sick of Sid complaining about my being late for work, so I came up with what I thought was a reasonable solution. I started to sleep at the office. I would *appear* to leave the agency at 6 p.m., then I'd sneak back in after I saw Sid drive away. I slept on a not-very-comfortable post-modernist sofa in the reception area, stowing my pillow and blanket and some clean clothes in the back of the closet where we store demo dvds. I was already keeping a toothbrush and a few toiletries in my desk drawer, so that was no problem. Sure, there's no shower in the building, but I would slip into the men's room down the hall early, before anyone came to work, and manage a sponge bath. I even figured out how to wash my hair, by leaning over the sink and pouring cupfuls of water over my head.

Sid got wind of it, though, and put the kibosh on it. I think the cleaning crew narced on me, even though I'm always nice to them and even try to speak Spanish to them, however ineptly.

So now I'm back to being late every day and Sid is back to complaining about it every day. You think he would have been happy about my resourcefulness. *I* was happy, since I was able to use my evenings for writing instead of sitting in a car for hours, barely moving.

I'm commuting again. No matter how early I leave, it's not good enough because everyone else in L.A. is leaving earlier and earlier, too. Should I break my lease (and take my chances with the Russian-mafia-building owner) in order to find a place (that I probably can't afford) that's closer to my job (even though I hate-hate-hate my job?)

I feel so stuck.

CHAPTER EIGHT:
TWENTY DOLLARS FOR A DIAPER

There had always been angry chemicals in Lester Vinson's brain. They usually slept peacefully until some unexpected event roused and roiled them into a dangerous soup, in much the same way that stomach acids get activated and cause no end of trouble to their host. A big, refrigerator-shaped man with a sun-seared face and a normally genial expression, Lester knew about the chemicals and sometimes tried to head off their effects. This worked best when he was able to keep busy.

The batteries on his hand-held solitaire game had long since run out of juice, and he had no handy replacements. He was out of water and just about out of cigarettes, so he was hoarding his remaining three. Every once in a while he'd shake the pack and stare into it, as if a fourth or even fifth cigarette might have magically appeared alongside the others, but there were still only three.

When was the last time he'd been able to move his rig forward? It had to be at least two hours ago, and that had been for only a few feet. Lester cursed himself for not sticking to his guns with Herb and insisting on taking only East Coast and Midwest runs. "Oh, it'll ease up by the time you get there," Herb had promised. "I mean, c'mon! They can't let it *stay* like that, can they? With nothing moving? Plus, I'll sweeten it up for you with a bonus."

Bonus. With all the delays, Lester was going to end up earning about a nickel an hour on this run. Bernice's car was gonna get repo'd and he'd never hear the end of it. Ho boy. And he really, really had to take a leak.

A sinus headache felt as if it were cemented to the right side of his face. That and the burning, bad-flavored grit layering his tongue and the back of his throat had to be from this lousy air. He always thought the stink of that soybean-processing plant in Illinois he used to pass was the worst thing he'd ever smelled. That was *nothing* compared to this. Why didn't more of these idiots turn off their engines? They must think they'd get the chance to move at any moment, so they should be ready. And because they kept their engines idling, the air got thicker and more foul by the minute. Beautiful. He could feel his ruddy face shining with what felt like a thin layer of grease. His thinning, strawberry-blonde hair was plastered onto his scalp. His beefy, freckled arms felt disgustingly damp.

A wide-bodied dude on a Harley passed beneath the window of his truck, going slowly but still going, his long gray ponytail hanging limply down his leather-vested back. Lester scowled as he passed by. Motorcycles. They were the only things able to squeeze between the lanes and keep traveling. He knew his irritation was not rational, but that didn't stop it from intensifying as he looked around and saw more bikers winding slowly, steadily forward in the narrow channels between columns of plugged up traffic.

"Sono le tre meno dieci," a woman's tinny voice said somewhere nearby. A man repeated, uncertainly: "Sono le tre meno dieci." Lester saw him: a wavy-haired, soft-featured man in his 50s -- a fruit, no doubt -- talking back to a CD playing in his BMW's stereo. Probably getting ready for his next trip abroad. Those people always seemed to have lots of money to throw around, at fancy restaurants and on the kind of furniture that was pictured in those magazines Bernice liked to look at. They didn't have to spend it on kids that weren't even his, like he did, Lester thought bitterly, wondering why Bernice's lawyer didn't do a better job of shaking down her first husband for money.

He popped a piece of sugarless gum into his mouth. "Well, Peter," he said to his truck, a Peterbilt, "looks like we got another long wait. Looks like another day has gone by and those useless politicians have once again not done diddly about this. More money out of my pocket, Peter, but what do they care? What do they care about the little guy?"

The little guy -- who, in fact, weight 269 pounds -- realized that he couldn't ignore his near-to-bursting bladder any longer. He'd already scoped out the landscape, hoping to find a tree or *anything* that would provide a little cover, but the roadside was featureless. He couldn't exactly stand there in the street and drain the dragon. He eased his door open just a few inches, wishing the cab of his truck were lower to the ground, and unzipped his jeans. He tried to release his urine in a controlled trickle, so as not to attract attention, but it'd been too long since the last pit stop and something more like a waterfall cascaded from his cab to the ground below. A fat broad sitting in a Ford Bronco in the next lane heard the sound and looked over, then quickly averted her eyes in disgust. Too bad, lady, he thought. He wasn't gonna wet his pants just to protect her delicate sensibilities.

Feeling greatly relieved, Lester climbed down from the Peterbilt, taking care to avoid the yellow puddle below his door. Once on solid ground he stretched both bulky arms to the sky, losing a little of the tension that had lodged in his back. He glanced back at his load: eight shiny new Chevy Sonics, headed for a dealership in Van Nuys. Just what La La land needed, he reflected. More cars. Beautiful. He scuffed the toe of his cowboy boot on the road a few times then started walking, trying to work the kinks out of his legs.

"Does anyone have any diapers?" a woman wailed in a desperate, I'm-about-to-go-over-the-edge tone. "I'll pay twenty dollars for a diaper!" Lester was glad he wasn't in *her* car.

What a freakin' circus it was. People were mostly outside of their vehicles, talking to each other or on their cell phones. A tall blonde chick sat on the hood of her Jeep, typing on a laptop computer. Some guy was doing push-ups next to his car. Several people stayed in their vehicles and slept. One couple was in their back seat, but not sleeping. Did they really think people couldn't tell what was going on underneath that blanket? He watched them for a few minutes, trying not to be too obvious, but hell. They were doing it right here, in front of everybody, weren't they? Wasn't *him* that was the pervert. It was almost better than pay-per-view porn.

A skinny guy in a white Chevy Cavalier trimmed with rust was on his phone, sounding wheezy and frustrated. "Yes, Sid, I can call him from here, but I CANNOT CONFERENCE YOU. Not on my cell phone. If you need to talk to him right away, why don't you dial him up yourself? I can give you the number." He paused, listening. "Sid, I don't know what you want me to do.

49

I'm stuck here. I can't move." He waited again, glowering. "I *am not* exaggerating the situation."

A loud argument raged in a blue SUV. "You didn't think it was important to tell me that?" a woman stormed at the unlucky man sitting behind the wheel, his expression set in stone. "You didn't think you should mention that you've had a *vasectomy*?"

Lester moved on quickly. Bernice was pestering him to get one of those and he didn't want to even be reminded of it. He was damned if he was gonna get snipped *there*.

He was suddenly knocked to the ground. What the hell-? Shaken but uninjured, Lester leapt to his feet and saw what had struck him: a freakin' motorcycle. It was bad enough that these bikers got to keep moving when no one else would. No, they had to run innocent bystanders over in the process, just to rub a little salt in the wound.

"Son of a bitch!" Lester shouted. "Watch where you're going, you asshole!"

The biker, a short, stocky Latino, stopped and looked over his shoulder at the angry Anglo who was getting to his feet, shaking his fist and yelling something in English. The Latino shrugged and offered an apologetic half-smile. This had the opposite effect, lighting a flame under the angry chemicals simmering in Lester's brain and bringing them to a rolling boil. When he roared in outrage, he expected to be feared. Instead, this Mexican was smirking at him. The som'bitch probably wasn't even in this country legally! Who was he to go around running down American citizens? Even if he was going real slow.

Sensing danger, the Latino started forward again, but he wasn't able to proceed very quickly and Lester caught him with him in a few strides. Lester grabbed the handlebars and wrenched them, knocking the rider off balance and off the bike. A crowd quickly swarmed around them. People who were already out of their cars got the best viewing positions. Others had to climb on top of vehicles to see. The air was thick was nitrogen dioxide and anticipation. Few would have admitted to actually wanting to see a fight, but the boredom was so intolerable and had gone on for so long that even those who considered themselves civilized and progressive were ready for a little action.

"You owe me an apology, asshole!" Lester's breathing was shallow and raspy. Ferocity made him seem larger than he was, which was already pretty large. This was not lost on the biker, who got to his feet slowly, looking around for an escape route, assessing his options. He was not happy to find Lester's massive hand suddenly clamped onto his forearm.

"You understand English?" Lester demanded. "You almost ran me down and I wanna hear that you're sorry. Comprendo?"

The Latino did *not* seem to understand English. He *did* seem to understand that Lester was a very angry man. A very angry, very big man. He tried to break free from Lester's grip.

"Stop it!" a woman cried out.

"Hey, take it easy, man," said someone else in the crowd. "It was an accident. I mean, he was barely moving. You're not injured, are you?"

Some multi-tattooed bozo chimed in: "Not exactly a fair fight, brother. You got about a hundred pounds on him."

These voices stirred the toxic chemicals in Lester's brain into an even more volatile broth. "Shut the fuck up!" he roared.

Still holding the Latino's arm, Lester gave him a hard shove from behind, propelling him face-first into the side of a black Buick Regal. As the biker got shakily to his feet, holding the nose that was now dripping blood, Lester grabbed his shoulder and swung him around to face him. He bent the smaller man backwards over the hood of the car, shouting in his face.

"It's bad enough that I'm stuck here in this hellhole, losing money by the minute."

He punched the hood of the car right next to the Latino's face, to scare him and let him know what might be coming. It hurt, but the terror on the Latino's face was worth it, as were the horrified gasps he heard coming from the crowd. The biker ineffectually struggled to push the larger man away from him.

"Assholes like you gotta make things even worse."

Lester swung hard, meaning to connect this time, but the tattooed man leaped forward and grabbed his arm, jacking it up behind Lester and locking his own arm under Lester's chin, holding him in an immobile, impotent rage.

"That's enough, man," said the tattooed man. "You gotta chill out. This guy didn't mean nothing."

Lester sputtered and struggled.

"You're not the only one who's stuck here, you know. Everybody's on edge. Nobody's happy."

The biker took advantage of the distraction to burrow through the crowd, collect his motorcycle and get away.

"Why are you sticking up for that piece of shit, you freak?" Lester couldn't believe the injustice of it all. "He ran me down! And he's not even an American!"

"Hey, man, I'm a peaceable guy, that's all. He didn't mean to hit you. And be honest- he barely touched you. You gotta chill out. We're all in the same boat here. Let's not make it worse."

"Screw you!"

The tattooed man tightened his arm, pressing on Lester's throat. "Look, man. I *want* to let you go. I really do."

Lester, his face now the approximate shade of a Beefsteak Tomato, responded with angry choking sounds.

"You gotta promise me you'll relax. Will you do that, man? If I let go of you, will you walk away? No more trouble."

A cell phone conversation coming from somewhere nearby penetrated Lester's consciousness and pushed his brain into eruption mode. The voice was recently familiar, the breathing labored. "I told you, it's a fight! Somebody's going to get hurt bad. You're telling me that the police *just can't get here*? That's what you're saying?"

At the edge of his peripheral vision, Lester could see the skinny guy in the Cavalier looking in his direction, a cell phone up to his ear. The little shit. The little tattle tale. Somebody always had to call the cops. Just like that time at that bowling alley in Meridian, Mississippi.

"What do you say, man?" The tattooed guy was still talking. "You ready to relax?"

Lester jerked his head, but in a way that was difficult to interpret. The tattooed man released him and stepped back quickly. Lester wheeled around and swung at his face, but the other man easily ducked his blow. Before he could even admit to himself that he missed, Lester was clubbed with a roundhouse punch by the tattooed guy. Lester slammed into a bus and fell to the ground but he wasn't done yet, oh no, one punch was not going to do it. He shook his head like an angry bull and half-rose, but before he could get to his feet, the tattooed man sent the steel toe of his steel-toed work boot deep into Lester's groin. Lester collapsed onto the roadway, a quivering heap of pain.

The tattooed man shrugged. "You shouldn't oughtta messed with me, man. I been in prison." He walked away. Several people clapped him on the shoulder, which would have aggravated Lester if he wasn't in agony.

Lester eventually braced his back against the tour bus and, after a few minutes of concentration, was able to slowly raise himself to a standing position. A few people still stood around, watching, but he ignored them. He limped slowly back in the direction of his truck, his crotch feeling as if it were on fire.

The skinny guy was still babbling into his cell phone, so intent on his call that he didn't realize the action was all over. "Well that's just great," he said irritably. "Yeah, I KNOW there's a traffic problem. So does that mean the police just don't do their jobs now?"

Lester honed in on the voice as if he were a sound-seeking missile.

"You can't get to the scene of a crime, so the criminals do whatever they want? Well *that's* good to know."

The skinny guy looked up just in time to see Lester's flying fist, coming at his face like a hairy club.

CHAPTER NINE:
LICK IT

blog entry
iraorileysblog.wordpress.com
August 21

Sorry I left things hanging with that last post. I heard Sid coming down the hall and had to conclude the story prematurely.

The worst part wasn't even getting a black eye from Cro-Magnon man when I was misguidedly trying to be a good citizen. (I honestly thought somebody was going to end up dead.) The worst part was that after I got sucker punched, I did get out of my car and try to hit the big golem back, but by that time I was having a full-blown asthma attack and couldn't even catch my breath, much less swing my arm. (My spaghetti-sized arm.) It was truly humiliating. Cro-Magnon man looked puzzled, like he thought I was faking it. Finally he just laughed and laughed. It was disgusting, because it made his ginormous belly shake so hard I thought he was going to cause an earthquake. I could hear his guffaws as I got back into my car to look for my inhaler. He continued laughing while I sucked on it – the sight must be more amusing-looking than I thought. I wanted to vanish -- poof! -- but of course I was stuck there, in my car, trying to breathe. I ignored him and he finally went away. I practiced my stupid relaxation techniques that don't really work until traffic finally started moving again.

By the time I got back to the office, the right side of my face was a pulpy mess. Naturally, Lupe Sevá happened to be there, dropping off some hair "product" for Sid. For the briefest of moments, I thought maybe the black eye made me look macho. Maybe it did. I'll never know, because after chastising me for taking so long, Sid told me that his cleaning lady can no longer get from her low-rent district to his Beverly Hills condo because the buses, like everything else, are barely moving. So...guess who Sid sent to clean his condo? (In front of Lupe Sevá.) Yeah. Me. Told me where the toilet brush was and everything. Like the candyass that I am, I didn't tell him to lick it.

If he doesn't find a replacement maid soon, and if I do a good job cleaning his place, it may be added to my job description permanently. Oh joy. Oy vey.

CHAPTER TEN:
HER MAJESTY'S GANGSTA

INT. COFFEE SHOP - DAY

IRA O'RILEY, a handsome, confident-looking young man, sits at a table, sipping a latte. He writes in longhand on the yellow legal pad in front of him.

In the b.g. we see HUGH GRANT standing near the counter, a beverage cup in his hand. He is looking at Ira intently.

CLOSE SHOT: HUGH GRANT, COMING TO A DECISION

He walks up to Ira.

>   HUGH GRANT
> *Ah, excuse me. Ira? It is you,*
> *isn't it? I don't know if you*
> *recall, but we met at a party at*
> *David Geffen's house? I'm*
> *Hugh Grant.*

Ira looks up and smiles. They shake hands.

>   IRA
>   *(cordially)*
> *Of course, Hugh. Good to see*
> *you again.*

He gestures.

>   IRA
>   *(CONT.)*
> *Would you like to sit down?*

Hugh Grant eagerly takes a seat.

HUGH GRANT
*Thanks. That's, uh...that's just
great.*

IRA
*I didn't know you came here.
I'm addicted to their lattes.*

Hugh Grant drinks from his cup and smiles.

HUGH GRANT
I'm an espresso man myself.

He drinks again and gags, making a face.

IRA
You don't seem to like it.

Grant grins ruefully.

HUGH GRANT
*Ah, well, that's just it. It seems
you've, sort of, caught me.
(looking around)
I've never been here in my life,
actually. And I'm not even sure
what espresso is. Or why we
have to say espresso instead of
expresso, which is the way
everyone wants to say it, really.
And it tastes dreadful. To be
brutally honest. Bitter. How can
people rave about it? Are they
just pretending? Is Starbucks
practicing some form of mass
hypnosis, to make everyone
think that this swill is actually
tasty?*

Still smiling and friendly, Ira nonetheless tilts his head in puzzlement.

                    IRA
          You've lost me, Hugh. What do
          you mean, caught you? I'm
          afraid I don't... follow.

                HUGH GRANT
          Well it's just that...I heard that
          you come here. And I've popped
          in here from time to time,
          hoping to, uh, encounter you.
                    (earnestly)
          It's Stowaring, Ira. As soon as I
          read your brilliant screenplay, I
          knew I had to play Stowaring.
          It's exactly the kind of role I've
          been looking for. He's half me --
          or what the public's come to
          expect of me, anyway, and half
          more. What a stretch he'd be for
          me. What a delicious stretch.

                    IRA
          How did you get hold of the
          script? It's not even really in
          play yet. My agent's in talks
          with a few people but--

TWO BEAUTIFUL WOMEN walk by the table, ogling Hugh Grant. He doesn't notice.

                HUGH GRANT
                  (vehemently)
          That's just it! I had to speak to
          you before any deals were
          struck.

IRA

*You'd be great as Stowaring,
Hugh. I mean that. But I don't
make casting decisions.*

HUGH GRANT

But you could.
(nodding)
*You could put it into your
agreement that you get approval
over casting.*
(fiercely)
*You've got that kind of clout,
Ira.*

IRA

*How did you even hear about
it?*

HUGH GRANT

*That's not important. What's
important is that you've written
a brilliant screenplay with a
role in it that would take my
career to a whole new level.
Break things wide open for me,
so to speak. I can't do romcoms
forever, Ira. Can't go on
playing these devilishly
handsome, charming cads when
I'm...a man of a certain age.
Sooner or later, even I must age
out of that sort of role. And...I'm
bored, Ira. Ready for something
more substantial. You've made
Stowaring so vivid, so fully
realized that he practically
jumps off the page. He's got a*

rich core, tremendous texture --
yet he's a rugged man of action.

         IRA
Well I'll certainly think--

      HUGH GRANT
Ira! It's the kind of role that
comes along only once or twice
in a career! The arc of his
character...is breathtaking. He's
so much edgier than anything
I've ever played. Under that
polished exterior, he's brutal. I
love that about him.

DIFFERENT ANGLE - COFFEE SHOP - DAY

DWAYNE "THE ROCK" JOHNSON enters, looks around, sees
Ira and Hugh grant deep in conversation. Frowning, Johnson
strides quickly over to their table. People look up. Several
recognize him and stare.

      JOHNSON
Ira! Wait! Don't make any
decisions until you've heard me
out.

Ira, surprised, looks up. Uninvited, Johnson sits beside Hugh
Grant.

      HUGH GRANT
You're interrupting us, Johnson.

     DWAYNE JOHNSON
You can call me The Rock

> HUGH GRANT
> *(to Ira)*
> *He's all wrong for Stowaring,*
> *Ira. Surely you can see that.*

> DWAYNE JOHNSON
> *Stowaring? I want Moses*
> *Muldoon.*
> *(leaning toward Ira)*
> *I AM Moses Muldoon.*

> IRA
> *(reluctantly)*
> *I don't know, man. That tooth*
> *fairy movie-*

> JOHNSON
> *My agent talked me into doing*
> *that. Ira, you've got to listen to*
> *me-*

Ira, lying alone in his bed, reveled in the fantasy, until he realized that he was being an idiot. Who cared who played Stowaring and Muldoon? What about the hot babe who would provide the sizzle in the script? The love object for Muldoon or Stowaring...or both? My God, that would be brilliant: a love triangle.

Which actress should (in his imagination) suck up to Ira for the role? It was difficult to flesh out this version of the fantasy, since he hadn't conceptualized the female lead much past figuring out that he needed to have one. Was this woman going to be a secret agent? A terrorist who turns good in the end? An ordinary person who finds herself mired in frightening yet exciting circumstances because she's in the wrong place at the wrong time -- and thus has no choice but to join the two partners on their dangerous mission?

Ah...which actress would join him unexpectedly in the coffee shop, sitting very, very close to him and purring in his ear about how she'd do anything for the role? Kirsten Dunst? Eva

Mendes? Eva scared him a little, but in a good way. She'd be a brilliant choice for the not-yet-fleshed-out female lead. A smokin' hot spicy dash of Latina exotica to contrast with the working class Irish-Jewish Muldoon and the stuffy oh-so-Anglo Stowaring. Wait a minute, wait a minute. He was forgetting Megan Fox.

He tried hard to reset the coffee shop scene in his mind so that he could recast it with Megan Fox. It was no good. Anxiety about getting to work on time trumped lust. He reached over to his bedside table and reset his alarm clock, for a half an hour earlier. Would that do it? If he could figure out a way to not sleep at all, he'd be in great shape.

Up until last week he'd been able to crash on the sofa of a guest house in Holmby Hills at which a buddy of his was house-sitting. It was a real stroke of luck. Ira was able to commute by bicycle to work every day, and a rather beautiful route it had been. Rolling through exquisitely landscaped neighborhoods on his clunky ten speed, mentally choosing which mansions he would consider buying when he became rich and successful, he'd made it to work in good time and in a good mood each day, albeit sweaty and out of breath.

Unfortunately, the home's owners returned from their sojourn in Mustique. His buddy's house sitting services were no longer needed. Ira briefly considered secretly making a spare key and sneaking into the guest house every night, but he knew he could never get away with it. The property, naturally, was wired with an elaborate security system.

He mourned the loss of the temporary solution to his commute problem but wondered, really, how long the traffic mess could last. Surely somebody would do something about it soon. Surveying the SUVs and sedans, the delivery trucks and pickup trucks and semi-trailer trucks, the minivans and sports cars and luxury cars that he wheeled past, he tried to take comfort from the realization that he wasn't the only one being inconvenienced by this nightmare. Gridlock was a great leveler. The rich, the poor, and everybody in between were equally screwed.

He closed his eyes, trying to squeeze out just a few more minutes of fantasy before sleep overtook him.

CHAPTER ELEVEN:
A NEW ROUTE TO HELL

Blog entry
iraorileysblog.wordpress.com
August 24

It almost sounds as if the rest of the country is taking some satisfaction from our misery. Network pundits and nationally syndicated talk shows are airing many hours of jabbering on the topic of Southern California's intractable traffic impasse, almost always with an unspoken yet unsubtle subtext: those spoiled Los Angelenos are getting what they deserve.

There is also the well-what-did-you-expect camp. Conservatives are blaming liberals. Liberals are blaming conservatives. Libertarians are blaming the government. Some analysts are viewing it as a symptom of a larger, systemic disease which will soon ravage the entire nation. Op ed writers are calling it the fault of spineless leaders, greedy corporations and a self-absorbed populace unable or unwilling to change its lifestyle for the common good. I think they're jealous. Everyone envies L.A.; the glamour, the weather.

Environmentalists are jubilant, those self-righteous bastards. They are happy with the sudden impotence, however localized, of the previously mighty automobile (never mind about all the auto workers and car salesman who have lost their jobs). TV and radio talk show hosts are thrilled that they have a new crisis to beat to death. They're trying to whip up the fear that the plague will spread from the left coast to the rest of the nation, and it's not that much of a leap. I hear that rush hour traffic in Chicago and Atlanta, New York and Houston and Boston is already nightmarishly slow.

The general sense in the media is that the United States is, as a society, going to hell, and a new route just opened up. In California, naturally.

Everything starts here.

Chapter Twelve:
The Army of the Anonymous

"Did you vote, Leon?" Cap Lessing's voice boomed out in thousands of cars, thousands of homes, thousands of radios.

"Naaaaah. I don't vote. Ever. Because it's pointless."

"Then you have no right to complain."

"I'm gonna do it anyway."

"Not on my radio show you're not." Cap drew his finger theatrically across his throat, giving his producer the "kill" signal. Leon was abruptly disconnected, leaving Cap free to launch into one of his diatribes.

"This mess is YOUR fault, people. That's right. YOU caused this mess, so take some responsibility for your actions, for a change. You're selfish, materialistic and lazy. So am I. We ALL saw this coming. Is there anyone out there who did NOT see this coming? Do the math. There are x number of roads, and y number of cars and the number of cars keeps expanding geometrically. We can only build ourselves so many roads. We can only build them so fast, because road-building takes time, and because every time someone proposes a new road or an expansion of an existing road, someone always screams, 'Not in my backyard! You're not going to knock down my house or use up some of my property for the common good. Oh, no!

"How many of you who are listening at this very moment are sitting in a car all by yourself? Did you even try to get a few people together for a carpool? Did you check out the possibility of taking a train or a bus? Some of you don't live all that far from where you work. Ever think about getting off your fat ass and riding a bicycle to work? No? How about walking? It's a foreign concept, I know. Walking. Heard of it? People in other countries do it all the time. Maybe that's why they're thin and we're fat."

Cap, who was fat himself, looked at the computer screen in front of him, scanning the list of callers who were waiting on hold to talk to him. "Somebody give me a new idea. Anybody.

I'm begging you. Kenny from Thousand Oaks, what's your solution?"

"That one councilman had a good idea, about holding a lottery," said Kenny from Thousand Oaks. "And people whose numbers are picked have to give up their rides."

"Why don't we just stone them to death?"

"Huh? I don't get ya, Cap." Kenny sounded deeply confused.

"Famous American short story, Kenny. '*The Lottery,*' by Shirley Jackson. Maybe you read it in high school, along with the rest of us?"

"The woman who was in *The Partridge Family*?"

Cap killed this call, too. "Kenny has just given me an idea, folks, although he didn't mean to. I say we administer IQ tests to all wanna be drivers. People in the moron range would not be granted drivers licenses. I'm afraid that would include you, Kenny. But let's give Kenny the benefit of the doubt for a moment, and examine his suggestion with all the seriousness it deserves. Let's say we hold a lottery, and the people whose numbers are picked are losers, not winners. They'd lose all driving privileges, or maybe lose them for a period of time, like a year. It would be completely random. Who could possibly object to that?"

He paused. Waited. Then punctuated the airwaves with a voice that sounded like a blast from a rusty trumpet. "LAWYERS, THAT'S WHO! They're already circling the idea like the vultures that they are. They're going to claim that it's not fair to make some people and not others give up their cars. They'll cite hardships -- and they'd be right. This would cause hardships. They'll launch a bunch of writs and lawsuits and they'll tie up the courts with their nonsense. And all the while that's going on, the traffic mess will get worse."

He shifted his inflection abruptly, leaning close to his microphone and purring intimately into it as if he were confiding to the stranger on the phone about a highly personal matter. "Dimitri, you're on the Cap Lessing Program on K-Talk-L.A., Hot News and Provocative Views. What's on your mind, Dimitri?"

65

"We should close the borders, Cap," said Dimitri, with spirit. "No new people in the state. California's already too crowded."

Cap laughed, an ugly brassy bark that was utterly without humor.

"Hilarious, Dimitri. All these years we've worried about the border with Mexico, but you're talking about the borders with our brother states in these here *United* States, aren't you? Keeping out other *Americans*."

"I was talking about Mexicans, too. But, yeah. People from other parts of the country shouldn't just get to come here. We're overpopulated."

"And you're not bothered by the fact that many of those other Americans -- your fellow Americans, I might remind you -- come here to spend lots of tourist dollars. So now, under your plan, you've got Disneyland and Universal Studios and hotels and motels and golf courses and restaurants and those crappy souvenir shops on Hollywood Boulevard and Ripley's Believe It Or Not Museum and the Queen Mary all losing big bucks. Plus, all the people who work for those establishments are going to be out of work. You don't see a problem with that?"

"We could make exceptions--"

"And what about the gorgeous national parks we have here? *National*, Dimitri. They belong to Uncle Sam, not Cal-i-for-ny-ayyy."

"We could buy the national parks from the federal government. That way we could--"

Cap cut him off. "Another one who wouldn't make it past the moron test. Delbert from Pasadena, you're on the Cap Lessing Program. Del, old boy, my producer tells me you're going to defend the governor. He's yanking my chain, right?"

"You can't blame Olmstead for this. He hasn't even been in office for that long. This problem has been building up for a long time."

"You've got a point there, Delbert, but however long Jorge the Jerk-ay has been in power -- and regular listeners know that I believe him woefully inadequate to the office that he snuck into -- he's going to have to nut up, be a man and DO something about the traffic problem."

66

"Olmstead's done a lot for African-Americans, Cap."

"And you're telling me this because...?"

"Well..." Delbert stammered uncomfortably. "I thought you'd...be a supporter."

"Why is that? Because I'm a black man, Del? Or, if you prefer, an *African-American*. You think I should give Olmstead a free pass because he's a mutt? The product of old money and new arrivals? Because his white father married the Mexican housekeeper's daughter and produced good old Whore-Hay, you think I should feel some mysterious, men-of-color connection with him? You think that my entire focus is on my ethnicity? Maybe I can't grasp any issue besides race. Is that it? You lefties just kill me. According to you people, I'm only allowed to talk about race relations. Not about politics, or the economy or international relations -- unless it's about the *racial* implications of those subjects. Come to think of it, maybe I should only take calls from callers who are African-American. Yeah. New rule. Listeners, when you call in, you've got to tell my screener what *race* you are."

"I didn't mean--"

"Mean what?"

"What I meant to say was, it's really the mayor of Los Angeles' problem."

"Do you own a map, Delbert? This mess goes beyond L.A. city limits. It's paralyzing a good chunk of Southern California. It's hurting business. That state is losing money. Workers can't get to their jobs. Customers can't get to stores to buy things but that won't matter soon because the trucks that deliver goods to stores can't move. People can't even get to hospitals when they're having heart attacks."

Delbert persisted. "If *you* don't have a solution, Cap, what do you expect the governor to do about it?"

Cap took a deep, audible breath -- a sign familiar to his regulars, who were legion and fanatically devoted to his flamboyant, abusive style. "Resign. He should get out right now and take his wishy washy lieutenant governor with him. They're both worthless."

"He's the kind of guy who learns from his mistakes. He's not perfect, but he's a Rhodes scholar with a Ph.D in economics. That's gotta count for something."

"Jorge Olmstead ran for office on a whim," Cap said, with the same level of revulsion he might use to say, "Jorge Olmstead collects *child pornography*."

He went on. "He's in power because he's an ex-drunk and an ex-cokehead who got sober and went public about how *sorry*, how *very sorry* he was. We've turned into such wimps in this society that we glory in people's flaws. Olmstead wasn't even a legitimate third party candidate. His *party* was a coalition of twelve steppers. They thought he'd be a real leader of men, did they? Well it's crunch time, Jorge. There's an actual crisis underway. You're going to have to do more than seek serenity and turn your problems over to a higher power. Julie from Culver City. Have you got a solution?"

"Cap, baby! I love your show!"

"Yeah, yeah, yeah," he said in his patented, gruffly-pleased tone. "You and everybody else, Julie. Now say something interesting or I'm gonna hang up on you. "

"Wait! I've also got an easy fix for what you're talking about. If we could just get all the illegals off the road, with their broken-down, uninsured piece of crap cars, there'd be enough room for those of us who are actually *supposed* to be here."

"Thanks for not disappointing me, Julie. I knew it wouldn't take long for someone to use this as an opportunity for a little immigrant-bashing."

"*Illegal* immigrants, Cap. There's a difference. And you sound like a liberal when you stick up for these people."

"Well, if you're going to call me names... There's only one problem with your idea, Julie. We shut out the illegals, who's going to clean the houses of the rich? Who'll be nannies for their kids? My God!," His voice rose in mock horror. "White people are going to have *change their own babies' diapers*? Mow their own lawns and trim their own hedges? *Wash their own cars and scrub their own toilets*? Ha! You're not thinking this through, Julie. Always remember that the needs of the rich come first, and you'll have a clearer understanding of how public policy is determined in this country."

Cap glanced at his computer screen, where his producer had typed in: Line 6 - Phillip - Olmstead supporter.

"We've got Phillip on Line 6," Cap announced derisively. "Says he's a real fan of our blubbering woosie of an ex-drunk governor. Let me guess, Phil. Are you a reformed drunk, too?"

"AA saved my life, and I'm not ashamed to say it."

"Glad to hear it, Phil, but it doesn't make you qualified to run a state, does it? And what I find most amusing about Alcoholics Anonymous and Narcotics Anonymous and Nicotine Anonymous and Masturbators Anonymous and Nail Biters Anonymous and Nose Pickers Anonymous and all the rest of those outfits that cater to the whiny and self-absorbed is that every time I meet one of their members, you can't wait to tell me about how you belong to this so called *anonymous* organization. Can't wait! My neighbor's car has a bumper sticker on it that reads, 'Friend of Bill W.' How anonymous is that? And you people have your own special language. And your own special rules. Face it, Phil. You're in a cult."

"It's not a cult, Cap. Twelve step programs have helped millions of people to save their own lives. Just because you're frustrated with Olmstead--"

"It's still a cult," Cap baited him. "If it's a cult that works for you, I'm glad, but don't kid yourself. It's a cult. And by the way, if they give you any Kool Aid, I wouldn't drink it if I were you."

"Fortunately, Cap, thanks to AA, I've got the serenity to not let assh--" -- the remainder of the word was bleeped out -- "like you bother me." Phillip nonetheless slammed down his phone.

"Well, see, that's just the problem," Cap went on. "The governor of our fine state is so busy working the program and doing the steps, turning his crap over to a higher power and making amends for all of his screw-ups that he's NOT DOING HIS JOB!" Cap fairly shouted that last bit, his pitch piercingly high. His dedicated fans, the Cap-lets, loved that pitch, because it meant he was winding up for a big segment finish going into a spot set.

"Phillip, you and Olmstead and all of your spineless 12-step cronies who conspired to put him into a position he couldn't handle are EXACTLY what's wrong with this state. Heck, did I say 'state'? I meant this COUNTRY! You're not a *symbol* of what's wrong. You ARE what's wrong. This country was built into a superpower by strong, self-reliant, resourceful people, not professional whiners. People with backbone and vision. People who handled their problems themselves, not in groups. But you, oh soldiers in the army of the anonymous, you are spineless wimps, perpetual crybabies who are bent on dragging the rest of us down to your level. You LOVE being weak! You revel in it! You find empowerment in it!

He paused. "After the break, we'll change gears and talk to Evan Ketchell, author of 'The Teeter Totter Manuever.' Ketchell tells business types how to jump off the teeter totter when their company is down, so that your competitor who's on top falls down on his ass. You're listening to the Cap Lessing Program on K-Talk-L.A., your station for Hot News and Provocative Views."

Chapter Thirteen:
The Fat, Funny Friend

This guy was gonna pop a gasket, thought Luanne Sajewski. As she punched the buttons on her radio in order to find something less irritating than talk radio, her crimson-colored fingernails flashed anxiously as if movement -- even just the movement of her fingers -- would make the cars around her go faster. The dial landed on some hip hop music and she kept it there. It was lots better than that Cat Blessing, whoever he was. Did people really want to listen to him rant and rave like that? They must. Some must, anyway, or he wouldn't have his own radio show.

She sighed miserably and looked around in disbelief. Of course she'd heard about L.A. traffic being pretty bad, but this was ridiculous. It couldn't be normal. If it were, no one would live here. There must be some accident or toxic spill, for it to be this bad.

She was bored, bored, bored. She'd already propped her feet -- one at a time -- on the dashboard and painted her toenails hot pink. She hated the color but happened to have the bottle in her purse, so went on the theory that toenails painted any shade were better than bare toenails. She accidentally got a dab on her jesus sandals. Hopefully she could get that out later, with nail polish remover.

What street was she on? Santa Monica Boulevard? It had been so long since she'd moved, she'd forgotten. Her AC was busted, naturally, so she had no hope of avoiding the god-awful, superheated air blasting in through her open windows. Sure, she'd thought about getting the AC fixed before leaving Chicago, but repairs would have bitten too deeply into her meager nest egg. Once she got settled and found a job, she'd get the Corolla taken care of. Clearly, living here without a working AC in the car was not an option. Would she be sweating this much if she wasn't overweight? Served her right. Her t-shirt clung damply to her back. She could feel sweat sliding down in slick streams between her breasts, collecting like dew on her upper lip, moistening her scalp and making her fine hair even flatter looking, she was sure. Fortunately, there was no one in the car with her to see the disgusting puddle that she was becoming. She looked like a hot tranny mess.

Her cell phone rang.

"Luanne? Where the heck are ya?"

She tried not to allow her irritation to transfer to Jeff. This gridlock wasn't his fault."Stuck," she said glumly. "Going nowhere fast. I won't be getting to your place anytime soon, Jeff. Sorry, I hope I haven't screwed up your day."

"No, no. I thought I'd wait for you, give you a real welcome, but..," he hesitated awkwardly. "Since we don't know what your E.T.A. is, would you mind if I went out and got something to eat? There's this new Indian restaurant that opened up just down the street. Within walking distance, which is pretty important these days. A friend and I wanted to try it out. We can wait until you get here, though. If you want. Maybe you're closer than you think."

"Go," she said. "Don't wait on me. You could bring me a doggy bag, though. I'm partial to samosas." The thought of genuine, hot food made her stomach spasm with desire. She'd polished off her "travel cuisine" -- Nacho Cheese Doritos, Diet Cokes, power bars and peanut butter and jelly sandwiches -- some time ago. The blue and white Igloo cooler on the floor of the passenger side of the front seat was empty. The brown paper grocery store bag resting atop it held only crumpled wrappers, empty pop cans and sticky baggies. Normally she would simply pull over at some convenience store and restock her rolling larder (and replenish the rolling larder on her ass and hips, she thought ruefully). Even if she were able to move out of her current position, she'd never be able to get back into the lane of traffic. She dared not risk it. Did she? Traffic would have to get rolling soon, wouldn't it? She'd get to eat at some point.

"You and your friend have a good time," she told him. "Is he cute, by the way?"

She got a laugh out of him with that line. Of course the friend was cute. Jeff was adorable, boyish and fit, with a sunny personality and an irresistibly friendly manner. He'd been one of her closest friends in Chicago. They met when they were both cast in a one act about a young married couple trapped in an argument, forced to have it out again and again in different ways with a different outcome each time. Hilariously, they had chemistry onstage, and, as two newcomers to Chi-town, they quickly bonded offstage as well. Jeff, unlike hetero men, paid attention to her. In all ways but sex, they enacted the rituals of courtship, with he being teasing, warm, occasionally gallant, and she being his sounding board, his cheering section. They met in her flat to run lines or watch bad reality shows while eating microwave popcorn and drinking cheap merlot. They shopped together at thrift stores for inexpensive clothes that were more shabby than chic. They alerted each other to upcoming auditions, went to each other's plays, talked about writing a play together. Jeff was as crazy about acting as she was. What's more, he made her feel good about herself -- something that rarely occurred outside the performance of a role, when she could lose herself in a character. Their rituals had to be put on hold now and then when Jeff would find a new beau. Although he always made an effort to include her in his new relationships, she felt awkward, an impediment to his fun. Jeff would try to include her in his plans, but she was inevitably convinced that the new boyfriend -- whichever new boyfriend -- couldn't possibly want her around. She would retreat to her own life at these times, to her temp work in whatever downtown office she was placed in for however long, to auditions and acting workshops and a succession of diets that always left her as fat as ever, or sometimes even fatter.

She thought she must be mad, bringing her pear-shaped body to L.A., the Land of the Gorgeous People. She was absolutely confident of her talent. She had it, in spades. When she was able to get a director to look past her size-16 ass and size 32A breasts and cast her in a play, she worked a magic with it that she was supremely sure of, because she felt it, again and again, from audiences: a collective intake of breath, or teary sniffles, or raucous laughter just where she wanted it.

She filled up a role like she was unable to fill up certain vital corners of her own life. Onstage, she was at home. She felt most real, most activated when she was immersed in a role. Her voice was richly versatile: a sledgehammer-like weapon, a plaintive wail, a shy whisper, a coy deceit. It could be youthful and exuberant, ragged, accented, teary, serene. Onstage her body was a remarkable tool instead of the unattractive, disproportionate hindrance that it was in the real world. In the magic world of the theatre, it moved in magical ways.

She was inventive, seemingly spontaneous, courageously vulnerable in scenes that called for it, despairing or gleeful, serious or exuberant or shocked in scenes that called for those emotions. Her characters' relationships with other characters were far more vibrant, more electrifyingly alive than anything she'd ever experienced in her offstage life. She inhabited each part so thoroughly that she often forgot who she was until the final curtain applause had crested and started to recede. She was damn good. When she'd headed to Chicago from Altoona, Pennsylvania she'd been hoping to eventually crack the major theatres, the Goodman, the Victory Gardens, but she never had. It turned out not to matter. For three years she worked so much in the smaller theatres that formed a passionate performance network throughout the big city that she felt artistically challenged and satisfied, finally deciding to head to California to take her crack at the movie industry. After all, Jeff seemed to be enjoying himself here. She had a box of new head shots ready for distribution and her resume was updated and (she thought) pretty impressive. She had a demo tape of some of her performances, had heard that theatrical experience was valued here. Of course, so were looks. She would never be cast as the beautiful ingénue, the object of love upon which so many plots turned. No, she was destined for the outcast roles: the oversized Josie Hogan in A Moon for the Misbegotten, the unwanted virgin Lizzie in The Rainmaker.

She could always play the fat, funny best friend. There was almost always a fat, funny best friend, someone the beautiful female lead can confide in, hang out with. Someone whose looks wouldn't challenge those of the beautiful female lead.

And as for the personal component...if all the women here were slim and beautiful and they were the ones who got all the men...well, her love life couldn't be any worse than it had been in Chicago, could it? She cringed as she remembered her most recent affair (she couldn't even honestly call if a relationship). It was with a marketing guy she'd met at one of her temp jobs. They hadn't had much in common, but she'd been so thrilled when he asked her to go to lunch that she thought...why not? After a few months of lackluster outings and mediocre sex, he'd stopped calling and she'd stopped caring. Some things come to a natural end, she thought philosophically. She'd already moved on to another office, a different administrative assistant position, so she didn't have to see him in the workplace. It was never clear to her why he'd asked her out in the first place.

"Here's something to look forward to, Luanne: my apartment complex has a swimming pool, so you can have a nice cool swim when you get here. If I'm not back yet, just come on in. I'll leave the key in the dirt of the potted bamboo sitting next to my door. Just root around a little."

"You can do that in L.A.?"

"I guess we'll find out," he said, and signed off to go with his "friend" to the Indian restaurant.

Jeff had told her she could stay with him until she found a place of her own. "It's a tiny apartment, but I've got a blow-up bed you can sleep on. It's not the best neighborhood in the world, but it's cheap and colorful. Right near the theater district. Little theaters, mostly, stuck in between liquor stores and pawn shops and car washes. There's a Jehovah's Witness that has services in English, Spanish and Russian, in case you want to convert. They have their services on Saturdays, you know. That could be a selling point. For the glamour factor, the CNN building isn't far."

She'd played along. "That's the best you can do for a glamour factor?"

Her car finally moved forward, maybe two feet. This was unbelievable. Was there an accident up ahead? She couldn't see any flashing lights. If there'd been a crash, it was affecting traffic in both directions. Eastbound was as bad as westbound. It didn't make any sense. She was starving. Was there any stray food in this car? Something she'd overlooked? She popped open the glove compartment and scrabbled around in it, rooting through fast food restaurant napkins and packets of ketchup, a few tampons, some crumpled maps and a flashlight with no batteries in it. Oh, no. Her fingers closed on a small cellophane wrapped container she hadn't known was there, since she'd quit smoking more than three years ago. Oh, no! Not now. Why did she have to find this now, when her defenses were low? She was hungry and tired and sweaty and irritable and... Maybe the pack of Salem Slim Lights was empty. It sure felt light. She tilted it and shook it gently, just as she used to do, and saw two cigarettes shift to the opening. After all this time, they had to be stale. Disgusting. Really stale. Besides, she probably didn't have a lighter. She threw all her smoking paraphernalia away when she quit. Almost as if they were bionic, and acting on orders from a brain that was not hers, her fingers rooted around in the glove compartment until they closed on a familiar object. She pulled out a book of matches. It was lavender, with gold letter in a scrolling font: Clarissa and Anthony, Sept. 25, 2004.

One little cigarette couldn't hurt. Not after all this time. She was powerfully curious about how it would taste. Probably awful, since it had been sitting in her glove compartment for years and years. Maybe the matches wouldn't work.

The first match she tried flared instantly into life. She held the tiny flame to the end of the cigarette and sucked in deeply. Oh, my God. She felt an instant high, a rush of pleasure into her lungs and brain that was even better than chocolate. She smoked hungrily, happily. The chemical rush somehow bestowed a feeling of freedom on her and she suddenly thought: *I'm not chained to this car. I can leave.* There must be a bar nearby, with a cool, dark interior and a whiskey sour with her name on it. And a cigarette machine. Did they still have those? She put the matches in her purse – just in case. What would happen, if she simply got out and walked away from her car? She probably had time to eat a decent meal before the traffic moved at all.

She got out of the Corolla, locked it and walked away, not looking back.

Cap, half-listening to the news, unscrewed the top of his thermos and poured some coffee into his mug, an oversized blue ceramic number bearing the legend, "I Hate Cats." He never drank the coffee from the coffeemaker in the station's kitchenette, claiming that he used a special blend: organic, heirloom, non-genetically engineered, free trade coffee grown from beans first cultivated by Incan kings and now, after being enthusiastically dispersed by migrating caffeine addicts, grown on sweetly sun-kissed hillsides in Hawaii.

Cap's special blend actually consisted of supermarket brand coffee mixed liberally with Scotch or sometimes -- when he was feeling festive -- Bailey's Irish Cream. Usually Scotch.

He didn't give a damn whether or not what he ingested was genetically engineered frankencoffee from beans saturated with toxic chemicals and picked by child slaves. All that "special blend" crap was just an ironic nod to his location. In L.A., you had to pretend that you cared deeply. About what depended on the day of the week.

If he heard one more person tell him that they were "really spiritual," he was going to throw up in his mouth.

Cap drank a large thermos full of his special blend every day during his show and every day his producer pretended not to know what it really was. Cap wasn't worried. As long as he'd been a fixture in this market and as strong as his ratings were, he'd have to kill somebody while driving drunk to even get temporarily suspended. And with traffic moving as slowly as it did these days, *that* wasn't likely to happen.

The "I Hate Cats" mug was a gift from his second wife, whom he'd assumed would be a sexual dynamo because of the size of her breast implants. She turned out to be perfectly average in the sack – even ungenerous with her enormous and expensive breasts, as if they were only for show.

His second wife grew tired of his peccadilloes even faster than wives #1, #3 and, #4. In his few introspective moments, he knew he should have wondered why four beautiful women had found him -- at least for a short time -- attractive enough to marry. While his mirror showed him grizzled hair atop a jowly, egg-shaped face, small bleary eyes and a paunch spilling untidily over his giant, cowboy-style belt buckle, he saw, instead a star. He knew he was a star because of the amount of money he made, the number of emails and calls that poured in, the thousands of requests for him to emcee events and endorse products.

Radio was a glorious medium in which an ugly man could win his spurs before his listeners knew what he looked like. Or even *if* his listeners knew what he looked like. He had never considered plastic surgery. It was too gratifying to look like he did and get the reactions he got in a place like L.A., where appearance was almost everything.

When Cap Lessing glanced in a mirror, he saw a wildly popular talk show host who made more money than he'd ever thought possible. He saw a man whose agent was working on a syndication deal that would spread his fame even farther, and make him even *more* money. Of course, the money went out as fast as it came in. He was currently supporting two of his four ex wives. (The other two had found new, even wealthier husbands.) He was also paying for the three children that he knew of, legally fighting off an expensive paternity sought brought by a woman he wasn't sure he'd slept with, subsidizing the meth habit of his current girlfriend, a 22-year-old model/set stylist, paying off and maintaining his 35-foot cabin cruiser, vintage car collection, 2009 Porsche Carrera, a swanky condo that was only a ten minute walk from the station, a house in Malibu Colony, and yet another beach house, in the Caribbean, even though he rarely got there. He should probably sell that one, he thought. Same for the boat. He almost never took the boat out on the water, but was loathe to get rid of it, since it was his love of boats that had inspired his on air moniker, "Captain" -- eventually shortened to Cap. His real name was Duane. He didn't like it.

Cap loved his flaws. Gloried in them. Embraced them and used them frequently in his show - except for the drinking, of course. He wanted to be able to take shots at recovering alcoholics because, according to his therapist, he was unwilling to confront his own problem with the bottle. He was a self-hating alcoholic. Screw that. That wasn't it. He just enjoyed jerking them around. Aside from that one, he talked about his faults fondly and excessively, crafting his own legend out of the turbulence and drama that perpetually swept around him. There'd been two bankruptcies, an arrest for assault after he punched Ex Wife #3's snotty lawyer during a deposition, a short-lived scandal over some illegal betting on sports. He'd had more affairs than Bill Clinton (and with better-looking women, he thought smugly), used way too much cocaine, made ill-advised investments in questionable schemes whose originators later ended up under indictment. He'd smoked cigars with presidents and Mafia kingpins (though not at the same time), caused a sensation when he allowed himself to be tearfully reunited -- on television -- with his father, who'd abandoned the family when Cap was only 7. Once the cameras stopped rolling, Cap gave the old son of a bitch opportunist a check for $5,000 and instructed him to never even *think* about getting in touch with Cap again. Publicity was one thing. Unwanted family ties were another.

Cap lived large and regretted almost nothing. He'd made a lot of enemies and taken many wrong turns, but he rarely looked back. Why should he? He was a black man who'd made himself hugely successful in an industry owned by white men. He was an ugly man sought after by beautiful people. He was very, very good at what he did. The number of people he pissed off each day was a testament to his talent. He'd climbed to the top of the broadcasting mountain and stayed there for a long time. Many had tried, but no one had been able to pull him down from his perch. Not yet, anyway.

Chapter Fifteen:
Actin' Like Husband and Wife

Ira was surprised when the female lead of "Her Majesty's Gangsta" popped up and introduced herself. She wasn't at all what he'd expected.

INT. HOTEL HALLWAY

Muldoon strides confidently down the hallway toward his room. Suddenly he stops and stares—

CLOSE SHOT: A HOTEL ROOM DOOR, SLIGHTLY AJAR

He pulls out his gun and nudges the door open with his foot.

ANGLE ON HOTEL ROOM

The door opens wider to reveal a lamp turned on, a television screen lit up.

SFX: TV SOUNDS

CAMERA FOLLOWS Muldoon's P.O.V. as he creeps further into the room, then peers around a wall toward the beds.

ANGLE ON WOMAN, SITTING STRETCHED OUT ON THE BED, DRINKING A BOTTLED WATER.

She looks over and sees Muldoon, aiming a gun at her. Startled, she spills water on herself.

> SABRINA
> (exasperated)
> Damnit, Muldoon!

Muldoon holsters the gun.

                    SABRINA
                (CONT.; annoyed)
            Would a burglar be sittin'
            around watching Judge Judy?

                    MULDOON
            You're a long way from the 4th
            Precinct.

SABRINA WEATHERLY is 30ish and fit, with more character in
her face than beauty. Still, there's something about her
personality that draws men to her, and she knows it. She swings
her legs over the side of the bed and sits up straight, trying to
look more professional.

                    SABRINA
            Interpol decided you needed a
            wife, to look more like a tourist.
            They wanted to supply you with
            one of their own, but Loo
            convinced 'em you needed
            someone who knew you.
            Someone who could keep you on
            a short leash.

Muldoon sits next to her and puts his arm around her, attempting
a kiss.

                    MULDOON
            So let's start actin' like husband
            and wife.

Sabrina fights him off and jumps up.

                    SABRINA
            You're so predictable. You know
            what my real assignment is

here? To keep you from
embarrassing the Department.

MULDOON
What's the matter, Sabrina?
Where's the love? Have you
turned into a lesbian?

SABRINA
Maybe I just have good taste.

MULDOON
You didn't think I was so bad
the night of Harrison's
retirement party.

SABRINA
I was drunk.
(angrily)
What a pig. No wonder your
wife left you.

Muldoon looks genuinely wounded.

MULDOON
Where did you hear that? My
wife didn't leave me. She died.
Breast cancer.

CLOSE SHOT of Sabrina's face, processing this information,
deciding that it must be true.

SABRINA
Oh my God. I'm sorry. I'm
really sorry. My big mouth, you
know. It gets me in trouble a lot.
I didn't mean to...

There's a long, awkward moment of silence. Then:

82

MULDOON
Just kidding. She did leave me.
Said I was a jerk.

Furious, Sabrina picks up a pillow and hits him hard with it on the back.

CHAPTER SIXTEEN:
TENNIS PLAYER LEGS

Cody Torrance wrapped up his phone call with his business manager and realized that the limo wasn't moving. Had not moved for awhile, in fact. Where were they? He was going to be late for a meeting with Maj Remoshi, the director of Torrance's next movie, "Choke Holder and Wiser."

Cody pushed a button to open his window. No, that was the wrong one. A panel inlaid with glossy burled wood slid back to reveal stereo controls. Or were those the TV controls? He was no good with technology. He tried another and felt an inward whoosh of rancid-smelling hot air that made his nostrils contract in self-defense. He let the window down a little, just enough to see that they were only in West Hollywood. He gazed out at the stilled traffic in irritation.

This new limo driver, Bran, wasn't exactly at the top of his game, was he? Why hadn't he taken Malibu Canyon Road to the 101? Oh. That's right. Something about the 101, like all the freeways, being too slow. Cody didn't pay much attention to traffic reports. Since wrapping up the promotional tour for his last movie and divorcing his latest wife, he'd retreated to his Malibu beach house for some much needed rest and recreational drugs. Not much – just a little medicinal weed, along with a little medicinal wine. There really was nothing like smoking dope at sunset, on a balcony, while gazing out over the churning, mysterious majesty of the ocean as the sun withdrew its fiery splendor and darkness rose up to turn the relentless waves black, the beach sand cool.

The ocean was where he found his center, his calm. "Whatever we lose like a you or a me, it's always ourselves that we find by the sea," he murmured to himself in satisfaction. He loved e.e. cummings.

The longer Cody looked out at the bizarre tableau before him, the more forgiving he felt toward Bran, who seemed like a good guy, after all, and was only trying to earn a living. Bran couldn't be blamed for this mess. He'd probably done the wise thing by taking the Pacific Coast Highway to Sunset, which curved its sinuous, luxurious way inland - although Sunset wasn't exactly speedy in good times. Cody thought suddenly that he really should buy that estate in Idaho his realtor had mentioned to him. Bolt this appallingly overpopulated city and escape to somewhere green and peaceful, like Kurt and Goldie, and Demi and Ashton – when they were together. Maybe they had the right idea.

L.A. was shallow and crass and now, on top of all that, impossible to navigate. Wouldn't he love to be back amid mountains again, like when he was young? Ah, but who was he kidding? He was thoroughly spoiled. He could never leave this weather. Cody rolled the window back up so he wouldn't have to look at the other cars and thus be reminded that he wasn't moving. Besides, he was naked.

The smoked glass wall that divided the back seat from the front slid silently back. Just a few inches, as he'd specified. Wouldn't do to have the limo driver know he was sans clothes at the moment.

"We're almost out of gas, Mr. Torrance, because we've been stuck here so long," Bran announced respectfully. "I'm going to have to go and get some. We'll never make it to a gas station."

Cody was put out. "You didn't see this coming?"

"This limo doesn't get very good mileage, sir. And, well, you wanted to keep the air conditioning running so I couldn't shut off the engine..." His voice trailed off but his meaning was clear: the gas situation was not his fault.

"All right," Cody said in resignation. "And while you're out there, see if you can find an alternate route. Ask at the gas station. I've got to get to this meeting."

"I know, Mr. Torrance. I'm doing my best."

"I know you are, Bran."

Bran left the limo, closing the door behind him.

Cody thought about putting his clothes on. He enjoyed riding around in the raw, knowing that the tinted windows of the limo hid him from the world beyond, the world of ordinary people who were forced to go about clothed, prisoners of convention. Nudity was a great freedom to him. He practiced it discreetly, mainly at his beach house, which was on a road secured by a gate that could only be opened by a combination known only to the few homeowners living behind its protection. Going about in his birthday suit in his own home was pleasant enough, but it lacked the sheer relish he got from riding around Southern California completely naked, with no one even guessing that he was in this condition. When he was going somewhere alone – without his assistant or agent -- he generally took his clothing off as soon as he got into the back seat, away from the curious eyes of whoever was driving that day. He then dressed before exiting the vehicle. After all, he wasn't a pervert! His nudity was between himself and...himself. Somehow, transforming his appearance to his most elemental state lessened, at least a little, the uneasy chasm that existed between who he appeared to be and who he actually was.

No, he wouldn't put his clothes on just yet. He had time. It felt too good to lounge absolutely free of restriction, his bare flesh meeting the smooth surface of the leather seat, his skin tickled by the cool, steady flow of air conditioning.

So Cody Torrance, a.k.a. Floyd Minterling, settled back and turned again to the script he was reading. The name Cody Torrance was his agent's idea. "Sounds rugged. Kind of cowboyish. Cody is a city out west somewhere." Even though Sid had lived in L.A. for more than twenty years, he still geographically viewed the world in terms of its relationship to New York. "Also makes you think of Buffalo Bill Cody, doesn't it?" Floyd was glad that the sweet, absent-minded grandfather for whom he'd been named, Grandpa Floyd, was already dead when he was rechristened. The proud family name of Minterling was replaced with equal ease.

Cody Torrance was just about the most famous man in the world. It was still a bit of a surprise to him. A dreamy boy who loved stories and movies, an indifferent student raised by a widowed bookkeeper in a small New Hampshire town, he'd tried out for a high school play on a whim - to impress a girl. He also wanted an excuse for missing a month's worth of basketball practice, which involved lots of running and sweating. In his tiny school, any boy who had two functioning legs was expected to play on the basketball team, regardless of ability or desire. Floyd had gotten the role in the play and the girl, and the link between the two became firmly fixed in his mind.

"You're nothing but a pretty face," his first wife said scornfully to him in the last weeks of their decaying union. "A no talent." It stung, as she'd intended it to. It pushed the button of doubt that periodically tortured him. He knew he was an ordinary man, only moderately talented as an actor. He also knew that he had a look, a quality, a charisma that the camera adored.

When he'd gone on to drama school, his classmates anxiously plumbed the unfamiliar depths of Shakespeare's rich language, agonized over how to interpret characters created by Albee and Williams, Ibsen and Miller, strained to develop techniques that would allow them to express and emote, physicalize and internalize. How they struggled, while he held the small audiences in the drama school theatre *spellbound* with what amounted to instinct. He failed to master accents, proved clumsy at stage combat and didn't even project all that well, but it hadn't mattered. The spotlight bathed him in glory, followed him as if it had nowhere else to go, loved him just as the camera would love him a few years later, when he made his way to L.A. and ventured into the movie industry.

The public loved him, too, even in the early days. His head shot -- an inexpensive, amateurish version of the slick photos that would represent him later, when he was a star -- was stolen again and again from its hanging place in the lobby of the drama school theatre. The suspects were numerous: schoolchildren and senior citizens who arrived in busloads for matinees, culture seeking ladies who attending evening performances. Floyd didn't mind replacing the photo, each time it went missing. He felt complimented by these first bright flashes of fame, which flared briefly and magically like heat lighting on a humid summer night.

Eventually, he realized that some of his fellow actors resented the thefts. He could hardly blame them. Their hard work, their accomplishments were greater than his but he had something – some quality - that made people tingle to hear him speak, or watch him make the slightest gesture. Although he didn't really deserve it, he was the member of the school company who got most of the attention.

Finally one night he stole the headshot of Ted, the most talented student actor (and the one most bitter about the lack of adulation). Floyd was gratified by Ted's reaction the next day. "It's the damndest thing, isn't it?" Ted remarked, since they were then in the same fraternity, a small select circle of heartthrobs. "Kind of a pain in the ass. Those head shots cost money." But Ted was pleased, Floyd could tell. Floyd stole Ted's photo again a few weeks later and several more times before he was graduated from drama school.

Once in L.A., Floyd Minterling had become, with relatively little effort, Cody Torrance. In fact he'd caught the attention of Sid Kirschenbaum, a top agent and the man who renamed him, so quickly and easily that he at first assumed it was that quick and easy for all would be actors to attract the services of top agents.

Sid put him together with casting directors, who saw in him the same thing that his earlier audiences had observed. What that was, exactly, was impossible to define or name, but it was irresistible and that was all that really mattered.

He was handsome, of course, with thick roan hair like a Kennedy and tennis player legs, a rangy upper body and a face that people couldn't stop looking at. Still, there were thousands of handsome actors in L.A. grappling for a place in the entertainment industry. After a few -- a very few -- smaller movie roles, Cody was cast as the lead in a major feature film, "Choke Hold." He played Buck (short for Buckshot) Buchanan, a tough cop with a heart, a character as good with a quip as he was with a fist, resourceful and cunning when placed in peril, capable of the rare tender moment, his habitual manly smirk now and then yielding to a fleeting haunted expression that reminded the audience of his tragic past (as shown in flashbacks). This past accounted for his cynical, shoot-first-and-ask-questions-later methodology. Buck Buchanan had no love of violence - no! He was, however, very good at it, each and every time he was forced into using it.

Women fantasized about drawing out the sensitive side they just knew was there, buried deep inside of Buck, while still thrilling to the protection of those muscular arms (chiseled to perfection under the direction of the personal trainer Sid recommended). Men admired his taciturn, cut-through-the-crap directness, his preference for action over emotion, the simple yet effective way Buck mowed down enemies with a 9 millimeter or a baseball bat, whichever was handier. At the end of the day, the bad guys were dead and the broad was in bed, waiting for a different kind of action. They were waiting for Buck Buchanan, the man other men wanted to be.

"Choke Hold" launched Cody like a rocket into the stratosphere of Hollywood stardom. The speed of his ascent was dizzying. He was not prepared for the attention that slammed into him with the force of a tsunami, nor had he expected that his fame would be worldwide. "Choke Hold," like so many movies that were heavy on action and light on dialogue and character development that might require cultural contexts, was easily exported to other countries. Action was simple to follow, satisfying in its cause and effect storytelling. The movie made a boatload of money.

He then starred in "No (Choke) Holds Barred," and a slew of other movies in which he played a tough cop with a heart, as quick with a quip as he was with a fist. In reality, he was quick with neither, but he soon noted that it did not matter to the people who met him. They only saw the glowing aura of fame around him, because that's all they wanted to see.

Buck Buchanan could kick the ass of ten or twenty bad guys, pleasure a woman, then kick a little more ass before calling it a day. Floyd Minterling had never even been in a fight. Floyd Minterling was afraid of heights, roller coasters and spiders. Floyd Minterling wasn't agile enough to be good at baseball or tennis or the sword fighting he'd practiced in stage combat classes. Until he made his way to Los Angeles, Floyd Minterling had never been in a big city and he was still (he admitted only to himself) intimidated by the sprawling, seething, untidy metropolis that was now his home. Floyd Minterling had once, from the safe confines of his limo, seen some thug grab a woman's purse and run away, leaving her screaming angrily in his wake, and Floyd Minterling had done absolutely nothing about it -- although he had briefly considered instructing his limo driver to chase the man. Instead, perplexed and indecisive, he rode on in silence. Cody Torrance would have kicked the man's ass.

His musings were abruptly interrupted when the door to his right swung open.

"There he is!" he heard Bran say excitedly.

A photographer aimed his camera at Cody and took pictures rapidly and ruthlessly.

Cody grabbed the door handle and tried to pull it shut, but the photographer blocked it open with his body.

No! This couldn't happen! Photos of Cody Torrance, naked in the back seat of a limo, all over the internet and splashed on magazine covers in every grocery store! Cody thrust his foot out and kicked the photographer hard in the knee with it. He probably didn't do any real damage to the knee, but the move did cause his tormentor to lose his balance and teeter, giving Cody the momentary advantage. He shoved the man back and pulled the door closed, hitting the "lock" button. He quickly pulled on his shorts (he never wore underwear) but heard an infuriating "click" as he reached for his shorts.Bran was using his keyless entry system to unlock the door. Cody pushed the "lock" button again, grabbed his shirt and slid his feet into a pair of loafers just as Bran got the door open again. The son of a bitch! How much was he getting paid by the photographer? Had he known that Cody liked to travel around in the buff, or was that a surprise that was going to get him a huge bonus?

Cody slid across the seat and sprang from the limo through the opposite door. Hunching over, trying to hide his face, he sprinted away from the limo, pulling his shirt on as he weaved through gaps between stopped cars. He glanced back and saw the photographer following, but the man was burdened with photographic equipment. Bran stayed apace with his co-conspirator, probably to protect his financial interests. Photos of Cody Torrance running away like a coward would be almost as good as the nude shots.

And that was the problem. Even if Cody evaded them now, they still had photos of him naked in his limo. Naked on a private beach in the Maldives wouldn't be so bad. Naked poolside in the south of France would be ok, too, image-wise.

But naked in the back seat of a car on a busy street in L.A.? It would be seen, or spun, as perverted. What would it do to his career? Nothing good, that was sure. Cody Torrance, tough cop with a heart and -- by the way -- pervert?

Fear and fury made him wheel about and leap at the paparazzi. Even though the man's legs were short and his broad body not built for speed, he'd managed to just about close the gap between them. He was shockingly close. Cody's move took him by surprise. Cody was gratified to see the paparazzo's eye's light with fear. His pursuer, who was now his quarry, executed a clumsy about face and sped away from him.

The parked cars and trucks around them formed a series of obstacles, making the chase a bizarrely slow motion one. Cody got close enough to the photographer to seize the tail of his faded army fatigue shirt and yank it hard in an attempt to stop him, but that only motivated the man to clamber over the hood of a motionless Honda, dodging wildly out of Cody's grasp.

After a moment's hesitation, Cody himself scrambled up and over the car, a little surprised that he was able to carry off a move that he'd seen his stunt double do in his movies. I am an action star! he thought. But he also hoped he wouldn't have to hit the man. He wasn't even sure how to do it.

The idled motorists, many of whom were lounging outside of their vehicles while waiting for traffic to resume, found this peculiar chase scene diverting, particularly when the tall, good-looking man unexpectedly turned around and started chasing his chaser. Some looked around for a camera crew and the big white trucks that would mean this was a scene being filmed for a movie. Finding none, they were even more intrigued. Whatever this was, it was real. Or maybe it was for reality TV. Bored, frustrated, and having nothing better to do, people drew closer to the two men, inadvertently ringing them in and bringing the pursuit to a close.

Up against a wall of people, the paparazzi tried to duck under Cody's reach, but Cody grabbed the camera strap and wrenched it over the man's head, taking possession of his camera, pivoting so that he could run with it. He'd been so intent on catching the photographer that he didn't notice the crowd, gathering and thickening like ominous gravy, until it was too late.

"That's Cody Torrance," a man announced in wonder. The name rippled through the crowd like an audio orgasm. "My God! It *is* him!" "It's Cody Torrance!" "Cody Torrance!" People pushed forward, trying to get closer. The paparazzo, who was trying to grab the camera back from Cody, was pressed against him briefly like a lover. He looked up at Cody with a belligerent bravado, sneering and reaching for the camera that Cody, who was taller, held up and out of his reach. Their inadvertent embrace was short-lived. The paparazzo was rolled out of the way by many arms. He disappeared into a sea of people before he could even utter a protest.

Pens and scraps of paper were shoved at Cody -- the inevitable autograph seekers. A woman fell under the force of the crowd and screamed helplessly. Cody finally realized the danger. There was no security here. No large men in dark suits to hold back the fans, as there were at movie premieres. No burly uniformed guards, like the ones who kept watch at the gates of the movie studio. He didn't even have his assistant or p.r. flack on hand to run interference for him. The situation was about to get dangerously out of control. He was going to be swarmed.

Was this payback, because everything had come so easily to him? Still holding onto the camera and thinking almost as fast on his feet as Buck Buchanan would have, Cody made for the weakest part of the crowd's inner circle: a woman in a wheelchair standing next to three children. He brushed past them easily, then zig zagged to punch through the crowd at its next thinnest point. He leapt to the top of a Nissan bearing a "Buckle Up With Jesus" bumper sticker, and then dropped down onto a mini Cooper. He jumped to the ground and zipped around the side of a building to remove himself temporarily from sight, then stretched his legs and galloped recklessly down the sidewalk, still clutching the camera in his hand.

He was surprised, really, at how fast he could run. Maybe he'd talk to Maj about doing some of his own stunts in the next Buck Buchanan movie.

CHAPTER SEVENTEEN:
STITCHES IN UNMENTIONABLE PLACES

"Yeah, it's hard to believe that the anti-smoking Nazis got their wish. The legislature just rolled over for them. Can't smoke in office buildings. Can't smoke in restaurants, OK. Fine. I understand that, people are eating food in those places. But not in bars, either? Like bars are health spas? I mean, people don't come in to places like this for their health. And it's not stopping there. You know in some towns in California, it's illegal to stand on a street corner and smoke? This is supposed to be a state where anything goes! You ever see the shit they sell on Venice Beach? Herbs my ass. Who are you bothering on a street corner, I ask? The air inside is one thing, but the air outside sucks anyway."

The uninvited diatribe was giving Luanne a headache. She was angry with herself for smoking the first cigarette, furious about smoking the second. When she left her whiskey sour and stepped outside the Mexican restaurant to do it, she found herself conversationally trapped with this chatterbox, another smoker taking a nicotine break. A fellow traveler. She nodded politely as he yammered on and on about the government suppression of his right to give himself cancer, and thought that when she politely excused herself to go back inside, she'd be rid of him.

No such luck. She sat back down at the bar and was about to order another drink when her new best friend sat on the barstool next to her, continuing his attempts to bond with her over their mutual bad habit. This is a granfaloon, she thought. But she felt a little sorry for him, because he was trying so hard to connect with a fellow human being whom he had met only seven and a half minutes ago. He was terribly needy.

The restaurant was artificially dark, cool and soothing. Ruby-glassed wall sconces illuminated large paintings on black velvet of brown-skinned people dancing, women with long dark hair grinding corn and holding babies. A dozen or so customers sat in captain's chairs around varnished wood tables or in booths

93

upholstered in deep green vinyl. The carpet felt spongy when you walked on it.

"I'm not really a smoker," she said. "I just found an old pack in my glove compartment and, well, today's been sort of frustrating. You know. The traffic. I actually quit four years ago."

"I understand," he said gravely. "I've slid down that slippery slope myself a few times. And I will quit for good, one of these days. But it should be my choice. Just as it's your choice. Not the government's. Not some self-righteous, anti-smoking Nazis. Cigarettes are still legal in these United States. We smokers have to stick together. I can help you with that, if you tell me straight out that you're not a cop or any kind of health department employee." He paused dramatically.

She couldn't help herself. "I'm an actress."

He smiled knowingly, his teeth eerily white in the bar's gloomy interior. "I should have known. Here-- take this. I'm Tom, by the way."

"Luanne." She accepted the business card and stared at it, puzzled. It contained only three phone numbers, each prefaced by an area code: either 323, 818, or 310. There was no name or company name, no email addy or snail mail address.

"You call that number, give whoever answers your location, and they'll tell you how to get to the nearest smokeasy." At her obvious confusion, he explained; "Smoking speakeasies. Bars where you can still smoke. Like in the twenties, during Prohibition. There were tens of thousands of secret illegal places where you could still go to drink. Same thing goes on today, all over California. People like to smoke and drink at the same time. They also like to talk to other people who are smoking and drinking. We won't be stopped. It's all just gone underground. You'll pay a lot more for your booze there, but most people think it's worth it. We like the combination."

She shook her head in disbelief. "You're not serious."

"Try it, next time you're in the mood. Some of these places won't look like anything on the outside. They'll appear to be abandoned, boarded-up buildings. Maybe in a warehouse district. When you call that number, you'll be given directions on how to find the entrance, plus a password. Don't write anything down.

You'll want to have deniability, in case you're caught. It's just a misdemeanor for you, but a hassle nonetheless. The smokeasy operators, though, could get in real trouble."

"Yeah, thanks," she said, without enthusiasm, slipping the card into her purse.

"You don't believe me."

"Not entirely." Luanne laughed. "It's a little cloak-and-daggerish for a bad habit, isn't it?"

"A bad habit that's illegal. Punishable by a hefty fine."

"Well, who's behind this, this network of smokeasies? What are they getting out of it? How is it funded?" The question she really wanted to ask was: "Are you clinically insane?" But Tom seemed quite calm. "It's a group called the Jean Nicot Society. He's the guy who introduced nicotine to the French court, after coming across it in Portugal. The French royals took to it right away, naturally. This group is very libertarian-leaning. Doesn't think the government should interfere with individual choice." He paused for a moment, frowning. "Although it may be funded by the tobacco companies. I'm not sure. Doesn't really matter to me. Your eyes are glazing over, by the way."

"I've had a long day, and it's far from over." *Or maybe it could be the conversation*? "Is there a convenience store near here? I need to buy some cigarettes."

"Down the street. But here-" He was scrabbling in his jacket pocket. "I noticed you smoke menthols, too. Take this pack – until you can get some more."

"Oh, I couldn't."

"Sure you could. We smokers have to stick together."

Why not? She put the pack of cigarettes in her purse.

He stirred his drink with a tiny straw. "So you're an actress. Have you done anything that I might have seen?"

Why should she bother? Luanne knew that if a pretty woman sat down at the bar, this guy would shift his attention away from her so fast it'd make her barstool spin. Not that she'd care. He was squat and sour-faced, maybe 45, maybe 50. Familiar in a disturbing way.

"Actually, I've just moved here. Today, as a matter of fact. From Chicago. I did a lot of theatre there."

He looked thunderstruck. "Now? You're moving here NOW? When things are like this? Boy, does your timing suck. Don'tcha even watch the news on TV? There's a crisis going on."

To hell with being polite. He'd gotten on her last nerve.

"Go away now," she said irritably, holding up her hand so that her palm was only inches away from his face while shifting on her barstool so that her shoulder was toward him. She grabbed a tortilla chip from a basket on the bar, jabbed it into a bowl of salsa and crunched on it savagely. Hot! The salsa was spicy! She'd mistakenly dipped her chip into the hot salsa, and her mouth felt as if it were on fire. She waved her hands at the bartender, trying to mime, another drink. Maybe she'd drink some and pour the rest in her ear, so that it would get plugged up and save her from listening to any more blather from her new friend. Of course, she could always leave. When she'd gone out to smoke that second cigarette, she checked the status of the traffic, a little concerned that her car might be causing some kind of obstruction. Nothing had moved. Her car was fine, still, right where she'd left it.

"Look, Luanne, I'm sorry," he said. "I know I can be annoying. It's my personality. Lots of people have told me that. Let me buy you a drink."

She chewed on another chip, this time without benefit of salsa. It was dry this way, but still satisfyingly salty. "Not necessary."

"Then let me buy you dinner. This place has great enchiladas."

She regarded him cynically. Was he really interested in her? Was that the vibe here? Hard to tell.

"I don't see a wedding ring. I know you probably get guys hitting on you all the time," he said, causing her to nearly choke on a chip. "I just... I hate to eat alone. Tell you what. I'm going to go visit the men's room, and you think about it. No pressure."

He slid jauntily off his barstool and headed down a hallway toward the back of the restaurant.

Luanne tried to think about what to do. Instead, she shamelessly eavesdropped on the conversation taking place at a booth somewhere behind her and to her right. It was a habit she'd developed to improve her craft (she told herself). It helped her study people and the way they interacted with each other.

"I hope you have an easier time than Janet," a man said. "Jeez. By the end of it, I was just begging her--"

"You were there with her the whole time?" interrupted another male voice. Luanne stared at the mirrored wall behind the bar, trying to see the speakers without too being obvious. She pretended to be examining the rows of liquor bottles lining shelves over a glass-doored refrigerated unit filled with bottles of Corona and Dos Equis as if she found them all very fascinating. There wasn't much need for the subterfuge. She couldn't really see them, so they probably didn't notice her. After a few minutes of careful listening, the group resolved itself into two couples, probably thirtysomethings.

"Sure did," the first man said proudly. "Got muscle strain in my arm from holding her leg in the one position for so long. The doctor said it could have developed into tendonitis."

"Would you flag down the waitress next time you see her?" a woman asked. "I want some flan."

"Janet was in labor for twenty-six hours," the first man said.

"Twenty-seven." This female voice had a sharp edge to it. "I was in labor for twenty-seven hours."

"Ok, honey. Ok. Whatever you say. Twenty-seven hours."

"Whenever you tell this story, you always say twenty-six and I always have to correct you. Every single time." Her anger bubbled just beneath the surface of her words like a hot spring. "Why is that, I wonder?"

"I said I was sorry," he said, getting irritated himself.

"No you didn't."

"Well I am. Boy, am I sorry. I'm sorry I made a minor error. Big deal. I was an hour off."

"It's probably hard keeping track of time when you're in a delivery room," said Man #2, clearly a peacemaker. "Although I can't wait to do it myself, honey, really." He laughed. Was he patting the hand of flan woman? "We're already interviewing nannies. The agency has even found us some that speak pretty good English."

"And that Irish one, don't forget."

"But I've told him about it before," insisted Angry Woman. "He does this every time. On purpose."

"Janet, you should just be happy that he was there, in the delivery room with you. A lot of men won't do it, even in this day and age," said Flan Woman.

"I am happy that he was there to share in the joy of the experience, but because he was there, he should know that for twenty-seven hours, I went through utter hell. Utter, absolute hell. Pain. Blood. Tearing. Stitches in unmentionable places. The works. Yet every time he tells the story, he shorts me an hour. He gets all of his golf scores straight. He can remember to the pound how much he can bench press at the gym. When he comes home from a fishing trip, he remembers the length and weight and the number of scales, for God's sake, of every single fish he caught. So why can't he remember how long I was in labor with our son?"

A long silence followed. Luanne listened hard. She had a chip clutched in her hand but was afraid to put it in her mouth and chew, fearing that it would be loud and she'd miss part of the dialogue. She waited.

"I thought we were going to try and have a nice meal," Error Man said finally.

The bartender was suddenly standing over her. "Ready for another?"

She started guiltily and shook her head. Did he know she was eavesdropping? "Yeah, sure." She ate the tortilla chip. The interesting part sounded over, anyway.

The bartender slid a fresh drink in front of her, took away her empty and went back to the end of the bar. He sat on a stool and picked up his book again. She wondered how he could see well enough to read in the dim light. He was young, Latino, short of stature but well-built, packed nicely into tight jeans and a snug black t shirt strained a little by his muscular biceps. He carried himself with a formality that discouraged small talk and familiarity. His mien lent a certain dignity to the profession of bartending. A tattoo of a happy-looking skeleton riding a motorcycle with a banner bearing words in Spanish decorated his left forearm. When he put the book down to bring someone further down the bar a Heineken, she was able to make out the title: The Little Book of Zen.

"So what do you say?"

Tom was back. She had the strange sensation that she knew him from somewhere.

"You're thinking that I look familiar," he commented.

"Yeah."

"But you can't quite place me, can you?"

"No."

"You ever watch 'The McDermotts'?"

"You mean that old show?"

"You remember the youngest McDermott kid, Mickey? The one who was always inadvertently causing trouble by telling everybody's secrets?"

"Yeah. Yeah, I remember Mickey."

"That was me."

She was surprised, but instantly knew this to be true. The big, mischievous eyes, full cheeks and perky chin that had made him adorable as a child star were sort of grotesque on his adult face -- like all of his features hadn't developed the way they was supposed to, or developed at the same time. He let her stare, pleased by the scrutiny.

"Wow," she said finally. "A real TV star. I'm impressed. Really."

"I'm Tom Motti, by the way."

The name did ring a distant, small-print-in-the-TV-Guide bell.

"I'm Luanne." She took a sip of her drink, wondering what to say in order to prevent him from returning to the topic of smoking. "So. That's really cool."

"Used to be. It's been a long time since I got any acting jobs," he said. "When you're a cute child star and don't stay cute when you grow up, you might as well have leprosy in this town. I used to get thousands of pieces of fan mail. My fan club was bigger than the Fonz' fan club. I'm not exaggerating. All that money I made the studio, and once 'The McDermotts' was cancelled, I couldn't even get past the guards at the gate."

He was back in Bitter Town. Luanne considered returning to her car and sitting in it, even though it would be boring.

Almost as boring as listening to Tom Motti. Maybe when she finished her drink.

He didn't even need her here for his ventathon. He seemed to be talking to himself. "What I don't get is, why were people so surprised when I wanted to get a little crazy and do some cocaine? It was the 80s. Everybody else was doing it, not just people in the entertainment industry. The whole country was snorting coke up its nose, but when everybody's favorite kid, little Mickey McDermott, got busted with those club kids, the public acted like I'd violated some sacred trust. I wasn't allowed to be a human being with flaws. You remember all those headlines in the tabloids?

As a matter of fact, she didn't. How old did he think she was, anyway?

The bartender finished wiping down one end of the bar and glanced over at her, his expression sardonic: *Yeah, I've heard this before. Now it's your turn.*

Tom Motti muttered darkly into his drink. "I was on top of the world! All that money. Sure, a lot of it went up my nose. And the women... God, the women. And let's not forget all the people I had working for me, when I was on top: my agent, my manager, lawyer, accountant, tutors, drivers, p.r. people, vocal coach, the woman who ran my fan club. My own parents were on my payroll, for God's sake. Half my relatives, too. I was a pint-sized industry. Leeches, all of them. Feeding off the cash cow, who was just a little kid, responsible for so many people. No wonder I had a couple of nervous breakdowns! America turned on me. I was so cute when I was young. Every parent wanted their kid to be just like me, cute little Mickey. Always saying such adorable things. Getting the laughs. But then I grew up. That was my big crime. Growing up. America wants to stay a kid, too, you know. Forever 17 years old, in jeans and a rock band t-shirt, making out with some girl in the back of a car, not thinking about the future. Sure as hell not thinking about the past. America doesn't want to be a grown up. It wants things simple. It still wants everybody to like it."

"Take it easy, Tom," the bartender said. "You're getting all worked up again."

"Yeah, Esteban," Tom said savagely. "I'll take it easy, all right. For Christ's sake! I peaked at the age of ten! Where do you go from there?"

"Everyone has troubles," Esteban said calmly. "Some people never even get a taste of what you got."

"I know." Tom sighed. "You're right."

"What do you do now, Tom?" asked Luanne. "I mean, it's good to move on. To let the bad things go."

Tom glared at her. Esteban shot her a look that said: *Be quiet. You're making things worse.* She shot him one back: *I just came in here for a drink.*

Jesus. Did Tom Motti live in the anger dome full-time, or merely rent a room there now and again?

"I did find a new career, after I got out of prison. And got clean and sober and earned my G.E.D. I was estranged from my parents because they took a lot of my money and I sued them over it, so there was no help from them. You don't know how hard it was to learn how to be a normal person, after a childhood like that. Didn't know how to pay bills, shop for groceries, make a dentist appointment. That stuff had always been done for me. So, I finally found someone who was willing to give me a chance. Selling cars." He sighed. "And I was really good at it. I had a gift."

Luanne waited. She wouldn't ask. She would not participate any more. If he wanted to continue, he could do so without her prompting, even though that's what he clearly expected her to do.

After a long moment, he commenced talking. "Talk about picking the wrong profession," he commented glumly.

"What do you mean?" she said, forgetting her resolution.

"You're kidding me, right?" His hostility was loud and palpable. "Do you not know what's going on out there?" He waved his arm wildly toward the door. "Nobody's buying cars right now, because they can't go anywhere in them. The guy who owned the dealership I worked for had his entire inventory airlifted out of there and taken to Nevada. You see that guy at the end of the bar? He's a bus driver. Buses can't move. He got laid off and is probably going to lose his house. And that couple in the corner? Sitting at the table near the jukebox? They own a couple of car washes. Used to do really well. They had to file for bankruptcy last week. They're going to have to move to Des Moines and live with their grown daughter and her husband, and they can't stand him. He's a jerk.

"I had one customer, a psychologist. Bought a new car every year. Like clockwork. A lot of his practice was based on counseling couples whose marriages were strained because they didn't see each other much, because they spent so much time commuting every day. Most of those people have lost their jobs so they don't have to worry about commuting anymore. They spend plenty of time together. My customer loses patients, and I lose a customer. It's not a trickle down effect. It's an avalanche effect. People's lives are getting ruined because nothing's moving out there, and you're asking me what do I mean?"

Luanne wished she'd never let him start the conversation, wished she'd never stepped outside for that damn cigarette. She felt sick to her stomach, worried for her own future. What had she done? Why hadn't she paid more attention to what was going on here? This idiot was right. Her timing did suck. She should have waited until the traffic crisis was over to pull up stakes in Chicago and head blithely west.

"Why don't you move?" she murmured, staring not at him but at his reflection in the mirror behind the bar. "The traffic's not like this everywhere." Maybe she could just turn around right now and go back to the Midwest.

"It will be. Someday." His tone was maliciously smug. "All trends start here and spread to the rest of the country. Besides, I've lived here since I was six. I can't leave this weather."

She stood, swigged down the last of her whiskey sour, grabbed her purse and headed down the hallway to the ladies' room, not bothering to excuse herself.

She finished in the stall and was drying her hands at the sink when just about the most famous man in the world ran into the ladies' room, breathing hard, carrying a digital camera that was off the hook.

"I'll pay you a thousand dollars if you'll let me use your cell phone!" gasped Cody Torrance.

CHAPTER EIGHTEEN:
A WAY AROUND THE FRINGES

Lester Vinson was out of breath. Walking and talking at the same time was harder than he thought, especially since the pace he and the other men were keeping up was pretty brisk. They had to reach the demonstration before it was over, or they wouldn't get paid.

"Baby, I'm tellin' ya, I'm coming home soon." He was getting a little tired of Bernice's nagging, to tell the truth. He'd tried and tried to explain the situation to her, but she just didn't seem to understand that he was pretty much stuck here until the government did something to fix this mess and free his truck. He hated the thought of just walking away without finishing a job. He also hated the thought of not getting paid for that job, which he wouldn't, not until the load was delivered.

"But what are you going to do about Herb's truck? He keeps asking about it?"

"Bernie, the truck is stuck. The truck ain't going nowhere. Nobody back there gets it: traffic is just not moving here. Don't you watch the news?"

"I don't have much time for that."

Something disturbing occurred to him. "What do you mean, Herb keeps asking about it? Why's he bothering you? He's got my cell number. I give him updates. I'll deliver that load as soon as I can and he knows it. What's he doing, talking to you?"

"Oh..." Her voice drifted away a little. "Herb just stops by now and then, to make sure I'm doin' ok. He fixes little things. He says he knows how hard these long absences are on the wives of the guys who work for him."

Lester's angry chemicals started simmering. "Well isn't that nice of him."

"Don't be that way, Lester. He's been very helpful. You know I'm not handy. The other day he fixed the garbage disposal. Just like that. It all of a sudden stopped working and wouldn't grind anything up, and he got it going again."

"All he had to do was push the re-set button!" Lester said heatedly. "Any moron could do that. He's not exactly a mechanical genius, Bernie."

"Don't yell at me, Les. You weren't here to help and he was."

"Yeah? What else has he been 'helping' you with?" The angry chemicals were heating up, bubbling and roiling.

Up ahead, Les could see people moving with purpose, gravitating toward a larger mass that was focused in a single direction. He and his group of rapidly striding men picked up their pace. They would either need to plough through the crowd or find a way around the fringes. Between the increased speed and his irritation with Bernice, he found it even harder to speak.

"How many times has Herb been over there, Bernie? Is he making this a regular thing?"

"A couple of times. That's all. But who are you to act so suspicious? Are you gonna tell me you're an angel when you're on the road?"

She'd all but admitted it! He should have known Herb would come sniffing around once he was out of the way. Maybe that was why Herb had sent him on this lousy run. He always suspected that Herb had a thing for Bernie.

"Goddamnit, Bernice! You better not do anything to mess us up! After all we been through, you can't wait a little while for me to get home--"

The leader of their group looked back at his men, frowning when he saw Les talking on his cell phone. "Time to wrap it up, buddy. Everybody ready?"

"I gotta go," Les said roughly, snapping his cell phone shut. He took a deep breath, telling himself that he was not scared, even though he'd never done anything like this before. Not for pay, anyway. Come to think of it, he wished he knew who was paying him.

CHAPTER NINETEEN:
A MARIONETTE'S LIPS

From the moment she saw Cody Torrance dash into the ladies' room, sweaty and disheveled, desperately needing help, Luanne believed that he'd come into her life for a reason. She recognized him instantly, of course. How could she not? But the bizarre dissonance of seeing him in such an unlikely place, in such an improbable state, jarred her into treating him like an absolutely normal human being. And he was so sweet! So grateful for her help. When she flipped open her cell phone and held it out to him, he reached for it eagerly, then stopped himself. "I don't actually have the money on me, at the moment." He was so charmingly apologetic! Also out of breath, in a really sexy way. "You see, I had to leave...where I was...rather quickly. I was being chased by...a crowd." He shrugged ruefully. "All I have are the clothes on my back. But I'm good for it. I'm--" and here he seemed almost embarrassed to reveal his name, as if simply saying it constituted boasting -- "Cody Torrance. I'm an actor."

Luanne realized with surprise that he was...shy. And nice. The rugged, usually snarling action star, the overpaid and overhyped celebrity, was a *nice man.*

"I know who you are, Mr. Torrance. And forget about the money. You're welcome to use my phone." She felt stupid, putting it like that. Why? Why did she feel stupid?

He accepted it and smiled at her. "You're very kind. And it's Cody. Please."

"Well then it's Luanne."

"Luanne." The way he said it, her oh-so-ordinary name sounded like a lullaby. Like a fragment of a poem. He started to punch numbers.

"I'll just step outside." And she started to, feeling that he should have some privacy, even in a ladies' room, but he reached out his hand and gently grasped her wrist to stop her.

"Luanne, I...would you stay? Please. If you wouldn't mind. I may need your help. But maybe you're in a hurry. Is your boyfriend out there, waiting for you? I promise, I'll explain this all to him, once I get my escape plan put together. This might look a little peculiar, you and me in a bathroom, but I'll make him understand." He grinned, and she suddenly saw a bit of the screen charm. "I'm pretty persuasive, I'm told."

She had to laugh at that.

He looked pleased, as if her reaction was unexpected. Or was he acting?

"I'll stay here, Cody," she said, still astonished that she was able to speak so normally to him. "It's not a problem. And there is no boyfriend waiting for me. I...I've just moved here, as a matter of fact. I'm free this afternoon. But maybe you should go in one of the stalls while you make your call. Just in case anyone comes in." She thought for a moment. "And you might not hear the door open while you're talking, so if anyone does come in, I'll tap on your stall door."

He stared at her, impressed. "That'd be just great, Luanne. Good thinking."

He disappeared inside the middle stall and in a minute, she could hear his voice, echoing off the walls. Trying not to listen, she washed her face in the sink and dried it with a paper towel. Her lips were chapped and she applied a cherry-flavored lip balm, but that was as far as she would go. She would not primp for him. She wondered why he'd guessed at a boyfriend and not a husband. Because he looked at her left hand and didn't see a wedding ring? Had he checked her out? Right, Luanne. Sure.

She was going to make a conscious effort to ignore the aura of celebrity that he radiated. She would not be a cliché. She would not fawn, or ask him for an autograph. They were both actors, after all. She would treat him as if he were an ordinary person.

As if.

She combed her hair, but only because it really needed it. It was limp from its long ride in an un-airconditioned car. Reluctantly, she dug into her purse and found her Wild Roses lipstick. She drew it over her lips unwillingly, as if she were a marionette and her hand was being manipulated by someone else. Wondering, as she always did, if even this subtle color on her mouth made her look like a clown, she grimaced as she blotted the lipstick with a tissue. But that was it. She would not do any more. She was what she was. She relented just a little, pulled a compact from her purse and dabbed at her nose, forehead and chin with it, subduing the sweat-induced shine in the notorious "T-zone" mentioned so often in the acne medication commercials. There. That was it. She would not do an instant makeover – even if she could – for this man, just because he was who he was. Of course – she admitted to herself – even if he wasn't famous, he would still be incredibly good-looking, not to mention charming.

Luanne knew that she was a nice person, most of the time. She would have helped him out of simple human decency, regardless of who he was, but really: if he wasn't Cody Torrance, would he be pursued by a mob of fans and have to run down and alley and use the back door of a Mexican restaurant and charge into a bathroom and ask to use a stranger's cell phone?

Cody finished his call. She heard her cell phone snap shut and a toilet flush. A moment later, the stall door opened.

"I'm afraid that I have to ask for a few more minutes of your time," he said apologetically, while washing his hands. "If that's all right. Unless...maybe I could buy your cell phone from you?"

She was aghast. That phone was her only connection to...anywhere, at the moment.

He must have known from the look on her face what her answer would be.

"You're right. Not a good idea. I'm sure you need it. But my agent is going to come up with something and call back, in just a few minutes. Would you mind waiting, Luanne? I promise it won't be long."

Luanne relaxed. She had nowhere to go. Nowhere that she could possibly get to, anyway.

"Sure, Cody. No problem."

He smiled at her fondly, as if they'd known each other for a long time.

"That shade of lipstick suits you." He'd noticed. Then: *did he really mean it?* Then: *did it really matter?*

"Thank you."

107

So far, Luanne was finding L.A. pretty damn exciting.

Chapter Twenty:
Like a Beautiful Boy

It was hard for Ira to imagine feeling more miserable than he did at this moment. Fatigue burned painfully in his fast-pedaling thighs. His inability to catch his breath was alarming. Bicycling on smoggy days was not generally one of the activities recommended for asthmatics.

His bike hit a bump and jarred him. He was going to be late again. Sid was increasingly unhappy with Ira's chronic tardiness, even though pretty much every Los Angeleno was regularly late to work these days. Sid wasn't aware of that because Sid lived in a splendid little bubble that Ira liked to think of as SidWorld. In SidWorld, everything went the way Sid wanted it to go. Sid seemed to think that if Ira simply planned ahead and left a little earlier for work, he could make it. He failed to grasp that the traffic catastrophe was worsening by the day, if not the hour.

Today, for instance, Ira left his house well before dawn. When Lankershim ground to a frustrating halt, he'd ditched his car on a side street in Toluca Lake, taken his ancient red ten-speed from his trunk and struck out on two wheels instead of four. He got onto the 101, ignoring the irregularity of a bicycle on the freeway. There were no rules anymore. There was also no danger. He was not likely to get knocked down by a car whizzing along at 70 miles per hour. He even passed a police car sitting stationary, in impotent authority, in the center lane of the freeway. One of the cops sitting in the front seat was reading a newspaper. The other looked unconcernedly at Ira as he rode by and nodded. There was a new normal. Any method that allowed you to get from Point A to Point B was allowed, and no cop was going to stop you for it.

Although the shoulders of the road were filled with cars, there was still enough space between lanes of vehicles to make it through on a bike. He was not the only one using this strategy, however, and there were occasional near-collisions with motorcyclists and other bicyclists who were going in the opposite direction and felt the need to occupy the same space he did. He tried to be aggressive, to own his own space, but his concentration tended to be focused on breathing, so he was forced to yield to others again and again.

The 101 took him southeast when he needed to go southwest, but it was the only way he could get over the hill on a bike. He exited at Highland and persevered, pedaling as fast as he could. Sunset wasn't his best westward route, but Santa Monica and Melrose were clotted with cars, so he rode on. This was an insane plan, but he had no alternative. By the time he reached Beverly he was wheezing harshly, sweating lavishly and, despite all of his efforts, once again late for work. He turned west and struggled onward with all the speed of a leaky ship in a stormy sea, striving to reach the landmarks ahead: CBS Television City, the Beverly Center, Cedars Sinai and beyond all of that, the golden mecca that was Beverly Hills.

He stopped briefly near Pan Pacific Park to use his inhaler. Too many people were still keeping their engines running, hoping idiotically that they'd actually be moving soon. Driving had become a cutthroat, highly competitive endeavor, albeit a competition in slow motion. If a space opened up in front of you and you didn't move forward immediately, a car from an adjoining lane would bolt into your lane. There didn't have to be sufficient space for the car to pull entirely over -- just enough for it to plug part of its front end into the gap, thereby gaining a few feet. Dents and dings were commonplace. So was the type of argument that was in progress a short distance away.

Two women in expensive designer outfits were squaring off, screaming profanities that Ira was surprised to hear coming from, well, women in expensive designer outfits. Both combatants were sleek and stylish, but their styles were quite different.

The tall brunette with collagen-plumped lips, silicone-plumped breasts jutting from her otherwise bony body and henna-hued hair moussed into dangerous-looking points was probably a mid to upper level studio type, he decided. She had that aura of power. The exquisitely maintained silver-blond confronting her was more of the my-husband-sits-on-several-boards-and-I-host-charity-galas kind of gal, and older -- although how much older was hard to tell. It would be useful, Ira thought, if you could tell a person's age by counting the facelifts in the same way you can determine how old a tree is by counting the rings. The blonde's face looked late-40ish, but the sun-spotted hand she shook in the other woman's face suggested something more in the 60-plus range.

Ira stood next to his bike, trembling with fatigue, willing his breathing to return to a useful level of function. He wondered if the two shrieking women were really going to fight and if they were, would manicures determine the outcome? The brunette had longer fingernails, shellacked in a menacingly dark eggplant color, but they were trendily squared as opposed to the blonde's sharper, almost knife-shaped, mother-of-pearl colored nails. Let the tigers come with their claws, he thought.

The blonde was older and smaller, but she wore more rings: massive, diamond-rich miniature sculptures of gold encircling most of her fingers. They were Beverly Hills matron-type rings that could do a lot of damage to a face. In addition, the blonde shook with rage and indignation. Normally Ira would put his money on the fighter showing the most fury, but if the brunette really was of the studio breed she had to be one tough mama, no matter how willowy she looked.

"You didn't move fast enough, you old witch!" the brunette shouted into the other woman's face. "You snooze, you lose."

Ira saw that the front bumper of a silver Benz was jammed into the side of a vintage Jaguar. It was almost tragic, cars that beautiful being marred with dents and protrusions that looked like malformed wings. Broken glass was scattered on the ground below the unhappy coupling, from a headlight that would need replacing.

"Do you know how much this car is worth, you little tramp?" The silvery blonde's insult was as vintage as her car. "I'll see that you pay dearly for this."

Who was writing her dialogue? Ira wondered.

The brunette shoved her adversary hard with both hands and the older woman tumbled backward, landing in an oil stain. When she got to her feet, she had grease on her Armani suit and thunder in her eye.

Ira lost sight of her for a moment as the people watching jockeyed for better positions, temporarily blocking his view.

When he next glimpsed the blond, she was holding a tire iron high over her head, advancing on the brunette.

Her opponent leaped back, trying to get out of harm's way, but she teetered awkwardly on her Bruno Maglis and lost her balance, falling hard on her tightly toned ass. She thrust her arm defensively in front of her face. "You'd better not, you lunatic," she warned. "My boyfriend's a lawyer and he'll--"

The blonde swung the tire iron as if she were channeling Babe Ruth, putting whatever weight she had into it and bringing it around her body in a powerful curve.

The crowd gasped a collective gasp. Would she really-?"

Some bystanders were visibly and audibly relieved, others noticeably disappointed as the blonde connected with the Benz' windshield rather than the brunette's face. Safe for the moment, the brunette struggled to stand, gaining strength and fury by looking at the network of cracks in the glass.

A small, balding man moved amid the crowd, taking money and writing notes on the back of a sushi restaurant's paper take out menu. He stopped in front of Ira. "You want in on the action? It's three to one in favor of the brunette."

Ira, still rationing his breath, simply shook his head, disgusted with himself for watching as much of the altercation as he had. What was happening to everybody? Are we becoming animals? No! Animals didn't bet on fights. We are worse than animals. We are monsters. Or just really bad humans.

He forced himself to suppress his curiosity and turn away, boycotting the rest of the fight in his own small way. He would rise above this. It wasn't easy. The crowd cheered lustily at something. Ignoring the noise, he resolutely wheeled his bike around a corner, looking for a peaceful place in which to rest for a short time. Instead, there seemed to be a disruption in progress nearby. Was it another fight? No, this had a different tone.

A stocky, curly-haired man stood in the bed of a Dodge Ram truck, shouting into a bullhorn, while the people milling about in the streets -- an involuntary audience who couldn't leave the scene even if they wanted to -- gathered closer to hear him. A couple of dozen supporters ringed the speaker, standing in the street below him, holding signs aloft and shaking them vigorously when he hit an especially compelling point. One sign in particular caught Ira's attention: "ASTHMATICS for CLEAN AIR". There was also: "L.A.: 6 MILLION CARS AND COUNTING" and "The VALLEY BREATHERS." One group of demonstrators looked for all the world like gang bangers; they were scowling teenagers in low-slung baggy pants and knit caps who held signs bearing the word PULMONATION alongside a graphic of a clenched fist next to an inhaler.

The eclectic, racially diverse group of demonstrators included men and women in suits, men and women in dreadlocks, health care workers in scrubs made from cartoon character prints, vegans in Birkenstocks and hemp clothes, a selection of the Tragically Hip (both genders, all sexual orientations), Midwestern-looking types who probably lived in Burbank, Armenians from Glendale, Iranians from Beverly Hills, Latinos from all over, white hip-hoppers, black investment bankers, actor-activist types, people who could have been rock musicians, people who could have been stand-up comics, people who looked famous but weren't, hyper-tattooed men and women in black wife-beaters and skinny jeans, angry-looking mothers holding the hands of sickly-looking children, an assortment of feisty seniors and surfer dudes, including one who aimed upward with a video camera to tape the speech.

Ira also noticed a tall, leggy girl with boyishly short blonde hair whose sign read, (cheerily, he thought): "GENERATION AIR: RECLAIMING THE FUTURE!"

"You see this as a crisis," the curly haired guy was saying. "It's not. It's a warning. A wake up call. Most of all, it's an opportunity. We have a chance to make fantastic changes in our world, to make things BETTER, for ourselves and for future generations. Our vision, our new way will rise like a phoenix from the ashes of this failed transportation system. This...stoppage will finally make those in power listen to our ideas."

Megaphone Guy was a rousing and effective speaker, Ira realized. His speaking style was part black Baptist preacher, part motivational speaker, part next door neighbor. Surprisingly compelling. Was he an actor?

The people standing near him were listening, although it was hard to tell from their expressions whether they were in agreement or whether they had nothing else to do at the moment.

"Our twisted love affair with the conventional automobile is the worst kind of dysfunctional relationship because CARS ARE KILLING US!" Megaphone Guy swept his arm in a dramatic gesture, indicating the vehicles at a standstill around him. "Auto emissions -- from conventional engines, anyway -- are destroying the ozone layer and putting our very habitat at risk, yet we continue to put more and more cars on our roads. The greenhouse effect is REAL, people, and it's going to kill us. The air quality is deteriorating -- can you feel it? The incidence of pulmonary problems has gone up 47% in the last six months. Sixty-one percent among kids."

The squadron of mothers shook their heads in agreement and stared at the crowd as if daring anyone to contradict the speaker.

"Kids are at particular risk because their lungs are still developing. However, this affects all of us. WE CAN'T BREATHE, AND WE'RE DOING THIS TO OURSELVES!"

"I'm just trying to get to work, buddy!" someone shouted.

"And you'd be getting there on a decent, non-polluting mass transit system, if our politicians weren't in the pockets of Big Oil and Big Auto Manufacturers," Megaphone Guy shot back. "We've been brainwashed by advertising to believe that cars give us status, mobility, independence." He pointed to the car-cluttered street. "Is this mobility? And are we independent? No! We're completely DEPENDENT on foreign oil, thanks to our addiction to cars."

"Not all of us can afford hybrids," someone called out. "They're expensive."

"That's because the government hasn't gotten behind alternative transportation research the way it should have," said Megaphone Guy. "With dollars, tax subsidies and research grants."

Ira tried to listen, to understand the larger issues. He'd been so mired in his own misery that he'd failed to understand the bigger picture of the traffic mess. He only thought about the environment when he was arranging for one of Sid's high-profile clients to appear at some fundraiser to accept an award for saving dolphins or raising money to slow down global warming. These appearances were great for photo ops. The celebs could get warm and fuzzy press coverage while wearing tuxes or really hot gowns borrowed from designers.

Ira did recycle, when he thought about it. That was something that helped the environment. And he didn't consume much, but mainly because he couldn't afford to. His carbon footprint was the size of a Chihuahua footprint.

"So what are we supposed to do," a woman called out sarcastically. "How do you expect us to get around? On horseback?"

This got a big laugh. Megaphone Guy didn't join in, but he was savvy enough to smile and pause to allow the guffaws to subside.

"Are you getting anywhere now?" he demanded. "Are any of you moving in these cars you love so much?"

Several people shook their heads in disgust.

"We must DEMAND action from our elected leaders," he said firmly. "We can't let them restore the traffic to 'normal' because normal will be our downfall. Our destruction. Join us. We are Generation Air. We are reclaiming the future. We WILL have a livable planet. We've got petitions here today that we're asking you to sign. That's one easy thing you can do. Join us as we DEMAND that the government start building decent mass transit systems TODAY!"

"That'll cost too much," shouted a man in shorts and a mesh muscle shirt.

"Do you know how much THIS mess is costing us?" Megaphone Guy demanded. "How much productivity is being lost because people can't get to where they need to go? Two hundred and seventeen companies in Southern California went under last week, because their workers couldn't get to them and their goods or services couldn't get to their customers. And let's not forget the sick people who are dying because they can't get to hospitals fast enough. How much more of that can we afford?"

Ira knew he should continue his journey to Midwood, but his chest still heaved and tightened with the effort of simply breathing. People jostled against him carelessly as he stood on the crowded sidewalk, swaying weakly, his bike leaning against his side. Ignoring them, he closed his eyes and did his visualization exercises, imagining his lungs as buoyant pink sails on a clipper ship bounding over a sparkling blue sea, the sails filling easily with air, rippling with vitality, expanding and contracting, expanding and con--

"Are you OK?" When he opened his eyes, a new vision swam before them. The leggy girl who'd been accompanying the speaker stood close to him, her expression anxious and concerned. She held a clipboard. He hoped she wasn't about to ask him to sign a petition. He didn't want her to see his hand shaking.

"Sure," he said, only it came out as an inward wheeze: "Hhhhuuu." He attempted a casual grin but couldn't hold it in place. His mouth trembled. He suspected that he conveyed the impression of being about to cry.

"What is it? Asthma?"

He nodded.

"Maybe you should...sit down?" She looked as if *she* was about to cry. "I'd call an ambulance for you, but..." She shrugged helplessly. They both knew that a call to 9-1-1 would be futile. No ambulance could get through. Paramedics had taken to rolling what gear they could through the streets and responding to summons on foot, but this, naturally, took a great deal of time and left many emergency calls unanswered. People were dying who would not die in better times. The herd was being thinned out.

"Be all right...in....a...minute," he managed. He sat heavily on the sidewalk, hoping that no one would step on him.

She crouched down next to him. "Nathan was a medic in the army," she said. "In Iraq."

"Nathan?" he wheezed.

She waved toward Megaphone Guy, who was still speaking. "Maybe he can help you. I'll get him. By the time I get up there, he'll be finished with his talk." She smiled. It was dazzling, and for the briefest of moments he was held captive by its shimmer. Then she was purposeful and serious again. "I know, because I helped him write it." She jumped up gracefully.

Ira caught her by the arm, unwilling to share her just yet. "This will take effect soon," he gasped, showing her his inhaler. She looked at it with great seriousness, her large, brown, doe-like eyes narrowing. Her features were clean and streamlined, made even more feminine by the short, masculine cut of her light brown hair, which was silky and shot through with gold streaks. Her limbs were long and slender, her attire simple: jeans and a sea-green hoodie over a white tank top. She was like a beautiful boy. Ira couldn't stop looking at her and he thought, with relief: I can still think about sex. That means I'm not going to die today.

"I saw you over here and knew you were in trouble," she said. "My name's Oceana. Ocean, with an 'a' on the end."

"Ira," he said. "Ira O'Riley. I'm OK. Better. I just--" He didn't know how to finish the sentence. He *was* feeling better, but didn't want her to think that he was well enough for her to leave. He was happy that his words were finally recognizable as words instead of gasps. "So. You're with them?" He nodded in the direction of the demonstration.

"Yeah. Generation Air." She pulled a business card from her pocket and handed it to Ira, who tried to conceal his elation. He'd gotten a phone number from her! Maybe just the number for her organization, but still... "You should think about joining us," she was saying. "We've formed a coalition with lots of other groups, including lots of RAs." His puzzled look prompted her to explain: "Radical Asthmatics."

Ira smiled a tremulous smile, waiting for the punch line. He handed her his own business card, which had his cell phone number on it in addition to the office number. "Radical? Asthmatics? Those two words together? You're kidding, right?"

"Not being able to breathe makes some people very, very angry," Oceana said. "Don't you ever get pissed off? Don't you ever think to yourself; 'I have the right to breathe freely'? Ira, it's a fundamental human right! It should be spelled out in the Constitution."

He shrugged. "What can you do? It's a disease."

"Which is made much worse by air pollution. Look at you. You're suffering more than you should be."

Ira felt unmanned rather than moved by her sympathy. He wasn't feeling strong enough yet to stand, but struggled to his feet anyway. Oceana took his hand to help him. He decided to let her. When fully upright -- albeit in a shaky stance -- he was pleased to note that he was a few inches taller than her. He felt a wild, brief impulse to seize her in his arms and kiss her, to show her that he was not a weak, sickly Peabody. There was more to Ira O'Riley than defective lungs.

Screams erupted suddenly, along with a human commotion, a flurry of movement near the Ram. Someone had Megaphone Guy -- Nathan -- by the arm and was pulling him down from the pickup truck, despite his attempts to lunge away. He disappeared in a tangle of bodies and Ira saw fists swinging downward. He could hardly believe what he was seeing. Was this real? Or staged? A group of thugs was beating Nathan and his fellow demonstrators to pulps, blatantly committing this attack in front of many witnesses. One of the goons realized that the surfer dude was videotaping the whole things and the unfortunate cameraman became a next target. His camera was seized and his face smashed by a flying fist. A few of the demonstrators fought back valiantly, if ineffectually, jabbing their attackers with the sticks that held their posters, kicking and hitting. Most tried to run away. Ira could hardly blame them. They outnumbered their attackers, but were not, generally speaking, combative types. Parents quickly herded small children away from the violence; Ira was relieved to see that they, at least, were ignored by the goons.

The watching crowd seemed stunned into immobility by the speed and ferocity of the assault. Finally, a few men moved forward and tried to intervene. They were shoved viciously backwards into a cluster of bystanders, several of whom were knocked down.

"Headbreakers hired by the oil industry!" Oceana cried. "They warned us, told us to stop holding demonstrations or there'd be trouble and we'd get hurt. Nathan said we couldn't let them prevent us from doing right. Oh, God... Nathan..."

She started toward the melee but Ira caught her by the arm.

"It's too dangerous!"

"They're my friends!" she said tearfully. "And I believe in what we're doing!"

Ira, confounded by her sincerity, released her. She spoke like a character in a screenplay but the sentiment was real. At least to her. He felt as if he should charge after her, protect her, but knew he could not. Standing was one thing. Running was another, currently impossible thing. His breathing was still shallow and insufficient.

Oceana plunged into the crowd toward the other Generation Airites and Ira tried to follow her progress, catching glimpses of the pale green top she was wearing. One of the big thugs looked familiar, but that was impossible. In a city this populated, what were the odds that the lumbering man with the ginger-colored crew cut and enormous beer belly throwing punches indiscriminately at anyone who even looked at him was the same man who'd clobbered Ira through his car window? It couldn't be. Could it? He forgot about Oceana for the moment and peered at the fracas, trying to sort out individual players. As busy as they were mixing it up, none of them stayed helpfully in one place long enough for him to get a visual handle on him. He did manage to spot Oceana again, pushing relentlessly through the crowd. He was relieved when the assailants broke off their attack before she managed to reach the worst of the trouble. The thugs ran away together, all in the same direction, as if by prearranged plan.

Intimidated by the violent unity the flying wedge presented, no one in the crowd opted to chase them. Instead, several people moved forward to tend to the injured. Nathan lay prostrate on the ground, surrounded by people. Ira glimpsed one leg moving slightly, and was satisfied that the Generation Air leader was conscious. He couldn't be that badly injured then, could he? Oceana was bending over him. Ira felt absurdly jealous. He'd known this woman all of five minutes.

Ira heard a familiar series of faint chords. He was so riveted by the bizarre scene that had just taken place that it took him a moment to identify the ordinary sound of his own cell phone.

CHAPTER TWENTY-ONE:
BEFORE THE GELATO MELTS

"Ira? You almost here?"

He tried to collect his thoughts. Where was he, exactly? How far from the agency? So much had happened in the last fifteen minutes that he was disoriented.

"Ah, yeah," he lied. "Pretty close. I'm on my bike, because no cars--"

'Great. Great." Sid could care less how Ira got to work. Just that he got there. Soon. Sid was finally cognizant of the traffic crisis because it was forcing him to actually walk the half mile to work each day. He still didn't understand how large a problem it was for Ira. "Listen, we got a problem. Cody is holed up in a restaurant off Sunset and there's a crowd milling around, waiting for him to show again. They got nothing better to do than stay on starwatch. He's really spooked. I called the limo company, but they said they can't get anybody in there. Not close enough to rescue him, anyway."

Rescue him, thought Ira. Oh, the drama. Oh, the humanity.

"You know anybody with a car around there who could pick him up and get him back to Malibu? Maybe you could get a cab? Cody sounded frantic when he called me. His meeting's off, anyway. The director couldn't get there, either."

"Sid, no cars are moving right now. There's no way--" He stopped, in idea taking shape in his mind.

"Well we gotta do something!" Sid's frustration always took the form of the royal "we." Ira was promoted to management only when the impossible needed to be done.

"I've got a solution, but it'd cost quite a bit. How about a helicopter? Cody would need to get to a rooftop. And there'd have to be a large, flat rooftop near him."

"Hmmmm. A helicopter. Sure, it'd be expensive, but Cody can afford it. He's desperate. We'll airlift him out of there. Call around and get somebody to do it, right away. Somebody used to dealing with celebrities. Get 'em to sign a confidentiality agreement."

120

Sure, Sid. No problem. I've got that form right here in my freakin' backpack. But it wasn't Sid's fault that Ira wasn't at his desk right now, using agency resources instead of his own. On the other hand, it wasn't Ira's fault either.

Sid gave him Cody's approximate location. "He's got some girl with him, so make sure they know it'll be two passengers. Oh, and I need you to stop at Alura's and pick up some lunch for me. First you gotta call and order it. You know Alura's? On Melrose?"

Sure. Melrose. It was out of his way, but what the hell. What were a few more miles on the old bike today? He fumbled for the small notebook he kept in his backpack. Heard Sid say something indistinct.

"What's that?" Ira asked.

"Oh, I was just talking to Palmer."

"Palmer's there?" What was that pesticle doing there? Most talent agent to casting agent business was conducted by phone -- especially these days.

"Yeah, he stopped by to chat. He and Ruben got into it and Ruben let him go."

"Really. Well maybe Ruben will reconsider. I thought he liked Palmer." Liked? *I thought he was schtupping Palmer.*

"Palmer thinks it's for real this time. Says it's been in the works for awhile, and that Ruben is OK with it. Palmer's ready for something new."

Quite a chat they'd been having, Palmer and Sid. Sounded downright chummy. Sid never talked with him like that. As if he were an equal. Sharing feelings, as if Sid was interested in his plans. His future.

"What do you want for lunch, Sid?"

"The tangerine-glazed Sonoma quail," Sid said. "And make sure it's lightly browned this time. It was medium browned last time. They tried to tell me it was lightly browned, but I know the difference. And a spicy cucumber salad. And some gelato for dessert. Just a minute." Sid apparently covered the phone, then: "Ah, you better make that two. Of everything."

Ira seethed. Now he was fetching lunch for Palmer, too? Sid never bought him lunch!

"And make sure you get here fast, before the gelato melts."

How could someone so rich and successful be so dumb, Ira wondered bitterly. Sure, Sid. I'll get there fast. On my BIKE!

"And don't forget to take care of Cody. He's our biggest paycheck, remember."

Chapter Twenty-Two:
His Rags Were About to Become Riches

Ross Faber was thinking several thoughts simultaneously: thank God for barf bags; it was great to be back up in the air again; and when was Cody Torrance going to stop throwing up so that Ross could start a conversation with him and subtly introduce the topic of a screenplay Ross had written, which had a role in it that would be just perfect for Torrance. Or, if he didn't want to be in it but still liked the screenplay, maybe he'd recommend it to some producer he knew.

What an opportunity to have blown his way! Bored and broke since being laid off, Ross was happy to get the call today, even before he found out that his passenger would be a high-profile A-Lister. It hurt, to get the axe, but he didn't blame the TV station for cutting costs by getting rid of him. Why waste energy taking it personally? It made business sense. All the stations in town were grounding their traffic choppers and laying off their pilots and traffic reporters. Not only was there almost no movement to report, but media research showed that the mere mention of the word "traffic" during newscasts now made people so aggravated that they changed to a different channel or, shockingly, turned the TV or radio off. Ross understood their pain. After all, he used to fly daily over the gridlock that trapped hapless motorists like flies on flypaper. If the government didn't work out a solution soon, and he didn't get his job back, he'd be living in a cardboard box. Or maybe his real career as a screenwriter would kick in and he wouldn't have to worry about being a wage slave, working for somebody else. His screenplay, "Traffic School," could be his ticket to ride. So to speak.

Ross guided the helicopter toward the coast, directing a silent but fervent 'thank you' to God for sending Cody Torrance into his life. His orders were to take Torrance to his estate in Malibu, then to drop the girl off wherever she wanted to go. He wondered what the back story was there. Who was she? What was her relationship to Torrance? Ross snuck glances at her, trying to figure her out. She didn't look like an actress, or like anybody in the business, really. Not slick enough to be an agent or p.r. flack. Maybe she was an assistant. That was a possibility. Her wrinkled pale orange cotton top screamed discount store and was cut in an unflattering style that emphasized the expanse of her hips rather than her small breasts. She had an ok face and limp, plain brown hair that cried out for highlights and a more up-to-date cut. The calves jutting out from her beige cotton Capri's were oversized, as were the thighs contained within. She wore the kind of shiny cheap sunglasses found at gas stations, and her brown pleather sandals were strictly Payless. She sure didn't look like somebody Torrance would be dating. If she was an assistant, she could possibly be an ally for Ross. Somebody who would put his screenplay in Cody's hands and say, "I've read this, and I think you should take a look, Cody. It's amazing."

Ross made a mental note to be really nice to her. You never knew...

He hoped, though, to be able to mention his work to Torrance directly. He had to find a way to introduce the subject, once Torrance was able to focus on something other than his motion sickness. Ross just happened to have a copy of "Traffic School" with him. Just happened to, right. As soon as he'd received the faxed confidentiality form and seen who his passenger would be, he grabbed a copy of the screenplay that he always kept in his locker, just in case. You never knew when you might get a chance to network with someone who had real clout.

He'd tried everything to interest agents, producers, directors, production companies, studios and actors in his script. He'd done submissions by mail and email, phone calls, query letters and, most humiliatingly, an impromptu, impassioned pitch in the men's room of a comedy club to a guy who claimed to be in Development at a major studio, but who'd actually been interested only in having sex with Ross.

It was discouraging. What he'd long since realized was that he wasn't the only one hawking a screenplay in SoCal. A teacher at a screenwriting workshop he'd attended advised the students to tell everyone they met about their screenplay. "Not only does it help you polish your pitch, but you never know when a casual contact might prove invaluable."

This technique had one major flaw. Everyone Ross mentioned his screenplay to turned out to have a screenplay of their own that they were trying to get produced: his chiropractor, his letter carrier, his ex-wife's new husband, the kid who worked at the store where he bought his last pair of shoes, his landlord, his mechanic, the girl at Kinko's, the guy on the next treadmill at the health club he used to belong to. It was demoralizing. Ross was convinced that his screenplay was terrific, but despaired of its ever rising from the masses of would-be cinematic stories that cluttered the landscape to be read by someone with enough juice to get it made, or even by someone who knew someone with enough juice to get it made.

In desperation, he'd flown off course after his TV station traffic duties ended one day and dropped a copy of "Traffic School" into the backyard of what he was pretty sure was Ron Howard's house. The damn thing flapped around like an ungainly white bird, pages shredding in the wind, finally coming unbound and descending to the earth in waves of papers, many of them drifting downward into the shimmering blue rectangle of a swimming pool where they hovered for an instant on the water's surface before becoming saturated with water and sinking to the bottom, soggy and, thankfully, illegible, because no one could know who to blame for the mess.

The next time, he made sure that the manuscript was tightly bound and safely encased in waterproof plastic. The latter turned out to be unnecessary, because his aim was better. With a satisfying thrill, he saw the bundle containing the fruit of his imagination land on a green sweep of lawn next to a sprawling mansion that allegedly belonged to Ben Stiller. Now there was a talented comedy director and actor! "Tropic Thunder" was brilliant. It satirized Hollywood moviemaking but let outsiders in on all the inside jokes. Line after line, scene after scene, character after character was just brilliant. Stiller as director could bring the best out of "Traffic School" and he could play the lead, too! My God – if Owen Wilson and Vince Vaughn would be in it, as well, success would be a slam dunk! Ross tried to think about what roles they would play in "Traffic School." Some characters would have to be reshaped for them, some scenes rewritten, but wasn't that always the case? It was a process, after all.

After his unorthodox script delivery, Ross had ridden back to base in an excited state, wondering if Stiller would read it. Well if he passes, I'd love to see what the darkly humorous Tim Burton would do with it. Stiller's not the only player in town. Still, he desperately wanted to hear from Stiller. You never knew...

Unfortunately, the incident had only earned him a reprimand from the TV station. Someone on the ground had seen the station's logo spread vividly across the fuselage and called to complain about the unsolicited delivery. "You could have killed someone!" the general manager raged at him. "One more stupid stunt like that and you're off payroll. And grounded for good, after I report you to the F.A.A." As a final stroke of humiliation, the home turned out to belong to a nobody, some rich investment banker with no ties to the entertainment industry whatsoever. What was someone like him doing taking up real estate in L.A.? Southern California was the nerve center of the entertainment industry, not the banking industry.

As a final humiliation, Ross was let go three weeks after that for simple economic reasons, not for his boneheaded play.

Today, though, everything could change for him. His entire life could morph into something magical. His $17,000 in credit card debt, one-bedroom apartment in the Valley and 12-year-old car in need of a transmission transplant could all be replaced by luxury and abundance. He could succeed in the most exciting, most creative industry in the world. It all hinged on this opportunity. The moment was almost upon him. It wouldn't be too long before he reached the coast and made his way northward to Malibu. He was going to have to make his move soon, whether Cody Torrance's stomach settled or not. His moment of destiny was nigh.

Tension flared in his throat, along with an unwelcome wave of heartburn. Unlike some people, who thought a couple of cups of coffee constituted an adequate start to the day, Ross made sure he was always fueled by something substantial and high in protein. The nutritionists were right. Breakfast *was* the most important meal of the day. The bacon, eggs and sausage platter he downed this morning left him feeling comfortably full, content and energetic. It didn't usually back on him like this. Maybe he should have passed on the cheesy hash browns. They'd been unusually greasy today, but they were part of his favorite Egg-spress Special at Alda's Diner. He was on a tight budget, but fortunately, breakfast was still a bargain.

Torrance straightened up in his seat slowly, his expression dazed, his skin the yellowish hue of a wax bean.

"Feeling better, Mr. Torrance?" Ross knew he probably shouldn't be so bold as to speak directly to the star. There were some big-name actors who had it written into their contracts that no crew members or extras were allowed to speak to or even make eye contact with them on a movie set. He thought he might get away with the presumption this time, though, given the circumstances. Torrance was vulnerable. And after all, Ross was only concerned with his passenger's well-being. Had his tone been sufficiently sincere?

Torrance didn't seem to mind the inquiry. He nodded slowly, deliberately, but then made the mistake of looking out the window, taking in the deep shadowed creases of the canyons below. He gulped. He gulped again. The vomiting resumed.

Damn! He'd been so close! Ross occupied himself with mentally rehearsing his pitch. Naturally he'd practiced reciting the logline for his screenplay many times. He could give the required "snapshot" descriptions of the major characters and sketch out the pivotal scenes. He had a few tantalizing details ready to toss in, should he get a long enough hearing. Now, faced with a mayor player, he knew he had to make some hasty changes in order to tailor the pitch to Torrance.

OK, so "Traffic School" was a comedy and Torrance didn't do comedies. Who's to say that Torrance wasn't ready to broaden his artistic horizons as an actor, go in a different direction, like Stallone did in "Stop, or My Mother Will Shoot"? Maybe that wasn't a good example. But…Torrance could have been looking for the right comedic script for some time. You never knew.

Or, if he absolutely wasn't interested in a comedy, then Ross could easily give the slapstick action a harder edge. Downplay the comedic elements. Add guns and explosions. The story was -- currently -- about a nebishy loser who gets sent to traffic school because of his lousy driving. While there, he ends up being unwittingly recruited as a getaway driver by a bank robber who has a worse driving record even than the loser. The loser thinks he's being hired for a legitimate job. Never fully grasping what's happening until late in the story, he ends up being the worst getaway driver ever and succeeds in foiling the robbery and saving the day pretty much by accident. The script contained lots of zany chase scenes and near-misses, a good-versus-evil theme and, of course, a romance. The main character hooks up with a shy, sweet bank teller who thinks he's a genuine hero.

Ross accepted -- yes, even embraced -- the fluidity of the creative process, especially as it applied to the art of screenwriting. Making a movie was such an enormous and collaborative process that even if "Traffic School" was accepted for production just as it was, it would inevitably undergo changes during the transformative process that morphed it from page to screen. "Don't fall so in love with your own words that you become unwilling to revise them," recommended one writing instructor. Good advice, he thought. Rewriting was not selling out. It was simply tapping into the fast-moving landscape of thought that was storytelling.

The chase scenes could go from wacky to destructive, with some of the near-misses ending in spectacular crashes. In this new version, his bank caper would lay waste to Burbank! The bookish bank teller would be reconfigured as a hot babe. Or, better yet, she'd still look shy and repressed, but at the end of the movie she'd take off her glasses and whip the pins (or whatever) out of her tight, spinsterly bun so that her hair flounced around her shoulders in a long, sexy mane. And underneath her plain, tailored, bank teller's suit? A black lace teddy.

Just as quickly and nimbly, Ross reimagined the nebishy main loser, seeing him now as a macho guy. A cop, yes! A cop who was only masquerading as a wimp in order to go undercover at traffic school because he knew the leader of a vicious gang of bank robbers would be attending at that time and he wanted to infiltrate the gang. Boy, are they surprised when the Class Dunce reveals himself to be their worst nightmare: a renegade cop out to settle a score! Because the bank robbers had killed his family! During a robbery!

Ross wondered if he should keep one of the cop's young kids alive, in order to give the cop a reason not to totally self-destruct. Maybe the kid could have witnessed the robbery/slayings and gone mute as a consequence, and he would regain speech at the end of the movie. No, no. That had been done to death. Maybe he could go blind instead. Was there such a thing as traumatic blindness? He'd have to look it up. If there was, the kid could miraculously recover at the end of the movie. (Maybe he'd recover when he got a good look at the smokin' hot bank teller and realize that she was going to be his new Mommy!)

Stay focused, Ross, he scolded himself. Stay on task. He reviewed the changes he'd just made in his story and congratulated himself on his willingness to be artistically flexible. He was not selling out. *Trust in the process*, he told himself firmly.

The new version was a perfect fit for Torrance, yet it still remained true to Ross' original vision. Sort of. He could always write another comedy later, once he had a producer's credit to his name. He was terrifically excited, flooded with the sudden conviction that everything would work out. His rags were about to become riches. Torrance would be in a receptive mood momentarily. He had to be. His stomach contents had to be close to completely ejected by now. Torrance would listen to his pitch. He'd agree to read (the soon to be quickly rewritten) "Traffic School." He'd see what a talented writer Ross was -- a recognition that would bridge the gap between world famous star and no name peon, because they were both artists. Torrance would understand that Ross' screenplay would be another big hit for him. He would get it.

Ross looked ahead, happily surveying the jagged canyons slicing deeply into the mountains below, their topsides softened a little by scrubby greenery and clots of small, stubborn trees. There were only a few roads down there, winding dizzily over the heights toward the Pacific Coast Highway, but he nonetheless noticed a number of newer houses, Mediterranean-style palaces, niched into steep slopes. Who would want to live in such inaccessible places? Nobody who had to drive to work every day, that was sure. Of course, these days one didn't have to live in a remote locale to have commuting trouble. But these nouveau riche must be regarded as an unwelcome, invading species to the old hippies that still, in some form, inhabited the canyons, their counterculture spirit still intact but in danger of being squeezed out of existence by the relentless press of money and hunger for property -- just like what was going on in the Hollywood Hills. He imagined that he was flying over 1960s-era VW vans, overgrown with vines, forever parked next to crumbling cabins. Relics. There were probably some interesting stories in these mountains. Maybe some material for future screenplays. He'd have to come back some time. Talk to people. Do a little research. Once he was a professional writer, he'd have the financial freedom to really cultivate his craft.

The heartburn came back in a sharp jolt. He wished he had some Tums. It was really uncomfortable. God, it hurt! No. No. No no no no. What the hell was happening? In a panicky epiphany, he realized that he was having a heart attack. No! Not possible! He wasn't old enough. He should speak to Torrance and the girl. Tell them-- Warn them-- He couldn't think. His brain went into lockdown, frozen with fear. The pain spread down his arms like hot lava. He tried to think. Had to land fast, but where? A terrible location. Canyons everywhere. No level patch of land that he could see. Bad pain. Jesus. Really bad pain.

CHAPTER TWENTY-THREE:
HIS OWN PRIVATE DISASTER

What a great story this was going to make. Luanne smiled to herself. The folks back home in Altoona would have a hard time believing it. On her very first day in Los Angeles, she'd met a movie star. In the ladies' room of a Mexican restaurant, no less. She'd helped him escape a mob of crazed autograph seekers by going outside -- after paying her bill and extricating herself from the conversational clutches of America's formerly cutest kid -- to scout out a landmark to describe to Cody's agent on her cell phone, so that the helicopter pilot could get close enough for a pickup. Then she'd gone up a back stairwell, looking out windows until she found the fire escape ladder. After that, it was a simple matter of retrieving Cody from the middle stall in the bathroom and leading him up the stairs, out the window and up the ladder to the roof.

She'd made as if to leave him there at that point, but he asked her to stay with him and she found that she couldn't say no. It almost seemed like Cody was afraid of heights. He huddled almost pathetically in the center of the rooftop, unwilling to glance at the landscape below even though it looked kind of interesting at this angle.

Luanne felt a little anxious about her car being in the way of someone, but after a few minutes of hard scanning, she was able to locate it by the grey luggage carrier strapped to the its roof. Traffic had not moved since she left it. Not one inch. The same vehicles that had been in front of hers and behind hers were still in the same positions. Amazing. Why not stay on this rooftop with Cody for awhile longer? She might as well go where the story took her.

She expected, though, that they would part ways when the chopper arrived, but Cody invited her to come along -- almost insisted, really.

"He'll drop you off anywhere you like. You can avoid this mess. Where do you want to go, Luanne?"

"Back to Chicago?"

His laughter was golden, throaty and bracketed by flashing white teeth. It was so wonderful that Luanne almost congratulated herself on eliciting it from him.

"Why don't you let me show you around my place in Malibu? At least stay for dinner -- I owe you that much. Then you can fly away, if you like."

She was surprised. "You cook?"

His smile was a self-deprecating one. "No, I didn't mean that. I have a housekeeper who does. A live-in one, so I don't have to worry about her braving the traffic to get to my house."

And so, like a fairy tale, Luanne climbed into the helicopter when it landed on the rooftop and flew away for her first such ride, to the oceanfront home of a famous movie star.

Pinch me, she thought, grinning idiotically as she enjoyed the dramatic scenery below, the browned mountains and carved out canyons. Cody's airsickness didn't detract from her pleasure at all, nor did it make her think less of him. Luanne was a pragmatist. She'd partied hard in college and found her face in close proximity to a toilet bowl more than a few times. And unlike her own experiences, this poor man had done nothing to bring on this abhorrent torrent. She felt bad for him. His face was a greenish gray, slicked with perspiration, his eyes haggard. She dug into her purse for yet another tissue, pressed it to the opening of her water bottle to moisten it and held it out to him.

He was still clutching the airsickness bag, so she mopped his forehead with the tissue.

"You must think I'm..." He couldn't think how to finish.

She shook her head. "It happens to a lot of people. It's pretty common, really. That's why doctors prescribe Dramamine."

He tried to grin. It was almost gallant. "Wish I had some now."

"I wish you had some now, too," she said, smiling.

He chuckled. "Oh, how the paparazzi would love to see me at this unfortunate moment. Cody Torrance, barfing. Wonder how much they'd get for those pictures?" He stopped suddenly and looked away from her, frowning at something.

Luanne had the strange sensation that she could read his mind. "I won't tell anyone that you got sick. I do want to be well known some day, but not for that."

Cody laughed again, took a deep breath. "I know you won't tell anyone. You're not that girl, are you?" He sighed a testing sigh. "I think I'm feeling better."

"Nothing more to bring up," commented Luanne helpfully. At his look, she explained: "I always try to look on the bright side."

"I can see that." He took her hand and held it reverentially, as if he were about to propose marriage. "You know, now that my stomach is feeling more settled, I think I actually might be able to enjoy myself."

She was the one who laughed. Pinch me, she thought again. She wished her cotton Capri's made her thighs look thinner.

Just then the helicopter lurched and bucked, sluicing sideways. Were they getting knocked around from winds churning up from the canyons? It didn't seem like a particularly windy day. Even if it were, wouldn't the pilot know how to cope with conditions like that? Maybe stay high enough to avoid them? They were so low that she could see ground-level features in vivid detail: steep, rock-dotted canyons curving harshly down toward golden brown grasslands and sparse groves of oak trees. It couldn't be safe to be this low. What was the pilot thinking?

His momentary good mood gone, Cody looked paralyzed with fear. Luanne struggled to inch forward, trying to keep her balance. The craft jerked and descended sharply, then rocked back and forth as if fighting to stay airborne. She grabbed at the pilot's arm, but he was too focused on his own private disaster to notice. He was all knotted up, straining for breath, his face the color of a beefsteak tomato. He suddenly went ramrod-straight, his eyes rigid with fear. Then he slumped forward over his controls.

The chopper dropped out of the sky.

133

Chapter Twenty-Four:
Your Walls are *Pink!*

He was going to have to quit. Now. Today. Give his two
weeks' notice, and hope to God he'd be able to find another job
soon, one that was closer to his apartment. It was a terrible time
to find a job in L.A., but he had to try. Ira wished he had a better
skill set. Beyond a few basic office skills – and the ability to
answer a phone nicely – he was not all that marketable.

Ira dropped his backpack at his desk and briefly considered
heading to the men's room to freshen up. The long bike ride had
left him sweaty and rumpled, not exactly a businesslike state in
which to formally conclude one's employment. This was the
fugliest he'd looked in a long time.

To hell with it. Let Sid see how he'd suffered to get here,
struggled to go out of his way even to get Sid's precious lunch.
Let Sid realize that he was losing a valuable worker. One who
literally went the extra mile.

He carried the take-out bags down the hall to Sid's office,
hearing laughter and conversation long before he got there.
Palmer, breezy and chic in Dockers and a wheat-colored
cashmere v-neck Ralph Lauren sweater, was lounging
comfortably in the leather club chair as if he and Sid were old
friends instead of two people from distinctly different levels in
the entertainment industry hierarchy. Palmer's potent attitudinal
wardrobe of arrogance and confidence must elevate him. Why
did he look so cool on such a warm day? He must have had to
walk here from Ruben's office, which was at least two miles
away. He certainly couldn't have driven here. Yet he was
perfectly preserved, immaculately coiffed, with no blush of
perspiration on his apparently poreless face, no hint of exertion
in his body, no suggestion of weariness in the dark eyes that
glanced at Ira from beneath epicanthic folds.

Palmer looked up at Ira as if Ira was merely a delivery boy,
and Ira hated every platinum-colored hair on his head.

In fact, Ira thought, he *was* a mere delivery boy.

"Ah, Ira. Good to see you in the flesh, old chap." Palmer turned back to Sid and stated the obvious: "Most of the time we ring each other up."

Ira wanted to grind his teeth in irritation. Could that English accent be any phonier? Sid didn't seem to notice. Or, if he noticed, he didn't seem to care. Sid was too busy lifting containers of food from the bags and distributing them to himself and Palmer.

Ira knew he had to play the game. "Nice to see you, Palmer. Sorry to hear that you and Ruben have parted ways."

"Well. Yes. We haven't really parted ways. He called me just a few minutes ago and gave me his blessing for...my plans." Palmer, who'd opened a container and helped himself to plastic utensils and a napkin, suddenly froze, looking quizzically at Sid. An awkward silence ensued. Sid stopped fussing over the food and looked at Palmer. The two men seemed in wordless communication with each other. Palmer put down his fork and stood. "I think I'll go have a washing up first." He nodded to Ira and left Sid's office.

Ira belatedly realized that one of the takeout bags was leaking a sticky fluid onto the glass top of Sid's desk. Probably the melting gelato. Or maybe the glaze from the quail. He braced for a rebuke from Sid, who had to see it. Sid saw everything. None came, however. Sid, distracted, didn't even notice the wet blob oozing onto his precious desk.

"You get Cody taken care of?"

"Yeah," Ira said, feeling stupid because he was still standing while Palmer, a fellow assistant, had gotten to sit during his audience with the Great and Powerful Sid. Maybe Ira should be bold and sit down without being invited to do so. Maybe he should sit in the very seat Palmer had just vacated. That would send a signal.

He couldn't bring himself to do it. Instead, he hovered. "It was no problem, and I even got a good deal. You know how many helicopter pilots are out of work right now because TV and radio stations have stopped doing traffic reports, because there's nothing to report? The stations are in a real bind. They own these incredibly expensive to maintain pieces of equipment that they're loath to sell, because they expect traffic to get moving again sometime. My inquiry was a welcome one."

"What about the non-disclosure form?"

Ira pulled a wrinkled paper from his back pocket and unfolded it. "I faxed it to them and got a signed copy back before I told them where Cody was."

Sid stared at it, frowning, smoothing it open with his hands. "This is just a faxed signature? Not an original?"

Sid had to be kidding! "There was no way I could physically get over there and get someone to write their name in ink on the form." Ira waved his arm expressively toward the window. "Sid, you do know what's happening out there, right? I mean, the best I could do was to find a copy shop with a fax machine." And Ira had thought that was pretty damn good, by the way. He wondered if he would ever get any credit for doing a good job, particularly under trying circumstances. Since he was hours late to work today, probably not.

"Anyway, the pilot should be calling any minute to let us know that Cody is safely back in Malibu."

"Did you give him your cell number? Or the office number here?"

"Both." What did that matter?

"Great. Just great." Sid was uncharacteristically distracted. "Listen, Ira. We gotta talk. This situation, with you coming in so late every day. It's just no good."

"I can't help it, Sid. I told you how the landlord won't let me out of my lease. I can't afford to pay two rents. And even if I could get out of it, finding affordable rent around here, in Beverly Hills, is not exactly--"

"I'm not saying it's your fault. In fact, it's not your fault. There. I'll say it straight out. You're a victim of circumstance."

That was big of him.

"But it's just not working out. We're not getting business taken care of here. I had to send the submissions out myself this morning. You weren't here to answer the phone. It's just no good."

"What are you saying, Sid?" he asked, even though he now knew what Sid was about to say.

"I'm gonna have to let you go, Ira. Of course I'll give you a good reference. And two weeks severance."

"It's Palmer, isn't it? You've hired that phony blonde Chinese phony English accented son of a bitch Palmer to replace me. That is just...craptastic."

"As a matter of fact, Palmer *is* joining the agency." Sid shrugged. "No reason to keep it from you. He'll fill your position. He has a genuine desire to be an agent, and it's OK with Ruben. Might even be helpful to Ruben, the way everybody scratches everybody else's back in this business. And Palmer lives close by, so getting to work on time won't be a problem like it is for you."

"How can he afford that?" Ira sputtered. "Are you going to pay him...what, five times what you paid me?"

Sid hesitated, trying to phrase things with delicacy. As crude as he generally was, he was a bit of a prude when the topic was homosexuality. "As a matter of fact, Palmer is Ruben's...roommate."

"Right," Ira nodded bitterly. "So that's the way it is."

"Ira, I need someone that I can groom to be an agent. I'd like to expand the business, but with the personal service we give to our clients, I'm really gonna need some help with that. You're a capable assistant and all, but you're just not agent material. You should accept this gracefully. Change is something we should embrace. Life is a processs. You've been...just great. This helicopter idea you came up with, for Cody – it's just terrific. You're so smart like that. Resourceful. I'm really going to miss you, on some levels. But I need to take Midwood to the next level, and Palmer's the guy who can help me do it. He knows how to talk to people. And he just...carries himself like a winner."

"Meaning what? I carry myself like a loser?"

Sid blinked nervously. "I didn't call building security to escort you out because I thought you'd be mature about this. It's just business. That's all. Nothing personal."

"You son of a bitch. After how I've slaved away here. All the stupid scut work I've done for you. I cleaned your toilets, for God's sake!"

Sid shrank back in his chair, unpleasantly surprised.

Ira derived some small satisfaction from the knowledge that Sid was, at least momentarily, afraid of him. Afraid of skinny, wheezy, spaghetti-armed Ira. It was not enough satisfaction, though. Ira reached into the leaking takeout bag and picked up the container of gelato, removed its plastic lid and then thrust his arm forward. He would shove the melted dessert into Sid's astonished face, like Jimmy Cagney had ground the grapefruit half into that woman's face in "The Public Enemy"! But Ira lost his nerve at the last minute and instead turned the container upside down so that its contents spilled down into a shapeless blob on top of the pile of scripts sitting on a corner of Sid's desk. His own script was somewhere in that pile, but he didn't care.

Sid shook his head in disgust. "You disappoint me, Ira."

Ira shuffled through the soggy, sticky scripts until he came to his own. Pulling it out of the pile, he clutched it in his white-knuckled hand. "And you're a liar. You never meant to read this, did you, Sid?"

Sid didn't answer.

Ira, taking his script with him, turned to leave but turned back. "By the way, Sid. Your walls are *pink*. A really ugly shade of pink."

CHAPTER TWENTY-FIVE:
THE LOOTERS MUST BE LAUGHING

Blog entry
iraorileysblog.wordpress.com
September 4

What a craptastic day this has been. I just got fired. I feel like I've been kicked in the stomach by a horse. After all the dues I paid, all the scut work I did hoping against hope that someday I'd get a useful connection from that gig -- I'm out. Sid won't feel the slightest inconvenience; he's probably had my replacement lined up for some time. Palmer Lu is the sort of naturally ass-kissing Ralph Lauren-wearing jerk who will rise as quickly in this industry as bubbles in a glass of ginger ale. Suddenly I understand workplace violence. When I think about how I was Sid's pathetic little gopher and fetcher, I want to cringe. Then I want to shoot him. Today, I figured out a way to get Sid's biggest client, Cody Torrance, out of a real jam. And what was my thanks? Right. The axe. I would have liked to see Palmer figure out a better solution.

So what? I didn't want to be an agent, a leech sucking the blood from true talents. I wanted to be the one getting my blood sucked. Then why does it sting so much, to be dismissed as if I was a nobody? When I've had a chance to calm down and think about it, I may very well be grateful I was fired. Maybe Sid did me a favor. I'm still going to reserve the right to hate him, though, especially if I can't find another industry job quickly. My office skills are minimal, my resume unimpressive. Academically, I am the worst possible thing I could be: an English major who didn't even get my degree. I was too impatient. Didn't bother fulfilling those pesky requirements in math, science, etc., because they didn't interest me. I wanted to get to Hollywood and get going on my screenwriting career right away! Brilliant decision, Ira.

I have almost no savings. And, no, I'm not a spendthrift. I just made crapola in the way of a paycheck and even in the Valley apartments ain't cheap. I'm going to shoot out some resumes right now, but who am I kidding? The entertainment industry is as crippled as the traffic right now. Every part of the local economy is stagnant, because no one can go anywhere.

I'm typing madly on my laptop in this wireless café even though I should already be on my bicycle, making my way home. Or, maybe I should get back to where I ditched my car this morning. It's closer to my apartment but pointless to retrieve it because it's official; traffic is now at an absolute standstill. The news came over the radio a few minutes ago. The governor has declared martial law. He said he's sending National Guard troops to L.A., because there's been a lot of crime on the freeways and the inevitable looting of stores, but when I heard his warning I thought, like others must have; how are the troops going to get here? They'll have to walk, because their trucks can't get through any more than other vehicles. The looters must be laughing at the extra time they're being given.

People are just walking away from their cars and heading home, presumably.

The really funny thing is that my family back in Michigan was always more worried about Los Angeles (and me, in it) getting destroyed by an earthquake. They never dreamed of apocalypse-by-automobile

It's hard to imagine how all of this is going to end.

CHAPTER TWENTY-SIX:
THE ELITE FLEEING FROM THE UNWASHED

"Your last caller wasn't hallucinating, Cap. I was there, too. Cody Torrance was running down Santa Monica Boulevard and this big mob was chasing him. Why not? They had nothing better to do."

Cap laughed heartily. "Sounds like one of those old vampire movies, doesn't it? The angry villagers, carrying torches, chasing the villain to his castle?"

"They weren't angry, Cap," said Rick from Altadena. "Just all excited at seeing a movie star right in their midst, with no security people around him. They were chasing him like he was Jesus Christ. Like they wanted to touch him and be healed."

Cap sipped his coffee and pictured it. "Now you know that civilization is finally collapsing, Caplets. When you have movie stars at the mercy of the masses. The elite fleeing from the unwashed. The unimaginably famous being set upon by the anonymous rabble." He paused. "Poor Cody Torrance. All those action movies and he can't even fight off a few thousand crazed fans. Has to run from them like a scared rabbit."

"Ah, come on, Cap," protested Rick from Altadena. "You would have done the same thing. If you had any fans, that is."

"Ha ha ha, Rick. I get it. Very funny. Too bad I gotta drop you now. I can't allow anyone on my program who's funnier than me. Besides, as enticing as a celebrity lynching is, I'd like to stick to the main story of the day. The only story, really. Governor Jorge Olmstead, after failing to solve the traffic problem that has us all stuck where we are as if the freeways were made of quicksand, has declared martial law. Has there been a natural disaster? An enemy attack? No. There's a simple little problem of too few miles of roadway for too many cars. A manmade problem that should have been alleviated by a manmade remedy by now, if only our leaders -- starting with Olmstead -- had any balls." Cap stopped, squinting at the computer screen in front of him. "I'm afraid we have to leave that topic for the moment and get back to Torrance Talk. My producer tells me we have a caller waiting with some breaking news. Rachel from Santa Clarita, what's this about Cody Torrance missing? Missing? That can't be right. If you've been listening, you just heard from two eyewitnesses who said that earlier this afternoon, Torrance was seen high-tailing it down Santa Monica Boulevard."

"Cap, my brother knows a guy who got hired to pick Cody up and fly him out to his place in Malibu. My brother just called and said that the helicopter is missing. He called me because he knows what a huge fan of Cody I am. I've seen all his movies so many times I can--"

"Rachel. Focus. What do you mean, 'missing'?"

"They've lost contact with the pilot. Last time they heard from him, he was headed over the Santa Monica Mountains."

"Rachel, don't take this the wrong way, but is your brother generally a reliable source of information?"

"Well sure, he--"

"Is he on any medication?"

"Just for acid reflux--"

"Has he had any psychiatric treatment? Ever?"

"Of course not, Cap. He's absolutely sure that--"

"Or, my dear Rachel-from-Santa-Clarita, is there any chance your brother is pulling your leg? Because you know, if you listen to this show on a regular basis, that Caplets tune in for vitally important and *accurate* information. K-Talk-L.A. is about 'Hot News and Provocative Views.' The *last* thing I will allow on this radio program is for people to spread panic by airing unsubstantiated rumors. We take the high road here, Rachel."

"It's true, Cap," she insisted. "I listen to you every day. I know how you are about people getting their facts straight. My brother was very serious when he told me about it. He would never make something like this up."

"If what you're telling me is true, Rachel, then we've just broken a sensational news story here on WQMR. Cody Torrance may have been in a helicopter crash this afternoon. He could be dead or dying at this very moment. He might have just joined the legion of celebrities to die tragically, before their time, in air disasters. Glen Miller. Carole Lombard. Patsy Kline. Richie Valens. Kim Kardashian. Oh, that's right. I just wish Kim

Kardashian would die in a plane crash, so we wouldn't have to hear about her anymore because YOU, KIM KARDASHIAN, ARE ONE OF THE MOST USELESS HUMAN BEINGS TO EVER SUCK AIR ON THIS PLANET AND YOU DON'T EVEN DESERVE TO TAKE UP SPACE, MUCH LESS GET ALL THE ATTENTION YOU GET!"

Cap permitted himself one of his long, trademark pauses -- several minutes of dead air that most radio personalities would not dare to attempt, could not tolerate, really, so ingrained was their habit of filling time with sound. He knew how to strategically use silence. His lulls were always potent with possibility. His listeners were enthralled with suspense. Had he gone around the bend? Had a stroke? Suffered another of his famous rumored nervous breakdowns? Would he be fired for wishing death on someone? Suspended? Would he be sued (again)? He'd been reprimanded by his station several times for launching into extreme, deliberately offensive, nearly hysterical diatribes on subjects far more serious than Kim Kardashian. Wishing a public figure dead was mild compared with some of his past verbal transgressions. Each time he was suspended, he and the station had waged explosive wars of words via columnists in several L.A. publications, volleying insults and charges back and forth at each other in print until some agreement was reached by lawyers for the two parties and a fine paid by Cap. His return to the airwaves would be heavily promoted. The public loved the drama.

Just when his producer looked ready to launch himself over the console and talk into Cap's mic himself, or pop in a CD and play a song -- anything to break the excruciating silence -- Cap continued. "Course, I still wouldn't mind seeing her naked. If anyone has a copy of that sex tape that was circulating on the Internet and wouldn't mind duping a copy for me... But I digress. I need to stay focused. To continue with my list of celebrities who've died horrible deaths in plane crashes: JFK Jr. The Big Bopper. Lynrd Skynrd, or most of them, anyway."

Cap had forgotten to "kill" the call from Rachel from Santa Clarita, giving her the opportunity to interrupt him.

"What about Reba McIntyre's band, Cap? Remember when a bunch of them died in that plane crash?"

"Not celebrities," he snapped. "Can you name even one of them, Rachel? No. You can't. So they don't belong on this list. They belong on a list of nobodies who've died in plane crashes. Now let me see. Where was I? Aliayah, because just like every other woman, she took too much luggage with her. Hope you're enjoying being fashion forward in heaven, Aliayah. And now, Cody Torrance. Rachel, my producer has already alerted the WQMR news department and our reporters are jumping on the story. For anyone who's just tuned in -- and where've you been? -- Cody Torrance has reportedly been in a helicopter crash somewhere in the Santa Monica mountains, as desolate a place as you'd ever want to crash in. Cody Torrance may be dead. Rachel, I'm going to go out on a limb because I'm pretty sure we're not going to get a bigger news tip than this one for the next couple of weeks, so I'm going to officially name you 'Cap Lessing Show Caller of the Month.'"

"I can't believe it, Cap! I never win anything."

"You'll believe it, Rachel, when you come to the station and pick up your official Cap Lessing Show t-shirt and K-Talk-L.A. bumper sticker, along with a gift certificate for a free haircut from Le Style salons, with 38 convenient locations throughout Southern California."

"But I can't get to the station with the traffic--"

"Now Bran from Culver City -- my producer says you claim that Cody Torrance was posing for pictures this morning NAKED in the back of a limousine? Tell me more..."

CHAPTER TWENTY-SEVEN:
CALAMITY IS GOOD FOR BUSINESS

Ira rode for a while in a trance-like state, which would have been dangerous if the cars on the roads he crossed so absentmindedly had been moving at their usual spastic pace. Fortunately, they were now stationary objects, and he squeezed his bicycle through gaps between bumpers without being very aware of what he was doing.

He'd been fired. He'd been fired from his job. He tried to tell himself: big deal, he didn't like the job anyway, there were other jobs, Sid treated him like shit on a stick, but the harsh fact was that his being fired was a veritable rupture in his carefully tended identity. He'd never thought of himself as the kind of person who ever would be fired. He was the kind of person who left a job when he was ready to leave it. Sid's dismissal burned in his brain far worse than the many rejections he'd received from women. Those he actually understood.

This was different – and disturbing. He felt cast adrift. No, it was worse than that. He'd been on a beautiful cruise ship (albeit as a purser, but one still got to enjoy the views, the sunsets and the ambiance) and he'd been thrown overboard, with no rubber raft in sight. No one was even standing at the rails, to yell "man overboard!" or at least wave poignantly to him, acknowledging his departure from their glittering midst.

It was a tremendous jolt to his world to be suddenly, abruptly unemployed. He had no financial safety net. The little money that was in his checking account would go fast. Saying that L.A. was an expensive place to live -- even when trying to do it on the cheap -- was like saying that hemorrhoids were uncomfortable. He could call his parents for some emergency funds, he supposed, but he would hate to do it. They would suggest, sweetly but firmly, that he come home. To Detroit. A place he fit into even less than here.

He made his way north past Wilshire. How was he going to get over the hill on a bicycle? The 101 seemed a million miles away. Might as well be. Should he use Laurel Canyon?

Normally, he'd never think of taking it on two wheels. It was a road laid out by a lunatic, some ambitious planner who refused to accept that certain mountains should not be roaded. On a map it didn't look that bad, a squiggly but useful north-south route through the Hollywood Hills. Once you found yourself actually on it, though, it was like being on a carnival thrill-ride that was much scarier than you'd expected, and you had no way of getting off until the ride ended and the road dumped its endless load of cars onto Sunset Boulevard. Once you made the foolish decision at Ventura Boulevard to use Laurel Canyon to get over the hill, your fate was pretty much sealed, unless you wanted to take some equally insane side street that would lead you miles out of your way, up mountainous, absurdly narrow roads with undersized guardrails that wouldn't do much to keep you from plunging into the deep, dangerous, jack pine-covered ravines they bordered, through neighborhoods favored by middle-aged rock stars, former centerfold models, owners of hip music clubs and coyotes. He'd learned, for instance, that "Lookout Mountain" meant "Look out for death." Even motorists who drove Laurel Canyon every day took deep, calming breaths, gripped their steering wheels with both hands, and prayed to whatever God or spirit force they were currently embracing to help them survive the terrifying series of ascending and then descending curves that offered no visibility of what lay beyond whatever sloping embankment they seemed -- at any given moment -- about to smash into.

Ironically, people drove Laurel Canyon fast. Residents of any other region of the country, when dealing with such a road, would go sensibly slow, feeling their way, taking their time to navigate carefully around each harrowing hairpin curve. Not so Los Angelenos. It was possible that some drivers sped down Laurel Canyon because they were so frightened they wanted to get off it as quickly as possible. Others probably viewed it like some extreme sport. If one wished to drive at a moderate speed, one was shit out of luck. When the car behind yours was kissing your tailpipe because the car behind them was kissing their tailpipe, you had no choice but to drive fast enough to not get rammed from behind. It was like a bizarre motorized cattle stampede that went on day after day. Flatlander that he was, Ira knew he would never get used to it.

In Southern California, people made desperate navigational decisions based on their need to keep driving time within reason, relative to Southern California. Thus, Laurel Canyon was a popular route.

Or it used to be, anyway. He felt a warm flush of nostalgia, thinking of the time when cars moved. All of that fast-paced aggravation was gone now. He could take Laurel Canyon on a bike today, except that it was incredibly steep. Which would give out first? His legs or his lungs?

The scene around him finally penetrated his wounded preoccupation. The surreal specter of trapped traffic in a city in which everyone and everything moved all the time forced him out of his self-absorbed daze.

Ira began to question his assumption that things would inevitably return to normal, just because they had to. Now, looking around, he was not so sure. The air was apocalyptically thick and raw, darkly layered with car emissions that hung visibly in the sky like angry ghosts, trapped in their auto afterlife by a stubborn coating of marine moisture drawn inland by high pressure from the east. Cars stoppered up every traffic route like some monstrous form of urban constipation. People walked about slowly, uneasily, unsure of their destinations. They were prepared for earthquakes, hazardous materials spills, multi-car accidents, terrorist attacks. But this…this was such a *quiet* catastrophe.

Ira pedaled slowly, trying to keep the wheezing in check. His chances of getting all the way home to North Hollywood tonight were not good. He was already exhausted. Damnit! Why couldn't L.A. be flat, like the plain, noble heartland from which he'd sprung? Traveling on two wheels would be a lot easier if he didn't have to take the terrain into account whenever he tried to map out a route in his head. He was a long distance from his apartment. He could always spring for a motel room, but the thought of spending money when he was jobless sparked a fresh pang of anxiety in him. Besides, with so many people stranded, there were probably no rooms available. If he could make it to his car he could sleep in it overnight. He found himself actually pleased at the prospect.

Think, Ira! He tried to orient himself. To the southeast lay CBS. Paramount Studios were due east, beyond Warner Brothers' Hollywood Studios. Over the hill lay Universal City, Disney, Warner Brothers' main studios. He had mainly an entertainment industry grasp of the local geography, which did him no good at this moment. The afternoon was rapidly aging. He needed to figure out what he was going to do for shelter tonight.

He was now in West Hollywood. The boys in Boys Town seemed to be making the best of a bad situation. Gripping the handlebars of his bike, wishing it had a basket -- however girly or dorky -- into which he could shove his heavy backpack, he looked around in increasing amusement. A gigantic street party was in progress, like Mardi Gras but without the topless women. Dance mix music blasted from the open windows of parked cars. Laughing, talking, getting-jiggy-with-it humanity packed bars and restaurants and spilled out onto the sidewalks. Alcohol and hors d'oeuvres were circulating freely among the riotously cheerful crowd, as was the unmistakable scent of marijuana. Lots of people were wearing costumes, or parts of costumes. Ira wondered where they'd gotten them, or if West Hollywoodians simply kept costumes handy in order to be ready for any festive occasion.

A man wearing a shirt and tie, a shiny green grass skirt and a Statue of Liberty headdress was offering passers-by chips and guacamole he'd set up on a card table festooned with a Caribbean-themed tablecloth. "No double dipping!" he admonished Ira cheerfully. He sipped something blue from a martini glass while slouching comfortably in a jaunty yellow canvas director's chair. He raised a digital camera, framed a bit of nearby revelry, and clicked off a few pictures.

"What's going on?" Ira asked, eating a chip. It was probably a stupid question, he reflected.

"We can't go anywhere, so we might as well enjoy ourselves," the Statue of Liberty/Hawaiian dancer said.

He was joined by an older man carrying a cooler. The newcomer wore a business suit, but over his shoulders was a harness sprouting wings made of gold-flecked white tulle stretched over wire frames. His chunky necklace proved to be a dingy collection of oversized plastic molars strung together. "Luckily, I still had this get-up in the trunk of my car from Halloween," he said to the other man. He put the cooler down and sat in the other director's chair, adjusting his wings upward so that they didn't get bent by the armrests. At Ira's quizzical look, he explained, "I'm the tooth fairy. It's an old joke but still, I think, a good one." He opened the cooler and extracted several cans of beer, offering one to Ira and opening one for himself. "You look like you could use a cold adult beverage, my young friend."

Ira smiled wearily, lay his bike down, accepted the beer and gulped at it enthusiastically. "You're a Good Samaritan. Thanks. This does hit the spot." He looked around, stupefied, still trying to comprehend the scope of what he was seeing. He felt as if he had a serious buzz on -- much more than he could be getting from the beer. He was hallucinating. Dreaming. Seeing elements of reality that were familiar, but in a context that was all askew.

"Par-TEE! Par-TEE!" a drunken man yelled as he walked by, one arm encircling a busty blonde woman who walked in step with him, the other periodically bringing a bottle of vodka to his mouth. He noticed Ira staring at him. "Par-TEE!" he screamed, somewhat belligerently this time.

Ira held up his beer and manufactured a fake smile to show his solidarity. "Par-TEE," he managed.

The drunk, satisfied, moved on.

A woman with fox-colored hair and enormous brown eyes hurried toward them. "Gill, it's official," she said excitedly to the Statue of Liberty/Hawaiian dancer. "I just heard it on someone's car radio over there. The governor has officially declared a traffic emergency in Southern California. The last bit of detectable movement came this morning. Now, everything is frozen."

"Can't put anything past Olmstead, can you?" Gill said sardonically. "Thanks, Reva, for the news flash."

His sarcasm was wasted on her. "I knew you'd want to know," she said before moving on, eager to spread the news.

Three young men doing acrobatic routines in the street nearby were drawing a crowd, many of whom dropped money into a jar labeled DONATIONS set strategically in front of the performers. One finished doing a series of backflips to terrific applause.

Nearby, standing in the bed of a shiny new Silverado was a middle-aged woman playing an acoustic guitar. She wore black jeans and a gauzy black blouse of an indeterminate shape, probably to conceal her own indeterminate shape, thought Ira. The top's winglike sleeves reminded Ira of a gypsy moth. She strummed the guitar, finished "Four Strong Winds" and went on to "Landslide." The TIPS sign propped up in the open guitar case next to her was working. Ira saw several people drop in bills and coins.

He sipped his beer. "But what does it really mean? The governor's big announcement. Does it change anything?"

Gill shrugged. "What you really mean is, does it fix anything? Probably not. It just makes official what we've seen coming for a long time. This is a disaster of epic, if quiet, proportions. A crisis with no precedent. Olmstead must have had to do it in order to go for FEMA funds, but what's he going to do with them if he gets them? Money won't fix this mess. He leaned forward intently, really warming up to the subject. "So Olmstead declared martial law. Called out the National Guard to maintain order. Problem is, the Guard has to *walk* to the neighborhoods at greatest risk, so it's going to be awhile before any real security is in place."

The other man, the Tooth Fairy, nodded in agreement. "I heard on the Cap Lessing show that Olmstead imposed a curfew, but then had to do some quick backpedaling when it was pointed out to him that no one can get home -- at least anytime soon -- so that ordering people to remain in their homes won't work. The curfew is unenforceable. What are you going to do? Arrest everybody?

"Did you hear about the looting?" Gill asked Ira. "It's already started. In Hollywood, Santa Monica, Pacoima, Compton. Hell, they're going to be breaking in the windows of those jewelry stores on Rodeo Drive pretty soon. Not enough security guards around to stop them."

The Tooth Fairy shook his head grimly. "Not Rodeo Drive. Horrors! It's getting surreal."

"At least it looks like people around here aren't too upset," Ira observed.

Gill dipped a cracker in the guacamole and crunched on it appreciatively. "I think I put a little too much lemon juice in it this time, but it's still good," he said to the Tooth Fairy, who nodded. He turned back to Ira. "Sure, people are having fun tonight. It's a new situation. Exciting, in a perverse way. But already you can anticipate the problems. Every hotel and motel is booked up. Some people might get resourceful and start renting out their spare rooms or even their sofas, but still, a lot of folks are about to get a taste of what being homeless is like, and they're not going to like it. They'll be sleeping in their cars tonight, if they have cars. Or parks, but there they might be targets of crime. Accommodations will be a problem beyond tonight, in fact. Well into the foreseeable future. The middle class is not used to being uncomfortable. Hygiene will be an issue. So will communications. People who are sticking with their cars and who have cell phone battery chargers in them will be all right for a while, but lots of people have abandoned their cars and started walking home. Their cell phones are going to die, eventually. Good luck finding pay phones these days. Families are separated, people will be anxious. What about parents who need to get home to kids? Caretakers who need to get to sick and elderly patients? Workers who have to get to essential jobs? What about hospitals and power plants?" He sighed. "If we are not mobile, we're screwed."

"Yeah," said the Tooth Fairy. "What's it going to be like when the next shifts don't come in, and the workers unlucky enough to get stuck on duty there get tired or just jump ship and go home? You remember the rolling blackouts here a few years ago? Or how about that big power outage back east? Remember the havoc that caused? This is going to be much, much worse. It's almost enough to make me want to leave California."

"Almost?" Ira queried. He'd been thinking yet again that maybe it was time he left himself.

"I would," the Tooth Fairy sighed, "But for the weather. Moved out here from Pittsburgh 17 years ago and now I'm completely spoiled. Don't even remember what snow looks like. Don't want to."

"The experts aren't brave enough to venture guesses as to how long it's going to take before we can resume something like normal daily life," said Gill. "Right now, it feels like summer vacation, but the party atmosphere will evaporate pretty quickly. People will lose jobs. Homes. Those who can't adapt will fall through the cracks. If this thing goes on too long..." He shook his head sadly, opened the cooler and removed a covered plastic tray whose various compartments held crackers, cubes of cheese and chunks of melon and strawberries. From the cooler he also extracted a pile of snack size paper plates, a container of multicolored toothpicks and some cocktail napkins. He laid the items out artfully on the table next to a stack of business cards.

"Have some more chips," he said to Ira. "How about some cheese and crackers? We've got plenty."

"Thanks." Ira, hungry, slid a cheddar cheese-topped multigrain cracker into his mouth. He chewed thoughtfully for a few minutes. "You guys don't seem that worried."

The Tooth Fairy laughed. "We live nearby, so we're not homeless. Our office is close, so we can walk to work. But more to the point, we're lawyers who specialize in civil suits. Calamity is good for business."

"*Great* for business," amended Gill. He took a business card from the stack and handed it to Ira.

Ira read: Rafe Luster and Gill Steingold ~ Attorneys at Law.

"*Our* business, anyway," Rafe was saying. "This mess is going to cause a lot of suffering. And someone's at fault, naturally. It'll be our job to get appropriate compensation for the victims. Off-hand, I'm thinking the state of California is going to have to pay off lots and lots of people. The Department of Transportation has screwed up big time. And the longer it goes on, the greater the suffering and the bigger the compensation."

"But if the state pays, that money comes out of our pockets, right?" Ira said. "The taxpayers are the ones who ultimately foot the bill. So the politicians and bureaucrats won't be the ones who'll be punished. We will. We'll be sort of...paying damages to ourselves."

"By Jove I think he's got it." said Gill, giving him a little salute.

"Then what's the point?"

"Justice, grasshopper," answered Rafe. "Justice for all. And attorneys' fees for us."

Ira wanted to be angry with them but he was drinking their beer and eating their food. "And if the cause is beyond anyone's control? Simply a matter of too many people being here? Overpopulation? In other words, what if no one is to blame?"

They regarded him with amusement. Gill shook his head. "You starry-eyed young optimist, you. Someone is *always* to blame."

Chapter Twenty-Eight: How Would Glenn Close Handle This Situation?

Darkness. Darkness that was darker than the darkest night she'd ever known. She might as well have been on a different planet, or on the dark side of the moon. The streetlights and headlights, neon signs and gleaming windows of civilization were far away. If there was a moon tonight, its glow didn't penetrate into this particular slash in the earth's crust, this canyon at whose bottom rested a crumpled helicopter and three people, at least one of whom was quite dead.

The night was awash with unfamiliar sounds, most of them scary. Who knew which of the noises emerging from the darkness signaled something dangerous? There were feathery creakings that could simply be tree branches moving slightly in the breeze, or some sort of creature rubbing wings or legs together in a mating ritual. Did animals mate at night? Some were nocturnal, but were they screwing or just hunting and eating? Owls didn't trouble her, but rats were nocturnal, too — weren't they? How about snakes? But didn't they prefer it warm, and wasn't it warmer during the daytime? *Sleep, snakes, sleep*, she thought fervently. *I command you.* She heard throaty blotches of sound off to the east that might be a bird. Maybe it was a special bird, a vulture, staying awake for this very rare feast: a late night snack of human flesh. Maybe he could smell death. She couldn't, not yet, but possibly animals were aware of the odor sooner, reactive to it like to one of those high-pitched whistles only dogs could hear. Were there even vultures in California? She had no idea. She was a newbie. And let's face it: even if she'd been here longer, she wasn't exactly nature girl.

The image of a single vulture gave way to a scarifying assemblage of winged and four-legged scavengers, hovering in the gloom just beyond where she could see them but waiting to ravage the body of the poor pilot and then, strengthened by their meal, move on to the (slightly) more lively food possibilities offered by herself and Cody. She might pose more of a challenge than a dead man, but with her extra pounds of flesh, more of a reward as well. She felt that she should protect the body of the pilot from being eaten -- or at least gnawed -- but had no idea how she might accomplish that task.

Luanne rested the back of her fingers gently -- why gently? -- on the cheek of the pilot again, hoping that she'd made a mistake the first time, or that he'd miraculously revived. No. Still cold. Cold and hard and curiously smooth, like the stone bench her Mom had in her front yard. The guy may well have died before the crash. It had looked like he was having a heart attack. *Just your luck, Luanne. You think you're about to have the adventure of your life, flying away with Cody Torrance, and you get a pilot with a bad ticker.*

Stop it, she told herself. *It's not all about you. The poor man is dead.*

But she was afraid and overwhelmed. She had to find Cody. She knew he'd survived the crash because when she came to, she heard him making sounds. Crying, she thought, then amended it to: moaning. He wasn't moaning, at the moment, so she couldn't use the sound to guide her back to him. The silence unnerved her. As long as he was making those horrible, pained noises, she knew he was alive. Please don't be dead, Cody. I can't be all alone here. She shuffled around, her feet bumping into pieces of wreckage and other objects she couldn't identify.

"Cody?" she whispered, then wondered; why am I whispering? Worried about waking up Big Foot? "Cody!" she called out loudly.

How long until the sun came up? How bad would that pilot look, when it did? She tried to prepare herself for what could be a horrific sight. In the meantime, she wished for a flashlight. And some water. And the pack of cigarettes she had in her purse, which could be lying somewhere nearby or miles away. No telling how far the debris had scattered.

Smoking is bad for me. Gotta quit -- again. She almost laughed at the mantra that came automatically into her head. *Helicopter crashes are bad for me, too. Gotta quit having them. After this, no more.*

How long had she been unconscious? Her entire ride side ached, the shoulder throbbing and the ribs hammering out a jagged rhythm of sharp twinges. It hurt when she took a deep breath, but if she kept her respiration shallow, she was able to move around all right. Maybe the ribs were just bruised. That would be good. She could feel blood crusted on her right temple and in her left palm. The gash in her hand felt pretty deep, but it wasn't bleeding anymore. She sensed instinctively that none of her injuries was life threatening. She was going to live. Of course, that might only mean that she was going to live long enough to die of starvation or exposure.

A sob arose from the black stillness. Cody! She followed the direction of the cry and nearly tripped on him. Kneeling down, she felt his body with her hands.

"Cody! Can you hear me? It's me. Luanne. Remember?"

He babbled something, an undertone of anguish beneath the half-formed words. She groped at him like a blind woman, uncovering his legs and searching for clues, her finger stopping when she encountered a sticky mass of blood on his side. Jesus! He was really hurt bad. What was she supposed to do here? Call 911? She'd already tried that. Even though she knew the impulse was futile, she took her cell phone from her pocket, powered it up and cursed at the symbol displayed on the small lighted screen: no signal. Of course no signal. They were in the middle of nowhere. The fucking wilderness. L.A. was supposed to be such a big fucking city. How could there be all this wilderness so close to it? And how could it have been her bad luck to get stuck in it? If they had to crash, why couldn't they have crashed by the side of the freeway, with thousands of witnesses in cars who would use their cell phones to call 9-1-1. Were the circumstances of this crash some cosmic message? Was she getting slapped down by Fate because she, the oh-so-ordinary Luanne Sajewski, had the temerity to want to be an actress? (A famous actress, she admitted to herself.) Should she survive this bizarre little outing, was she meant to immediately take her oversized ass back to Altoona and settle down into a life of...what? She couldn't even imagine.

A helicopter downed in the black depths of a barren canyon. You never saw this scene on a postcard from L.A. Only palm trees and suntanned, cellulite-free people on beaches. Stars on the Hollywood Walk of Fame. That's what you saw. The realization that she was freezing was a fresh hell. It was cold!

156

Cold! In California! It made her furious. How could it be cold in California?

There was absolutely no fairness in the world.

Sobs erupted from her throat, coursed through her body and filled the canyon in loud waves. The crying jag had its way for awhile, fierce and unstoppable. She felt crushed by anxiety. On her very first real day in L.A. she'd been involved in a horrific crash, and now found herself in a remote canyon with no food, water, warm clothing or toilet paper, and she really, really had to pee. There were fuzzy dark shapes nearby. Bushes? Trees? Should she make her way over to them to relieve herself? Why? One potential spectator was dead, and the other was so out of it he wouldn't notice. Besides, she was hearing more strange noises. Crinkling. Crunching. Snapping. Was it a hungry mountain lion? A bobcat? A snake? Something waiting for her to move away from the other living human so that it could attack her? Whatever it was, it was wildlife, and that couldn't be good. Or maybe it was just a rabbit. Silly wabbit.

The point was: she had no way of knowing whether it was dangerous or not.

Cody wailed briefly then went silent. Luanne cursed herself for her inability to remember much from that first aid course she'd had to take all those years ago in Girl Scouts. Stop bleeding. Apply pressure. Elevate....something. The wounded limb? She wasn't even sure what all was wounded on him. He could have internal injuries. What if he was bleeding inside? Poor Cody. She wished she could at least help him with the pain. Despite his mostly unconscious state, he seemed to be feeling something.

Luanne decided that someday she was going to use this experience to inform her acting. It would actually end up being a very positive experience in her life, if she lived through it. It would give her a very exciting story to tell, in years to come. Damn! Maybe she could turn it into a one-woman play! Once rescued, she'd have to really use the media coverage that would no doubt come her way, just because of Cody's involvement. But she'd have to get a play together pretty quickly, to stretch her fifteen minutes of fame into something longer. And then...a movie? Nia Vardalos had done it with "My Big Fat Greek Wedding." Chaz Palminteri with "A Bronx Tale."

Once daylight hit, she'd have to find a pen and some scrap paper and start jotting down notes.

Feeling slightly more optimistic, she had the sudden but firm conviction that it was not her destiny to get eaten by a mountain lion while she was urinating. The universe was sending her ideas, plans for the future, which meant she would survive. She squinted into the black void around her and realized that it was not such a void after all. The grainy outlines of trees materialized from the shadows. The crumpled hump of the downed helicopter was almost comforting in its solidity, like a friendly beached whale. She compromised on her "pee plan" and went halfway to a copse of trees, squatted and did her business, then pulled her pants back up and tried not to think about how strange it felt not to wipe. There was tissue in her purse, but God only knew where that was. Cody couldn't have heard the quiet tinkle, could he?

She found her way back to the dead pilot with difficulty, her shuffling feet bumping into flotsam and jetsam she couldn't identify. She hoped none of the things she was inadvertently kicking would turn out to be a severed limb. The morning sunlight would bring some welcome clarity to the situation, but it could also reveal horrors hidden by the night.

"Sorry, guy, but you're not going to need this," she told him, as she stripped off his long-sleeved shirt. It wasn't easy removing it from his rigid, unyielding torso, but she wrestled with his unbending arms and flipped him onto his stomach, inching the garment from him until he finally surrendered it. She wondered idly if he had any tattoos. *Stop it! Focus*!

Taking his pants off was easier. She briefly considered leaving them on him, to preserve a little of his dignity, but pragmatism won out. She needed every scrap of clothing she could lay her hands on. She wished she knew a little something about the pilot. The poor guy had died in the company of a pair of strangers who didn't know him from Adam. Adam. The Bible. Should she say some kind of prayer over him? What if he was a Catholic and was supposed to have Last Rites? She wasn't terribly religious, but it seemed like something should be said to acknowledge his passing. How would Glenn Close handle this situation, if Glenn Close was playing a character in a scene in which she had to say something profound over the dead body of somebody she barely knew?

Luanne thought hard for a moment. Something was coming back to her, nudging at the half-closed door of her memory. "The Lord is my shepherd," she recalled slowly, whispering, then wondered why she was whispering. "I shall not want." Her voice sounded strange, echoey. A voice in the wilderness. The whole damn night was biblical. "He leadeth me... He leadeth me...somewhere. To green pastures. With goodness and mercy." She gave up and got to her feet. "Sorry, guy. I don't remember the passage, but I wish you...well. Although I'm a little late, because you've already gone to wherever it is you're going." She paused briefly, staring down at him, unable to make out his features in the gloom. "I hope it's a nice place."

Back at Cody's side, she placed a folded-up portion of the pants leg against his bloody side, applying firm pressure with her hand for a while before tying the pants around him to hold the makeshift bandage in place. The first aid stuff was coming back to her. It was just common sense. She'd always been a practical girl. Now that she felt calmer, she'd either remember what to do or figure things out for herself. Stop the bleeding, treat for shock. Stop the bleeding, treat for shock. Cody's hand was cold when she took it in hers. Was that from shock? Or just from being in this godforsaken canyon at night wearing only shorts and a light cotton shirt? The pilot's shirt became his blanket, although a woefully inadequate one, not even big enough to cover his bare legs. Still, she tucked it tightly around his upper body, hoping that it would stop his shivering. She found something nearby that felt like a piece of the chopper. It had no jagged edges and was about the right height, so she propped it under Cody's feet to elevate them. That was something from the first aid class, she was almost sure.

What time was it? How many more hours before daylight? Luanne was growing confident in her ability to find a way out of this mess, once she could see clearly. Maybe there was still a working radio in the helicopter. Maybe her cell phone would function tomorrow. Maybe the pilot had a cell phone with a better carrier and she'd get a signal. Or, they'd make it without communications. She couldn't carry Cody, but she could...drag him out, maybe. On a piece of wreckage that could serve as a sort of sled. She could make her way to a house or a road. Flag someone down, knock on a door, get help. Get medical attention for Cody. He wasn't going to die here. Not like this.

Her optimism was fragile, though; exhaustion threatened to down her barriers and allow anxiety to move in. Cody was badly injured and they was lost. She should probably try to sleep a little. Could she do that, with unidentified wild beasts probably hovering nearby, waiting to pounce? She stretched out on the ground, trying to make herself comfortable, trying to ignore the fact that she was cold. Some kind of plant life pricked her uncomfortably in the lower back and she shifted to one side, her hand encountering a familiar object. Could it really be...? Yes! The gods were good! It was her purse, with the pack of cigarettes and matches in it. She sat up excitedly, tapped a cigarette free and got it lighted, inhaling deeply. It actually gave her a rush. The satisfaction was intense. She savored the charged buzz that flooded through her.

Things suddenly didn't seem quite so bad after all.

CHAPTER TWENTY-NINE:
LEG ROOM AND FREE DRINKS

Ira curled in a fetal position in the back of a parked BMW he'd found unlocked on a side street off Santa Monica Boulevard and dreamed of Detroit. Half-dreamed, really, since he was only half-asleep. He wondered what his family was doing at that moment. It was a safe bet that none of them were sleeping in some stranger's car.

This would make a funny story. When it was all over and everything was back to normal, it would be a pretty amusing tale to tell. His parents probably wouldn't be amused, though. Thinking of his mom and dad brought on a dull sort of brain pain that felt like separation anxiety. He was awash in loneliness, hollow with alienation. If he wasn't too old to be homesick, this awful feeling would be homesickness.

He shivered, wishing for a blanket, wondering why it was cold at night in SoCal, even during the summer. It was wrong, a kink in the natural order of things. He tried to use his mental powers to invoke memories of hot, sticky, mosquito-laden Michigan summers, willing himself to hear the drone of lawn mowers, the hissing of sprinklers, the baritone shifting of air conditioners as they powered up to do battle with sticky air that was heavy and sluggish with humidity. It didn't work. He didn't feel any warmer.

He imagined himself walking down his suburban street on a sunny day in June. The animals that had been driven off when the subdivision replaced the original woods were brought back representationally, sometimes whimsically. Bronze deer lurked, perpetually alert, in the patchy shade of maple trees. All-weather aluminum rabbits crouched under bay windows. Faux antique brass songbirds perched on painted birdhouses. On front porch after front porch, concrete geese engaged in a fashion competition, finding themselves dressed in cunning pilgrim costumes at Thanksgiving; red, white and blue capes for the Fourth of July. Stone mallard ducks led their stone babies across chemically greened front lawns toward ponds which no longer existed.

Thinking about the animals depressed him. Where did they go, the real ones, when families like his moved in?

There were only three different styles of homes in the sub, so people did their best to individualize their front yards. Ira's mother planted impatiens around the base of the mailbox that stood like a sentinel at the curb, lined up with all the other mailbox sentinels. The Farbers had a fake brick wishing well on their lawn. If you tossed in a coin, it fell approximately two feet to land on the patch of dead grass beneath the fake wishing well. Herb Miller made the bold decision to replace his standard durable weather-resistant polymer putty-colored mailbox with a painted aluminum miniature turreted castle, with a drawbridge that opened to admit the day's bills. Instead of hedges, Mrs. Larksen put a bed of polished white stones under her front window and populated it with statues of characters that were dear to her. A large Virgin Mary, her robin's egg blue robe fading a little more each year, enjoyed pride of place, centered as she was just under the large front picture window. St. Francis of Assisi stood amiably to her right, undaunted by the company of Snow White on her left. The seven dwarves were arrayed on either side of the religious figures, mixing it up with two medieval-looking stone gargoyles, a giant brass tortoise with a happy expression on his face and two garden gnomes wearing tall pointed hats.

At night, from the sidewalk, you could see the blue lights of TV screens flickering in living rooms up and down the block, hear katydids chirping their sweet, sultry, choruses, sounding like so many tiny saws.

Raising the details from his memory did not make Ira feel warmer but it did cheer him up and make him feel closer to his family. They did not understand him, but they certainly loved him. He knew they were hoping he'd fail out here, so that he would come home and be one of them, even though he never really had been.

He could not conceive of moving back to Detroit and giving up this weather. He would visit, sure, especially once he was successful and wildly famous, flying back first class with leg room and free drinks, landing at Metro Airport in style, then taking his parents out to dinner downtown. Then they'd see. Then they'd believe.

His mind strayed toward Lupe Sevá – someone else he wanted to believe in him. Lupe, Lupe, Lupe. Would he ever have a chance with her? Would he ever even see her again? Despair deepened the chill he felt.

He thought suddenly about Kim Lefertowski, wondered what she was doing these days, wondered why he was even wondering about her since he didn't know her all that well, aside from the fact that she'd relieved him of his virginity the night of their junior prom. He was a skinny geek, she was a fat goth/steampunk girl. It seemed like a mismatch on the epic level of Romeo and Juliet, but not really, because they were both outsiders. Defectives. They were both smart, too.

They snuck out of the banquet hall and into her father's Cadillac to drink the bottle of the Jagermeister she had stashed there. An inexperienced drinker, Ira downed the powerful elixir in gulps, as if it were ice water on a hot day. He oozed confidence and alcoholic fumes, shedding his anxiety over why Kim should have invited him to the prom as quickly as he helped Kim shed the black, scarlet-ribbon laced goth corset that contained her considerable girth. As he rolled around with her in the back seat of her father's car, amazed and thrilled at her proportions, he felt as if he were both having the experience and watching himself have the experience,

Hovering at a distance.

When it was over, he thought they must be in love. They spent the last of the school year and the early part of the summer together in a tender, tentative daze, having as much sex as they could sneak away and have, until Kim went away to fat camp.

When she returned in the fall she'd lost a great deal of weight, along with any interest in Ira O'Riley. Slender and streamlined, stylish and snotty, her hair having changed to a natural shiny brown and her fingernails polished a creamy pink instead of hard black, she breezed past Ira in the hallway with an indulgent smile, as if he was someone she pretended to remember out of sheer politeness. She was no longer a defective. Within two weeks, Slim Kim was dating a jock.

He turned in the borrowed BMW so that he was still in a fetal position but lying on his other side. Now he was facing the seat. Maybe it would block out memories. The past sucked. The present wasn't so great, either. He knew he had to get some sleep tonight so that he could face whatever tomorrow brought him. He would have to be resilient and resourceful.

The future, his future, would be much, much better. As always when he turned his thoughts toward "Her Majesty's Gangsta," he grew happy. It thrilled him to work on the screenplay, even if – as he was at this moment -- only making notes about it in his head. Actually typing on it was even therapeutic, though. The longer the document in his laptop grew, the more he was able to block out the frustrations of his life.

He realized that he should do a cloud backup of the screenplay but got distracted when an idea struck him. He'd have Muldoon rappel down Big Ben! Yes! Using that iconic structure in such a startling new way would be brilliant! He'd just have to work out why Muldoon would have to do such a thing. And why he would happen to have a really long rope with him.

Ira was pleased to have a problem to work on that did not have to do with being homeless and jobless.

He began composing his acceptance speech for the Best Original Screenplay award he was going to win for "His Majesty's Gangsta," reasoning that it was never too soon to start. He assembled some sentiments that sounded suitably humble yet subtly victorious but then got pleasantly distracted imagining the expression on Sid's face when Ira's name was announced as the winner and Sid's former office drone strode to the stage to accept his Oscar. Ira backed up his fantasy a few steps in order to insert Lupe into the seat next to him. When Ira's name was announced they both jumped to their feet and Lupe gave him a soulful kiss.

Still shivering but also smiling, Ira finally fell asleep.

Chapter Thirty:
Lumpen Solitarians Live Alone

It couldn't be real. Just couldn't be. She wanted so badly to see a house that when she finally saw one, she was afraid it was just a manifestation of her longing -- especially since it was such an incongruously refined building in this wild setting. The house -- what little she could see of it -- was backed up against the base of a hard mountain and secured by a high, brick-hued stucco wall broken only by a wide, lavishly ornate iron gate that bore the inscription: "Hyacinth House." Towering eucalyptus trees ringed the perimeter of the property, which gave way to a wild, unkempt landscape of lavender and goldenbush and tall plants that looked like telegraph poles decked out with sprays of yellow flowers. Only the top portion of the building was visible beyond the wall. It was Spanish hacienda in style, the same sun-baked brick color as the wall, rising to a weather-greened copper-tiled roof that shimmered in the midday sun. Two snarling stone lions kept guard on either side of the gate which was, she discovered, locked.

Luanne stood still for a moment, puzzled. Who the hell did they think was going to break in here? There were no neighbors. None of the human variety, anyway. She saw no doorbell. No intercom box. No address. Was she missing something, because she was so hungry that she could not order her mind rationally? These people must get deliveries. Everybody got deliveries. How did they know when the UPS truck brought them the tchotchkes they got from eBay? The gate and wall were the same forbidding height, offering no toeholds that would enable her to climb over. Everybody had a doorbell. Everybody but the freaks who lived here. She was furious with them. How dare they live this way, when she needed help?

"Hey!" she shouted weakly. "Hey! Anybody there! I need help! There's been an accident." She sank to the ground, weeping hiccupy-sounding sobs. "A helicopter crash," she muttered miserably.

Was there even anyone home? She wondered if the place was abandoned. Peering through the densely coiled iron curves of the gate, she saw no movement in the courtyard within. No cars were visible. The front door, if there was one, was out of her visual range.

Luanne had been walking since daybreak, scrambling over rugged slopes and scuffling through dry ravines with little sense of the directions she was taking. Before she left Cody, she'd collected bits of debris from the crash site and put them in a canvas sack she found. It must have belonged to the helicopter pilot. The sack had held only a typed manuscript entitled "Traffic School" which she'd tossed to the ground to make room for her breadcrumbs, as she thought of the pieces of junk that she'd dropped behind her as she walked, to help her find her way back to Cody. When she left him he was alive but unconscious, warm to the touch -- that was a good sign, wasn't it? She'd taken a quick, horrified look at the wound that extended from the inner edge of his ribcage to his right side. It looked like the bleeding had stopped, but the darkly swollen purplish mass that was his ribcage hinted at things that could be crushed in there. It was hard to tell just how bad the gash was because she didn't want to reawaken the bleeding by cleaning the site. This was convenient, because it grossed her out to look at it, much less touch it. Was she supposed to be Florence Nightingale all of a sudden, just because there was an injured person around? Not to mention that dead one, as well. Her fingers located a big knot on the back of Cody's head, and when she pried one of his eyelids open with her fingertip, his pupil looked enormous -- a big black blob engulfing the iris. She was pretty sure that was a bad thing. What if he'd fractured his skull? What if he had internal injuries -- bones broken, important organs leaking blood into his body cavities? Injuries that she couldn't even see? Poor Cody Torrance. He was just about the most famous man in the world, yet he was lying all alone at the bottom of a canyon, possibly dying. If he came to, he'd find himself all alone. He'd think she'd abandoned him.

Luanne would never do that, even if he hadn't been a celebrity. She'd gotten lucky in the crash and he hadn't, but it could just as easily have been her lying there, depending on

166

someone else to get help for her. Besides, in the few minutes of vomit-free conversation she'd had with him, he'd seemed like a pretty nice guy. Not that he would ever think of her in that way. They might as well be from different species.

Luanne wished she'd been able to move the dead pilot further away from Cody. He was going to start to stink soon, wasn't he? That wouldn't exactly make Cody feel better. How long before a body started to putrefy? She'd grabbed the guy's ankles and tried to pull him toward a grove of sycamore trees, but he was too heavy -- a fact made visible when his shirt, hiked up toward his arms by the dragging -- pulled up far enough to reveal a white whale of a belly. The shrub-covered ground did not make for a smooth track, either. After a few feet she simply gave up, telling herself that she needed to save her strength for going for help for Cody. It was true, too.

And now, many hours later, having found a road and even a house, she was apparently no closer to making contact with a live human being than she'd been at daybreak.

"HEY!" she screamed in frustrated hysteria. "Goddamn it! Is there somebody IN THERE? ANYBODY?" She ran out of steam, paused, listened. Her throat felt raw, but she pitched her voice even louder and higher. "Goddamn it! Have some compassion! I KNOW somebody's in there! There's GOTTA BE! Listen to me, YOU FUCKER! I've been in a helicopter crash and there's a guy who's badly injured and WE NEED HELP!" Sobs shook her, although she tried to keep up her tirade. "I...can't...do...this anymore," she cried. "I'm not... I'm not that girl. I need some freakin' help and I NEED IT NOW, before he dies!" Luanne, in a wrinkled heap at the base of the lavish stone gate, stamped her feet on the ground like a child and raged. "And I'm really, really hungry and I have to pee and THIS TIME I WANT TO DO IT WITH SOME GODDAMN TOILET PAPER!"

Exhausted, defeated, and just plain pissed off, she cried stormily for the second time in 24 hours. That was unusual for her, but she didn't judge herself for it. These were unusual circumstances. She sobbed loudly, making no effort to restrain herself. Why bother? If a woman cries in the wilderness and no one hears it, does it count? Besides, it felt good to get it all out.

Soon she'd have to pick herself up, pull some new energy out of her ass and hike some more, hoping to encounter a road and a Good Samaritan motorist before she died of hunger. Or thirst. Thirst would kill her first, she dimly remembered.

She didn't have a clue about which direction she should take. What time was it? How long before it got dark? Oh, no-- what if nocturnal animals, emboldened by nighttime, went after the helpless Cody? She couldn't bear to think about it. Maybe she should retrace her steps and stand guard over him until tomorrow. If she did that, he might die because of the delay. Maybe that would be a better way than being torn apart by...whatever. At least he wouldn't be alone. Still, she couldn't decide.

"I don't get many visitors."

"Jesus!"

Luanne shot to her feet, her heart seizing in a brief convulsion of fear. Even once she had a chance to gape at the ordinary-looking man behind the iron gate, her pulse continued to pound alarmingly fast for a few minutes, her heart slow to get the "stand down" message.

The man staring at her with veiled blue-gray eyes was maybe 65, although from his dry, sun-baked skin he evidently spent a lot of time in the sun, so he could have been younger. His head was shiny bald and tanned on top, with wispy brown fringes of hair hanging down untidily on either side. Too long for a guy his age, thought Luanne, but at least it wasn't in a ponytail. Old guys who tried to compensate for going bald by wearing what hair they did have in a long ponytail just looked absurd, in her opinion. He was medium tall, skinny and sinewy except for a prominent belly that bulged beneath his black t-shirt, which bore the name of a band too faded to read. His jeans were low-slung and flared at the cuffs in a retro style.

What was a guy like this doing in a house like this? Did he work here, as a caretaker, maybe? Or did he own it? He *did* look like the kind of guy who'd live far away from other people.

"Yes," he said. "I live here. Alone. I'm a Lumpen Solitarian."

"Jesus," she said again, thinking: *great, a wacko.*

He gazed at her, unruffled. "Are you having a religious experience?"

"I...no. I'm just a little rattled right now."

"Was there really a helicopter crash?"

She stared at him in disbelief. "Why would I make up a thing like that?"

He didn't answer for a long moment, chosing instead to look around, beyond her. What was he expecting to see? Why so suspicious?

"Where is this man?" he said finally. "The one who's hurt."

So he had been listening to her, the son of a bitch. Making her wait. "Out there," she said, irritably waving her arm toward the direction from which she'd come. "I can find him again. I left markers as I walked. He needs to get to a hospital fast. I'm not a medic, but he seems pretty badly injured to me."

His eyes unfocused, on purpose, she thought. She'd never met anyone as unhurried as this man. Her acute sense of urgency and alarm, which must be rolling off her in waves of agitated energy, was having no effect on him at all. She made a deliberate effort to control her confusion and anger, restraining her impulse to grab him and shake him into action. Whatever was going to happen was going to have to be on his terms, apparently.

After a few minutes, he sighed and snapped back into real time. "Pacific Coast Highway isn't moving -- maybe as far north as Zuma Beach, and certainly back past Santa Monica and Venice. He'll have to be taken by an inland route, by car, if the rot hasn't spread that far west yet. My housekeeper will come in three days, with a car, if she can get here. You can take him to a hospital then, if he's still alive."

She was dumbfounded. "You...don't have a car?"

He blinked. "Don't need one. I don't go out much. The few times I do, I borrow my housekeeper's car."

"Can't you call her and tell her to come sooner?"

"I don't have a phone."

"So you use...*what* to communicate with the outside world? Homing pigeons? Smoke signals?"

"Email. But not with her. She doesn't have a computer. She simply comes on Thursdays."

Well, that was something, she admitted. At least he owned a computer. He wasn't a complete freak. Still, it wasn't an ideal method for summoning emergency help. "Do you have any neighbors who own a phone?"

He exhaled serenely before he answered. "No one lives near here. That's why I live here. Lumpen Solitarians live alone. Apart from others."

Was it her huge hunger that was making this conversation sound so bizarre? She tried hard to suss out what he was saying but it didn't track. "Are you some kind of...religious order?" *Cult,* she was really thinking.

"No. We are a sort of network of people who live all over the world. We share the principles of Solitarianism with each other through websites and emails. Never instant messaging -- that would be intrusive. We use usernames only - no real names. We like to be alone, that's all. Some have always liked it that way. Some came to Solitarianism because the world was too much with them. They got tired of the crush of the multitudes. Colliding values. The bruising encounters with the giant family."

Bruising encounters? With his fellow human beings? He *was* a freak. Her tired mind started briefly down a peripheral, useless path, wondering how he managed to make a living, take care of practical needs in this splendid palace that was set down amid a barren canyon before she righted herself and focused on more pragmatic thinking.

"He's rich," she said. "The injured guy. Really rich. Money is no object. We can get a helicopter in here to pick him up. He can afford it."

The stranger smiled a close-mouthed smile.

"That didn't work out so well the first time, did it? This is a narrow, treacherous canyon. Unpredictable winds cut through these passes. If we can get him up to higher ground, then a helicopter would be feasible. But he'll have to be feeling strong enough for us to get him up there." He looked at her placidly, his blue-gray eyes fixed on her face as if he'd been looking at her for a thousand years. "If he's meant to live, he will live. You are doing your part. I will do mine, whatever it turns out to be. He will do his, whether it is to survive or to go to the next place. It is beyond our control. You must let it play out. You cannot

170

interfere with someone else's path, no matter where it happens to lead."

She was too tired to argue. Plus, her shoulder ached and her ribs throbbed. The day after a crash, she was realizing, was when the real soreness asserted itself. She swayed slightly, light-headed and strangely nauseated from hunger. "Whatever."

He swung the gate open for her. "You'd better have something to eat first."

She felt just a little bit guilty about not returning to Cody right away, but found that she was too famished to sustain the feeling.

CHAPTER THIRTY-ONE:
DOIN' THE NASTY

Governor Jorge Olmstead was surprised at how nervous he felt. In spite of all the public speaking he'd done during the campaign -- and those damned debates -- he found that his mouth was as dry as sand. The hand that clutched the telephone, however, was damp and sticky. It was trembling a little, too. As he waited his turn, he made sure for the fourth or fifth time that the rubber band holding the tissue over the phone's mouthpiece section was secure. It would be terrible if the napkin fell off in mid-conversation and he was outed. It was a disposable cell phone, so there shouldn't be any problem there. But what if Lessing had some secret, high-tech way to trace the call? It would be just like the bastard. Still, the main danger came from his fairly well known voice.

He waited, listening to Cap Lessing's show while on hold. If only Lessing were limited to L.A. - then Olmstead wouldn't have to listen to him, or hear *about* him. But, no, thanks to the marvels of syndication, Lessing's irritating voice boomed out from radios all over Sacramento, as well as central California.

What would this call accomplish? Nothing, probably. No. That wasn't right. It would make him feel better. That was something. He had a momentary panic attack: what if he was interrupted? He'd buzzed his assistant a moment ago and told her he was not to be interrupted, but what if something urgent came up and she felt she had to override that directive? He could just hang up. This was a terrible idea. He should hang up right now. No. Terrible idea or not, he was going to do it. He couldn't help himself.

"George from Sacramento, you're on the Cap Lessing Show," he heard, as if in a dream. Panic gripped him, made him shake. Lessing would know. He would know it was Olmstead using an alias and he would ridicule him and Olmstead would have brought the public humiliation on himself!

He tried to speak and choked a little. It sounded, to his ears (ears burning uncomfortably with embarrassment), like a death rattle.

"What's that you say, George? Are you too scared to talk? I'm not surprised. My screener tells me you're another of Olmstead's timid defenders. I would really, really, really like for someone to give me one reason -- just one -- why Olmstead shouldn't resign today. No. Wait. Not resign. He should fall on his sword. That would be more honorable."

"Olmstead's doing the best he can," sputtered Olmstead, feeling ridiculous and wondering if he was sufficiently disguising his voice.

"Ha!" barked Lessing unattractively. "The emperor has no clothes, George. I knew it long before the election, but he conned a lot of people into thinking he was fit for the position. Now, most people in this state realize that he's buck naked. Tell me, Holden, why we shouldn't launch a recall election. And I mean immediately."

"This problem was in the making long before Olmstead got into office."

"You're right. That's why he should have seen it coming. We're in the big leagues here, Holden. This is a big, important state with a big population and big problems to go with it. We needed a big man -- or woman -- to step up and show some leadership. We're not talking about some township commissioner post in Yuma, Arizona. Olmstead is an ordinary little man -- a mediocrity with no vision and no real leadership skills -- who woke up one day and decided that he could handle an extraordinary job. A lot of rich people are like that. Growing up privileged gives them ambition beyond their actual talents, but they're too arrogant to see the gap. Remember W? Well now, in our very own state, we have J."

"This traffic problem would have happened no matter who was in office!" Olmstead's voice cracked a little, but he tried to remain resolute.

"Would it?" Lessing thundered. "Would it really?" He knew how to use his voice as if it was a weapon. "Everyone with eyes could see what was happening. How bad things were getting. There was time for Jorge the Joke-ay to take some preemptive action. In English or in Spanish, I don't care which. Instead, Jorge the Joke-ay sat on his multicultural hands. Or maybe, as a caller who claimed to know suggested earlier, the good governor was too busy with erotic extracurricular activities to care about something as mundane as traffic. Did you hear that call last hour, Holden?"

Olmstead froze. What call? "No. No, I missed it."

"Well, the governor is supposedly having an affair with a strip club hostess named...what was it? Busty? Chesty? No. My producer is telling me it was Misty. That was it. Could be just a rumor, but a night clerk at a hotel on Sunset that he prefers not to name because he wants to keep his job says the governor and this stripper are regular customers there. He says the governor wears glasses and a fake mustache, but he can tell it's him."

Olmstead's throat seized. They knew! They knew about Misty! My God! He'd been sure that the mustache looked realistic. What would Sheila do? If this really hit the media (what if there were pictures?) and turned into a big story, what would his wife do?

She'd *kill him*!

"...just a rumor, but if it isn't, it might explain why Olmstead can't address important state problems. He's too busy getting Lewinskeed by a hooker. Sorry, I mean a stripper. Cause there's such a big difference."

Olmstead made the mistake of trying to speak. "A...fake mustache? That sounds...ridiculous." He attempted a laugh, but just sounded as if he were being strangled.

"It's too bad you missed hearing the call. The night clerk was pretty convincing. Says he snapped some photos last time the gov and his lady love were at the hotel. Apparently, there's one special room that the staff knows about. A room with a view, so to speak. The view is from the adjoining room, actually, through a peep hole. The clerk says he got photos through the peep hole of Whore-Hey the Joke-ay and this woman going at it hot and heavy. Doing the nasty. Says he's got some of the celeb gossip sites involved in a bidding war. So what do you say, George? Still want to stick up for your guy? Even though he's fiddling -- or letting some woman play with his fiddle -- while California burns?"

"I'm surprised you'd sink so low as to participate in rumor-mongering, Cap," Olmstead said, suddenly calm. A sense of fatalism moved through him like a strong laxative, purging him of something unpleasant. He realized that, on some level, he'd *wanted* Sheila to find out. "Why don't you stick to the real issues and not wallow in character assassinations?"

"Your voice sounds kind of familiar, George. Have you called before?"

Olmstead plunged on, oblivious to the danger. "The traffic mess is the inevitable result of overpopulation. No one's saying it, but it's true. Are you going to blame Olmstead for that? For too many people moving here? Living here? It's the Promised Land of sunshine and opportunities. Are you going to limit the number of children people can have, like they do in China? Because controlling the size of the population is the only thing that could have prevented the problem. And L.A. is not the only city feeling the pain. Unless something is done on a national level, traffic paralysis is going to strike city after city, all over the United States. It just happened here first. We always start the trends, good or bad."

"I've got it now. You know who you sound just like, George? It's uncanny. You sound just like-"

"That's all I had to say, Cap. There are just too many damn people in this state!" Olmstead snapped shut the disposable cell phone quickly, as if disconnecting the call would end Lessing's sentence. A radio rested in a red oak armoire behind his desk. He'd turned the volume down, as instructed by the screener, to avoid feedback when he spoke with Lessing. He briefly considered turning it back up, to hear Lessing finish his thought. To know or not to know -- which would be worse? How humiliating would it be if Lessing announced that the governor had called his program and defended himself using a phony name! He should have had the balls to call and challenge Lessing directly, as himself.

Wait a minute. He calmed himself. Lessing can't prove anything. He may think he recognized my voice, but he can't possibly be sure. Anxiety rippled through him again. When had Lessing ever felt the need to be sure of his facts before speaking out?

175

L.A. was full of actors. Impressionists. Plenty of people could do credible imitations of him. That would be his defense - that whoever had just called the Cap Lessing show had impersonated him. If this whole thing blew wide open, he could hire an actor to confess that he'd done it. Just like in that movie, "Dave." Brilliant.

His secretary buzzed him, in spite of his "no interruptions" order, startling him into shooting several inches up out of his chair.

"Sorry to interrupt you, Governor, but your wife's on the line. She said it's urgent." There was a pause, then an unwilling addendum: "Sir, she sounds pretty upset."

CHAPTER THIRTY-TWO:
A LATE NIGHT SNACK OF CORPSE

Just about the most famous man in the world was being trundled back to Hyacinth House in a large, rusty wheelbarrow that smelled like manure. Blake -- for that was their strange savior's name, Blake -- had thoughtfully lined the barrow with some old burlap sacks, to soften the hard metal for his unconscious passenger, but that elegant bedding didn't diminish the earthy fragrance. Cody was still unconscious, and mercifully unaware of the pitiful picture he made.

Cody was a tall, leggy man -- not a good fit for a wheelbarrow. His torso was sort of folded into it, with his legs dangling over the side and his feet brushing against the ground, making an erratic trail as they moved.

Luanne wasn't about to complain. Blake didn't own any vehicle that used fossil fuels. Of course not. Mr. my-house-is-powered-by-the-sun was not about to go roaring over this rough terrain in an ATV just for fun. It was almost un-American that he didn't own anything that used gas and made a loud noise. Would an ATV help them get Cody to someplace where he could get medical treatment faster? Maybe they could have rigged up some sort of wheeled stretcher to attach to the back of the ATV, strapped him onto it and gotten him the hell out of this hellhole. Pardon her. This beautifully wild, unspoiled canyon.

At least Nature Boy was the one doing all the work. Blake gripped the handles of the barrow with his glove-covered hands and strode steadily, if not quickly. Not as fast as he'd started out, anyway; Cody had to be pretty heavy. Quite a load, to move in this cumbersome way. In spite of his exertions, Blake was still able to keep up a running lecture on the landscape they crossed.

Luanne had gotten a small second wind from the sandwich Blake had made for her, but not enough to allow her to focus very clearly on what he was saying, even if she wanted to take it all in. And she didn't want to.

There was a lot about the "fragility of the ecosystem" -- that would be why he didn't go around in anything motorized, she guessed. He kept pointing out varieties of plants as they passed them: Palmers goldenbush, California buckwheat, cliff aster, milkweed -- and telling her when they bloomed and why they grew where they grew. She tried to pay attention, just to be polite. She was just too tired, having moved into a zone of realization that she would survive, that she was no longer the only one responsible for Cody's survival.

Oh, God. Wouldn't Blake ever run out of breath and shut the fuck up?

"This is chaparral country," he said. "More shrubs and bushes than trees."

"Wouldn't you like me to take a turn now?" she offered half-heartedly, hoping to distract him from his flora talk.

"No."

She was glad. That Cody-filled wheelbarrow looked heavy.

"See that growth on those slopes? That's Manzanita."

Manzanita. Sounded like a really delicious dessert. She imagined eating some Manzanita. Would it be creamy? Or chocolatey, with a cake-like texture, maybe in layers with nuts and caramel in between? Or would it would be fruit-flavored, sticky sweet and colorful and crunchy? Hmmmmm. Manzanita. Would it be on a South or Central American menu? Italian? Spanish? Manzanita. Her mouth watered just thinking about it.

"That's Cody Torrance, isn't it?"

So he did recognize him. She wasn't sure, until this moment.

"Yes."

"I've seen some of his movies."

Yeah. Him and everybody else in the world. Since Blake was going to continue to do all the heavy lifting, she realized that the least she could do was to entertain him. She told him the parts of the story that Cody had told her, while they waited for rescue in the bathroom, about his naked run-in with the paparazzi, getting mobbed by fans, fleeing from both the mob and the photographer. She was able to add more of the details after she crossed paths with Cody, and described in rather thrilling terms how they climbed the fire escape to the roof of the building, got into the helicopter to be spirited away to Malibu, and crashed after the pilot had some sort of medical catastrophe.

She couldn't tell him much more about the pilot, except that he was dead.

Blake listened in silence, offering little comment. He grunted occasionally, but Luanne couldn't tell whether that was because she'd said something particularly interesting or whether he had to put in extra effort to get the wheelbarrow over a bumpy patch of ground.

When they reached Hyacinth House, exhaustion made Luanne feel as if she were home. She let Blake tend to Cody, although she hovered in the background to make sure that he did a good job. He did. Armed with an impressive first aid kit, Blake cleaned and bandaged Cody's wounds, frowning at the bloody gash in his side. Luanne was even more concerned about the possibility of a skull fracture, or whatever terrible thing could be happening under the monstrous, pulpy mass of purple bruises that constituted the left side of his head. She also noticed that his left leg looked...weird. At a wrong angle. How had she missed that before? Was it broken? If it was and it wasn't set quickly, would he have a limp for life? It might work for Buck Buchanan, she supposed, since the character did live a fairly hazardous life. However, she was pretty sure that Cody Torrance, Real Person, would not appreciate a permanent limp. Of course, that would only be a concern if he actually lived.

Blake tried to give Cody a little water, but it just dribbled down the side of his chin and down his neck.

Cody's eyes fluttered open.

"Hey," Luanne said. "Do you remember what happened?"

He stared up at her in confusion.

"Do you know your name?"

"Floyd," he murmured.

She frowned, turning to Blake. "He is really out of it. Doesn't even know his own name. That worries me."

"There's not much more you can do right now," said Blake. He turned out the light and left the room, with Luanne following. "How about some dinner?"

"Lizard," Cody whispered, so softly they didn't hear him.

They ate at an enormous dark wooden slab of a table. She wondered: why such a big table when he lived all alone? She also wondered: where did all this fresh produce come from? It's not like this guy gets to the grocery store often.

"A lot of this I grow myself," he said.

Damn! Were these Solitarians psychic? Was that from spending so much time by themselves? Or was the reverse true? Did they become Solitarians because they were psychic, and they couldn't stand the constant mental chatter of other people in their heads all the time? And wasn't there an old Twilight Zone episode about that? And why was her mind spinning out of control, in nonsensical circles?

She felt so peculiar.

The good news was that she and Cody were safe, probably -- unless Blake turned out to be a psycho. She was eating real food and would get to sleep in a real bed, far from the predators that stalked the canyon at night. She tried not to think about the dead helicopter pilot, lying alone in the cold white moonlight. She and Blake had tried to cover the man's body with a few pieces of wreckage, but after hearing about the mountain lions and bobcats and coyotes that inhabited the area, she felt that the improvised shelter would not keep it from being turned into a late-night snack of corpse. She also felt pretty happy that she and Cody had not been accosted by those animals the previous night, when they were vulnerable.

The only things she'd taken from the crash site were her purse and that damned camera that Cody had been so intent on keeping with him. She felt protective toward him. In spite of their obvious differences (he: international movie star and she: ordinary person) they'd been through hell together. She wondered what would happen once this episode was all over. Would she ever see him again?

Her cell phone was charging while they ate, with the charger she'd gotten from her purse. Although she knew she wouldn't get a signal here, she would be able to see the last number Cody had called, maybe look it up online, find a website and email whoever it was. That would have to yield faster results than waiting for Blake's housekeeper to arrive, if she was even able to make it through the traffic. Blake's serene, let-happen-what-will-happen philosophy was getting on her last nerve.

Dinner, though, was surprisingly cordial. She sipped the very nice pinot noir that Blake kept refilling her glass with, content to listen while he talked and talked. For someone who chose to live alone, he sure liked the sound of his own voice. Did he even realize how lonely he was, she wondered? It was a little sad. And why so much wine? Was he...trying to loosen her up? She wasn't sure how she felt about that. What a strange man he was. Not young. Not good-looking. Yet, there was something terribly charismatic about him.

"What do you do?" she blurted out suddenly. "I mean...how do you afford to live here? If it's not too personal a question."

Of course it was too personal a question, but it didn't seem to bother him.

"I'm a poet."

"Really!" What she was really thinking was: *Damn. Poetry must pay a lot better than I thought.*

Things turned kind of ugly when she tried to put her email plan into action. It turned out that Cody had dialed something called Midwood Artists Agency, in Beverly Hills. Accessing their website using Blake's satellite internet service proved easy. Finding an email link on the site for a Sid Kirschenbaum -- presumably Cody's agent, the Sid she'd spoken to on her cell phone -- also easy.

Providing the details to Mr. Kirschenbaum that would get Luanne and Cody the hell out of this canyon, not so easy. After typing in the highlights: that there'd been a helicopter crash, that the pilot Sid had sent was dead but Cody Torrance was alive and injured and would need medical care quickly, Luanne turned to Blake for help with their location.

"I have to think about how to do this," he said thoughtfully.

"I realize that you probably don't have a street address, since you don't have a street, but you have to have some way to describe where you live. To...people who have to come here. What's the name of this canyon? It has to have a name, doesn't it? Or how about the nearest freeway? Or even longitude and latitude? Something that will help them find us."

"That's not the problem."

"What is the problem?"

"I don't want to be invaded."

She nodded in agreement. "Sure, sure. I totally understand that. We'll be out of your way as quickly as we can. I promise."

"It won't be that simple. He's famous."

"That's not his fault."

"The media will come."

"They probably can't get here. I'm not even sure search and rescue people can get here, and they're used to out of the way places."

"They'll find a way. All of them."

She slumped in her chair, stymied, then alarmed. "So what are you saying? Are we prisoners here?"

"You're welcome to leave at any time. Cody, too."

"And I'm supposed to, what? Carry Cody out on my back? Or maybe you'll lend me that smelly wheelbarrow?"

"I just need to think about how to do this so that I will be left alone."

She moved beyond frustration into the edges of fear. What if this Blake character grew more than lettuce and zucchini out back? An illegal crop of marijuana would explain both his lavish estate and his love of privacy. Persisting in this might just put her and Cody in danger.

"Maybe tomorrow or the next day Cody will be strong enough so that we can move him away...from my house. Out of sight. Then we can let his people know, and they can come and get him. Or maybe my housekeeper can make it through, and he can be taken out in a car."

She couldn't help herself. She had to try. "But he could be--" she groped about for a strong word -- "Hemorrhaging internally."

"There's nothing anyone can do tonight, anyway," he said calmly. "It's dark. No rescuers can come. And your Mr. Kirschenbaum probably won't pick up that email until the morning. I will think about this overnight."

"Look," she said, trying to be sound reasonable but firm. A little playful, even, so if he was growing criminal crops, he wouldn't realize that she suspected as much. How would Sandra Bullock play this scene? There would be a subtle flirtatiousness overlayering the subtext of urgency. The wine wasn't exactly helping her hit the right tone, but she felt that she was coming close. "I totally respect your privacy, I mean - hey, this Solitarian thing you've got going has some real advantages, I would imagine. No obnoxious neighbors. Nobody playing loud music when you're trying to sleep. I get it. You can think in peace. Commune with nature. I don't want to interfere with any of that. In fact, with Cody and me gone, you'll be back to zero distractions. Zip."

He wasn't buying it. Maybe if she actually looked like Sandra Bullock it would be working.

"Why don't I show you where you'll sleep?"

She followed him resentfully, feeling like Dorothy, having braved many terrors to reach this splendid Emerald City-like palace in the middle of nowhere. She was being taken care of yet still felt trapped, beholden to her host for her ride home.

CHAPTER THIRTY-THREE:
THINGS ALWAYS WORKED OUT FOR HIM

As he had during much of his life, Cody felt as if he were a chess piece, moved around on a big board by forces beyond his control. It wasn't necessarily a bad sensation because so far, those forces had done pretty well by him.

At present, he rested on someone else's bed, feeling as light as air, as if he were levitating. He was dimly aware that something bad had happened to him recently. There were parts of his body that hurt, but not too much. There was a deep black well of panic where his memory would be, so he simply avoided it. The something bad that had happened had to do with falling, falling, falling. He remembered stark fear but from a great remove, as if it were a distant train whistle which he heard but was unaffected by.

It was always better to live in the moment. In this moment he was safe and warm, being visited once again by a beautiful angel whom he somehow knew and liked. It gave him a comforting, easy feeling to think about her, although he couldn't remember why.

The angel was accompanied by a helper, a man who sounded somehow familiar and who hovered uneasily in the background, judging by where his voice came from. Was the male angel just learning? The female angel knew just how to lay her hand on Cody's forehead so as not to disturb his serenity. She did so now.

"Doesn't feel feverish," he heard.

She was very gentle in the way she open his jaws with her fingers and poured a little orange juice into his mouth, although the juice tasted funny and he tried to resist swallowing it. She lifted his head a few inches above the pillow with her hands and felt the back of it with her fingertips.

"Still got that big old knot on the back of his head. What if he fractured his skull?" The angel sighed.

"Are his pupils dilated?" It was the male angel's voice.

He felt his eyes being pried open, glimpsed her looking down at him with concern. He felt grateful. She cared about him. He had a sudden revelation that almost made him cry. Maybe she was his long-dead mother, come back to take care of him when he needed her most.

"I don't think so."

There was relief in her tone, and Cody relaxed. Soon, he thought, he'd be moved again on the great chess board. Despite the angel's presence, he didn't think he'd be moved to heaven. Not yet. He was utterly certain that he would, eventually, be fine. Just fine. Things always worked out for him.

Cody saw their shadow forms glide out of the room. He felt sleep coming over him like dusk on a summer night back in New Hampshire. It was a gentle, peaceful feeling that rose up from the floor and surrounded the bed like gossamer netting.

"Mother," he whispered happily. Then he surrendered himself once again to pleasant oblivion.

Chapter Thirty-Four:
So We Got That in Common

ESTABLISHING SHOT: GLITTERING EUROPEAN CASINO -
NIGHT
INT. CASINO - NIGHT
It's a glamorous setting filled with glamorous people. Men in
evening wear and women in jewel-colored gowns enjoy
themselves at the roulette wheel, poker tables, etc.

FAVOR ON MOSES MULDOON

Despite his tuxedo, he still manages to look like an unkempt
rogue. He takes a seat at a poker table, openly ogling the
BEAUTIFUL WOMAN standing next to him in spite of the fact
that she is clearly in the company of A SINISTER BLACK-
HAIRED MAN who wears an eye patch. The sinister man glares
at Muldoon. Unintimidated, Muldoon reacts blithely, then shifts
his attention to the DEALER as he places chips on the table in
front of him.

MULDOON
How much?

ANGLE ON OTHERS SEATED AT TABLE
The THREE MEN and a WOMAN register subtle disgust at
Muldoon's less-than-refined style.

DEALER
(haughtily)

Fifty, sir.

Muldoon slides some chips forward.

SHOT: STOWARING, MOVING CLOSE TO THE TABLE AND
WATCHING

DEALER
(CONT.)
Fifty thousand, sir.

*Muldoon reacts: are you joking? He quickly recovers and tries
to look nonchalant, surveying his paltry pile of chips.*

MULDOON
*Ah, I just remembered
something I have to do.*

*He scoops up his chips and, with a last lecherous glance at the
BEAUTIFUL WOMAN -- who looks lecherously back at him --
he leaves the table. Stowaring catches up to him as he strides
through the casino.*

STOWARING
*I thought I told you not to draw
attention to yourself.*

MULDOON
*I was blending in. Now where
are the nickel slots?*

*Stowaring stops him, keeping his voice low but not bothering to
conceal his irritation.*

STOWARING
*You imbecile. There are no
nickel slots here. This is the
high-roller area, as I believe I
told you. Now listen to me. That
man in the eye patch at the table
you were at? He's our target.*

Muldoon glances back at the table.

MULDOON
He's got good taste in women.

STOWARING
(exasperated)
In his country, he could have
you killed for the way you just
looked at his girlfriend.

MULDOON
Really? Same as in my
neighborhood in Detroit. So we
got that in common.

Stowaring angrily grips Muldoon's arm and gets in his face.

STOWARING
Will you stuff it and stop
treating this entire thing as if it
were a lark?

Muldoon peels Stowaring's hand off his arm and bends his wrist
backward. The two men are engaged in a quietly intense,
painful, low-key struggle and yet manage, miraculously, not to
draw any attention to themselves.

MULDOON
(through clenched teeth)
Listen, Sir Brokeback. I'm done
takin' orders from you.

Stowaring, stronger than he looks, is able to shift the balance of
power back toward himself. Muldoon is surprised and a little
discomfited by his adversary's move.

STOWARING
You clod. You think I'm
enjoying being your keeper? I'll
have you know--

Ira was startled by a sharp, insistent rapping sound. It took him a few moments to remove himself from the fabulous confines of the European casino and bring himself back to the present.

He was typing on his laptop, sitting in the back seat of a BMW he didn't own, with his back against the side wall and his long legs stretched out along the leather-covered seat. He realized with some surprise that it was fairly late in the morning, judging by the amount of sunlight bathing the street. This was when writing was best: when it swept him away so thoroughly that he lost track of time and place. But there was that damned rapping sound again...

The noise came from the hairy knuckles of a uniformed cop, being applied authoritatively to the window next to Ira's head. Both the cop and the worried-looking elderly woman standing next to him peered in at Ira as if he had a bomb strapped to his body and he was about to detonate it. Seeing Ira finally paying attention, the cop gave his knuckles a rest and stopped knocking on the window. He used his hand to make a gesture to Ira that was easily understood: come on out of there.

Ira saved the changes to his document, snapped his laptop shut, shoved it into his backpack and scrambled out of the car, feeling foolish.

"This lady says this is her car. She's got the registration."

Ira prided himself on having a fairly fertile imagination, but he could never have imagined being in this particular situation. "I was just..." He shrugged. Why lie? "I slept in it last night. I didn't do any harm. Just...slept in it. And this morning, I know I should have left right away, but I had a few ideas I had to get down. I'm a screenwriter," he offered. He was not surprised when that description failed to impress.

The cop actually yawned. "You write anything I might have seen?"

Ira realized the error of his gambit. "No," he admitted.

"So what you really are is a wannabe screenwriter," the cop said in a tone that clearly implied: I caught you in a lie.

The woman looked horrified. "You slept in my car?"

Ira directed his comments to the cop, who, though disdainful, seemed more rational. "I couldn't get home. Couldn't get to my car. You know how it is."

"So you broke into *my* car?" the woman demanded.

"It wasn't locked. Look for yourself. There's no damage. I just needed a place to sleep."

The cop stared at him skeptically. "You got any outstanding warrants on you?"

"No! I've never been in trouble. What do I look like?"

"You look like a rumpled mess," the cop said, then, turning to the woman; "That laptop he's holding -- is that yours?"

She shook her head. "I don't have any use for computers."

"Look inside the car and make sure that nothing is missing."

She stuck her head in the backseat, then opened the front passenger door and examined the front seat as well. She sniffed the interior of the car suspiciously.

Ira clutched his backpack as if afraid that it would be taken from him. Then the cop *did* take it from him. He opened it and rooted around in it with one hand, then handed it back to Ira.

The woman opened the glove compartment and peered into it, flipped the visor down, opened a few interior compartments. She finally straightened up and spoke to the cop in a grudging tone, ignoring Ira. "Everything looks as if it's still there."

The cop turned toward Ira. "Go on. Get outta here. And stay out of other people's cars."

"Aren't you going to arrest him?" The woman was clearly not happy about the way this was being resolved.

"Ma'am, we've got a few other things going on here at this time. You may have noticed. This is one of those 'all's well that ends well' situations. Your car is fine. Nothing is damaged, nothing stolen. I think he's learned his lesson and I'm sure he will not do anything like this again."

Ira nodded enthusiastically. "You got that right. I certainly won't."

The cop added: "And I hope that you've learned a lesson about locking your car doors."

The woman glared at both of them and pushed the button on her keyless lock device before walking away.

190

The cop watched her and shrugged. "She just came by to check on her car, see if she might be able to move it forward a little. She got scared when she saw a stranger in it."

Ira slid the straps of his backpack over his shoulders. "If I could have found a motel room, I'd have spent the night in a real bed. Trust me."

The cop patted the top of the BMW approvingly. "At least you got good taste."

Then, looking bored, he sauntered away, a lawman on foot amid a surreal landscape of unmoving vehicles.

Chapter Thirty-Five:
A Nice Little Garden of Potential Death

"Stop," Blake said. "Don't move."

What, was she about to step on one of his prized perennials? Luanne had to admit she was enjoying the tour this morning, after having checked on Cody and found him sleeping peacefully, but Blake was a bit of a control freak when it came to his flora and fauna.

Although she still thought Blake a weirdmobile, once she awakened in the morning and was led through his house, she had to concede that he did have exquisite taste. Flooded with daylight, his spacious rooms were cleanly beautiful; creamy-walled, with oversized modern furniture in neutral colors. The earthy, understated palette directed the eye to the vivid accent pieces, which she thought were Native American. There was a bronze sculpture of a flute player, a set of skin-topped drums, a grouping of arrowheads on a wall next to an amazing-looking woven blanket. A large, tile fronted fireplace opened onto both the living room and the kitchen. A den held built-in shelves lined with books, and she wished she could see a few of the titles, but Blake was a rather speedy tour guide. He seemed eager to move her to the lower level, and she could see why. This house in the middle of nowhere boasted what appeared to her to be a state-of-the-art media room. There was an enormous high def plasma TV, a Bose stereo system and lots of other things she couldn't identify. She caught a glimpse of a tidy, compact home office next to the media room. Black and white photos of what looked like Paris hugged the walls.

They emerged from the house into a garden that was lush with abundance. Backed up dramatically against the sheer side of a mountain, tightly bordered by either house or iron gate, the expansive plantings nonetheless seemed to get plenty of sun and were flourishing amid strange-looking structures she assumed comprised some sort of irrigation system. There were ascending terraces of citrus trees and flowers, ornamental grasses and bloom-covered bougainvillea whose thorny arms wove their way through wrought-iron trellises. She didn't see any marijuana plants.

Two hammocks were strung on wooden frames (two? she thought), and wrought iron chairs circled a glass-topped table. For a hermit, his place was ideal for entertaining.

He appeared to be proudest of his large, organic vegetable patch, explaining the vertical gardening techniques that allowed him to maximize production in the relatively small space. He'd been pointing to various rows, naming the varieties, when he'd issued his strange command.

"Don't move," he said again.

She froze in place.

He pointed to the ground, a few yards from her feet. Following the line of his outstretched finger, she gasped, but resisted the urge to jump out of her skin. A primitive fear shot through her; she instantly felt cold. There was a slippery sound from below, but she also heard her blood thundering loudly in her ears, her heartbeat rocketing in her chest. She was feeling so many loud noises.

The rattlesnake had to be four feet long. He was very close to her, moving slowly, deliberately, in her direction.

Her fear was thick and raw, an intimation of immortality. She hadn't even been this scared when the helicopter was going down. That had been too quick, too confusing. But the inexorable advance of this snake reminded her in her very bones that death was not only possible, it was inevitable. And could be imminent.

Her thunderous heartbeat was drowned out by a new, sinister noise: the shaking of rattles. The snake watched her as he writhed at one end. She found herself locked in his gaze. Don't look at him! He'll hypnotize you! Or was that just a myth?

"He has many rattles," Blake remarked. "That means he's old. A survivor. He's making that sound because he feels threatened by you. He's warning you off."

"Great. He feels threatened by me?" Her teeth were clenched so tightly she was surprised she could speak.

"Stay perfectly still."

"Can I just pee in my pants?"

"If he remains afraid of you, he'll strike. It'll be lightning fast. You won't be able to move out of the way."

"So I won't suffer long? Nice to know. Nice location you have here, by the way." She hated Blake at that moment.

"Just...stand there."

She did. Years passed. An airplane droned in the distance. She began breathing again, even found the panic subsiding enough for her to study the snake, as it studied her back. It was almost beautiful: sand-colored, with dramatic brown markings that began as rough circles at his head and turned into stripes at his tail. The rattles were smooth and precise, shiny segments that grew smaller toward the tail. The snake flicked its tongue, which scared her more than the rattling. It was long and thin, a stiff ribbon of menace.

"He's smelling you."

When this little encounter was over -- if she survived -- she was going to kill Blake with her bare hands for his ill-timed little nature lesson.

The snake, without warning, suddenly collected himself into a muscular bunch and launched himself away from her. With startling speed, he moved in a wavy motion toward a cactus garden and presumably, hopefully, toward escape through the grill of the iron fence beyond it.

The day returned to normal. The sunlight lost its harsh edge. The reassuringly familiar sound of an airplane grew louder, reminding her that civilization -- sans snakes -- was not all that far away.

"Goddamn it!" She felt quite explosive. "You could have warned me!" She was furious with him, even if she couldn't quite figure out why. "Nice little garden of potential death you've got here."

He smiled, making her even angrier.

"It's nature. He's part of the west. Remember, even the garden of Eden had a snake in it."

She was in no mood for poetic reflection. "Do you get little visitors like that often? I guess that explains why you don't have any pets."

"I had a cat once. La Chaise. Coyotes got her, while she was out hunting one night. I heard the shrieks and ran outside, but it was too late. All I found the next day, when it was light, were a few tufts of her fur stuck on a bricklebush." He looked genuinely sad, nature or no.

"Jeez. That's--"

Suddenly, the garden exploded with action. Large, heavily muscled men rappelled on ropes down the face of the mountain and landed in the strawberry patch, to the deafening thump-thump-thumping soundtrack provided by the bizarre-looking aircraft that slid into view overhead. What the hell? Luanne had never seen anything like it. It looked for all the world like a modified Hummer sprouting helicopter propellers from its roof. With a growing sense of unreality, Luanne watched, open-mouthed, as sturdy tires emerged from the underside of its boxy body and flipped from horizontal to vertical positions. The helicopter noisily descended into the far reaches of the garden before touching down on a terraced vegetable bed almost too narrow to support it. Its blades rose up and closed in a tight formation. Luanne was sure that it would topple from its inadequate landing pad, but its wheels spun into motion, allowing it to drive downward through Blake's meticulously cultivated levels of crops, crushing most of the squash, zucchini and hot pepper plants she'd admired earlier before rolling onto the flat, paved terrace, where it scattered and toppled furniture. The beveled glass top of the table was one noisy casualty. An enormous glossy ceramic pot holding a dwarf orange tree was another; the trunk of the small tree snapped as if it were a brown spine. The flying-rolling thing finally came to a stop near Luanne and Blake, who stood motionless, paralyzed by disbelief.

Blake's carefully maintained serenity was gone, replaced by a thunderstruck scowl and cheeks flushed red with rage. He crouched, tense and coiled as if ready to flee, but instead stood dazed amid his destroyed garden, stunned by its leafy carnage and fruity chaos. The now-lifeless corn stalks appeared to bring him special pain. They lay strewn over the ground, beheaded by the whirring blades of the invaders' aircraft. Plump purple cylinders that moments ago had been viable eggplants were flattened, as were ruffled green lettuce leaves and bush beans. The strong metal cylindrical cages that held the fragrant, bountiful tomato plants upright and contained were reduced to impotency, mere wires twisted and tangled up with the leafy arms they were supposed to protect, the immature tomatoes mashed into pulpy green pancakes, the pink ones that were closer to ripeness leaking seeds and moist flesh.

The men who'd descended from the cliff quickly detached themselves from their ropes and fanned out through the garden. Their black t-shirts were so snug they looked as if they were painted onto their massive biceps and marbled chests. Were they military? They wore camo pants and webbed belts, but they had no weapons. None that she could see anyway, thought Luanne. One of the men stared back at her, not meeting her eyes, his expression neutral but alert. He, like the others, held to a taut pose: a slight forward incline, arms raised in a ready position. Ready for what?

The pilot cut the engine abruptly. A door opened downward and rested on the ground, ramp-like, allowing a colorful assortment of people to leap energetically out. A number of them wore elaborate headsets with mouthpieces. The helicopter, or whatever it was, held more passengers than Luanne had thought possible.

A man and woman in scrubs rolled a compacted gurney off the aircraft, then speedily adjusted its height upward and raced off towards the house. They were followed by others, similarly dressed. One gripped a pole on wheels that had several fluid-filled IV bags attached to it. Others carried duffel bags and official-looking coolers. Medical supplies?

A tall blonde clutching a large zippered leather case stumbled briefly as she zigzagged through the fallen furniture on the ruined patio. Right behind her came a tall, African-American...something. Her cheeks were contoured with subtle shadows, her dewy lips glossy and pink, her eyes lined dramatically and her shoulder length hair drawn back in a severe yet stylish pony tail. But the body was definitely male. The grey sleeveless shirt he wore fit snugly over a muscular chest and exposed well-developed arms. Luanne was confused. He (or she) had an elaborate tote bag under his arm, and proceeded into the house with the Hispanic woman.

A tall, formidable-looking woman in khakis and a pink polo shirt did not follow the others. Instead, she aimed a camera at

Blake and Luanne, not turning it away or off even when Blake held up his middle finger in an unmistakably hostile gesture.

Next to emerge from the vehicle was a pint-sized man whose tawny brown hair was perfectly coiffed, despite what might have been a fairly rough ride. Luanne was fascinated in spite of herself. He had such an aura about him. She found that she could not stop looking at him and the satisfying picture he made in his streamlined, two-button gray wool suit -- a microphone clipped to one lapel -- a crisp, sky blue pinstriped Oxford shirt and neat leather loafers. Compared to the t-shirt ensembles on the military types his outfit must be warm, but she saw no sheen of sweat on his perfectly tanned face. He looked so cool. He probably always looked so cool. Just then, he pulled a white handkerchief from a back pocket and pressed it to his chin, cheeks and forehead so quickly and deftly that she thought she was imagining things. In an instant, the handkerchief was out of view again. A compact appeared in his right hand. He opened it and Luanne saw a glint of mirror captured by sunlight as he turned it to one angle and then another, examining his face before snapping it shut and putting it away. He was so quick she felt as if she was watching a magician's act. He signaled the camerawoman with an abrupt, decisive gesture, causing her to swing her camera away from Luanne and Blake and toward him. He instantly assumed an expression so animated that it looked as if he'd slipped on a mask. He began talking to the camera.

Luanne realized that she'd better try and understand what was going on. She shook off her stupor and shifted her attention to a blonde man with Asian features, newly disembarked and wearing the attitude of one was in charge.

"What the HELL?" shouted Blake. He'd finally found his voice and at an impressive volume. "What the FUCK do you people think you're DOING HERE?"

The blonde Chinese man, unperturbed, held up an index finger, and Luanne realized that he was listening to someone on his headset. He nodded intently. "Right, Sid. We've secured the perimeter." The accent sounded British, or maybe watered-down Australian. He listened for a moment then looked at Luanne and Blake as if he'd just noticed them.

"I'll be with you shortly." Then, into the headset: "Yes, Therese and Brionne are with him now. No, I couldn't reach Lupe."

Luanne noticed that the commandos had taken up positions around the house and were staring up at the cliff top and through the iron gates as if they were anticipating an armed invasion at any moment.

"Who are these people?" Luanne asked. "And who are they expecting?"

"Who *aren't* they expecting?" The blonde, surprisingly, gave her his haughty attention. His tone suggested that the answer should be obvious. "Our deal with StarWatch 24/7 is an exclusive one. If there's been a leak and someone else manages to get some film or photos of the rescue, we'd lose millions."

So that was why the miniature man looked so familiar to Luanne. Why he had an aura. She'd seen him on TV, many times.

"You're kidding me." Luanne shook her head. "You're trying to profit from Cody having been hurt in accident? Who *are* you people?"

"I am Palmer Lu, acting on behalf of my employer, Cody's agent, who has only Cody's best interests at heart. And you must be Luanne *Sajooski*." He held out his hand and Luanne shook it reluctantly. "We're ever so grateful to you. We were so relieved when we got your email. We made arrangements straightaway. Tracked the email to the computer at this location, assembled a team and, well, here we are."

Did he always talk in the royal we? It's Sigh-ef-ski," she said.

"The indisputable fact is that someone will profit from this tragedy. Many someones, probably. This story is worth a great deal of money. Entertainment Tonight, TMZ, Access Hollywood, People, the E! Network, the National Enquirer, the cable networks -- all of whom have celebrity coverage -- several thousand web sites...they have hundreds of operatives desperately combing Southern California as we speak, trying to find Cody Torrance. All Mr. Kirschenbaum has done is to ensure that Cody's story will be covered in a respectful way, by people we trust. That's why there are hair and makeup artists with Cody at this moment. So that he will look his best when his fans see him."

"And StarWatch 24/7 will get its money's worth." Blake spat out the words.

Luanne was thinking: *hair and makeup artists? Seriously?*

Palmer shrugged. "Mounting a private rescue operation like this is not an inexpensive proposition. The Hummercopter that flew us here, for instance, is very new, but just what we needed. Very costly, even to rent. The only buyers so far have been Saudi oil sheiks. Those security men? Ex-Special Forces. Navy Seals. That sort. They don't come cheap."

"What are they going to do if they see a camera crew flying overhead?" Blake inquired snidely. "Shoot them down?"

Palmer continued his narrative, ignoring him. "And the medical squad is comprised of a top-notch emergency room doctor and the best team he could assemble on short notice. If we'd allowed the police and EMTs in on this, it would be all over the internet as soon as they could snap photos on their cell phones. We needed our own people to manage the situation. People we can trust."

He suddenly waved to the camerawoman and TV correspondent. They hurried over.

"This courageous young woman is the one who saved Cody Torrance's life. Luanne Sajooski. And this is the homeowner who so generously took Cody and Luanne in after they were stranded in the wilderness."

Blake scowled.

"What's that?"

Luanne realized that Palmer Lu was listening to his headset again. She turned to find the camera aimed at her, and felt unexpectedly self-conscious. The correspondent stepped closer. "I'll just clip this on you if you don't mind." He reached forward to attach a small microphone to her wrinkled shirt, but never finished the task.

"They're ready for you." Palmer announced crisply. "He's upstairs. Second room on the left."

The two TV people spun around and practically sprinted toward the house. Not having her hands free, the camerawoman lagged behind the pint-sized correspondent, but she made good time nonetheless.

Palmer turned to Blake and Luanne. "You'll have to excuse me. I've got to manage the event." Then he, too, hurried away.

Blake lifted a chair from the ground and set it upright. He crouched down, picked up mashed plants and dropped them back down onto the ground in disgust. "Well. Lots of material for the compost heap. Isn't that just wonderful."

"I'm....so sorry." It was horribly inadequate. "I brought this down on you, didn't I? I...didn't know this would happen."

He sighed. "I should have. The vultures." He stood. "It's not your fault. He was injured. What else could you have done?" He stared off into the distance. "And it actually could have been worse. We could have been swarmed with media, instead of just this one group of wackos."

"All the way out here? And with traffic the way it is?"

"They'd have found a way. For a story this big, they'd have gotten here."

In a few minutes, people began streaming out of the house, in a different order than they'd gone in. First came the camera woman, walking backwards awkwardly as she documented the dramatic parade that unfolded. The correspondent stood in the forefront, to the side of her field of vision. He was talking, but Luanne couldn't hear the words. The camera's focus slid from him to the prone body of Cody, resting on the gurney that was rolled along by the dedicated-looking medical staff. In spite of the IV attached to his arm, Cody looked surprisingly good - better than when Luanne had checked on him an hour earlier, anyway. His hair was simply yet attractively styled. The pallor of his face was warmed to a healthier shade, by makeup, she presumed. She knew his mouth should be a worrisome ashen tone, but it was rosy. Sensuous, even. Lipstick? The stylists had done their jobs well, she thought. The two of them came well behind Cody and his rescuers, taking care to stay in the background. So did Palmer, who was talking, again, to his headset.

Luanne lost her sense of disconnection long enough to remember her purse. She couldn't reenter the real world without her I.D. and credit cards. She hurried into the house and snatched up her purse, then saw the impressive-looking digital camera that she'd left on the floor next to it. This camera had seemed important to Cody, those several lifetimes ago when they met in the ladies' room. She grabbed the camera as well.

When she got back outside, the medical team was loading Cody's gurney into the Hummercopter. The stylists, security types and pint-sized correspondent all boarded. Luanne was surprised to see the camerawoman and Palmer remain on the ground as the aircraft took flight. Why were they being left behind?

They were not, it turned out. After a noisy liftoff and short ascension -- filmed intently by the camerawoman -- the Hummercopter descended once more.

Palmer saw her puzzled look. "Had to get the footage of the Hummercopter flying away. Very dramatic and all that. Now we'll really be on our way." This last was directed to Blake.

"Great. And what about my property damage? This is the thanks I get for taking in an injured man?"

Palmer surveyed the devastated garden with little interest. He dug into a pocket and pulled out a business card, handing one to Blake. "Ring me up and I'll refer you to our accountant. You'll be compensated, I assure you." He stiffened attentively. "What's that, Sid? Oh, we're just leaving. No, he's still unconscious, but I'm told he's stable. Whatever that means. We'll meet you at Cedars. Right. The celebrity wing."

As he started for the aircraft, Luanne realized that she was about to be stranded.

"Wait! What about me?"

Palmer paused. "Oh, right. I'd almost forgotten. I suppose you can come to Cedars with us. Sid will want to debrief you, anyway."

Luanne suddenly felt ungracious about her abrupt departure. Contrite, she turned toward her host. "Thank you. Thank you for…you know. Saving our lives." She shrugged. "And I really am sorry about all this. I know how you Lumpen Solitarians like to be alone. At least you're about to get your peace back."

He snorted. "Others will come. Media vultures. After all, Cody Torrance was here. I might as well sell tickets."

He was right, she conceded sadly. "What will you do?"

"Leave. Maybe I'll sell this place and start all over somewhere else. Or it might be enough to just disappear for awhile, until they forget about it. I've done it before."

"How long will that take?"

He squinted toward the sun and smiled wryly. "Dunno. Forty days and forty nights?"

"Ms. Sajooski! If you're coming--"

"Bye!" Feeling awkward, she kissed him on the cheek. Clutching the camera strap in one hand and her purse strap in the other, she turned and ran toward the Hummercopter.

CHAPTER THIRTY-SIX:
BLANKETS OF STARDUST

Ira drifted north and east in a daze as the marine layer burned off and a timid sun made a feeble appearance over the Los Angeles. He gripped the handlebars of his bicycle and pushed it alongside him. The streets were too full of stopped cars, the sidewalks too clotted with people to ride the bike here. The Tooth Fairy's predictions were coming true. An ugly mood asserted itself among the hordes of pedestrians, some moving purposefully, and some, like Ira, meandering aimlessly in random directions. Many simply stood still in confusion, bumped and cursed by others, waiting to be rescued and restored to normalcy. An angry, unfocused restlessness gripped the city.

He wondered if it was worth it to go back to his apartment, which might as well be a million miles away. What, really, did he own that was of any value? Clothes. Toiletries. An old TV and sofa bought from a thrift store. The bed came with the apartment, abandoned by a previous tenant. There was his shrine, though. Damn, he thought. The pictorial homage to the Great Screenwriters wasn't worth anything monetarily, but it was the thing he'd miss most of all. He hated the thought of some stranger tearing it thoughtlessly from the wall.

He was only paid up for another six days. It would probably take him that long to get to the apartment, and when he did, he'd have to come up with next month's rent out of savings that would not be replenished any time soon. The hell with it. Nyet! He'd abandon his lease – and to hell with the Russian mafia building owner. Come and find me, comrade. Good luck with that.

It was almost a relief to see the same schlocky costumed characters selling themselves as usual in front of Grauman's Chinese Theatre on Hollywood Boulevard. The routine was enjoyable to him just now. Captain Jack Sparrow, a clone trooper, Wolverine, and a skinny, sort of creepy Spiderman posed for pictures with tourists and collected tips as if it was any old Wednesday. It *was* Wednesday, wasn't it? Ira panicked a little, realizing that he wasn't sure. The structure had been ripped away from his life.

He flinched at an eruption of glass breaking violently just a few feet away from him. He stared in disbelief at the man who'd just swung a golf club through the glass storefront of a closed shop, continued to stare as the man and several companions leapt into the shop and emerged with armfuls of souvenirs: shiny plastic replicas of Oscars, stacks of glossy movie stars' pictures, silkscreened t-shirts and piles of plates on which various Hollywood landmarks were painted. The last thief to leave had sensibly found some plastic bags and filled them with his loot. Ira glimpsed a jumble of snow globes with what looked like tiny white jumpsuit-clad Elvis Presleys in them near the top of one of his bags. As the man scrambled awkwardly out through the broken window, he locked eyes with Ira. Fear flickered momentarily on his face, but it was quickly replaced by defiance. He ran on, after his fellow thieves. No one, Ira included, did anything to stop them.

Ira thought: souvenirs? Seriously? People are looting *souvenirs*?

He found a restaurant and got a hamburger and some lemonade to go, because the interior was so noisy, so seething with loud, distressed humanity that he was reminded of "Soylent Green" and almost lost his appetite. Lacking a more comfortable option, he sat down on the sidewalk to eat, leaning against a building to minimize his chances of being stepped on. He could, he supposed, eat his burger standing up, but he refused to relinquish this one small measure of humanity. Still, sitting cross-legged on the pavement, he felt like a homeless person. Then he realized: I *am* a homeless person.

He was almost finished with his lemonade when he saw two men start a shoving match over...? He couldn't tell what started it. A few of the numerous bystanders nearby intervened to stop it. A long-haired Latina woman stood motionless a few yards away from the melee, clutching the hand of a small, bewildered boy. Both she and the boy were crying quietly, steadily.

Ira moved past her without speaking. What could he say to her, anyway, to make her feel better? That this insane situation was temporary? That it would right itself soon? Two women stopped to talk to the sobbing mother. Maybe they could think of something comforting to tell her.

A tidy-looking white man in a business suit shouted at passersby: "Woe, woe, woe to the inhabiters of the earth!" over and over again. Most people ignored him; a few shot him annoyed glances. One, a lanky teenager, deliberately collided with him and knocked him to the ground, causing him to temporarily stop his looped announcement. He quickly got back on his feet, though, and started shouting anew.

Ira tried to think rationally. How bad was his situation going to get, exactly? He wondered what he'd do when his money ran out, which would be soon if he couldn't quickly find another job. God only knew what effect this traffic crisis would have on the local economy. Should he call his parents, request a loan? Ask them to wire him money? They'd do it, no question, but how would he explain his predicament? It would sound absurd for him to tell them that he intended to remain here, in spite of the fact that he was jobless and living on the streets. And they couldn't support him indefinitely. They weren't wealthy people, after all.

He saw dozens – maybe hundreds – of people, moving north on Highland as if in a trance, like zombie extras from "Dawn of the Dead," but without the bloody mouths. They seemed happy, as if there was a pleasant destination up ahead for them. They must know something he did not know.

"Where is everyone going?" he asked a chunky red-haired girl in a pink tank top who was a part of the parade.

She shook her head. "I don't know. But…it's got to be someplace good, doesn't it? I mean, all these people are going there."

He caught up with a group of tanned and feisty senior citizens. They strode with pep, as if they were simply doing their daily cardio workout and not moving along with a massive wave of humanity during what was turning out to be a pretty damned unusual day in L.A.

"What's ahead?" he queried them. "Where are you going?"

"Don't know," said a small, sinewy man in white shorts and a pale blue polo shirt. "Beats standing around doing nothing, though." Like him, they were following others, who were following others, who were following others. The old man was right: even if they didn't know the destination, it was good to be going somewhere.

Ira followed, stupidly, hoping for some…hope. Going along with the crowd made him feel less alone. He fantasized that up ahead there was there someone in charge who had supplies and useful information. A plan. A prediction about when the problem would be fixed. Realizing that the day was wearing on, he knew he had to find a place to sleep tonight. Unfortunately, so did everyone around him. It was a safe bet that there were no rooms available at hotels and motels. Would some of these places open their doors and give temporary free shelter to the multitudes, letting people sleep in their hallways and use their bathrooms, like they did after earthquakes? Maybe the authorities would set up emergency operations in open places like public parks, erecting tents, dispensing food and bottled water. The phrase "refugee camp" flashed through his brain. He dismissed it, but not before it caused a ripple of fear and loathing.

He finally saw the beacon that beckoned to them: a solid white base bearing a scrolling electronic sign and topped by a curving white shell. Ah, ha! He and his fellow refugees were headed to the Hollywood Bowl, steps quickening and faces shedding worried expressions as if the fabled landmark was flowing with milk and honey. He wanted to shout: it's just an entertainment venue! He didn't though, because it *was* more than that. It was a symbol; a civilized little hollow in the wilderness. It was the kind of stylish refuge that could only be found in L.A., in which the newly displaced might sleep under blankets of stardust, in the shadow of a stage on which Sinatra had once performed. Now *that* was a way to ride out a crisis!

He'd never been able to afford a concert at the Bowl. Entertainment was not a top priority in his limited budget, but when he did partake of it he generally went to a movie, to learn something about his chosen craft. He'd passed the Bowl plenty of times, sometimes making the unfortunate mistake of doing so when crowds were pouring into it for an evening concert. At those times traffic was heavy even for a town accustomed to heavy traffic. The unruly streams of cars that usually zoomed frantically down Highland Avenue were not a problem now.

Once inside the seating section, Ira, like so many of his fellow pilgrims, gazed worshipfully at the enormous stage as if it were an alter, framed by soaring white arches, nestled amid the ivy-covered foothills of the Santa Monica mountains. Like an indication from God that the world was not coming to an end, the legendary "Hollywood" sign was right where it should be, roosting comfortably on Mt. Lee. Why he thought that it might not be there he couldn't say, but he found its familiar presence surprisingly reassuring.

As he looked around, reality fleshed out the more mundane details of his surroundings. The area near which he stood was divided into smaller seating sections by ugly, weather-beaten redwood partitions joined by metal strips, not unlike office cubicles, but without their fuzzy grey charm. No one seemed bothered by the aesthetics. People were appropriating cubbies or grabbing their shares of the uncomfortable wooden bleachers as if they were miners who'd found gold nuggets and were eagerly staking claims.

It was just before sunset. The diffuse, gentle, orange-tinged light from the west did little to soothe the pandemonium around him. Thousands of agitated cell phone conversations buzzed through the hollow. Some people stood paralyzed, as lonely as clouds. There were a few families, their members clustered together in a way that Ira envied. He guessed, though, that most people were stranded far from their loved ones when traffic stopped. Many were alone, like him. Others quickly gravitated toward fellow travelers. He was amazed that, even among strangers and in unfamiliar settings, humans sought to divide themselves so quickly into special interest groups, thanks to sloppily improvised but effective signs that had evidently been written by hand. It was a relentless drive, perhaps a biological one. Do we fear losing our identities in a large population unless we separate into smaller, more manageable units? Does bestowing names upon those units give us the illusion that we are bringing order out of chaos?

A calm crowd surrounded a man holding a pole on which hung a banner with the Christian fish symbol on it. He was leading them in prayer. Heads bent, they murmured quietly, heedless of the swirl and ebb of others around them. Near them was a petite, spirited woman holding a "Proud Parents of Trannies" sign, and talking animatedly to several people who'd joined her. He recognized a Kabbalah group by the red ribbons tied around their wrists. Young Republicans and Baker Street Irregulars congregated over to his left, Ice Chewers in one redwood cubicle and Southern California Progressives up near the stage. Vegans were sharing food that several of them seemed to have brought in backpacks. Libertarians sat together on the stage. Pagans stood around an improvised bonfire, chatting quietly. Ira wondered: shouldn't they be *dancing* around the bonfire? Adult Orphans collected in the bleachers, greatly outnumbered by Red Hat Society members. There were gatherings marked by SAG jackets and Teamsters caps, fast food uniforms and chauffer's outfits. Those around him seemed like strangely stinking animals, until he realized that he was one, too.

Inevitably, people sought out others of their own race. That distressed him and he wasn't sure why, since he himself had gravitated away from a heavily Latino section and drifted toward a cluster of Caucasians. Too bad he couldn't narrow it down to Irish-Jewish Detroiters. Then he'd really feel at home.

There were some scary-looking gang types but they, like everyone else, seemed a little dazed by their surroundings. Too dazed to victimize their fellow campers? Ira hoped so. Most of them skulked in the corners, disdainfully watching the scene from a slight remove.

Ira recognized a "PULMONATION" banner, waving right in front of the stage so that no one could miss it. It was striking, he admitted to himself, almost admiring the stark outline of the inhaler next to an angrily clenched fist, and under that, the words, "Taking back the air." He'd seen it at that demonstration...when? My God, was that only yesterday? So much had happened since then. He wondered where Oceana was at this moment. PulmoNation belonged to the same coalition her group did. Like the pagans, the PulmoNationers were having a bonfire, but theirs was large and threatening, sending dangerous sparks into the dusk. With growing irritation, Ira realized that they were tossing in inhalers that hissed and crackled explosively, their plastic hulls melting and emitting offensive, probably toxic odors. He thought there was probably a fairly high danger of wildfire here, like there was in most of L.A., most of the time. The PulmoNationers obviously didn't care. They shouted loud chants -- "Hell, no! The cars won't go!" -- and reveled in the furious glares that came their way. Ira fumed. Who the hell did these asthmatics think they were? What made them feel so entitled? And why didn't he, as a fellow asthmatic, feel as angry as they did?

Many women were collected around a WWOD sign and he mused about its possible meaning for longer than he should have, trying to decipher the acronym by determining what the followers had in common. He finally concluded that they had nothing in common – except that all of the adults were females, and some had children with them. The women chatted and laughed as if they were among old friends at a cocktail party. He approached one on the outer edge of the group and asked her, reluctantly, what WWOD meant, feeling like a crossword puzzle-solver who was flipping to the back of the book for an answer.

"What Would Oprah Do," she said. "You see, Oprah will have some ideas for how to cope with this. She's probably – at this very moment – planning a special show for her network on the crisis, with experts and everything. Maybe they can use those big screens alongside the stage to broadcast it. I think everybody would benefit from it." She nodded sagely, just like Oprah would nod.

"Ira! Ira O'Riley!" The shout saved him from having to come up with a reply. He turned to find Lupe Sevá making her way toward him as if one of his fantasies was coming to life.

She reached him and hugged him hard, fervently, like he'd just pulled her into a lifeboat. "Oh, thank God! Somebody I know!" She was crying, dampening his shirt with her tears.

He put his arms around her gratefully, a little thrill coursing through him. Of all the gin joints in all the towns in all the world, she walked into this one. It was meant to be. This was the scene where the two leads were thrown together and finally realized their attraction for each other. He would comfort her, protect her, take care of her, and she would understand that *he* was the man for her. She would draw strength from his manly confidence. Sometimes it took a crisis to make you see things clearly. The two of them would be an island unto themselves, safe from the chaos around them. God, she felt good. He could hold her like this forever. Except that he was starting to get an erection.

Trying to conceal his embarrassment, Ira awkwardly peeled her away from him, still holding her by the arms. "It's OK," he said, his tone soothing. "It'll be all right."

"Will it?" she sniffed. "I've been walking for hours, trying to get somewhere. Anywhere. I barely even remember where I left my car – not that that matters. I don't know when I'll get to drive it again. Where will we sleep, Ira? What about food? I thought that maybe the government or *something* would give us supplies, then I realized: how would they *get* the supplies to us? It's not like any trucks can get through. We're on our own!" Here her voice rose to a wail. She looked around in panic. "It'll be dark soon. What will we do? What will all these people do?"

She sounded dangerously close to hysteria.

Ira slid his backpack from his shoulders and reached almost furtively into it, afraid to let too many people see that he had a plastic bottle of water. He uncapped it and held it out to Lupe, who stopped crying and accepted it eagerly, as if he were offering her life itself.

"Oh, thank God!" She gulped, spilling some water down her chin. Ira thought that looked adorable. "Thank you so much, Ira! I was so happy when I saw you standing here. Someone I knew."

He smiled reassuringly, his tone firm. "You're not alone now. And everything will work itself out. You'll see. Things could be a lot worse. After all, this isn't an earthquake, with lots of damage. No one is dead, or injured. The weather's ok. This will turn out to be just a temporary inconvenience. I'm sure the mayor or the governor is working on it right now. Oprah, too," he added, remembering the WWOD woman's certainty.

He couldn't help staring at her as she drank more. It was wonderful to see her here, a fantasy materialized in a place that was far, far away from that fantasy-killing office he used to work at. "You look great," he blurted out.

She laughed. "I look like a hot mess, Ira." Then: "You're sweet."

She handed the water bottle back to him and he jammed it nonchalantly into his backpack, relieved that it still had some water in it. He was starting to feel thirsty himself. With an arm around Lupe's shoulder – just to comfort her, of course – he guided her over to a space in the bleachers, taking her hand when they had to climb up a few rows. She followed him without question, which he took as a sign that she had faith in him. He hoped that people were watching. He was with a beautiful woman. To all appearances, they were a couple. He felt very proud.

They staked out an unoccupied section of bench, with Ira trying to calculate how he would spoon with her as they slept, given the narrow width of what was going to be their bed that night. Damn. Would they have to sleep end to end? He wanted to touch her, to feel her. As it was, he willed the nightfall to hold off just a little longer, so that he could stare at her exquisite face for as long as possible. When it was dark, he would recreate her features in his imagination. What was important was that they had this time together. The intensity of the occasion would accelerate the feelings that had been there all along, in a subtle form. Possibly so subtle that Lupe hadn't known of them.

She sighed deeply, leaning against him. "Oh, Ira. I feel so much better." She chuckled, a rueful expression on her tear-streaked face. "You think I'm silly, don't you?"

"Not at all. This is an upsetting situation. No one knows what's going to happen next."

Damn. He saw by her look of alarm that it was the wrong thing to say.

"I mean, there's some uncertainty, but, in the end, it'll be all right."

She turned hopeful. "Will it? Will it really?"

"Of course. I'm sure it will."

A pleasant silence hung between them for a moment. He smelled the sweet fragrance of eucalyptus trees in the hills, heard children singing on the stage. He felt her shiver.

"I guess I'm a little cold," she said apologetically.

He took off his light denim jacket and handed it to her. "Here. This'll help."

"Oh, I couldn't," she demurred.

"Sure you could," he insisted. "Take it. I'm not cold at all."

She happily put it on and snapped it closed, rolling up the too-long cuffs. The body of the jacket was too big on her, too. Skinny Ira's jacket was too large for Lupe Sevá.

Her stomach growled and he wished he could do something about food, but he had nothing edible in his backpack. She seemed to sense this, talking, instead, about her upsetting day.

"It was terrible! I was so fraught about not being able to get to work on time, but then I realized I wasn't going to get there at all! Not even close enough to walk the rest of the way... I saw people stealing things from trucks, Ira. From stores, too. And no one could stop them. It was like all of a sudden, there was no law."

"It was surreal, wasn't it?" Why was he referring to it in the past tense? Did he think that tomorrow, when they woke up, order would be restored?

"My mother is so worried about me. I'm glad she's at home, safe. Oh!" She straightened up. "I'll call her and tell her I'm with a friend. She'll feel so much better." She grabbed her cell phone out of her purse and flipped it open. "I've been trying not to use this too much, because I only had my car charger with me. As it is, I'm down to two bars."

"Use mine," he said gallantly.

"Really?"

"Sure." He handed his over to her.

She dialed and conducted a brief but emotional conversation in Spanish with her mother. Ira listened carefully for his name, reasoning that he was not really eavesdropping, since he couldn't understand Spanish when it was spoken quickly. He was excited when he heard her say, "Ira," and then, after listening for a moment, "Ira O'Riley," followed by what was presumably an explanation of how she knew him. In a way, he was being introduced to her mother! It was a new phase in their relationship.

She finally snapped his phone shut and handed it back to him, her smile dazzling to his eyes. She could use up all his minutes and then some, he thought.

"Feeling better?" he asked tenderly.

"Much." She sighed. "Whatever happens, at least I'm not alone. Thank you so much, Ira."

"For what?"

She chuckled. "For giving me your water, your jacket, your phone. Just for being here. I always like seeing you, at the agency. You make me smile."

He let that thought linger, then said: "You always make my day better. It's too bad—"

"Lupe! Lupe!"

She jerked upright. "OMG. Gary?"

Ira saw a blonde man in a black motorcycle jacket pushing aggressively through the crowd, coming their way.

Lupe fairly flew down the bleachers, inadvertently kicking a few people who were in her way. "Gary!" she screamed happily. "You found me!"

Their embrace was epic, a prolonged, exuberant hug worthy of Baby and Johnny, at the end of Dirty Dancing. They were so close that it was hard to tell where one body ended and the other began. He enfolded her. She clung to him. Their bliss made them seem like they were on a different plane, above the petty inconveniences of this world.

Their reunion drew lots of attention. People were glad for a diversion, especially a positive one. When the hug turned into a deep, soulful kiss, a few turned away, but others clapped.

Baby and Johnny didn't notice. After what seemed (to Ira) like hours of kissing, they finally stopped to let their lips recover. He couldn't hear what they were saying to each other, but their smiles were plain enough, even in the gathering darkness. Lupe took Gary's hand and led him over to where Ira sat like a stone in the bleachers.

"Gary," she beamed. "This is Ira. He works for Sid. Remember? I told you about Sid?"

"Hey, man." Gary gave him a friendly wave. "Thanks for taking care of my girl, here." He pulled Lupe to him possessively, his handsome face bemused.

"No problem." Did he sound as wooden as he felt? Of course she would have a boyfriend. Women like her always had boyfriends. Ira had never had a chance.

"I had to borrow a friend's motorcycle to come and get her. My car couldn't get through."

Lupe turned to him. "I didn't know if you got my message."

"I wanted to surprise you, babe." Gary turned back to Ira. "Anyway, we'd better get going. I have to get my girl home and feed her. Sorry we can't take you, too, Ira, but there's no room on the bike. Nice to meet you, though."

With a last look at Ira, Lupe turned in synch with Gary as if they were dancing in a ballroom. They glided off together, two gorgeous people blended into one striking couple, escaping past the sweaty rabble to roar romantically into the night on a motorcycle.

Close to despair, Ira snapped open his laptop and tried to work on his screenplay, but the only scene he could think of was the one that had just played out painfully in front of him. What a schmuck he was. Talk about delusions of grandeur. Even if she didn't have a (great looking) boyfriend, a woman like Lupe would never go for a man like Ira. He surrendered to his morose mood, slid his laptop into his backpack and stretched out on the bleacher, willing himself to shut out the conversations around him and fall asleep quickly so that he could blot out the reality that was his life. For just a little while, with Lupe, he'd been able to forget what a loser he was. No job. No money. No place to live. No girlfriend. He tried hard to resuscitate his fantasy about winning an Academy Award for "His Majesty's Gangsta," but the image of him onstage clutching an Oscar refused to materialize.

He realized that he was cold. Lupe had taken his jacket. He curled up in a fetal position, trying to conserve what body heat he had, and eventually fell asleep.

When he woke up at dawn, damp with dew, thirsty and sore from his hard bed, he reached for the water bottle in his backpack and found it…gone. His entire backpack was gone. His wallet with his cash, ATM card and credit card -- gone. Panic pressed down upon him. He felt as if he was suffocating. When he grasped the full extent of his loss, he wished he was dead. His computer and back-up disks were gone and with them, "Her Majesty's Gangsta."

CHAPTER THIRTY-SEVEN:
A CRYSTAL BALL FILLED WITH ANSWERS

Luanne felt deeply confused. She sat in a waiting room at Cedars, hoping to hear an update of Cody's condition, even though she doubted that anyone would tell her anything about him. They would probably not be allowed to. His celebrity status would make them even more protective of his privacy, or it should. She was not his wife. Not a relative. She was not anything to him, really, except a woman he'd gotten into a helicopter crash with. She knew that she'd saved his life, but she didn't want a reward from him, or even thanks. Not really. What she wanted was to hear how the story was going to end. Cody's injuries seemed terribly serious. He might have been quietly dying the entire time she was eating and drinking and sleeping on clean sheets in that strange mansion in the wilderness. Even though Cody spent most of their relationship in an unconscious state, she still felt a strong connection to him. She *cared*.

Besides, she was not eager to make the decisions that had to be made. Logically, she should find a way back to her car, get as many things out of it as she could carry and get the hell out of L.A. There was still great theatre being done in Chicago. The movie career could be postponed. She could let the temp agency know she was back in town, and available for office work. Why stay here? This was an impossibly tough time for a newcomer with no connections to gain a foothold in the entertainment industry. Maybe if things weren't so strange...

"You're Luanne Sajooski?"

The man addressing her was tall, with a ridiculously thick head of silver hair that perched on his head like an upside down nest. The color must be premature; he was in his middle years, not old. His face was homely and interesting, its expression managing to look sleepy and cunning at the same time. He was dressed casually. Expensively casual, that is. He did not look like a doctor, which made her suspicious. Who was he?

"Yes."

"So you're the one who helped Cody?"

She had no idea how to answer him. Was he a reporter? If so, a legitimate one or a parasite from a tabloid? Was there such a thing as a legitimate entertainment reporter? Should she be hostile to him, just to be safe? Why bother? After all, the details of the story were going to come out sooner or later. Just about the most famous man in the world was lying in a hospital bed, recuperating from a helicopter accident. It was news.

The silver-haired man was eyeing the camera she still held. "That's it? That's the camera Cody had?"

"Yes."

"The memory card still in there?"

Luanne nodded.

"I'll take it." He reached for it as if he owned it.

Instinctively, she took a step away from him, wishing she had a few more clues to help her decide on a course of action. The camera was important to Cody. She was sure of it. When he'd stormed into the ladies' room he was clutching it as if it meant the difference between life and death to him. Unfortunately, between his airsickness and his unconsciousness, there hadn't been much of an opportunity for him to confide its significance to her. If he even meant to. Maybe he would have kept his secrets.

The man smiled knowingly. "Oh. I get it. And you're right."

"I am?" She was?

"It *is* worth something." He shrugged benignly. "That's the way the game is played, isn't it?"

Was it?

"I'll give you $5,000 for the camera." His tone turned stern. "Assuming the memory card is in there and that you haven't made any copies of anything. You haven't, have you? Or did that hermit guy have a printer?"

The figure was shocking to her. $5,000 was a lot of money in her world. What was the big deal with this camera? She tried hard to suss out what was going on.

He sighed. "You're holding out. That's a mistake. Have you seen the pictures in this camera?"

She didn't answer.

"You really think you're going to make a lot of money from them?"

"I...I..." she faltered, unsure where to go with her objection.

"You won't. Trust me. I've been in this business a long time, and I know what's what. But you've kept the camera safe, and just to make sure that you're compensated for your trouble, I'll give you $10,000 for it -- provided you sign a nondisclosure form saying you won't divulge any details about what happened with Cody. But that's all. Not a penny more."

Damn! Whatever was in this camera was worth a lot to this stranger. Luanne was tempted to turn it over for the cash, even though it did not belong to her. She curbed the impulse with difficulty. Giving the camera to this man felt like a betrayal. Cody trusted her, or at least he did when he had all of his senses working. She could not screw him like that.

Just then, the platinum blonde Chinese guy emerged from a nearby hallway. He hurried over to the tall man and addressed him with some urgency: "He's awake, Sid. He wants to see you."

Sid. This had to be Sid Kirschenbaum, Cody's agent. He was not a reporter. Not a danger. Sid nodded at the blonde man and looked at her expectantly. "I know you don't want to hurt Cody's career. You helped him. Saved his life, really. And $10,000 is a lot of money. You seem like a reasonable girl. Do we have a deal or not?"

"No." She smiled, suddenly knowing exactly what she should do. "$10,000 won't work."

Sid frowned, clearly caught off guard. "Jesus. More? Look, sweetheart, you're not going to hold that camera hostage for more than ten thousand. And if you try to, I'll have you arrested. It's not your camera."

"I don't want your money. I'm an actor. I want you to represent me."

He looked irritated, then disbelieving.

"Look, Ms. Sajooski."

"It's pronounced Sigh-ef-ski."

"Whatever. That's not the way things work in this town."

Could he sound more patronizing?

"Not for nothing, but I get hundreds of actors submitting headshots and resumes to me every week."

She held the camera up, nice and high. "Yeah well they don't have this, do they? And by the way, when Cody wakes up, he'll put in a good word for me. He said he was very grateful for my help."

He actually laughed. "You got balls, I'll give you that. Any talent to go with 'em?"

She nodded just like Glen Close would nod, if she were playing a character in this situation. The gesture was simple, powerful and assured.

"Oh, yeah," she said, her tone firm. "I've got talent."

Sid shook his head as if dumbfounded. He pulled an expensive-looking cigar from his shirt pocket and jabbed it into his mouth, making no move to light it. "You're a piece of work, you know that?"

She didn't answer, just smiled what she hoped was an undaunted sort of smile and waited.

Sid took the cigar out of his mouth and studied it pensively, as if it were a crystal ball filled with answers. Finally he looked up at the ceiling and sighed, then turned his attention back toward her.

"You got a head shot and resume you can give me?"

PART TWO

Chapter Thirty-Eight:
Antidepressants and Jesus All Rolled into a
Big Orange Ball

Ira came awake gradually, by now accustomed to the sound of voices nearby. He stretched thoroughly but carefully, mindful of his spatial limitations. He reached over and turned on the coffeepot whose modified cord was plugged into his car's cigarette lighter. He'd come to think of his new abode as cozy. The notion would have been absurd before the B.S. – the Big Stoppage – but now he was far from alone in embracing it. Millions of his fellow Southern Californians lived in their cars, too. Some, like Ira, even liked it.

He swept back the green plaid windshield curtains and gazed appreciatively at the dawn. The clean, deep blueness of the sky was immensely gratifying to him. He never took it for granted; not for an instant. Once all of the engines in all the cars and trucks and SUVs and limos and buses switched off, the air over L.A. began to heal itself and became, after a time, clear and azure blue in a way that no one could ever remember it being before. No one was that old.

Ira still had a newspaper clipping stuck in his visor: a story about how at the West San Gabriel Valley Air Monitoring Sub region, the raw data for ozone, nitrogen dioxide and carbon monoxide showed such a rapid and dramatic reduction that the operators initially thought equipment failure to be the cause.

For days, people who generally never looked too far past their steering wheels sat at sidewalk cafes or stood on streets or rooftops or balconies and simply stared upward, open-mouthed, in wonder, as if they were beholding the second coming of Christ when all they were really trying to do was to absorb the idea of a blue that pure, a sky that clear.

For Ira – and many others -- it was more than a visual pleasure. Every day that the air remained so clear, that the car engines stayed still, was another day that he could breathe freely. He had no idea how long this condition would last, but vowed to enjoy every lungful of clean air that came his way.

It was funny, he mused. Had he in known in advance of the changes that would wash over his life like a rogue wave, leaving him sputtering and turning round and round and contacting solid ground only when he crashed painfully into it, he would have resisted them more. He thought that losing his job was the worst thing that could happen to him. His job was the font from which almost all things flowed: his paycheck, his health insurance, his 401K (without any matching funds because Sid was too cheap), his paid holidays (secular, Christian and Jewish), his measly paid one-week-per-year vacation (important, even though he couldn't afford to go anywhere). It was his place to go every day and, most important, it gave him the illusion of prestige and superficial status in the eyes of people outside the entertainment industry who hadn't realized how lowly his position in it had been.

Worse than all that, though, much worse, had been the loss of his screenplay-in-progress. He grieved for "His Majesty's Gangsta" for a long time, mourning the witty dialogue, despairing that he would never come up with such elegantly executed plot developments, hoping that he'd someday bump into the characters he'd brought to such vivid life, maybe while grocery shopping at Ralph's, or rollerblading at Venice Beach. (If he ever learned to rollerblade.)

His fictional friends deserted him. Moses and Stowaring and all the rest, the secondary characters (some of whom didn't even have names yet), went off to their glamorous casinos and mean streets and sexy adventures without a backward glance, not caring that their creator, the Dr. Frankenstein who'd raised them from the dust of his imagination, was stranded in a parallel dimension in which his life sucked.

His synapses had stopped firing. His ideas dried up like a piece of ripe fruit that had the juice sucked out as if by one of those late-night infomercial gadgets. His momentum, finding itself with no constructive outlet, flailed helplessly, careened out of control and finally tumbled over a cliff, crashing on the rocks below and flattening itself into a sad little heap of woe. He was bereft. He felt like he'd lost his lover to a tragic, untimely death. He was inconsolable.

Then it grew worse. He tortured himself by speculating that whoever stole his laptop would read his screenplay, realize its worth and steal it. They would finish writing it, get it produced, win the Academy Award and -- by the way -- become filthy rich. In his more rational moments he told himself that was impossible. Only he knew how the story was going to play out, how the various subplots would be cleverly braided together and brought to a thrilling climax. Only he held the secret – in his mind – to the upcoming role reversal of the two men. He would engineer it so that Stowaring would have to act like Muldoon and Muldoon like Stowaring in order to defeat the terrorists. It was this stunning scene, this *masterpiece* of a scene, that would finally cause the two men to respect each other, almost too late, because one of them would nearly be killed while saving the Queen or whoever. Maybe Kate Middleton. Ira hadn't yet decided who would be saved and which man would almost die. He was patient. This important point would reveal itself in good time. It was a process. He tried to take comfort in the fact that, while a great deal of the screenplay was in vulnerable files in his laptop, a lot of it was still germinating in his head.

At times, that notion invoked terror. How could any thief – any literate thief -- not recognize the potential of "Her Majesty's Gangsta"? Its brilliance fairly leapt off the monitor! Anyone gutsy enough to steal a backpack that lay beside its sleeping owner might have the chutzpah to finish the story himself. Ira had a few panic attacks over that possibility. It wouldn't be difficult to recognize what a great premise he had. He'd established the main characters quickly and masterfully. What were the chances of a thief either being a wannabe screenwriter or knowing a screenwriter that he could show the script to? In L.A., the chances were pretty damn good. What if some schmuck took Ira's story in a completely stupid direction and ruined it?

Fortunately, Ira was not able to dwell on his lost screenplay for long, because he had too many real world problems with which to contend. His small salary hadn't allowed him to put together much of a safety net. When he fell out of the ranks of the employed his paltry savings barely broke his fall. They certainly couldn't sustain him for more than a month or two. His efforts to find another job were confounded by circumstances.

The Big Stoppage left L.A. in a terrifying stasis. No one knew how to plan for the days and weeks and months ahead because no one knew what, if anything, would happen with the traffic. More than ever, Los Angelenos focused on living in the present.

Over time, Ira's personal misery eased with the realization that he was not alone. The Big Stoppage disrupted millions of lives, not just his. People could no longer get to their jobs – if they still had jobs. They could not easily get home, or to stores and restaurants and banks and dentist appointments and post offices and schools and hair stylists and dry cleaners and dog groomers and kids' soccer games and karaoke bars and golf courses and movies theatres that were not within walking distance of wherever they found themselves when The Big Stoppage hit.

Ever resourceful, Los Angelenos quickly imprinted entirely new patterns on their lives. It was an anthropological anomaly: a brand new culture that skipped the usual millennia needed for development, springing up, instead, almost overnight. Rather than fighting the inevitable, as he might have done in the past, Ira relaxed and went along with the changes.

While his coffee was brewing, he got his toilette kit and a clean towel from the storage unit bolted onto his trunk and walked to the row of pay portable toilets a half mile distant from his car. He could have rented a car that was much closer to the toilets, but unlike some people, he wouldn't put up with the smell just for the convenience. Now that his nose was working properly, foul odors caused him a sort of sensory pain. I smell all things in heaven and on the earth, he thought to himself, paraphrasing Poe just a little. I smell many things in hell. He supposed if he was an old guy with prostate trouble who had to pee three or four times a night he'd tolerate the smell just to be close to relief. Or, he'd do as some were doing and use an old-fashioned chamber pot. It was funny, how remnants from the past were reemerging as solutions to the present dilemma.

Fortunately, there was never much of a line at the portable toilets. People tended to get in and out rather quickly. Conditions inside the johns were kept as clean as possible by self-appointed attendants, Mexicans or Filipinos or newly-arrived Chinese who popped in between users and tidied up, working for tips, but an outhouse was an outhouse. There was only so much you could do.

Next he stepped into one of the auto-showers that had been erected on the shoulder of the road. It was an ingenious device that dispensed lukewarm water in pre-measured amounts, five minutes' worth for a quarter. You dropped your coins in a slot and washed as quickly as possible. He'd learned to be ready, with the caps off his shampoo and conditioner and his plastic soap container open. Had this coin-operated wonder been invented just because of the B.S., he wondered? The bank of auto-showers was fairly primitive, a series of vertical plastic enclosures with cheap-looking showers heads that looked as if they'd been hastily jerry-rigged to the walls of the enclosures. Had some do-it-yourselfer seen an opportunity and run with his idea? If so, it was an American dream come true. The auto-showers were springing up all over the Southland. It was environmental, too. When you're paying for every drop of water, your showers are fast and efficient.

After he towel-dried himself and dressed in the clean set of clothes he'd brought with him, Ira headed back to his car. Like many others, it had been converted into a mini-apartment by a mobile converter, a guy who used to work out of an auto body shop but took to the road when the B.S. hit. He did a good job and his rates were reasonable. (*Why not? He had low overhead.*) In Ira's car interior's new configuration, his bed folded up and out of the way during the day. There were shades on the windows and small tables that extended from the dashboard. A mini refrigerator was now installed in his trunk, although he generally bought his food fresh, preferring not to store too much. He could have gone with one of the stove models that used the car's own engine for heat, but he felt that would be wrong. He was enjoying the way his lungs worked these days. Firing up the engine to cook when there were other means available would be hypocritical. The little cooking he did do was on a small grill he kept stowed under his car. For other needs he purchased time on a nearby portable generator which powered innumerable appliances for auto-dwellers in its vicinity. Like the auto-shower, it was another small business that had sprung up in the wake of the B.S. The entrepreneurial spirit was alive and even thriving in this bizarre corner of the world -- at least for some people.

The car that he'd turned into his living quarters wasn't exactly a Cadillac, but it was surprisingly comfortable. Inviting, even. He enjoyed coming home to it after a day's work. He passed an empty Aston Martin and sneered. So expensive and stylish, and yet so useless in times like these, because of its small size. Nobody but a dwarf could live in an Aston Martin.

And many people *were* living in their cars, at least during the workweek. Some commuted home for the weekend, if home wasn't too far away. Many, however, rented out their homes to people who needed to stay near their jobs.

With all of this car-dwelling going on and interior space, naturally, limited, the living quickly spread outside. Welcome mats lay beneath car doors. Tiki torches and plastic tables and chairs appeared, shaded by striped umbrellas. There were even attempts at landscaping. Tiny patios were established by painted trellises blooming with hot pink bougainvillea, blue morning glories, honeysuckle and night-blooming jasmine and bordered by terra cotta planters filled with impatiens and ornamental grasses. Luminarias glowed at night.

The luckiest people in this new order were those with really big vehicles. Ira heard a story about one couple – vacationing senior citizens from Iowa – who'd gotten stuck in Century City. They sold their Winnebago (the story went) for three million dollars to some wealthy hot shot who lived in Pacific Palisades but worked near where the Winnebago got stuck. The price may have grown by exaggeration by the time the tale reached Ira's ears, but he'd heard enough similar accounts to know that it was probably somewhat accurate. If a buyer had the means and the necessity, he'd pay whatever he had to in order to get a vehicle that large -- and one that was already a fairly comfortable weekday living space was highly sought after. Ira was sure the buyer did the necessary upgrades to the Winnebago: marble countertops in the bathroom, post deconstructionist Italian lamps in whatever passed for the living room, 800 thread count Egyptian cotton sheets custom-fitted to the bed.

Some large vehicles that had been abandoned were up for grabs. City buses deserted by their drivers were seized by squatters who tore out the seats and slept on air mattresses on the floor. Untended big rigs were looted and liberated, their cargo stolen and their trailers turned into makeshift motels and other businesses. Ira knew of at least one truck in the vicinity that was being used as a brothel. Small businesses really were the backbone of the U.S.

It wasn't necessary to go anywhere for sex, however, if that's what one wanted. Like other goods and services, it was newly mobile. Vendors of all kinds strolled along the rows of parked cars with some regularity: prostitutes, religious missionaries, holistic health practitioners, police officers, Botox-injectors, security guards, manicurists, bicycle repairmen, political poll-takers, pet hypnotherapists, repairmen and panhandlers. Ira could buy a sack of oranges, a cell phone, ink pens, batteries, a therapeutic massage, a deck of cards, a haircut, condoms, bug spray, athletic socks, a photograph of his aura, potato chips, a joint, a music CD, a six-pack of beer, a magazine, a sub sandwich, razors, soap or a flashlight without going more than a few steps away from his car. Most brick-and-mortar stores were still open, but proprietors who were smart hired traveling salespeople to do outreach business. Online sales, on the other hand, were very much down in the Southland, since the previous means of delivering online purchases were rendered useless by the Big Stoppage.

This morning he got a banana-nutmeg-cranberry-juice-and-tofu smoothie from a woman who pushed a cart up and down the line of cars, mixing juice concoctions to order. From another merchant-on-wheels he purchased a sesame seed bagel with cream cheese. He shook his head, "Not today," to the woman who came around and collected dirty laundry for washing, then unfolded a small chair he kept under his car and sat in it while he ate his breakfast, warmed by the sunshine, entertained by the scene around him. He never used to be able to spend much time outdoors, or to be able to eat a leisurely breakfast. Like many, he had not known his neighbors. Now, circumstances put people in close proximity to one another with few barriers in between. Neighbors knew each other now, just like in the Midwest. In spite of the occasional territorial dispute, most dealings were friendly.

"Hiya, Ira!" The Tanners waved at him from above. As usual, they were lounging in the cockpit of their cabin cruiser, which sat atop the boat trailer that was hooked up to their pickup truck.

Ira waved back.

"Join us for an eye opener?" Marzipan Tanner leaned out and held her own drink aloft to entice him to come aboard.

Eyeing her black bikini-clad body, Ira noted that adding champagne to her morning orange juice did not harm her figure in any way. He tried to remember what she'd been before she got married. Was it an actress, or a model? Did it matter? He'd seen this male-female paradigm again and again since coming to L.A.: a beautiful woman married to a rich, often homely guy who was many years her senior. Marzipan was mid-thirties and terrific-looking, although she was at that hyper-tanned stage where her skin would begin to look like leather very soon. For the moment, though, her lustrous bronze hue made her legs and arms appear lean and sinewy. Her hair was streaked in many shades from golden blonde to coppery red to nut brown and her eyes changed color depending on the day, courtesy of tinted contact lenses. Today they were a bottle green.

Phil Tanner was also tanned. At least his balding head, his broad face and thick-fingered hands were. Ira could glimpse a somewhat tanned belly bulging sloppily over the waistband of Phil's shorts, although most of the man's upper body was mercifully hidden by a wildly colored Hawaiian shirt that he wore unbuttoned. Phil sat in the pilot's chair, as he usually did, with a Mimosa on the table beside him and an unlit cigar in his mouth. He tapped at the keyboard of a computer he held on his lap. Ira knew from Marzipan that her husband, after a successful career as a restaurateur and entrepreneur, sold off all his businesses and now lived strictly off his investments. One of the ways in which Phil had made a boatload of money, she confided to Ira one day, was with a highly successful diet plan called ChocoLose, a weight loss program that required its followers to eat diet candy bars five times a day. The only problem: they weren't diet candy bars. Ira dimly remembered the ChocoLose furor. It turned out that Phil, on the hunt for potentially lucrative liquidations, came into the possession of a warehouse full of

226

aging candy bars that were available at a cut-rate price. He repackaged them as diet products (getting very creative with the nutritional labeling), aired infomercials featuring happy, slender clients (in reality, anorexic actors) and sat back on his considerable haunches while the profits rolled in. By the time the fraud was uncovered, he'd made so much money that he didn't mind spending a fraction of it on some highly competent attorneys. In the end he paid a fine and agreed to get out of the diet business. That was all right with him, since he was just about out of ChocoLose bars. The funny thing was, Ira recalled, many people were angry about the government's interference in their inalienable right to choose the weight loss plan they preferred. A conspiracy theory raced around the internet: the medical establishment made so much money from obesity-related illnesses that its lobbyists pressured the Justice Department to crack down on ChocoLose, a product that really worked! Fat people agitated for more ChocoLose bars, and soon counterfeit bars with similar packaging popped up on the market.

These days, according to Marzipan, Phil busied himself with monitoring and tinkering with his portfolio. That was probably what he was doing right now.

Ira shook his head at the offer of a drink, not bothering to note that it was pretty early in the day to be boozing it up. He suspected that there was more than friendliness behind Marzipan's repeated invitations, in spite of the fact that they were usually made within earshot of her husband, who rarely went anywhere. Although Ira was tempted, he knew it would be a terrible idea to get involved in an adulterous affair with a woman – one almost old enough to be a cougar, no less -- who lived ten feet away from him. Nowhere to run, nowhere to hide. He shook his head, feigning regret. "Maybe later, Marz. I've got to get to work."

Disappointed, she gave a sad little wave and sipped at her drink while unrolling her exercise mat and beginning her Sun Salutations. Whatever excesses she indulged in, she never skipped her yoga routine.

The Tanners were people to whom things seemed to come easily, Ira thought, although he did not envy them as much as he would have pre-B.S. Caught in the Big Stoppage like everybody else, they had comfortable sleeping berths in the boat and lots of extra space in the pickup. The Tanners did not have day jobs to worry about. They held raucous parties onboard their boat, drawing fun, frivolous people who climbed up and down their ladder all night long, laughing indiscreetly, tossing empty beer cans overboard, talking loudly and sometimes sneaking into the pickup truck for noisy trysts.

Ira admired the Tanners' joie de vivre. Stuck in an unmoving ocean of cement, as idle as a painted ship upon a painted sea, they nonetheless managed to squeeze tremendous enjoyment from life just as they squeezed every last drop of juice from their oranges each morning. With limited space, he was sure they had to do without many household necessities, but by God, they had a juicer!

Ira finished eating, put away his chair and freed the bicycle rickshaw he kept chained to his rear bumper. The bike-shaw appeared in various manifestations on LA. streets soon after the B.S. The Pakistani from whom he'd gotten his did a nice job of constructing a narrow wheeled cart with a comfortable seat that attached to the back of his bicycle seat. Some people used bike-shaws for transporting family members behind them. For Ira, it was a moneymaker. With a prominent "For Hire" sign wired to his handlebars, he set off to earn the day's wages.

Ira O'Riley, former up-and-comer in the entertainment industry, former rubber-of-shoulders with Big Name Stars, now rode a wheeled taxi for a living. He laughed whenever he thought about it.

He loved it.

The B.S. turned out to be the best thing that ever happened to him. Because of it, he'd been transformed – had transformed himself, really – from a pale, wheezing, loser of an office worker to a strong and suntanned entrepreneur. OK: a manual laborer. He didn't mind that label at all. Once the smog lifted and his breathing eased, Ira discovered that walking, running and bicycling were actually *exciting*, that having a fully functioning cardiovascular system and sufficiently oxygenated blood pumping freely throughout his body gave him a strength and energy he'd never thought possible. He built up his endurance, day by day. The changes were internal as well. He no longer agonized over his career strategy or despaired of ever selling a script. If Sid called him tomorrow and begged him to come back to work, Ira would turn him down flat. When he thought about it, he was embarrassed by the petty scheming, the pointless one-upmanship he'd engaged in while sitting at his desk at Midwood. All that now was but a fiction, a dream of passion. His life was simple and satisfying and entirely under his control. Ira drove his bike-shaw every day he felt like it, picking up fares, meeting new people and making more money than he'd ever thought possible. When he wasn't working he was writing on his new laptop, the one he purchased with his bike-shaw earnings. His growing confidence enhanced his productivity. Once his depression over the loss of his screenplay lifted, he tasked himself with remembering everything he could about "His Majesty's Gangsta." Surprisingly, his memory yielded up a great many scenes. Some fragments of dialogue escaped his recall but he refused to get upset about that, choosing instead to believe that it was because better dialogue was waiting to be written. The newly realized story was coming along nicely. The newly realized Ira was serenely convinced in the inevitability of its being snapped up by a major studio and made into a highly successful movie. He had no doubts.

He no longer wrote in his blog. He didn't feel the need to write an ongoing letter to the world that never wrote to him. He did not read self-help books or listen to personal development tapes or attend screenwriting seminars. The time for learning was over. The time for doing was upon him.

"Hey! Hey! Over here!" He was being hailed by a clown in whiteface and a bright orange fright wig topped by a cartoonish straw hat. The long, rubbery-looking false eyelashes it wore made him guess it was a woman. She wore orange overalls, an oversized white blouse covered with enormous orange flowers and black clown shoes whose toes curled, elf-like, back toward her feet in stiff little leather waves. She waved her right arm enthusiastically in his direction, even though he was already headed toward her. In her left arm she held a listless Jack Russell terrier.

Ira continued angling his bike-shaw through slow-moving streams of pedestrians until he reached her.

229

"Thank God I saw you. It's just too far to walk." It *was* a woman. The bright red smile painted from ear to ear was at odds with the real mouth it engulfed, which was tense and unsmiling. Up close, the greasy white makeup appeared to be gradually sliding off her face, with a flesh-colored gap of forehead visible just below the wig. It was a hot day and the elaborate clown suit must be making her feel even warmer, Ira thought.

"It's all right about the dog, isn't it? You take dogs?"

"Of course," Ira assured her. "Unless there's a chance he'll bite me in the ass when my back is turned."

"No! Never." She sounded horrified. "Mr. Bojangles may be a little hyper, but he doesn't bite. He's a good dog." She petted the terrier's head and caught Ira's smile. "Oh. You were kidding, weren't you?"

Ira leaned his bike on its kickstand and helped her onto the cushioned seat of the bike-shaw – an unnecessary gesture but one which, he found, increased his tips dramatically when performed with female customers. Just to show that he was, indeed, a kidder, he patted the terrier on the head. Mr. Bojangles looked as if he'd *like* to nip at Ira, but he settled for baring his tiny white teeth at him.

"You can hold him in your lap?"

She nodded and gave him an address of a building a few miles distant. "I've got to get Mr. Bojangles to the vet. Poor thing. I was doing a kid's birthday party. Mr. Bojangles is part of my act. He's really well trained. Does all kinds of tricks. I told the people to keep their psycho Dalmatian inside, but the big bully pushed his way out the door and just went after Mr. Bojangles, who is about a fifth of his size. Mr. Bojangles shrieked and squealed. It sounded like he was being torn apart. I grabbed him and got him away from that psycho Dalmatian as fast as I could."

Ira pedaled hard, not minding the exertion at all. He nodded his head to show her he was listening. "Is Mr. Bojangles bleeding?"

"I don't see any marks, but there could be internal injuries."

Ira sized up the smaller of his two passengers in his side view mirror. Mr. Bojangles looked pissed off, not injured. "Maybe he's just shook up. You know. Scared."

"Or he could be in shock. It was a vicious attack." She looked doubtful. "I just have the feeling it's something serious. I gave him a tiny smidgeon of one of my Zolofts, because he was so upset. The vet said to get him there right away. I noticed you looking at my outfit, earlier."

The sudden shift in topic confused Ira. He tried to look as if he had been looking at her outfit.

"And I bet you were thinking: that's a lot of orange."

Ira, guiding his vehicle in between two parked cars, said: "Exactly what I was thinking."

"Orange is my favorite color. It reminds me of sunshine and vitamin C," she said. "I don't trust people who don't like the color orange. They usually don't have a very positive energy."

But they could always get one, with a few choice pharmaceuticals, he thought. He glanced at the clown in the mirror, wondering what kind of figure lurked beneath the overalls, and caught her looking at his back with an expression both admiring and speculative. Their eyes met.

"Are you an actor?" she asked.

"No."

"This job must be a great workout for you," she commented. "You're really cut. Ever thought about being a personal trainer?"

"I like what I'm doing. The freedom of the open road, and all that. Ok, the road's not exactly open, but you know what I mean. I like being my own boss."

"I'm really an actor, but clowning around pays the bills. I perform as a mime, too, although people don't seem to like mimes much anymore."

Did they ever? wondered Ira.

"I also like clowning because it got me into a group called Clowns for Jesus. We use laughter to bring Christ's message of hope to people in prisons and nursing homes. Are you a Christian?"

"Half," he said, feeling no need to elaborate. Neither of his parents were particularly religious. He was not lapsed, fallen away or self-hating. He was Catholic and Jewish by cultural embrace, not practice. His mother made latkes and occasionally used an expressive Yiddish word, as in, "Here, let me get that

231

schmutz off your sweater." Every December his father put Christmas lights on the big bushes in front of the house, but mainly because he loved the way the colors glowed when coated with freshly fallen snow.

To Ira's great relief, they arrived just then at her destination. She disembarked, still holding Mr. Bojangles. The little dog looked drowsy, but not unhappy.

"Maybe you could wait and take us home when the vet is through with Mr. Bojangles. I'd pay you for your time, of course."

"I'm afraid I've got a pick-up to make in the other direction," he said, trying to sound regretful. "I sure hope your little dog is all right, though."

She disappeared inside the clinic and he resumed riding. He knew the clown had more in mind than a ride home. She was a little too complicated for him. The drama potential was high. Antidepressants and Jesus all rolled into a big orange ball. Clowntastic. Besides, it was impossible to tell what she looked like under the clown face.

Why couldn't she be Lupe Sevá? That would be convenient, wouldn't it? If she could see him now, Lupe might have a whole different reaction to him now. Maybe Gary was history by now; just another good-looking guy who broke Lupe's heart. Did she still work at that salon in Beverly Hills? He should Google her. Ira would love to track her down, make it seem like an accidental meeting. Let her get a good look at the new Ira.

It was an unexpected benefit of his new reality that female passengers (along with more than a few males) hit on him at an astounding rate. He discovered that the percentage went even higher when he didn't wear a shirt. Although still lean, he'd bulked up enough to have some real definition in his arms and chest. Daily pedaling while pulling extra weight had turned his legs into powerful pistons. Wearing shorts and frequently going shirtless left his formerly pasty skin looked tawny.

Apparently there was something about a bronzed, sweaty man breathing heavily on their behalf that aroused women. He sometimes accepted their sexual offers. He always accepted their excessive tips. Ira finished work each day a happy man.

He liked the independence as well. He could have had more security with one of the large bike-shaw companies that formed quickly after the B.S. Someone from The Shiksa's Rickshaws contacted him to offer him a job that would have included a guaranteed weekly wage, rain or shine, plus health insurance. He'd declined. It was better, much better, to be a sole proprietor. He was racking up a big bundle of profits, which he securely stashed in a safe that was welded to the undercarriage of his car.

State and federal and local tax assessors went on foot among the auto-condos, sniffing about to find post-B.S. entrepreneurs operating cash businesses who weren't reporting their income. They almost always returned to their posts at the end of the day with no new businesses to add to the rolls. The scofflaws were legion, crafty, and abetted by their fellow citizens. People were particularly incensed that the state government would have the nerve to try and collect taxes, since Sacramento had done so little to prevent the B.S. That some of the dislocated were enterprising enough to wring profitable new businesses out of the mess was a testament to inventive individualism, not the result of any assistance from the government.

Ira wasn't worried about being caught. He was paid in Yankee dollars and kept no records. He was off the grid! To hell with the government. Being an honest, law-abiding, tax-paying citizen had never gotten him anywhere but broke and homeless.

He paused for a drink of bottled water in the shade of a Jacaranda tree then resumed his runs. He enjoyed a steady stream of customers until midday, when he found himself near a public library and decided to take an air-conditioned break while checking out the new fiction titles. Maybe he'd grab some lunch after that. A pita wrap sounded good. Ira was sitting at one of the library's tables when a tinny version of Tom Petty's "Freefalling" erupted from his pocket. His cell phone was ringing.

"Ira? It's me. Oceana."

"Oceana." He drew a blank.

"From the anti-car demonstration? I was with Generation Air, remember? We were there with the Valley Breathers and the PulmoNation. We got attacked by some oil industry goons. You were having an asthma attack and I came over and talked with you."

"Yeah. Yeah! Of course I remember you. It just took me a minute to place your name." *I would never forget what you look like, though.*

"Yeah, well, no wonder. It's been awhile. I found your card and thought I'd call you."

How long had it been since that day, he wondered? That turning point of a day. Weeks? Decades? So much had changed in L.A. since then that it felt like it had been a lifetime ago, but it had been less than a year.

"How are you, Oceana?" He pictured her with pleasure: big doe eyes, sexy rumpled boy-short hair, long slim legs. The man at the table next to his looked over at him and glared meaningfully. Ira got up and left the library.

"Just fine. Busy. How are you feeling these days, Ira? Better, I hope?"

"I'm a different man. I can breathe now."

"Yes. I'm happy to hear it, but not surprised. We're hearing that a lot. And it's funny that you should mention it. It's why I'm calling. Have you given any thought to joining us? We can use all the activists we can get."

"How do you mean?"

"Our organization. Generation Air."

"I'm not really a joiner. Definitely not political."

"Ira, how can you say that?" Her voice was musical, with an undercurrent that was friendly, rather than overbearing. "You above all people should know what a difference clean air makes. You're feeling it these days. You're not breathing easier by accident, you know."

His impulse was to shut her down as an annoyance, but he paused. She had a point. She wasn't just another one of the many special-interest zealots – ok, kooks, that thrived in the Southern California sunshine. His life was infinitely better than it had been before the B.S. He was strong and athletic, full of energy. That was indisputably due to the vast improvement in the air quality. Still, the word activist made him cringe. And yet…she was hot. No harm in getting together with her and her little group and hearing them out. Letting her see the new and improved Ira up close. He was cocky enough now to think that he could get a woman like her -- a woman who would definitely have been out of his league, pre-B.S. In fact, he should probably make her work hard to win him over to her way of thinking. It might take several social outings, where she'd do her best to persuade him to join the activists while he did *his* best to get her drunk and horny.

"What do you have in mind?" He tried to sound sincere.

"You heard about that heli-lift the government is planning for tomorrow at noon?"

"What the hell is a heli-lift?"

She didn't catch his comedic lob. Did she have a sense of humor? He concluded that he didn't care. He was funny enough for both of them.

"They're going to use helicopters to airlift vehicles from key intersections in an attempt to get traffic flowing again. It's madness, because there's still no serious plan developed for reducing the total number of cars. Even if this works, it'll still just be a temporary fix. It's mainly a media event, to make it look like Olmstead's actually doing something."

"Yeah, no surprise. I stopped paying attention to the news because the politicians and business leaders have been wrangling over a solution ever since the B.S. happened, and they've come up with nada. Nothing. Squat. I'm a little surprised that they've even managed to agree on this...heli-lift."

He heard a familiar blast, saw a familiar fireball. Still clutching his cell phone, he quickly ducked back inside the library's solid brick vestibule to avoid bits of flaming wreckage raining down on the street outside. Pedestrians scattered in panic, looking for cover. A piece of fiery fuselage landed on a canvas awning shading a florist's shop, setting it on fire. A man wearing a green apron over his clothing ran out of the shop with a fire extinguisher and aimed it upward, although its foamy contents didn't shoot high enough to reach most of the flaming awning. Other bits of debris were hurled to the earth by the force of the blast. Ira watched in horror as a heavy-set woman was nearly hit by a large chunk of...something. It missed her, but she shrieked as if it had scored a direct hit.

He couldn't blame her. As often as this scenario was being played out every day in the Southland, it was still terrifying. Many people developed a sense of fatalism to help them cope with the possibility of sudden death from the sky. When there were injuries, paramedics would be summoned to treat them, but since they were still forced to respond to emergencies on foot, pushing their gurneys in front of them, the mortality rate was high.

Rich people were idiots, he thought angrily. They refused to be inconvenienced by the B.S. like the common folk, so they bought or hired helicopters to carry them high over the unattractive gridlock that marred the landscape below. They built helipads at their estates, and at golf courses and resorts and casinos and atop buildings which housed trendy restaurants or high-end stores. They hired their own pilots when they could, luring them from all over the United States with exorbitant salaries, but demand still exceeded supply because very few people wanted to move to Southern California right now. Thus, quickie flight schools sprang into existence, allowing inexperienced owners to illegally and egoistically fly their own craft in the increasingly crowded skies. Bribes were paid, licenses issued before the required number of hours logged in the air. There were many, many crashes, but that didn't stop the practice.

"That sounded close," Oceana said. "You OK?"

"Yeah. Fine." He turned his back on the disturbing, all-too-routine scene.

"How about it, Ira? We need all the warm bodies we can get, to show the governor that we mean business. It's important that we don't go back to the insanity we used to have here, and you know politicians. They're all in the pockets of corporations and special interests. We need to form our own lobby, Ira. Create a whole new way of life here. To do that, we need the help of people like you."

She still talked like a movie script, but Ira didn't mind. She was hot.

CHAPTER THIRTY-NINE:
THE BEST METHOD FOR KICKING PUPPIES

"Can I have your autograph, please?"

"Me, too."

Luanne wondered if she would ever stop being thrilled at hearing this. Not anytime soon, that was certain.

The bike-shaw driver she'd flagged down waited patiently while she obliged the two teenage girls who held out school notebooks for her to sign. The excited, surprised expressions on their faces when they saw her walking down the street was something she was going to savor for awhile. It was as if they couldn't believe that Luanne Sajewski – a TV star! – was right here in their midst.

"No one's going to believe me." The taller of the two girls was so overcome that she nearly choked, trying to get the words out.

"We love 'Aunt Mom," said the other. "You are so funny. You are the best one on that show."

The taller one found her voice. "I'm your biggest fan."

"Well thank you," Luanne said. "I appreciate your watching the show." It sounded stiff. Like she was trying too hard to be a regular Jane. She'd have to come up with something better than that. Was there a secret handbook of helpful clichés for successful actors? Things to say to fans? Sound bytes for the red carpet? Could she really consider herself a successful actor? It was only one show. (*Stop being so modest, Luanne: it's one MONSTER HIT of a show.*)

The girls took turns standing with her and snapping photos with their cell phones, and then hurried off, talking on cells, no doubt reporting the celebrity encounter to their networks of friends.

Luanne shrugged and smiled at the bike-shaw driver, as if embarrassed. Damn, he was cute! His eyes were grey-blue, his sexy mouth curved in an amused smile. His face was quirky and intriguing, not the kind of pretty boy face that was so ubiquitous in L.A. Underneath a tight black t-shirt, he had just the kind of lean, hard build she liked. His chest and arms were sculpted and looked rock hard. In a surprisingly courtly gesture, he helped her aboard the bike-shaw then seated himself. She was going to enjoy looking at his back during the ride. He had some serious body karate going on.

With the help of a personal trainer and nutritionist – whose fees each cost more than Luanne used to earn in six months as a temp, Luanne had lost a few pounds, but she was still plump and pear-shaped, at least by L.A. standards. Still, her newfound success had given her a tremendous confidence boost, as well as a budget that allowed her to buy figure-flattering clothes. Her sexual confidence was unleashed, although she wasn't entirely sure what to do with it yet.

"Where to?"

She gave him the address for Cap Lessing's radio station. He tapped it into a small GPS device strapped to his handlebars and got rolling.

Luanne wondered if he recognized her, or even watched the show. Although it hadn't been on that long, "Aunt Mom" was a ginormous hit. Although she'd been a celebrity for all of five minutes, she was astounded by the number of times she got recognized. It gave her keen awareness of the power of television. She was dazzled by the speed with which this had all happened.

True to his word, once Sid signed her as a client he did his best to represent her. Turned out that his best was pretty darn good. One of the actors in the pilot for a promising new sitcom didn't test well with audiences and had to be replaced quickly. It was only a recurring role but a juicy one, with lots of great lines -- not the fat, funny friend but the fat, funny sister of the lead role. Because of the traffic mess, Luanne practically had to break her neck to get to the audition. She couldn't pick up the sides in advance and had to do a cold reading, but as soon as she saw the frazzled producer's shoulders relax, heard the fat casting director laugh, she knew she'd nailed it.

The sitcom itself was in turmoil. L.A.'s paralysis prompted dramatic changes to many TV and movie productions. The set for this one was hastily moved to Las Vegas, which necessitated finding lodging for the cast and crew. Luanne barely had time to learn her co-stars' names before she was thrust in front of cameras, but she knew with all her heart that she had to rise to this challenge, seize this opportunity. Everything had happened for a reason, even the helicopter crash. What seemed like terrible events at the time were, in retrospect, the universe's way of nudging her toward her destiny.

She was an immediate hit. America laughed and laughed at her: her hilariously wry delivery, her brilliant comic timing, her uninhibited expressions and body language. She blessed the writers for giving her such great material. For the most part, her co-stars were happy to have her on board, because prior to her casting, the role was a black hole that threatened the future of the show. The star of "Aunt Mom," however, replaced her initial tentative welcome with a cold, professional demeanor. Luanne couldn't understand why. Rita Webb was an established actress with a long list of credits on her resumé. A star. Luanne was terribly excited about working with her and was always respectful in her dealings with Rita, hoping that the older woman would be her mentor.

"You don't see it?" Peter Walker, who played the husband, asked her one day. "You're getting more laughs than her. The audience loves you. You're the breakout star. The writers have been busy rewriting the scripts to give you more lines. You didn't notice?"

Well, yes, as a matter of fact, she had. She just assumed Rita was secure enough to handle a rookie like Luanne getting a little attention. When Sid called her to tell her that she was going from recurring to series regular, Luanne knew that she was living the dream.

The dream still didn't include a serious boyfriend, although she'd had a brief fling recently with a key grip. She wasn't sure of the etiquette, but if Julia Roberts could marry a cameraman, she supposed it was all right if she had sex with a member of the crew. When she realized that she would have to keep seeing him even after their little affair ran its course, it was awkward, and a lesson learned. Next time, she would avoid anyone associated with her own show. No fraternization in the workplace.

A pang of loneliness seized her unexpectedly. Next time, she hoped to have more than a fling. Her newfound career success, as welcome as it was, didn't fill the romance gap that she'd lived with for so long, and she worried that nothing ever would. What was it about her, that she couldn't attract true love? Where was her soul mate? The conviction that there was something fundamentally wrong, something fundamentally unlovable about her refused to be banished by the rush of fame. America (or a large portion of it) adored her, but when she went home at night, it was to a lonely suite in a Vegas hotel. Was she destined to spend her life without a soul mate? The fear made her terribly sad. Why *wouldn't* someone fall in love with her?

"You going to be on Cap Lessing's show because of 'Aunt Mom'?" the driver inquired.

So he did know who she was. "Yes."

He grinned. "You're brave."

Gosh, he was cute. His comment gave her pause. Lessing had a reputation for being an asshole. He didn't usually do lightweight interviews with actors, but Sid had lined this one up, along with a bunch of other promotional appearances, to fill her brief time off from taping the show. "His producer claims he's a big fan of the show," Sid had said. Sid wouldn't put her in a bad situation, would he?

"Oh, I'm sure it'll just be a friendly chat," she said. "A change of pace for him, before he goes on to his next segment, where he'll launch a campaign to do away with Mother's Day and then advise his Caplets on the best method for kicking puppies."

The driver laughed, meeting her eye in his rear view mirror.

"I've seen 'Aunt Mom.' I enjoy your work. You have a terrific comic ability and you make it seem so natural. You're a pleasure to watch."

She smiled, genuinely pleased. He was smooth. "Thanks. I still can't believe how well it's caught on. I don't hear good things about Lessing, but I guess you have to promote things." She shrugged nonchalantly. It was a gesture she'd practiced in order to look humble, which she was, even though she was on one of the top-rated TV shows in the country. "It's all still kind of new to me."

It was an opening, but disappointingly, he didn't take it. Instead he nodded, smiled again, then stopped the bike-shaw just long enough to slip ear-buds into his ears and turn on the mp3 player he wore in an armband on his right arm.

She'd thought they were having a moment, then chided herself: what did it matter? She didn't even live in L.A. full-time at the moment, although she was renting an apartment she seldom got to in Studio City. There was no point in entertaining fantasies about some stranger. Of course, the show would wrap not too far down the road and she'd be free to return to the Southland. Maybe traffic would be back to normal by then. She sighed and settled back in her seat to study her script for the next episode, occasionally glancing up at the driver. She liked the way those little muscles on the backs of his upper arms flexed when he gripped the handlebars. Watching him work up a sweat on her behalf was arousing in some primitive way.

Cap Lessing turned out to be a surprise. The few times she'd listened to his program, she'd pictured him as an obnoxious but compelling figure; tall and fit (his speech was so energetic that he must be, too). She pictured him in a crisp polo shirt and khakis – definitely not a suit. In person, Cap Lessing proved to be a disgusting slob. His navy blue t-shirt was marred by stains that did not look fresh, and did such a poor job of stretching over his expansive paunch that there was a bulge of bare skin visible above his belt. Appallingly, he wore an oversized silver belt buckle that drew attention to his gut. The buckle bore naked women in silhouette, seated back to back –the image so often seen on the mud flaps of trucks. Like too many men, he wore his jeans below his belly so that they hung limply in the back; when he turned she saw a hint of his buttocks crack, although she tried not to look. He had graying, unkempt hair that splayed untidily over his head like a mutant form of moss. His red-rimmed caramel-colored eyes burned with intelligence and unfocused hostility; she made a note to stay wary of him. Also, he was black. She hadn't expected that.

The commercial spot-set was coming to an end as Lessing's producer ushered her into the studio and made quick introductions. She didn't have time to get a reading on Lessing's non-radio personality, if he had one. The producer directed her to a chair in front of a microphone that was kitty-corner to Lessing's. She noticed Lessing gulping from a cracked blue ceramic coffee cup. It would have been nice if the producer had offered her coffee, or at least a bottled water. Just thinking about it made her mouth feel dry. Or was she nervous? This kind of thing – being interviewed – was still such a novelty. People actually treated her as if she was important, as if she had something meaningful to say! She thought she would never get tired of it.

With no warning, a red light snapped on overhead. Lessing abruptly began talking, not bothering to look at her. Luanne found it unsettling.

"We're back to the Cap Lessing Program on K-Talk-L.A., Hot News and Provocative Views. My guest today is Luanne Sajewski, the girl everyone's talking about. Luanne, of course, is the one stealing the spotlight on that hot new sitcom, 'Aunt Mom.' How does Rita Webb like that, by the way? You, a newbie, getting all the attention?"

Because he was still not looking at her, she felt sideswiped by the question. She stammered idiotically. "Well, she...I..."

Mercifully, he didn't give her much time to respond. "I hear she's a lesbian. Is that true? Has she put any moves on you?"

Luanne practically choked. "She's married!"

"And that proves what, exactly?" Lessing snorted. Or was that laughter? "So, no close, naked encounters, in the ladies' locker room?"

She was dumbfounded. "There's no lad—"

"Teasing, Luanne. Lighten up. Of course there's no locker room. I'm sure you highly paid, pampered TV stars have your own individual dressing rooms. I was just indulging in a little fantasy. Are you a lesbian, by the way? You do remind me of Rosie O'Donnell."

She sputtered ineffectually. Her heart pounded like it did when the helicopter was plummeting toward the earth.

"Never mind. If you are, I'm sure you're under strict instructions not to reveal it. After all, look how long it took Ellen to come out of the closet. Now Luanne, everyone is talking about your sudden rise to fame. Just remember: the quicker they rise, the quicker they fall. I've heard your back story. We've all heard your back story, because America loves nothing better than a rags to riches tale. You came to town right before the B.S. –

242

brilliant timing, by the way -- and miraculously managed to sign with a top agent, someone with the power to get you an audition for a network sitcom. How does that even happen, Luanne? Sid Kirschenbaum usually only takes on an actor after she's got a pretty solid career established in this town."

"Cap, I did a lot of theatre in Chicago. I had quite a lot of credits to my name before—"

Another snort. "Theatre in Chicago?" he said, in a tone that suggested that Chicago theatre was on the same level as a grade school talent show. "If you've just joined us on K-Talk-L.A., my guest today is Luanne Sajewski, star of 'Aunt Mom.'"

"I've been pursing my craft for a long time." She was determined not to be steamrolled by him. "Studying acting. Taking classes. Doing plays - show after show, in fact."

"I'm sure you did, Luanne." He nodded sagely, suddenly sincere, which threw her off balance. "You have a great deal of talent, and you've obviously honed your skills and put in a lot of hard work. But still, someone like you normally wouldn't even get in the door of that agency, much less get signed. A hundred Luanne Sa-joo-skis—"

"It's Sigh-EF-ski," she interrupted, not seeing the danger that was just ahead.

"Sorry. A hundred Luanne Sigh-EF-skis from Chicago or Portland or Savannah get off the bus here every day. A lot of them have been pursuing their craft and honing their skill. Many of them are beautiful." He paused, significantly. She hated him.

"One TV writer said that people like me because I look like them, not like some glamorous—"

"Oh, yes," he said. "You do look like someone we'd see at a county fair in Nebraska or North Carolina, strolling along the midway and eating one of those deep fried Elephant Ears. You know, the ones as big as dinner plates? With about five thousand calories each?"

She was flummoxed. She felt wounded, then furious. She really, really, really wanted to punch him, but she forced herself to aim for a light tone. Maybe this was still salvageable. If she showed that she could keep her cool with this jerk, that she could hold her own, she'd come out the winner. As it was, this train wreck of an interview was going to make her "the buzz" in the media for a few days at least. A sympathetic character. That was fine. She could live with that, but she wasn't willing to go so far as to play the victim.

She aimed for a light, teasing tone, but her subtext was: I am stabbing him between the ribs. His blood is splashing out in spurts. I am enjoying it. "What are you saying, Cap? And by the way, your listeners may not realize it, but you're not exactly a lightweight yourself."

"Oooooo. America's favorite new funny woman shows her claws! Touché, Luanne. You got me there. I'm a fat man. F-A-T, not P-H-A-T. I've got the perfect face and figure for radio. My Caplets already know that. But we're not talking about me. We're talking about you. On K-Talk-L.A., incidentally. You may be considered downright svelte in Altoona, Pennsylvania, but in this town, you're HUUUUUUUUUUUUGE. I don't pussyfoot around, like a lot of people in L.A. I call it like I see it. So the question you haven't yet answered is: how did you catch the eye of Sid Kirschenbaum? A man who represents some of the most gorgeous actresses in an industry full of gorgeous actresses? What's your secret, Luanne? How did you get Cody Torrance's agent to agree to represent you?"

It was as if, in an empty field somewhere, the ground suddenly opened up and missiles armed with nuclear warheads emerged, their sleek snouts pushing skyward, their menace becoming clearer with every inch of steel that rose above the land. He knew. He knew, or suspected. How much did he know?

How should she handle this?

After she and Cody were brought back to civilization, Sid Kirschenbaum thoroughly debriefed her, extracting a minute description of every incident that had taken place from the time she and Cody met to the moment the hummercopter descended on Blake's peaceable kingdom and demolished his garden. She could tell by the parts Sid dwelled on which aspects of the adventure bothered him the most. In the real world, they wouldn't have counted for much. They would have made for funny anecdotes to tell friends. In the world of the entertainment industry, where this story needed to be spun out to the media in exactly the right way, the scenes where Cody Torrance – action star – ran into a ladies' room and begged for help, sat in a stall of said ladies' room to call his agent, threw up during a helicopter ride and rode in a wheelbarrow reeking of manure were not details that would enhance Cody's public persona. "He's a human being," Luanne had said. "People know that." Sid shook his head impatiently. "No they don't, and they don't want to. And I don't want them to."

Sid got Luanne to sign a confidentiality agreement and gave her $5,000 for doing so. He added her to his client list but seemed pleasantly surprised by her demo video, as if he hadn't really expected her to be any good. However, would he be representing her if his most famous client hadn't barfed in front of her? Luanne had no idea if the rather severe penalties spelled out in the confidentiality agreement would be enforceable, and she didn't want to find out. If she were hauled into court over this, she could lose a lot: money (which she had some of, now), and Sid's goodwill. Sid could sink her career. She didn't doubt his power to do that for a minute. She was still new. He could make her disappear just as quickly as he'd caused her to vault to prominence. She'd be done in this town.

She was not going to let Cap Lessing engineer her destruction.

"He saw my demo and liked it," she said.

"Really? Because I have inside information that there was a woman with Cody Torrance when he was rescued from that canyon, after the helicopter crash. A woman who has never been heard from since, which is strange. If I was in an accident like that with a famous movie star, I would be all over Good Morning America and Entertainment Tonight, talking about it. I would claim my fifteen minutes of fame -- especially if I was a would-be actress who needed to jump-start my career."

She sputtered. "Inside information, Cap? What are you, the CIA?"

"I'm got a lot more sources than the CIA." It was weird how he still didn't look at her. It was like he was in his own little world inside this studio, on-air guest or no. "I've got lots and lots of sources, with new ones being added to my collection of Caplets all the time. Everybody wants to tell me something I don't know, so that I will turn around and tell it to the world. Now, as I was saying, this woman who was with Cody Torrance was described as being average-looking, with medium-length brown hair, brown-eyes and a big ass. Does that sound familiar, Luanne?"

She forced herself to stay calm. "That sounds like any number of—"

"My source heard this woman called 'Luanne,' by Kirschenbaum's assistant. He couldn't remember the last name, but thought it sounded Polish or Jewish. Sigh-ef-ski is Polish, isn't it, Luanne? And the name Luanne – not all that common, wouldn't you agree?"

She was busy thinking: Sid's rescue team wasn't as trustworthy as he thought, or maybe someone who was at the hospital was the "source," but she maintained her composure enough to say: "This is ridiculous! Whatever big secret you think you've uncovered—"

"Well that's just it, Luanne. What is the big secret? We all know Cody Torrance was in a helicopter accident. Good God— he received tens of thousands of get well cards, and gave interviews from his hospital bed. What we don't know is what happened in between when he was running from a mob down Santa Monica Boulevard and when he was rescued in the canyon?"

"How should I—"

"C'mon, Luanne. Give the Caplets some credit. My listeners have a much higher-than-average IQ. The fact that a woman with your first name, matching your description, was being represented by a powerful Hollywood agent just days after his biggest client was in a crash is just too much of a coincidence. We know that woman was you. We know you were there. How you came to be with Cody is what fascinates me. After all, you just got to town. You were a nobody. You sure don't look like the kind of woman Cody usually dates. And sometimes marries. For you to have been with Cody when he was rescued meant that you had to have been with him in that helicopter. Why not just admit it?"

She was overwhelmed with panic, even more so when she realized that for the first time, he was giving her a chance to answer. He stared at her. He waited. The dead air went on for an agonizingly long time.

"This is ridiculous," she gasped, realizing how stupid she sounded. "I thought you wanted to talk about 'Aunt Mom,'"

"We did talk about it," Lessing said. "Didn't we talk about Rita Webb being a lesbian?"

Oh, God. Would this never end? She should walk out right now. What was keeping her stuck in this chair? Didn't this awful man have to play some commercials or something?

"We're done with 'Aunt Mom.' What I want to talk about NOW on the Cap Lessing show on K-Talk-L.A. is Cody Torrance. So tell me, Luanne, what is it that you're not telling us about Cody? Did he cause the crash? Are you trying to keep the pilot's family from suing him over it? Was Cody on his way to visit his gay lover when the crash happened? Is that it?"

"Boy, you're really stuck on the gay thing, Cap," she said weakly, trying to sound humorous. "Why is that, I wonder?"

"You haven't answered my question. What do you have on Cody Torrance? What big secret are you holding over his head? I have to say, Luanne, I expected better from you. An honest, upstanding girl from the Midwest."

"I'm from Pennsylvania—"

"Whatever." He turned away from her to glance at his computer screen. "Oh, you Caplets. Lighting up my phone lines to talk to Luanne. I, too, want her to answer my questions, and not just keep dancing around them. Maybe you'll have better luck than me. Bert from Sherman Oaks, Vijay from West Hollywood and Lucy from Agoura Hills, stay on the line. You'll get a shot at Luanne right after this on K-Talk-L.A., Hot News and Provocative Views." The red light overhead went off.

She stood and grabbed her purse. "You son of a bitch."

"Whatever do you mean?" He pretended to be wounded.

"What a scummy way to make a living. You are an asshole."

He laughed. "I'm an entertainer, same as you. If you really do have nothing to hide, why not say so? Why not admit you were with Cody? The fact that you won't tells me a lot."

"Bullshit!"

"Stick around, Luanne, and you can set the record straight. This commercial break will be over in two minutes."

247

Lessing didn't seem at all surprised to see her hurry out of the studio. She couldn't get out of there fast enough. The producer, tucked away in a glass-walled studio adjoining Lessing's studio, was too busy pushing controls on a board to see her out. Mortifyingly, she was going so fast that she got lost in the labyrinthine radio station and got temporarily lost in the cubicle-studded area of what she guessed to be the sales department before finding the receptionist's desk and beyond that, the exit.

She was emerging from the elevator on the ground floor, still shaking with fury and embarrassment, when her cell phone vibrated. She pulled it from her purse and looked at the screen. It was Sid.

Great. Just great. She couldn't wait to talk to him. She lit a cigarette before she snapped open her phone. It was awkward, juggling both items, but it was worth it.

CHAPTER FORTY: BLAH, BLAH, BLAH

Cody Torrance was just a little sad that Victoria Stedwyck was gone, although she was a little noisy in bed for his taste. His delightful brunette co-star from "Choke Holder and Wiser" joined him at this idyllic spot for a time after the movie wrapped, but like so many of the überambitious actresses he coupled with, she was terribly focused on her career and had to go off and campaign for other roles and other projects after a short but sexually charged respite with Cody.

He was glad he didn't have to expend all that energy on his work. Projects came to him, not vice versa. Of course he realized that some day that could change, or that he might come to want different sorts of roles than the ones so consistently presented to him. He would worry about that then.

Oahu was the ideal place for not thinking about the future. When he was finished with Wiser and the traffic mess in L.A. still wasn't cleared up, his manager rented him this luxurious, secluded villa, right on the beach, complete with staff. Cody had no idea how much it was costing him, and he didn't care. It was paradise. A healing place. A warm, breeze-kissed oasis of white sand and translucent turquoise water where he spent his days windsurfing and snorkeling and his nights quietly, reading or watching television.

He put the mental trauma of the helicopter crash behind him rather quickly, possibly because he'd been too ill at that moment to fully apprehend what was happening. The physical consequences still troubled him a little. Surgery and intensive exercise eventually restored his broken leg to almost full function (Sid was afraid of a permanent limp), but Cody still had to work on it here three days a week, under the supervision of a local physical therapist, in a room of the villa that had been specially equipped with elaborate fitness machines. It was a shame, really. Paradise should not have a bossy, polo shirt-clad therapist named Maleko and instruments of sweat and torture in it.

The scar over his rib cage was prominent. He considered having plastic surgery to eliminate it, but wasn't sure he wanted to. Even Sid, usually so decisive, was on the fence about it. The jagged ridge of damaged skin – so close to the heart! – was kind of a perfect fit for Buck Buchanan. It would look good in those swimsuit pictures the paparazzi were always taking of him as he romped in the surf. Maj was so impressed with it that he made sure Buck had several shirtless scenes in the movie and didn't conceal the scar with makeup.

The headaches were another matter. Long after the concussion abated he remained plagued by episodes of dull, throbbing pain that a secession of neurologists said should not be there. Well they were. In the midst of some wonderful day, pummeling bad guys on the set as Buck Buchanan or here, swimming amid gloriously vivid coral and curious tropical fish, the heavy sensation would clamp onto his brain like a vise, fouling his mood, scrambling his thoughts. Sometimes the pain woke him up at night and he lay in stiff agony in his sumptuous, king-size bed, heart thumping resentfully, waiting for control of his head to be returned to him.

Victoria had given him massages which he pretended helped, although they didn't. The excruciating ache came and went on its own schedule, regardless of treatments. After getting little relief from conventional medicine he'd turned to alternative remedies: acupuncture, biofeedback, unpronounceable Chinese herbs that had to be burned and inhaled. They smelled disgusting and accomplished nothing. He used his prescription painkillers sparingly. He'd seen too many of his colleagues go the route of excess with those.

Tonight was, so far, one of the good nights. He relaxed hopefully. Maybe he would end the day and sleep through the night without a visit from what he'd started to think of as his little friend. He skipped his customary cocktail on the balcony at sunset and asked Kaki for an early dinner. It was, as usual, prepared in a simple but superb manner: a calamari salad followed by broiled red snapper. He ate with relish, although he found himself wishing he had someone to talk to. Kaki, the cook, customarily hid in the kitchen until he finished and retired to the den, at which time she apparently emerged and cleared away the dishes without a sound, because a short time later – if he bothered to look -- he would find an empty table, a spotless kitchen, and no Kaki. She seemed to be in awe of him.

Should he go back to Malibu, even if the roads were intolerable?

In the den he sank heavily into the plush white cushions of an oversized Balinese teak chair and tried to read scripts sent over by Sid, but he couldn't focus. His restlessness made him anxious. It was still early. What would he do with his evening? He could go and seek out some night life, although he had no one to run interference for him should some fans become bothersome, as some usually did. Maybe he should call one of his ex-wives, have a long chat. He tried to remember which one would be most likely to speak with him.

Cody put the scripts aside and turned on the television, clicking impatiently from one muted satellite-delivered channel to another. Sound sometimes annoyed him. He stopped at a 24-hour news station which was running a story about L.A. under the banner, "Breaking News." Something to do with the traffic. There was that bumbling governor, Olmstead, talking into a bank of microphones. Was the man finally going to do something about the problem? When you really thought about it, it was Olmstead's incompetence that caused Cody to get into a helicopter accident and end up with these horrific headaches. If Cody hadn't gotten stuck in traffic and chased by a celebrity-crazed crowd, he wouldn't have had to escape by air. Cody demuted the sound.

"…so we are unable to disclose, in advance, exactly where the heli-lifts will take place. We *can* tell you, however, that we anticipate immediate improvement in the freeways indicated on this screen." Olmstead gestured toward a large electronic map in which several lines now pulsed with green light.

"Governor Olmstead, do you honestly believe that these environmental activists you speak of—

"Environmental *terrorists*, Ron," Olmstead corrected.

"That they have the numbers and the will to disrupt a government operation as tightly coordinated as you say this one will be?"

"From what we've been able to determine, Generation Air has managed to put together a fairly large coalition of like-minded fanatics."

"You said, 'from what we've been able to determine.' Does the government have a confidential informant? Someone on the inside?"

"I won't discuss that, except to say that Mayor Luna assures me that the Los Angeles police department has excellent information-gathering abilities within the environmentalist community. The folks from Generation Air are, naturally, free to engage in peaceful, lawful demonstrations. They are not free to interfere with the helicopters that will lift the selected vehicles out of the way."

"You think they mean to do that"

"It's a possibility. That's why we're keeping the specific locations a secret until just before the heli-lift is to take place. The pilots won't be informed of their targets until just before take-off."

"But why would Generation Air block the heli-lift?"

Olmstead shrugged and smiled ruefully. "You'll have to ask their leaders that question. As best we can determine, they don't want things to get back to normal. They are contrarians. Malcontents. Anti-progress. We are, all of us, concerned about global warming, but these ecoterrorists want to send us back to the day of the horse and carriage, and that's just not realistic. They don't seem to care about the widespread misery that the Big Stoppage has caused for so many residents of southern California. Their agenda ignores that unpleasant reality."

"But Governor Olmstead, won't any improvement caused by the heli-lift be temporary? And limited to a few areas? After all this time, and all the wrangling we've seen among your office, state legislators and local governments, shouldn't there be a more comprehensive solution by now?"

Olmstead looked pained, but just for a second. He quickly found his smiling, confident politician face and put it back on, reminding Cody of why he took such little interest in politics.

"That comprehensive plan is under development and will be revealed as soon as possible. I don't have to tell you that it's a complex problem. If there were a simple solution, we would have implemented it already. In the meantime—"

Cody impatiently clicked the channel button and got rid of Olmstead's press conference, fearing that annoyance might bring on one of his headaches. It was pointless, anyway. Blah, blah, blah. Cody had little faith in this silly heli-lift. It sounded like a stunt staged for the media. What would moving a few cars out of the way really accomplish? It was just a good thing that Cody didn't have to return to Los Angeles soon. He could afford to wait this thing out. Hell, he could afford to never work again, if it came to that. He would be bored, though, he reflected. He must develop some interesting hobbies.

He landed on a new channel, paused, then smiled and set the remote on the end table next to him. Ah, "Aunt Mom." He loved this show. That Luanne Sajewski was just a delight. So funny! Such a magnetic quality. It was wonderful, how she'd managed to get successful so quickly, just like Cody had. Well Sid was a superb agent, wasn't he? Cody wondered if she remembered him, if she still thought of their brief, adventurous time together.

He sure did.

CHAPTER FORTY-ONE:
FARTING RHYTHMICALLY AS HE WALKED

Ira had never before had a girl pick him up for a date on a motorcycle. Or had a girl pick him up for a date, period. Not that this was really a date. It was, ostensibly, a recruitment. He was being drafted into Generation Air…or so he was willing to let her think. It was not going to happen. He'd been strong enough to resist Amway, as well as "spiritual" pursuits like Scientology and Kabbalah, even though the latter might have helped him a little with his screenwriting career. He'd thought about tying a red ribbon around his wrist, just to pretend an interest in Kabbalah, but knew that if any real Kabbalahites were to question him about it, he wouldn't be able to bullshit his way out of the deception. Back home, he'd managed to avoid both his parents' tradition-heavy religions – which they themselves largely avoided – and engage in the occasional good cause (volunteering a few times a year at a soup kitchen, making a donation to the Humane Society) without signing on in any really committed way.

L.A. was ground zero for causes and overrun people who believed they were passionate about them. Environmental causes were the trendiest and most competitive. He knew how quickly they tended to spring into tax-exempt, not-for-profit existence and start fundraising by the number of times Midwood Agency clients got asked to appear at this save-the-orange-roughy $800-a-plate dinner or that protect-the-Mt. Diablo-buckwheat $1000-a-plate dinner. He actually did care about the orange roughy and he would probably be concerned about Mt. Diablo buckwheat if he knew what it was. The cynic in him wondered how much of the funds raised in such a self-congratulatory way actually went to the threatened plant, animal or coral reef that supposedly justified these gatherings of the rich around the famous, where a fabulous gourmet meal and a few glasses of really expensive wine gave the attendees the satisfied illusion that they were doing something with their financial power. Some organizations were legit. Others, not so much.

Even if he was convinced of the cause, of the sincerity, Ira was not about to enlist with Generation Air. He was no tilter at windmills. He was a pragmatist who needed to focus on earning a living and finishing his screenplay. He couldn't spare time for activism and he especially didn't care about being spiritual – something referred to in L.A. about every five minutes, perhaps to counterbalance the intense pursuit of all things material. This was one of those places where Buddhists chanted for Cadillacs.

But he sure did want to get with Oceana. That conviction grew with each passing, recklessly navigated mile. Was he getting progressively more excited because she urged the motorcycle forward at suicidal speeds, cutting through streets crowded with pedestrians with the blithe confidence that they would simply scatter on time? Or was his excitement caused by the fact that he had to clutch her tightly in order to keep from being thrown from the bike? He wrapped his arms around her slender body, feeling panicky and thrilled, happy that he at least had a borrowed helmet to wear in case they were both thrown from the bike. For someone who wanted to save the world, she didn't seem to mind the prospect of killing a few of its inhabitants. So as to avoid seeing the terrified, furious faces of the people who leapt out of their noisy way, he squeezed his eyes shut and tried not to think about death – his own or anyone else's.

He enjoyed holding her close, even if it was by necessity. He wondered what she was thinking about their embrace. He was sure he'd seen a spark of surprise in her eyes when he rose from his camp chair to greet her. He was not the Ira she'd remembered. Women were a lot more subtle about checking men out than vice versa, so he couldn't be sure, but he thought she gave him an appreciative up-and-down glance with those mesmerizing doe-brown eyes just before she offered him a sweetly sensuous smile in an expression that seemed to be precisely midway between laughter and tears, but he could have been wrong. The moment passed quickly. Afterwards, though, he was certain, well, *almost* certain that there was a slight edge in her manner toward him. Maybe undercurrent was a better word. Women, he theorized wisely, could turn off their sexual mode when it wasn't needed or would be inconvenient. They had the ability to neutralize that portion of their selves and then reactivate it when the time, (or the person they were with) was right. Maybe she was attracted to Ira but felt that she had to stay on task. Focus on the mission at hand, which was, apparently, to draw someone new into the fold.

He guessed that she'd been expecting a semi-invalid: the asthma-ridden, helpless man-boy she'd encountered before. Instead she'd found...New Ira. Strong and self-assured. Sexy and somewhat enigmatic. At least he was working on the enigmatic part. Women, like men, enjoyed a challenge. He'd been cultivating a mysterious half-smile, practicing it a lot lately, but he forgot all about it when he saw her and just beamed. God, she was pretty. He suddenly flashed on summer vacations as a kid, swimming in green inland Michigan lakes, rising up out of the water and being dazzled by the sun bouncing on the lake's gently moving surface, seeing the people in the water around him only in brief, dazzling flashes of evanescence. It was if he were looking through a golden kaleidoscope. The effect was always disappointingly momentary. Once his eyes adjusted to the sunlight and he blinked a few times to shed droplets of water from his eyelashes, everything appeared normal.

Looking at Oceana reminded him of that dreamy, waterlogged, sunlit vision. He squinted at her happily, as if the plane she inhabited was in constant, shimmering motion. What were her parents like? What divine creatures must they be, that their commingled DNA could produce this mobile masterpiece of fluid features and long, perfectly proportioned limbs, of colors and shapes in a composite that Ira found irresistible. If da Vinci had sketched a Vitruvian *woman* with the ideal female proportions -- as he'd done for man -- Oceana would be that drawing come to life.

She'd given him a quick, obligatory hug. "Ira! You look great."

"I'm feeling good." He wanted very much to banish the previous impression she'd had of him. "The Big Stoppage hasn't been all bad for me. I have my own bike-shaw service now, and with riding a bike around all day, and working out, as well, I'm in great shape." He was talking too much. He stopped himself before he actually flexed a biceps muscle for her. Best not to be too obvious. "The asthma rarely acts up anymore." He cast about for a way to introduce the topic of his being a screenwriter.

She smiled, her tiny white teeth lined up in two rows of perfection. "A lot of people are feeling better, now that the air is cleaner. Nathan has us trying to collect statistics so that we can document the positive effects, but with so many people living in temporary places now, it's hard to get the data we need." She surveyed his rented car-apartment; its polished windows framed by plaid curtains, the meticulously swept pavement around the car, the synthetic, simulated green grass area rug that sat beneath his white plastic patio chairs near the small ceramic fire pit that held a few logs, ready for burning. His furniture and accessories were anything but expensive, but he'd taken care to assemble a comfortable, attractive outdoor setting. What did it all look like in her eyes, he wondered? He usually felt proud of his domicile. Now, though, he awaited her verdict with apprehension.

"Do you really live here?"

"Yes," he admitted, wondering what she meant by that. He couldn't read her expression. She seemed…surprised. What had she been expecting? A mansion? Lots of people were living in cars these days. What was *she* living in?

She reached for the handle on the driver's side front door, then paused politely. "May I?"

He nodded. "Sure. Go ahead." Then, aiming for a jovial tone: "The housekeeper was here yesterday."

"Oh, you have a housekeeper come by?" Her tone was sincere. Having opened the car door, she was peering inside.

"I was…just kidding. It's small. Easy to keep clean."

"It's amazing. Just amazing. You have everything you need in here," she pronounced, impressed. "You're so clever, Ira. So smart. This is, like, a perfect way to live. You're leaving such a small carbon footprint. I envy you. You're a much better environmentalist than I am."

Sure, *that* was the reason he lived modestly. Because of the environment.

"When I think of the house that I grew up in, I feel ashamed." She shook her head sadly. "It was ridiculously large. We needed a whole staff just to take care of it – housekeepers, groundskeepers, chauffers. It was so much more than we needed. It's obscene, when I think about it."

He tried to process this information and come up with an appropriate reply, but couldn't. "Care to have a cocktail before we get going?" he said instead, gesturing casually toward the plastic chairs. "Or something to eat? I could light a fire and cook something for us." Hell, he wouldn't mind if they skipped the Generation Air meeting altogether. He preferred to stay here and get to know her better. Let her get to know him. Although he was much more confident in his looks than he'd been the last time they'd been together, he knew that words remained his best tools. A woman like her was probably the object of a great deal of male attention, much of it – Ira guessed – clumsy and clichéd. Ira could do better than that. He was intelligent and intuitive. He could reach out to the woman within, the complex being who was – no doubt – tired of simply being lusted after for her beauty. Isn't that what we all want? he reflected. Someone who *gets us*?

"They're going to have food after the meeting," she said, "But I wouldn't mind a quick drink." She smiled charmingly. "I am thirsty."

She sat, accepted a cold can of beer he pulled from a cooler and sighed in contentment. Ira seated himself next to her, trying to think of how to distract her from the upcoming meeting.

"It's so good to see you again," he said tentatively. "You know, that day we met was a real turning point for me. I got fired, and it turned out to be the best thing that could have happened. You see, I'm actually a screenwriter, and I—"

She wasn't listening. She was staring in wonder at a tomato plant he had growing in a pot next to his car-partment. It was a magnificent plant, he conceded, with sprawling, octopusian stems bearing clusters of tomatoes in varying stages of ripeness. She put out her hand and gently stroked some of the sculptured green leaves, releasing their fragrance. She inhaled it deeply.

"Most nights, I'm usually working on my screenplay..."

She cupped one of the bulbous tomatoes in her hand. "And you even grow your own tomatoes. You're actually *doing* it, Ira. You're living the conscious life much more deeply than I am. I feel so...inadequate." She inclined her head toward the tomato plant and loosely encircled its green arms in her own, as if she were hugging a child. "They're such beautiful tomatoes," she said tearfully. "I've never seen such--such beautiful tomatoes before."

"Uh, thanks," Ira said uncertainly. "It's doing pretty well. I just have to water it every day, or else it'll dry out fast, being in a pot and all." He wasn't sure what to say next, because he had the impression that her microbreakdown was not really about his gardening abilities.

She looked at her watch, sighed, and put down her beer. "We should go. Nathan is a real stickler for starting things on time, and he says this meeting tonight is super important. We have to make our move, before the government screws things up again, or the human race might not survive, Nathan says."

Well, OK, then. If the very survival of humanity was at stake, Ira supposed he'd better go to the damn meeting. He wasn't pleased to hear that Nathan was still so active in the movement that captured Oceana's imagination, and not, instead, permanently out of commission due to the injuries he'd sustained at that fateful demonstration. Ira didn't want him to be a quadriplegic or anything. Just…non-participatory.

But it sounded like Nathan was back in action. Nathan, the fiery orator. The great liberator of lungs, the savior of oxygen. Was that what Oceana found attractive? Zealotry? Leadership? Was Nathan schtupping Oceana? Or was theirs merely an alliance of like-minded individuals? How could Nathan devote the proper attention to a woman like Oceana, when most – if not all -- of his energy was probably directed toward his organization?

Ira told himself that he had a shot.

"What kind of move is Generation Air going to make, exactly?" He was still considering skipping this little shindig. He'd initially assumed it was part of a membership drive, but it sounded more intense than that. He was not going to do anything illegal. That kind of trouble he didn't need. Nor was he going to get beaten to a pulp, like the Generation Airites sometimes did. He was not that guy.

If these environmental fanatics expected him to be instantly devoted to the cause just because he could breathe better (or because they'd sent a beautiful woman to fetch him), they were going to be disappointed. Ira O'Riley was not going to drink the Kool Aid. He was also beginning to doubt that he could strike up a genuine connection with Oceana. She seemed unable to formulate any thoughts of her own. He was getting a little tired of hearing about the great leader, Nathan. Should Ira even bother going with her? He'd been wrestling with a difficult scene in "Her Majesty's Gangsta," and was – he felt – on the verge of a brilliant solution. Maybe he'd be better off staying home tonight and working on it.

"I don't know what Nathan has in mind," she admitted. "But it's something big. He's got an amazing mind. You have no idea. He is really passionate about keeping the air clean. He's like, the smartest man I've ever met."

I'm smart! Ira wanted to say. Not rocket scientist smart, but smarter than the average bear smart. Jeez. What would it take to divert her adoring attention away from Nathan? Did the man have her hypnotized?

She suddenly smiled at him. Her smile was like a spotlight that shone over him, a powerful beam that revealed every flaw and imperfection, but also every attractive, admirable attribute of face, temperament and soul and ultimately rendered it all – every last detail that was Ira O'Riley -- beautiful. Valued. Maybe even desirable. That's the way he felt that he looked to her at that moment, anyway.

Forget the lake imagery, thought Ira. Her features were so clean, her face so out of place amid this ordinary, mundane location that he was convinced that she should always be seen against a backdrop of the Alps. Like Julie Andrews, twirling around and singing, but without the ugly clothes and repulsive haircut. Oceana deserved a more majestic, other-wordly setting than these city streets stopped up with cars and teeming with average people. There should be snow-capped mountains all around her, and air purer even than that of post-Big-Stoppage L.A.. Also, little Alpine flowers under her feet. Eidelweiss flowers.

She did look happy to greet me, he thought.

"I'm ready," he said. "Where are we going?"

"You'll see."

So, besotted with intoxicating possibilities, Ira put any further resistance aside and climbed aboard her motorcycle. As a writer and a lover, he knew he had to keep himself open to the universe and whatever it might send his way. They roared away from his car-partment in a torrent of thunderous engine noise, two bodies and a machine merged into one kinetic experience.

In the brief glimpses he got when his eyes were open, it looked as if they were headed in the direction of Los Feliz. They were. In fact, she zoomed into Griffith Park and came to a halt so suddenly that he was unbalanced and nearly fell off the motorcycle. He removed his helmet before disembarking, buying himself some time for his legs time to rid themselves of the rubbery, shaky sensation that fear had produced in them. He didn't want to tremble in front of Oceana. As he finally swung one long leg over the bike to get off, he felt like a modern-day cowboy.

"We're up there," she said, pointing to a destination well above them, up a steep and winding trail, over what he knew was rugged, chaparral-covered land split by peaks and carved with deep canyons. "That's where we've set up our headquarters."

Damn! He was fit, but, really, was she putting him through an endurance contest? Testing him?

"How do we get there?" he asked, trying to sound casual. "Hike?"

She beamed at him. "No, silly. That would take too long. And of course, we don't ride motorcycles in the park. That might hurt the flora and upset the fauna, Nathan says."

That Generation Air had located itself in this rustic, natural oasis that was smack dab in the middle of L.A. was not surprising. It was perfect, as a matter of fact. Thematically fitting. The park was a functional wilderness, especially at the lower levels, which hosted tennis courts and picnic areas, basketball courts, a zoo and a merry go round. As one climbed higher, he knew, the evidence of human activity became sparser, the dominance of nature stronger.

She gestured to the left, toward two horses tethered to sycamore trees.

"Do you ride?"

"No."

She laughed. "Oh, Ira! I never know how to take you."

His laugh was weak and insincere, but she didn't seem to notice. At Oceana's direction, Ira put his left, tennis-shoe clad foot in a stirrup. When he went to swing his right leg up and over the back of the rotund beast, the left stirrup dipped unexpectedly, unbalancing him a little. He kept a casual smile fixed to his face, determined not to let either the horse or the girl sense his fear. He was from the 313, after all (or at least, he lived near it). It would take more than a horse to scare him. Finally seated atop the animal, he found himself much higher off the ground than he'd expected to. WTF! And was this saddle supposed to be comfortable? Seriously? He made sure his right foot was tucked into the other stirrup. It gave him no comfort at all. His legs felt absurdly bent.

"For some reason, I wasn't thinking you were this tall," murmured Oceana.

"I was lying on a sidewalk the last time you saw me."

While she made some quick adjustments to the length of the stirrups, Ira surveyed his surroundings. He'd only been to Griffith Park a few times. It was amazing to him: a park consisting of thousands of wild acres on the slopes of Mt. Hood, its borders within a stone's throw of one of the most highly developed urban areas in the world.

Good God! They were lurching into motion. His musings distracted him from noticing that Oceana had mounted her own horse and was urging him to move forward. Ira grabbed the saddle horn in front of him as if the small leather protrusion could save him from death. He was a city boy, would always be a city boy.

Oceana was leading the way up the trail toward what he guessed would be Generation Air's secret compound. Ira could see no signs of it, but it didn't matter. He needed to focus on being in the moment, since in this particular moment he had to concentrate on not falling off of this damned horse. The difficulty in doing this wasn't the horse's fault. Their steep climb forced Ira to constantly adjust his balance and posture. The saddle – which seemed so substantial when he first sat in it – now felt flimsy and shifty. Was it loose? Was Ira about to find himself hanging upside down below the beast's belly, his legs clinging to its sides and his head brushing the ground? Yeah, that would be a great way to impress a woman. This was nothing like the frenetic, high-speed motorcycle ride that brought them here, yet it was almost as terrifying. He tried hard to take note of the details around him – as any writer should – but the patches of wildflowers, the occasional grouping of cacti, the groves of sycamore trees that gave way to short, tough-looking shrubs as they climbed higher – all this passed in an anxious blur.

After awhile Ira became accustomed to the horse's stride and felt himself instinctively adapting to it, letting his hips move forward on their own while his upper body swayed independently of them. He began to feel an empathetic connection to the beast, which seemed sort of…noble. He sensed a connection to the animal that made him feel compassionate toward it. Did it hate having this stranger on its back? What was it like to be slave to a smaller being that you could – if you wanted to – crush to death beneath your hooves? Did he (if it was a he) wonder about what type of person Ira was? Someone who was kind to horses, or not? Was the saddle itchy? The bridle uncomfortable? Was Ira working the reins properly? He was really not doing much more than holding them, since the horse was simply following the very large brown butt of the horse in front of him. Both animals seemed to know where they were going. Ira remembered "Animal Farm" and felt sad for his mount. What was the name of that horse, the one who worked so hard and was betrayed in the end and taken away to the glue factory? Napoleon? No, that was the pig. Boxer. It was Boxer. Poor Boxer. Damn, for an allegory that story really bummed him out. He felt sad all over again just thinking about it. And he hadn't even bothered to find out the name of this horse, before he climbed aboard.

Just then the horse veered abruptly off the path, nearly unseating him, and he felt a sudden hatred for it. "Hey!" Ira shouted angrily, startled by the equine mutiny.

His horse ignored him and stretched his broad neck out so that he could chomp on a tree branch and bite off some glossy leaves with his giant yellow teeth. He chewed calmly on them, ignoring Ira's increasingly insistent knee nudges.

As he watched Oceana and her mount recede into the distance, Ira kicked his horse gently with his heels. "C'mon, buddy! Snack time is over."

The horse chewed contentedly.

Ira kicked harder. "Let's go. Let's move on out!" It sounded like a cowboy thing to say. Or maybe he'd gotten it from a war movie. He couldn't remember.

Oceana had finally taken note of his dilemma. She turned her horse around and came back to him while he sat waiting impotently for his horse to finish dining.

"Just pull on the reins and give him a good kick," she advised, "Or he'll stand here all day, eating. You've got to show him who's boss."

"He's the boss," grumbled Ira. "He's much bigger than I am." Still, he did as she advised. Miraculously, the horse responded, turning back toward the trail. He resumed following the other horse, nose to butt. Ira suspected that the horse's apparent obedience had more to do with him being done with his meal than with Ira's ability to command him. The rest of the ride passed without incident or conversation. Aside from the occasional snort and the constant, regular thudding of hoof of earth, the only other sound was that made by Ira's horse, farting rhythmically as he walked.

CHAPTER FORTY-TWO:
HIS CARDBOARD CASTLE

For being mostly short little shits, these Mexicans sure were strong. And they were hard workers. He had to give 'em that. Lester grunted companionably at the stocky, black-haired man who was gripping the other side of the new, boxed refrigerator they were moving on a cart through the streets of Studio City.

The man, whose name was Arturo, said something to him in Spanish. Lester could tell it was a question because of the inflection. He wasn't entirely sure what the question was, but he'd been around these guys enough now to have picked up a little of the language.

"Está bien," he told Arturo. Yes, Lester had a good hold on his side of the box.

At first he was kind of pissed off about hearing Spanish all the time. They were in America, after all, not Mexico. People who came here should learn to speak our language, and not the other way around. He was definitely outnumbered in the park and for a time he thought about finding somewhere else to stay. Somewhere with more white people, if there was such a place in L.A. But these guys weren't so bad. That first night, before he really got settled in, they actually shared their rice and beans with him, and someone passed around a bottle of tequila. They sure did like their rice and beans. Cooked them all the time on their little cookstoves, along with tortillas, and sometimes meat that he hoped was chicken, although he didn't like to think too closely about it, because he usually bought his dinner from them. These boys were tight with a buck. Maybe they went to the store and bought chicken now and then, and maybe not. He wasn't going to worry about it. Whatever the mystery meat was, it was tasty.

"Caliente," he said. He couldn't work out how to use it in a sentence, because Spanish wasn't straightforward, like English. You couldn't just say, "I'm hot." You had to say something like, "I have heat," which didn't make too much sense to him. His one word was enough. Arturo knew what he meant and nodded in agreement. It was hot today, and doing this kind of work didn't make it feel any cooler. But he wasn't complaining. The sweatier you were when you showed up with the goods, the bigger the tip you got.

Lester made his living with his muscles now, and although there were nights when he was sore and tired, he found that he liked the simplicity of his existence. Besides, there were plenty of nights as a truck driver when he ended up sore and tired. In that job, though, he had complications: paperwork to do, weight limits to worry about, deadlines to meet, bad drivers to avoid. In this job, he picked things up and dropped them off. Period. Sure, the things he picked up were large and heavy, but that's why he earned pretty good money. It wasn't easy, navigating big appliances and pieces of furniture – like this 26 cubic foot refrigerator -- through crowded streets, sometimes uphill. It was too bad the B.S. couldn't have hit a city that was all flat. He made sure that he grunted a lot when moving the old appliance out of place and positioning the new one just so. Sound effects, like sweat, increased the amount of the tips.

"Tengo mucho hambre," said Arturo.

Lester was hungry, too. "Si," said Lester, groping around for the word for the right words. "Quiero el almuerzo." He thought that was: *I want lunch*. He couldn't think of how to say "soon," so he rubbed his belly and tried to look really hungry.

Arturo smiled ruefully and nodded again.

Day laborers were in demand in a way they hadn't been since before the recession, because distribution was all different now. The lady who was waiting for this new refrigerator was like everybody else in the Southland. People weren't going to let the B.S. stop them from buying new stuff -- even large items, like sofas and washing machines and big screen TVs. But now, because they couldn't be delivered by truck, these purchases were wheeled through the streets by strong men, like Lester.

The homeowner was thrilled to see them. "Oh, thank God," she said. "My old one quit on Tuesday, and the laundry is piling up. I've got three kids."

Lester and Arturo guided the new machine to her laundry room.

"What about the old one?" she asked. "Do you take that away?"

"Yes, ma'am," he assured her. "We'll get that out of your way." They'd take it a few blocks and dump it behind some building, to join the growing piles of debris that weren't making it to landfills because it was too much trouble to take them there. This wasn't like the old days. And, Lester reasoned, the company wasn't paying them to move the old washing machine.

The box the new one came in was a different matter. That wasn't destined for dumping. Lester would take that with him. It would be a great addition to his living quarters. He thought about how he could join it to his main box so that it'd be like a little alcove. It would give him more room to store his gear. Although a few of the guys in the box city had tents, most had setups like Lester's. Since it only usually rained during one time of the year in L.A. – unlike normal places – a cardboard home lasted a good long while. And when your box did wear out, you could easily replace it. Lester had his fixed up pretty nice. He'd carefully cut side windows which he propped open with sticks for ventilation.

When the B.S. first happened he was hell-bent on getting home ASAP, but after awhile he thought: why? He was done with Bernice, that lying, cheating bitch. Done with paying the mortgage on the house in which she was now sleeping with some other guy, (if it hadn't been foreclosed on yet). Done with making payments on her car. He hoped her Focus was already repo'd. He was through with paying for the braces for the teeth of her kid by that couldn't-hold- down-a-job first husband of hers.

Lester now worked for cash money and loved it. Even if Bernice could find him, she couldn't prove that he was earning anything. Neither could Uncle Sam, for that matter. Lester had thought about setting up a bank account in L.A., because it wasn't safe to keep his money in what he fondly thought of as his "cardboard castle." He did get an account, for show, but kept most of his money in a safe deposit box. That was the smart way. He'd go back to Missouri when he had enough money saved up and had figured out exactly what he wanted to do once he got there. He was in no hurry, though.

He and Arturo ate at a taco stand and did a few more deliveries before calling it quits for the day and heading back to the park. He washed up before dinner as he always did: with an outdoor bath. One of the guys had set up a sort of bathing area, for privacy, by placing an old sheet on a wire that'd been bent in a crude circle, and hanging the wire from a tree branch. Lester filled the communal wash tub with water, sat in it and soaped up, enjoying himself. This was the way his grandfather had bathed as a child, he knew from family stories. However, his grandfather was the youngest of nine children, so the wash water was none too clean by the time his turn came. Lester laughed out loud. Even with the B.S. changing everything, at least he had clean water.

"Lester!" an accented voice interrupted his musings. "There's someone here about work."

Lester got out of the tub, toweled off and got dressed. Usually, the men had to go and find by showing up at appliance and furniture stores every morning and waiting for assignments. The jobs didn't come to them. This was unusual. Maybe it was something better.

It'd been a long time but right away he recognized the tall white man who was talking intently to the group in the park. It was the same guy who'd hired him to help disrupt that gathering of environmental loudmouths awhile back. A Mexican stood next to him, translating his words into Spanish. Whatever he was saying did not appeal very much to those who were listening. Several shook their heads and turned away.

"What is it, Arturo?" Lester asked. "Qué pasa?"

Arturo frowned. "No quiero trouble with la policía," he said. "Don't want no trouble." He went to join others who were sitting around a fire in an oil drum, drinking Corona beer and listening to that bouncy, sing-song music they liked so much. Lester preferred country music, which he played on a battery-powered radio in his box at night. He knew what the problem was. These Mexicans were mostly illegal. They didn't want to do anything that would get them noticed by the police. Last time, that made the pay even better for those who were willing to sign on.

Lester approached the recruiter. "Remember me? I worked for you before."

The tall white man stared at him and smiled. "Oh, yeah. Les, isn't it?"

"Lester."

"Well, Lester, I'm looking for a few good men for a little job we've got coming up. It's real good money."

"Same kind of work?"

The man looked at him consideringly for a long moment. "Yeah. Same kind of work. Is that a problem for you?"

Lester didn't particularly like doing that kind of work, but those troublemakers did have it coming. Besides, the money was too good to turn down.

CHAPTER FORTY-THREE:
WE HAPPY FEW

Nathan began his speech just as the golden hour struck. It was that magical time before sunset when everything – every shabby, flawed detail of existence -- is bathed in a radiant glow and transformed into a kind of splendor, as if Rumpelstiltskin were on hand, spinning straw into gold. Ira had to wonder if the timing was deliberate. This was Hollywood, after all, where even the bus drivers and fast food workers knew the tricks of the trade, because most of them were wannabe filmmakers. Nathan was backlit, too, reminding Ira of a painting of Jesus that hung on the living room wall in his Irish grandmother's house: a Caucasian Jesus with blue eyes and light brown hair. Grandma Kitty's white-robed, serene-looking Christ seemed modestly unaware that his head was framed by a yellow halo, much like Nathan's was as he stepped up to the microphone and started to speak. Ira found himself temporarily distracted by the impressive audio set-up (how was it powered?) and the portable stage on which Nathan stood. They struck him as surreal features amid such a rustic setting. The enormous banner hanging above and behind Nathan read: "Generation Air: Reclaiming the Future."

Ira was surprised by the size of the crowd and the semi-permanence of the encampment. He hadn't had much time to take it all in, but estimated that there were hundreds of people gathered here. Unlike the diverse group of demonstrators he'd seen the day he'd gotten fired, these people were mostly young, in their teens, twenties and thirties. They looked like they were going to a Phish concert, not a demonstration. He saw no children, business suits or work uniforms. The attire tended toward t-shirts and flip-flops, do rags and halter tops, with tie dye accents and gauzy variations on the skirts. There were a fair number of black t shirted heavy metal types with low slung studded belts and angry tattoos, a baseball cap-wearing hip hop contingent, lots of Goths and several women in long, peasant dresses with tight, bosom-bearing bodices who looked as if they'd gotten lost on their way to a Renaissance festival. Beyond the fringes of the crowd he glimpsed dozens of tents erected on the shrub-dotted slopes. The water stations nearby and portable toilets situated at a discrete distance suggested that these activists were here for the duration.

"Those of you who are new to Generation Air, welcome," Nathan began. "You are all here because someone thought you might have a special interest in making sure Southern California's deadly air pollution is NOT allowed to return, just so corporate interests can resume making big profits by keeping us addicted to fossil fuels. We'd like you to join us in a very exciting event tomorrow. I'll outline the details of the plan in the morning. For tonight, I'd just like you to invite you to enjoy our hospitality. We'll be grilling up some food and we've got water, juices, power drinks and, oh, yeah, organic beer – for those of you who enjoy adult beverages." He paused for the chuckles that came his way. "We'll have live entertainment. You can spend the night, if you like. We've got plenty of room for you. And while you're getting to know us a little better, I'd like you to consider helping us make history. YOU" – he pointed into the crowd – "and YOU and, yes, even YOU" – he pointed to a pretty girl in a crop top and short skirt that revealed a skull-and-roses tramp stamp on her lower back -- "can help us make a real difference." The girl giggled, embarrassed by the attention. "We're going to let the government know that they must be accountable to US, and NOT to their corporate partners in crime, no matter how much money they get from them. We'll set an example for the rest of the country, as well. The TV cameras that will be gathered to document the state's ridiculous heli-lift will, instead, show what concerned citizens can do when they take action. The power of the government is NOTHING compared to the power of ordinary people, united behind a cause."

"Man, there are a lot of people here," Ira whispered to the guy next to him, who stood listening in rapt attention to Nathan. Oceana had disappeared as soon as they arrived, leaving Ira feeling peeved and uncooperative.

"We were each supposed to bring someone new," he whispered back.

Oh, God, Ira thought. This was just like Amway.

Whatever injuries Nathan had sustained the day Ira first saw him, he seemed completely recovered. His fit and compact good-enough-for-high-school-athletics-but-not-big-enough-to-get-a-college-scholarship build exuded vitality, communicated enthusiasm. Ira wasn't close enough to see Nathan's expressions, but he quickly realized that the man knew how to use his voice and gestures to great advantage. Was he an actor in addition to being an activist?

Nathan was still talking. "I'm not saying this is going to be easy. It won't. Here's what we're up against. Last year, the oil and gas industry spent $106 million on federal lobbying. Add in campaign contributions to individual lawmakers, and that figure jumps up into the billions. BILLIONS, people. They've got Congress in their pockets. The Citizens United decision opened the floodgates and corporate money is pouring into Congressional coffers. Big Oil and Big Gas are COMMITTED to keeping our roads crowded with fossil fuel-burning cars. Why do you think we haven't gotten farther than we have with alternate energy development? Why aren't there even better mileage hybrid cars by now? It isn't for lack of trying. It's for lack of funding. Lack of support. Big Oil and Big Gas – which, incidentally, are the same folks that own Big Coal – have deliberately blocked government subsidies for research. They don't WANT better, cleaner, less geopolitically volatile forms of energy. They sure don't want mass transportation. All that would mean money out of their pockets! Now, they didn't DELIBERATELY set out to cause irreparable damage to our environment, to make the air foul and cause climate change. They don't issue corporate memos saying, 'let's pollute the air so thoroughly in Southern California that people DIE from it.' That's just an unavoidable side effect. Can't be helped. Not if they're going to continue making OBSCENELY LARGE PROFITS!"

As Nathan's angry voice reverberated from speakers hung in the trees, Ira felt outrage bubbling up around him. Several young men performing tricks with crocheted footbags stopped what they were doing and listened, frowning. People holding out their cups for refills at the beer station turned toward the stage, their thirst momentarily forgotten. Some people held up their cell

272

phones and snapped pictures of Nathan, presumably, Ira thought, to capture what they believed would be an historic moment. An angry, stimulated haze settled over the crowd. Ira himself felt mesmerized and really kind of pissed off. Who did these oil companies think they were? He thought back to those times when he struggled to breathe. He had a sudden, terrible flashback to what it felt like to gasp desperately for every breath. Sure, he had asthma, but the air conditions had made it much, much worse than it had to be. How much of his pulmonary suffering could have been avoided if the oil and gas industry wasn't controlling everything?

Nathan took a drink of water from a cup sitting on a stool next to him. Nathan surveyed his audience. As if cued by a special effects coordinator, the Generation Air banner over him rippled suddenly, stirred by a cooperative breeze.

"So, here's where things stand," he continued. Our adversary is not the government, although it's going to look that way to some of those watching. These people will be persuaded by the public relations tool that is the media to see us as criminals, because they want really, really want to trust in their government. It gives them comfort to do so. Makes them think there's order in the world. They don't realize that the government is simply a collection of puppets, paid by various special interest groups to do their bidding. Keep that in mind. To some – if you join us tomorrow – you will be a bad guy. Your own parents might not get it."

"They usually don't!" someone called out, prompting widespread laughter.

"You got that right!" someone else added.

Nathan waited for a moment, smiling, then went on. "To those who understand, you will be a hero. I want to be clear about this. We ARE going to break the law, people! If you join us, you may very well get arrested. If that happens, we'll do everything in our power to help you. We've got money set aside for legal expenses. You won't be left dangling in the breeze. We take care of our own. Generation Air is a family, and I mean that. Keep in mind, though: you could end up with a criminal record." He paused and looked around. "I've got one. And I'm DAMN PROUD OF IT!"

Cheers erupted all around Ira.

"We CANNOT BACK AWAY FROM THE FIGHT just because there might be consequences. We've got to step up and do this. We've got to send a signal to the powers that be that we are NOT going to let things return to the way they used to be. Not on our watch.

"This is much more than a demonstration. This is ACTION! We are fighting for our very lives. For the future of our habitat. You" – he pointed at a thin, shirtless young man in a baseball cap and shorts. "How old are you?"

"Twenty-two."

"And you?" Another audience member was singled out.

"Twenty-seven."

"And you?"

"Twenty-four."

Nathan looked at them carefully. "It's your planet, man. It's gonna be your planet for a long, long time. For much longer than those old men sitting in corporate boardrooms right now, calling the shots that will mess up YOUR quality of life. Do you really want them to have control over you?

"Do you want to spend decades of your life wearing a breathing apparatus every time you go out of doors? That's no exaggeration. That's exactly what you have to look forward to, if we don't do something NOW to change things. Don't be lulled into complacency, just because the air is better now. The government is about to reverse that. Their heli-lift is aimed at sending us right back to where we were in terms of an intolerable air quality. We can't let that happen. We need to make our move before the breathing air is permanently gone. Before the sun is just a bright spot in the nighttime. And don't forget, we'll be doing what California always does; setting an example for the rest of the nation. Hell, for the world. The TV cameras that will be lined up to do the government's bidding will, instead, show people AROUND THE GLOBE what can be accomplished when a small group of determined individuals dare to stand up to the power structure. This is OUR Tiananmen Square!"

The crowd roared its approval.

Weren't those protestors massacred? thought Ira.

Nathan continued. "Henry David Thoreau said, 'If... the machine of government... is of such a nature that it requires you to be the agent of injustice to another, then, I say, break the law!'

"I can promise you that our operation will be dangerous. In the best tradition of peaceful protest, we are taking action in a thoughtful, deliberate way, but in doing so, we will be going up against armed adversaries. The spirits of Gandhi and Dr. Martin Luther King Jr. will be with us tomorrow, but make no mistake: those courageous men knew that you can't bring about change without a cost.

"What we do tomorrow may result in injuries. Maybe worse. I can't guarantee the safety of anyone here. The cops do the bidding of the corporate-controlled government. There could be mercenaries there, too – hired by the oil and gas industry. We've run into that before. The more of us there are, the better our chances of success, but if you want to leave now, or in the morning, we will totally understand. It's your choice. In that case, I hope that you will be with us in spirit. We also accept financial contributions."

Chuckles filled the pause that followed this, but they were tense. Subdued. Nathan took a drink of water.

"Even if we are left with only a few brave people to do this thing, we're still going to win. And in years to come, to the end of the world, everyone will know what we did here. Your children and your grandchildren will be grateful to you, for saving their air. For giving them a future. Those of you who join us in this great adventure will be heroes: we few, we happy few that will change the course of human history IN A SINGLE DAY!"

CHAPTER FORTY-FOUR:
PEOPLE AREN'T TIRED OF YOU YET

Luanne was puzzled. "I don't get it. You want me to be, like, a reporter?"

"No, no," said Sid patiently, speaking to her as if she was about five years old. "A commentator. You'll stand alongside an entertainment reporter and say funny things. Outrageous things, if you feel like it. Observations, like about what people are wearing, or point out dumb lines the politicians will use in their speeches. Your job is to spice things up."

"But..." Luanne felt that she must be missing something. "This heli-lift is a straight news story, isn't it? Kind of serious?" *Boring* is what she really wanted to say.

"That's exactly the point. The way it'll be covered by most of the media, it's going to be dull. Sure, there'll be a little action, when the helicopters lift the cars out of the way, but that's it. The governor will make a speech. The mayor will make a speech. Everyone will want to take credit, even though, between you, me and the fence post, I doubt that this heli-lift will accomplish much."

"So why does the Glitz! Network want in on it? Don't they usually show red carpet affairs? Talk to stars as they're going into premieres and award shows? Ask 'em what designer they're wearing"

"That's exactly right. That's what they *usually* do. The problem is, since the Big Stoppage, their normal programming has gone to hell. The Academy Awards were cancelled. So were the SAG and People's Choice Awards. Nobody can hold premieres these days. Sure, they can hold 'em, but the stars can't get to them, so what's the point? The Glitz! Network is scrambling to figure out how to hold onto their loyal audience until things get back to normal. If they can't wait it out, they'll be out of business. That's why they're thinking outside the box."

"So Glitz! is turning itself into a news channel?"

"They're going to cover selected news stories, but in a Glitz! way, with entertainment reporters covering events instead of real reporters. That's where you come in. You'll help Trask Weldon anchor the heli-lift. He'll describe what's happening and you throw in funny comments. And you get to wear a beautiful dress while you do it. Palmer had a stylist pick out some possibilities especially for you, especially for your figure. A bike messenger is headed to your house with them, as a matter of fact. You try 'em on and see what you think."

"You're kidding."

"No, he's pedaling as we speak. You pick out what you like and we'll have a stylist get you the jewelry and shoes. And don't worry about the fit. We can always get alterations done. Listen, Luanne, this is a part of the business. You gotta promote yourself. Let people see you, get to know you outside of the context of the show. You're doing real well with that so far—"

"Except for the Cap Lessing debacle."

Sid sighed deeply. "That's on me. I should have known better than to trust what his weasely little producer said. But you still kept your dignity there, Luanne. You stood up to Cap Lessing, which not a lot of people can do, I'm told. This will be completely different. Fun. No one will be taking pot shots at you. After this, you can return to Vegas. Production on 'Aunt Mom' starts back up pretty soon, doesn't it?"

"Yeah." She was eager to get back to the show, after this short hiatus. She loved, loved, loved doing 'Aunt Mom.' If this Glitz! gig would help her sitcom -- and her career -- she supposed she should do it. "But why me? I don't get it. I'm still a newcomer."

"That's exactly why. You're an *exciting* newcomer who's generating a lot of buzz. People aren't tired of you yet. Glitz! checked out the research on you before they extended the offer, although the head of programming over there is a huge fan of 'Aunt Mom' and was already looking for ways to use you."

"Research?"

"Sure. For someone who hasn't been on the scene for very long, your Q rating is very high. People *like* you, Luanne. Both genders, too, which isn't always the case. Women love you because you're so real. They see themselves reflected in you. You're relatable. Men want you to be their pal. You're not threatening to them like some women are."

Great, she thought. Their pal. Some things don't change.

Sid went on. "Kids like you because you're a riot. You're the crazy aunt they'd love to have. Everybody – across the board -- thinks you're funny. And nice. A girl next door type, but comedic. Glitz! didn't want to go with some gorgeous starlet who wouldn't have much to say. They want to tap that comic personality of yours!"

"Sid, you know a team of writers comes up with all those hilarious lines I say on the show, right?"

"See? That right there is funny! You'll be terrific at this. It's going to open a whole new door for you. And Luanne, let's not forget. This heli-lift is going to get some monster ratings. If the Glitz! Network promotes this right, a lot of those people are going to forget about boring old CNN and MSNBC and all the local channels, and tune in to watch you."

Sure, she thought. I just have to be as funny and entertaining – on the spot, with no script, in front of a LIVE TV cameras – as my fictional character.

No pressure there.

CHAPTER FORTY-FIVE:
PALM TREE PIPE DREAMS

Strolling past tents, hearing quiet conversations around campfires that blazed and crackled as they consumed dead, salvaged branches dragged uphill from the lower, big-treed portions of the park, Ira felt as if he were in a Civil War encampment on the eve of some great battle. He was pretty sure, though, that the boys in blue and gray didn't have any ganja to smoke, to help chill them out before they had to face potential death in the morning. The aroma of the herb mingling with the primitive scent of roasting meat enhanced the party atmosphere that settled over the canyon floor like a bright, gauzy layer of cheer. Was it his imagination, or was there a sobering apprehension that lurked beneath it, a fear that was being deliberately held at bay by those he encountered? He wasn't feeling it himself. He might stick around to watch events unfold tomorrow, but no way was he going to endanger himself for a cause. He was not that guy.

Some people used long sticks to toast marshmallows or heat hot dogs over the campfires, but more substantial cooking was being done on in a sort of communal outdoor kitchen area. Smoke rose from the bellies of many grills. Generation Airites and their would-be converts carried plates bearing hamburgers and vegan burgers (cooked on separate grills, of course), sweet corn and melon slices to camp chairs, stopping first at tables piled high with fresh fruit and packages of Doritos and cookies, coolers filled with smoothies, power drinks, bottled water and Mountain Dew. There was no judgment here.

Long lines formed up at the beer kegs, but no one minded. It was an opportunity to chat, and maybe meet up with someone who'd share your tent with you, or lie with you in one of the many hemp hammocks strung between the trees, bathed in a dreamy midsummer night's glow of red, blue and green LED lights tucked in branches overhead.

After Nathan left the stage, a band set up. Folk-flavored blues soon wafted out over the clearing. The vocalist was a thin, mournful young woman with choppy hair. Her bare arms were covered darkly in tattoos. The crowd gathered in front of the stage listened closely while snapping photos on their cell phones or eating from plates sagging with food. Some fanned themselves with fallen palm fronds. The singer's voice was rich and fluid and sounded older than she looked, like bourbon in a dark brown bottle.

Well I woke up tired in a cheap motel
On the edge of the desert on the edge of dawn
You were already up and havin' a smoke
Drinkin' gas station coffee, ready to move on.

Ira marveled at the organization behind this gathering. How many Los Angelenos would suspect that this complex, efficient little village had established itself amid the thousands of rugged, mostly-wild acres of Griffith Park? Generation Air had it together, and evidently did not lack for funding, either.

He looked around for Oceana, wondering if he would even talk with her again, or if, now that she'd brought him here, she was done with him. He tried to feel angry about that. He could leave, he supposed, but he admitted to himself that he was curious about what was going to happen tomorrow. He might as well stay the night here and think about it. Hell, if Nathan was right, the Generation Air activists thwarting of the heli-lift could be historic. Ira kind of wanted to be there, to see it firsthand. Maybe he could sort of hang out in the background. Lend moral support, rather than be right there in the thick of things. That was more his style.

Someone in the band was playing a mean blues harmonica, vamping silkily into the next verse.

Coyotes howl in the Hollywood hills
Or was that just another bad dream of yours?
And the mudslides tumble down on Malibu
It's a postcard paradise, but who's keepin' score?

He got in the beer line, reasoning that he wasn't accepting Generation Air's hospitality under false pretenses. He really *would* think about joining. He might as well get one of those veggie burgers, too. They looked good. And some vegetable chips.

The small, shirtless, heavily tanned guy in line in front of him turned and smiled. "They're amazing, aren't they? The Kool-Aid Wino Band. Dude, I heard them play at the Joshua Tree Music Festival. They're doing this gig for free, you know, just because they believe in us so much. Who did you come with?"

The sudden directional change momentarily confused Ira. "Oceana."

The other nodded sagely. He looked, thought Ira, as if both his current, young man self and the old man he would be some day were inhabiting his body at the same time. His grin was boyish, but it activated deep wrinkles extending from the corners of his eyes. The torso and the unusually short legs that carried it around looked muscular and strong, but the hair atop his head was already starting to thin its way toward eventual baldness, even though the sideburns arcing down nearly to his jaw were luxuriant.

"Oceana. Sweet Oceana. Poor little rich girl." The large gauge silver cylinders in his ear lobes gleamed dully, like extra, metallic eyes. Robot eyes. Numerous smaller, shiner piercings decorated the interiors and outer rims of his ears. His face, in contrast, was almost completely unmarked, except for a silver barbell protruding from his left eyebrow. Not all of his jewelry was embedded, Ira noticed. He wore a fringed leather cord around his right wrist and a macramé-and-shell number around one ankle.

"What do you mean?"

"Dude, I thought you knew her."

"Not well." Ira shrugged. He hesitated, then added ruefully: "But I'd like to."

"Dude, you and every other guy here. I'm Zed, by the way."

"Ira. How's it going?" They shook hands.

"Oh, here's the chorus. Listen! It's awesome. I downloaded this song, but it's sooooo much better live."

California's in the rear view mirror

281

Palm tree pipe dreams lapping at the shore
The more miles behind us, the more it gets clearer
I wanted you and you wanted more.

"She's a beautiful person, man."

"Who? The singer?" Ira, unlike his new friend, was having trouble switching quickly between music and conversation.

"Oceana. She's a beautiful soul. Beautiful on the inside, too. Not real smart, but sweet, you know? I worry about people taking advantage of her. These trust fund babies have it tougher than people realize. It's not as easy as you think, being filthy rich, especially when you didn't earn it yourself so you feel a little funny about it. Everybody lines up to take advantage of you. I myself am a working man. A mosaic artist. I do tile mosaics in swimming pools, showers, kitchens. Pretty much anywhere somebody wants one."

Ira was surprised. "You can make a living at that?" They both moved up a step, getting a little closer to the keg.

"Dude, I make a *great* living, cuz you can charge rich people anything you want to. See, let's say some rich guy in Malibu spends a boatload of money on a swimming pool, but then he realizes that it looks a lot like all his neighbors' swimming pools, because they spent a boatload of money on theirs, too. So he wants it to look different from theirs. Better. He wants to customize it. I'm the one who can do that for him. A few months ago I did a tile mosaic of a guy's trophy wife, naked, looking like a mermaid, on the bottom of his swimming pool. I was hoping she'd model for me, but he gave me a photograph to work from. He loved it. Shows it off to all his friends. The wife liked it all right, but I gotta wonder: will she like it thirty years from now, when she's in her 50s, swimming in that pool, and she has to look down at an image of herself when she was young and so beautiful? If they stay married that long, I mean. And dude, check it: I work only when I feel like it, which is when the surf is *not* up. You know what I mean? I don't live to work. I work so I can surf."

Hot winds blow through the valley of dreams
But you wiped my margarita tears away

282

We got lost on the billboard boulevard
Where the seasons don't change and the players don't play.

Stars in the sidewalk and signs in the hills,
dreams by the ocean are pulling me
Underneath the memory of who we were.
Your features now just a beautiful blur.

Ira really wanted to hear more about Oceana. He decided that he didn't care if he sounded obvious. "So…you know Oceana well?"

"Dude, I've known her since *last year*. Since she joined this fabulous freakshow. You know who her dad is, right? Or was?"

Ira shook his head.

"You remember Alex Harpey? From Putrid?"

"You mean the hair band?"

"Yeah, that's the one. That was her bioDad. Dude od'd a few years ago on prescription drugs, remember?" He sighed. "What a waste. I loved his music. He kind of inspired me. I'm in a screamo band, myself. And her mother was that Swedish model. I can't remember her name, but she was *hot*."

Was. "Is she dead, too?"

"No, dude. She just isn't real famous anymore."

California's in the rear view mirror
Palm tree pipe dreams lappin' at the shore
The more miles behind us, the more it gets clearer
I wanted you and you wanted more.

Applause followed the end of the song.

In the beer line, two girls standing in front of them blew bubbles at each other from brightly colored dispensers, laughing at each other, although they were both doing the same thing. Other people texted and tweeted, smoked cigarettes and joints, talked and talked. Ira and Zed reached the keg and accepted cups of beer from the men dispensing it. Ira gulped at his appreciatively. "Whoa. That is some fine beer. I'm a little surprised at them using plastic glasses, though. Not exactly environmental."

"Dude! They only look like plastic! They're made from corn. Completely recyclable. And the plates are made from sugarcane. And when you go to take a dump later on, you'll be doing it on a composting toilet."

"No kidding?" Ira tried to sound impressed, but he wasn't sure how he felt about using a composting toilet.

"And using a corn cob for toilet paper, just like in the olden days."

Ira was aghast. These people were taking things too—

"*Kidding*, man!" Zed laughed. "You should have seen the look on your face. Dude, there's actual toilet paper. Recycled, of course. Not—" he added jovially – "re-used. Hey, we may have a good time, and party a little, and smoke some doobies, and maybe hook up with hot women – a lot of the women who love the environment are hot, FYI -- but that doesn't mean we're not serious about saving the planet." He drank some more beer. "We just believe in enjoying ourselves while we do it. You know the sound system, the lights, the monster coffee makers they'll have going in the morning? All powered by generators that run on corn-based biodiesel fuel."

Ira was impressed. These Generation Air types walked the walk. He felt a little bit mean about his earlier doubts.

"Hey, guys! I'm glad to see you're getting something to drink."

Zed, hampered by the cup of beer he was holding in one hand, managed to give Oceana a half-hug. "How's it going, babe?"

Even framed by night Oceana was luminous, as if the waning moon overhead sought her out specifically to be a beneficiary of its limited light. For just a moment he tried to be annoyed with her for neglecting him, her guest, but he couldn't. She was probably a key player in the organization, with lots of responsibilities related to the big demonstration tomorrow. He couldn't expect her to baby-sit him. She hadn't gotten him here under false pretenses, after all. Hadn't suggested that it was a hook up. That had been all in his head.

But what was the relationship, exactly, between Oceana and Nathan? Was it platonic? Did she just…look up to the guy, because he was a leader? Ira remembered Nathan's inspiring speech earlier. There was a reason his followers treated him like a rock star.

"We're all ready, Zed. It's a great plan. Nathan has it all worked out, and he'll go over it in the morning. Ira." She turned to him. "I'm sorry I didn't catch up with you before this. Are you having a good time? Did you get something to eat?"

"I'm fine," he said. He gestured. "All this…is pretty amazing."

"It's big, isn't it?" said Zed. "Dude, there are a LOT of people who want to save the air. Oceana, why don't you show him the view of the city from up here? It is sooooo clear, now, since the Big Stoppage. I myself am going to go and get a burger, and then I'm going to check my equipment. I'm filming our little shindig tomorrow. TTYL," he told Ira, who suddenly realized that Zed was the surfer dude videographer he'd seen at that long-ago demonstration. Like Nathan and the others he'd gotten pummeled for his efforts, but here he was, ready for another go.

With a casual wave good-bye, Zed, the unlikely hero, left them and headed over toward the grills.

Oceana took Ira's arm and steered him away from the crowd, over a landscape he could only guess at in the darkness. He recognized the scent of sage, took in the sweet, lush aroma of oleander as they walked in silence. He enjoyed her touch, and missed it when they reached a promontory and she moved her hand from his arm in order to gesture toward the amazing tableau below.

Rocky, scrub-covered hillsides dropped off toward the dense arrangement of lights that was the city, still humming and alive in spite of the changes wrought by the B.S. White-gold lights against a black backdrop delineated the complex grid of streets, illuminated the shadowy forms of buildings, stacked upward in dowtown skyscrapers. He sensed something missing and laughed out loud when he realized what it was: the moving lights of traffic.

Ira found the sprawl strangely beautiful. He gazed at it with a sense of wonder. These people, these Southern Californians, were resilient and resourceful and inventive. Their very way of life was turned on its head, but they still went forward with great vigor, finding new solutions. New ways to succeed.

Despite their greed and phoniness, they were magnificent. He was proud to be one of them.

"I love it up here," she said.

"Yeah, me too." *He loved being here with her.*

She sighed deeply. "What a great view. I could look down at this all night. Too bad I still have work to do."

Ira, sensing a quick end coming to their idyll, sought to prolong it.

"Zed told me about your father. I hadn't known who he was. It must have been terrible, to lose him suddenly like that. And with all that media coverage about it."

She laughed softly. "Oh, I didn't even know him. He and my Mom split when I was a baby. The usual. Too many groupies. It was OK, though. My Mom had a really good lawyer."

He wasn't sure what that meant.

"I was real close to my stepdads."

"Step*dads*?"

"I mean, one at a time. They were really good to me. I didn't have any brothers or sisters, though. My therapist says that's why I love Generation Air so much. It's my surrogate family."

"You think that's true?"

She shrugged. "Maybe. But she doesn't give me any credit for having actual convictions, which I do. I mean, I don't think it's enough to just believe in something. You've got to act on it, if you want to make change happen." She shrugged. "Whatever. It makes me happy. These people make me happy. Isn't that what matters?"

"And you really do believe in the cause," he said, to let her know that he had greater insight into her than her therapist. He could tell how deep she was.

"Oh, yeah. It's like Nathan says, 'What's more of a fundamental human right than having air you can breathe?'"

Nathan again. The spell was broken. For Ira, anyway. Oceana still looked thoughtful.

"But enough about me. I'm not very interesting. What about you? What makes Ira tick? Didn't you say you're a screenwriter?"

Hope! He had hope again - she *had* been listening to him earlier. She was *interested* in him.

"I am. Haven't had anything produced yet, but I'm just about finished with my latest (his *only*) and I really think this is going to break it open for me. I must say, it is damn good."

She looked at him in surprise. "Wow. You are really passionate about your work. Your art," she corrected herself. "That must feel so good. My therapist says I have to work on that."

Wait, he thought. They were about to get off track. He wanted to talk about "Her Majesty's Gangsta" some more. Oh, hell.

"I believe in you," he said abruptly.

She came close, leaned in and, without warning, kissed him. After a moment of astonishment, he recovered his composure and kissed her back, gathering her in his arms, positioning his body against hers, hoping to not feel her move away. He didn't. She gave herself over to him, or at least for the moment. The kiss was long and soulful, igniting many small fires of deeper yearning within him.

"Oceana!" A voice he didn't recognize called out to her. In a moment, a tall girl wearing a tight black t-shirt, a short, plaid, pleated skirt and heavy black boots joined them. "Sorry. Don't mean to interrupt, but Nathan sent me to find you, Oceana. Says he needs you to do the transpo assignments tonight, because there won't be enough time in the morning."

Oceana patted Ira on the arm. "We'll talk more tomorrow," she promised, then walked away with the messenger.

Later, alone in the small tent assigned to him by the accommodations coordinator, Ira replayed the kiss again and again in his mind, enjoying the memory of the sensation of her lips, the feel of her lithe body against his. He eventually grew bored with that and turned restlessly over in his borrowed sleeping bag, trying to find a position in which he could fall asleep. He wished he had his laptop with him so that he could do some writing, but it was at home, safely locked in the trunk of his car-partment.

He started to rough out a pivotal sequence in his mind, although there was a danger in that. He might not remember every detail later. Important dialogue might be lost when he finally closed his eyes and slept. He decided to risk it, because thinking about "Her Majesty's Gangsta" was almost as exciting to him as kissing Oceana.

EXT. LONDON STREET – DAY

The street is full of cars, taxis and buses, moving steadily along. People stroll along the sidewalks.

SHOT: TOP DECK OF RED DOUBLE DECKER BUS

A BAD GUY hits Muldoon hard and he falls into some seats, flipping backwards, scattering frightened passengers.

ANGLE ON: People on the upper deck scrambling to get out of the way. Some are trapped in place by the furious fistfight that's going on nearby; others manage to escape to the lower level.

Muldoon leaps to his feet and punches his adversary. The two are well-matched. Muldoon's style is less subtle than that of his opponent, who demonstrates some moves that suggest martial arts training. The fight continues, with neither gaining much of an advantage.

SHOT: SIDEWALK, where pedestrians look up to the bus' upper deck, realizing that something strange is going on.

Muldoon, clearly frustrated, advances on his opponent, feints and – when the bad guy tries to dodge out of the way – clocks him in the head. The other man falls to the floor, stunned. Muldoon looks smugly pleased with himself. We see the bad guy getting back to his feet in the b.g. while Muldoon dusts himself off and straightens his clothing, checking out a PRETTY YOUNG WOMAN as he does so.

CLOSE SHOT: PRETTY YOUNG WOMAN. She's impressed by Muldoon.

SHOT: MULDOON, taking a step in her direction. Suddenly--

CLOSE SHOT: GUN BARREL PRESSED UP AGAINST MULDOON'S TEMPLE

> MULDOON
> Oh, this can't be good.

INT. LARGE, NEARLY EMPTY ROOM

It is dark save for a single central light, under which sits Muldoon, tied to a chair. The flesh around one eye is a pulpy, discolored mess. Blood drips from the corner of his mouth, down his chin and onto his shirt, which is torn.

Stowaring hurries into the room, goes around to the back of the chair and begins to untie Muldoon's hands.

> MULDOON
> You took your sweet time.

> STOWARING
> Rescuing you was not at the top
> of my list. I was a little busy
> finding out who the target is.

> MULDOON
> Yeah? Well I was busy getting
> the crap beat out of me because
> they were trying to find out how
> much we we knew.

> STOWARING
> Good thing you knew nothing.
> As Usual.

CLOSE SHOT: Muldoon, looking grim.

> MULDOON
> *What's the target?*

EXT. TOWER OF LONDON – DAY

TOURISTS in summer clothes walk around and into the tower.

MEDIUM SHOT: TERRORIST. He is wearing a jacket that appears somewhat heavy for the sunny day. He stays with a group of tourists as they move through the entrance to the tower.

CLOSE SHOT: TERRORIST. He is nervous, sweating.

INT. TOWER OF LONDON ROOM

TWO BEEFEATERS stand next to the doors.

VARIOUS SHOTS: VAULTS

We see gleaming crowns, scepters, rings and swords, laid out in magnificent settings. We get an idea of the enormous wealth and long history held in the vault.

SHOT: VAULT DOOR. It looks impenetrable.

INT. TOWER OF LONDON

The sweaty terrorist slips away from the group of tourists he's been with and hides around a corner, waiting until they're gone.

SHOT: TOWER STAIRWAY. The terrorist stealthily makes his way up the steps.

INT. TOWER

The terrorist peers around a corner at two Beefeaters standing at the end of a corridor. Beyond them, he sees:

SHOT: DOOR TO THE VAULT ROOM

CLOSE SHOT: TERRORIST

He is edgy, sweating profusely. He takes a deep breath and moves quickly around the corner, toward the guards.

MEDIUM SHOT: GUARDS

Startled by the intruder, they shift into a ready stance.

> TERRORIST
> *(in a heavy accent)*
> *Where is the lavatory? Can you tell me how to get to the men's room?*

They struggle to understand him. He gets closer. Suddenly—

CLOSE SHOT: HE'S GOT A TASER GUN IN EACH HAND

He zaps the Beefeaters. As they fall to the ground, he quickly moves beyond them and into the vault room.

INT. VAULT ROOM

The terrorist runs into the room, toward the vault door. The two Beefeaters in the room react, but not quickly enough to stop him. He gets to the vault door and turns to face them, opening up his jacket to reveal the bombs strapped to his chest. He reaches for some sort of button on the bomb pack. The brave Beefeaters take a step toward him.

> TERRORIST
> *(in heavily accented English)*
> *I wish to die, and embrace martyrdom. These crown jewels*

*are a symbol of Western
decadence.*

In the next instant, Stowaring and Muldoon—

Ira ran out of ideas and hit a blank wall head on. What, exactly, should Stowaring and Muldoon do here? Should they shoot the guy and risk setting off his bomb? Do they tackle him, which might give him the chance to set off the bomb himself? Knocking him to the ground might detonate it without him even pushing the button. Sure, they could negotiate with him, or maybe one could distract him with conversation while the other sneaks up on him. But that still left him with a boring potential victim. Although priceless, the crown jewels lacked the human element, the *pathos* that a room full of frightened, screaming people would have. Plus, you couldn't even see the crowns and stuff, unless you took the camera into the vault.

This scene wasn't going to work. He'd have to go back to his original idea, and have the guy somehow get into Parliament while it was in session, and threaten to blow everybody up. Maybe Kate Middleton would be visiting that day. Or the Queen. He'd been disappointed to find through his research that British lawmakers no longer wore white wigs. What was the world coming to, when the English couldn't be counted on to uphold traditions? It would have made a terrific visual. He could have had Muldoon and Stowaring sneak into Parliament ahead of the bad guys and then, just when the terrorist reveals himself, the two heroes would pull off their wigs and robes and start the smackdown! He played that scene over and over in his mind, loving it, even though he couldn't use it. It would *definitely* have been in the trailer. Muldoon, with his black eye and bloody lip, would have looked *brilliant* in a ridiculous white wig!

Drowsiness enveloped his thought processes, swathing his mind in cottony confusion, but he stubbornly struggled to resolve the problem before falling asleep. Once this scene was worked out, he was just about finished with the screenplay. Since there were no wigs and robes, there was no real point to staging the climax in Great Britain – aside from the fact that it was more exotic than a stateside setting. Why not have Muldoon and

Stowaring trail the terrorists back to the U.S., and stop them from attacking Capitol Hill? No, that wouldn't work, he decided. American audiences would *cheer* if Congress was blown up.

Disappointed because the scene was still unset, but excited and curious about what was to happen the following day with Generation Air – and with Oceana -- he finally let sleep pull him into its dark tunnel.

CHAPTER FORTY-SIX:
SKY BLUE SOMETHINGS

There was yoga at dawn. Once the sun rose high enough to light the upper reaches of the park, it drew dozens of lithe people to rows of yoga mats that were spread out on the ground. Led by a slim, ponytailed woman who demonstrated the moves on the stage in front of them, the early birds stretched and contorted their bodies while new age music composed of whale song and tinkling wind chimes issued gently from the speakers overhead.

Ira opted instead for some high octane wakeup fuel from one of the monster coffee makers. As he drank it, he eavesdropped on the conversations around him, trying to plug into the excitement he sensed from his fellow caffeinators.

"Dude!" Zed was wearing a t-shirt today, along with shorts, and, inexplicably, a knit cap that reminded Ira of Michigan winters. "How'd you sleep?"

"It wasn't bad," Ira admitted. "Pretty comfortable, in fact. What's for breakfast? And when does this shindig start?"

"Whoooah, dude. Chill. We've got plenty of time. The politicos have timed their big heli-lift for MME. Maximum media exposure. They want it to dominate the suppertime news, so it won't get started until later on. We've got to get there early, of course, and get all ready."

Nathan laid out his plans at a midmorning meeting. This speech, unlike yesterday's, was quiet and contained, detailed rather than inspirational.

"We know from our sources that the first heli-lift will take place at the 405-101 junction," he said. "There are more planned, but this is the first, and thus critical one. The one staged especially for the media."

Zed snickered. He leaned close to Ira and whispered: "They named it the 405 because, even in the good old days, you could only go four or five miles an hour on it."

"We don't know exactly which vehicles are targeted for removal, so we'll have to be ready to swing into our positions as soon as we see people putting slings under cars. They're to be lifted like cargo is loaded onto ships but instead of being attached to cranes, these slings will be attached to lines hanging from helicopters."

Off to the side of the stage, Ira could see a half dozen volunteers organizing into a sort of assembly line. They shuffled along, taking items from tabletops and placing them into blue nylon backpacks. There were binoculars, bottles of water, power bars, and devices that Ira thought must be walkie talkies.

"We will act as human shields. When the cars are being readied for transport, we will climb up onto their roofs and do our best to *stay* up there. Keep in mind: there will be local, national and even international TV news crews on hand, broadcasting live. Generation Air spokesmen will be giving interviews as the heli-lift is proceeding – or *not* proceeding, hopefully. That way, we will have some control over the spin that's given to the event. We will not be portrayed as crazy extremists who are simply anti-progress. The American people will get to hear our point of view. What they will not get are images of people falling to their deaths. The government won't risk bad p.r. like that."

Really? thought Ira. Because when Nathan was describing his plan, people falling to their deaths was *exactly* the image that came into Ira's mind. He'd been wrong: these activists *were* nutjobs.

"If we get atop the cars and stay atop the cars, they'll be forced to abort the mission. All of those cameras that will be on hand are our insurance."

Riiiiight. Keep telling yourself that, Nathan, you lunatic. Ira realized that he should have made a quick, unobtrusive exit the instant he heard the phrase, "human shields." In fact, as soon as he finished his plateful of rather excellent buckwheat pancakes cooked on large griddles by smiling Generation Air volunteers, he was going to jet out of here. He marveled at the freshness of the blueberries topping the pancakes.

"They won't completely guarantee our safety, though," Nathan said. "As I mentioned yesterday, we may come up against mercenaries, hired for the occasion by the oil and gas people who very much want this heli-lift to succeed. These hired thugs are the ones you want to watch out for. They may be able to pull people off the cars and assault them out of view of the cameras. That's a real possibility."

Ira saw Oceana, talking animatedly with one of the backpack stuffers. She was holding an armful of sky blue…somethings. He couldn't tell what, but they appeared to be made from fabric. At her direction, the volunteers starting placing the blue objects into backpacks. As with the other glimpses he'd gotten of her this morning, she seemed very busy. He wished he could get a minute to talk with her before this day all went to hell. Last night's kiss was magical to him. Had it felt the same to her? Ira felt as if he should go to the protest to keep an eye on Oceana, if for no other reason. Did she even understand how risky this undertaking was going to be? A poor little rich girl, Zed had called her. She'd no doubt lived a sheltered life. She probably had no idea that she could get hurt, seriously hurt, if she followed Nathan into this insanely ill-conceived scheme.

Far from seeming like a madman at that moment, Nathan sounded quite reasonable. "If all this sounds too intense for any of you, we understand. If you'd like to go with us but not engage in the most dangerous part of our protest, that'd be great, too. We can use the logistical support. We may have to make a quick getaway, and we need people ready to help us with that."

The now-full backpacks were lined up on tables, ready for wearing. Several large banners on long poles were placed nearby. Behind Nathan, two men took down the Generation Air banner that had been waving over him. They carried it away and set it down next to the others.

"This is a pivotal day," Nathan said. "It's impossible to overestimate the importance of what we're going to do today. We are taking back the very air that we breathe. Telling the power structure that we're not going to be led around like sheep. Oh, no. We are the ones who get to decide our destinies. I hope this day goes just as we've planned. We'll successfully block the heli-lift and no one will get hurt. That is my hope. It may not work out that way. Remember: we will try our utmost to avoid violence, but if we can't – if the other side starts it – then let's show these bastards that we have the courage of our convictions."

The assembly broke into applause and piercing whistles. Nathan beamed his approval at his minions.

Ira stared uneasily at some long, dark objects revealed when people moved away from a table at the perimeter of the crowd. Were those *guns?*

CHAPTER FORTY-SEVEN:
A WASPY CHORUS OF TRUTHS

Jesus. Were his hands going to shake like this when he was on live TV?

He'd really screwed up. Why he'd had a slip the night before the most important day of his administration was beyond him. No it wasn't, he realized. He'd had a slip precisely because it was the night before the most important day of his administration. He was so stressed out last night he wanted to scream. Even Misty was concerned. When she talked to him on the phone and heard the tension in his voice, she insisted on coming over. Said she'd never heard him sound like that before. No wonder it'd happened. He was only human.

The trembling of his fingers – which felt clammy -- made buttoning his shirt difficult, but he finally got that task completed. His legs were fluttery. Unsteady. He sat down suddenly at the end of his bed, wondering if he was going to be able to get through the gubernatorial appearance ahead. Fortunately, after his speech the only physical thing he had to do in the circus act that was planned for today was to look skyward toward the hovering helicopters and sweep his hand as if to signal the helicopters to "Come!" His advisors felt that using a military gesture would give him a commanderly air. It was, of course, purely for show. The helicopter pilots would be following instructions given via radio, by a controller on the ground.

Hopefully, at that point, all eyes would be on the aircraft, or on the cars swinging on cables beneath them. That sight would be so compelling that no one, presumably, would be looking at shaky Jorge. What did Cap Lessing like to call him? "Jorge the Jerk-ay"? Well today he deserved that nickname. After more than three years of sobriety, he would now have to start all over again.

He ran a hand through his hair, still damp from a shower. He didn't have to style it himself today. Marco, his usual stylist for public appearances, would be coming to the house shortly, along with a makeup artist booked for the occasion. He hoped this one was better than the last. When he'd looked at his "State of the State" speech, his skin tone was a hideous orange, and not the healthy glow he'd requested.

Maybe if he ate some breakfast, got something on his stomach, he'd feel better. He should at least try to eat a piece of toast. Unwillingly, he met his own eyes in the mirror. *You're weak*, he admonished himself silently. *If only they knew what a loser you are.* But then he thought: *It was just a few drinks! Not many at all.*

He wished to God he could cancel the heli-lift today, or postpone it for a week or two. Long enough for him to get his bearings back. It *had* to be the booze that was having this effect on him, because he didn't normally suffer from stage fright. Jorge Olmstead was a natural performer, at least on the political stage. Usually he blossomed in the white hot glare of the spotlight. He wondered if anyone watching today would be able to tell that he'd downed a shot of whiskey last night. *Now you're just being paranoid*, he told himself. It's not like alcohol gave a person a radioactive glow or something.

Misty had brought the bottle of whiskey, said it would calm his nerves and it did, at least initially. He took a tiny sip and waited a moment for something dramatic to happen – some Dr. Jekyll-Mr. Hyde-like-transformation – but nothing did. Then the whispers started, rising up from the depths of his regret-ridden past to scold him with a waspy chorus of truths: *It's been a long time; you can control it now...Just one won't hurt you...You're not like other people...It wasn't an addiction with you, it was a bad habit...* To numb the whispers into silence he drank another shot of whiskey. He soon realized the enormity of his mistake. The whiskey burned brightly as it took hold, made promises, assured him of its love, cried out for more, so that more promises could be made, more love could be given. Misty had helpfully kept pouring him drinks until angrily, he'd sent her away and shut himself up alone in the bedroom of his rented condo. If he just stayed where he was he knew he'd be OK. There was no alcohol in the condo. Of course, he could easily get some. But he wouldn't. If he stayed there and got through the night, he'd be safe. He'd felt a surprising, unwelcome impulse to call his wife, but stifled it. The lawyers were doing all the communicating now. The divorce was still in the angry, acute stage that he remembered so well. Years from now she might take his call and listen sympathetically to him as he talked about his problems, but not now. She was still too pissed off. He was sad about that, because she was a great listener. It was one of the things he loved about her.

The good news, he thought, was that one night of drinking didn't cause him to go on a bender, like it would have in the old days. Not that he was planning to test his tolerance. The point is: he'd dodged a bullet. He'd taken a big chance but hadn't really fallen off the wagon. Not really. Here it was, the next morning, and he was just fine. The alcohol was out of his system by now. He was clean and sober again. What happened last night was just a tiny blip on the radar screen, easily forgotten. He wished he could skip ahead a few weeks or even months to when the shameful episode would be well behind him.

He chose a tie from his extensive collection: a handsome cranberry silk number with subtle grey designs on it. He was starting to feel better. Stronger. Maybe he was overreacting to last night. After all, a lot of time had passed since he'd been a certified, rip-roaring drunk. He was a different person now. A governor, for God's sake. Was it possible that he could control it now? He chided himself for even considering the subject, when he had so many other things to think about this morning. Today was a huge day in his career. Although…a quick shot of whiskey would settle his nerves…

CHAPTER FORTY-EIGHT:
LIKE GODS FROM MT. OLYMPUS

They *were* guns, of a sort: smoke guns that fired dense, brightly colored bursts of vapor. They were developed by a games manufacturer for use in futuristically-styled indoor arenas in which teenage boys would use all sorts of non-lethal but spectacular weaponry to vanquish each other. Parents would love them because unlike paintball guns, they left no stains. Investors were being lined up. Franchises were being planned.

Ira watched, fascinated, as a rough-hewn commando-looking type demonstrated the pseudo-weapon to a group of activists standing in front of him.

"Do NOT, I repeat, do NOT fire directly at the helicopter. We don't want the pilots to lose visibility and crash. No fatalities, people. That is NOT what we're about!" He handed around belts holding large plastic cartridges, which his listeners slung over their shoulders like old school bandidos. These guns are already loaded. You probably won't need the extra ammo, but in case you do need to reload, you just break it open like this—" -- he cracked open the rifle – "replace the cartridges, snap it shut and you're good to go."

"Will it make a really loud noise?" one girl asked nervously.

The demonstrator shook his head. "Nahhhh. It's more like a popping sound. I'll show you."

The nervous girl and several others took a few steps back as he swung the rifle up.

"You hold it like this, sight down the barrel, and then, just before you pull the trigger…take a breath and hold it, to steady yourself." He did so, aiming at a shrub some yards distant and squeezing off a shot, accompanied by a dull thud that was nonetheless loud enough to cause a few people to wince. An impressively thick purple cloud enveloped the shrub, obscuring it completely. The effect lasted longer than Ira expected.

"As Generation Air sharpshooters—" -- a few people chuckled at that -- "your job will be to back up the human shields. If it looks like the government is going to go ahead and lift those cars out of there in spite of our people hanging onto them, then you will fire across the tops of the cars, so that when the helicopter pilots look down, they can't sight their targets. All they'll see," he said, in a tone of deep satisfaction, "are beautiful clouds of color: lime green, orange, aqua and the deep purple that just took out that shrub. Symbolically speaking, I mean. The shrub is unharmed. The vapor contains non-toxic chemicals that make it hold its shape for awhile before dissolving. Hopefully that'll be long enough to prevent the helicopters from doing what they're supposed to do, because they won't know where they're supposed to be. Any questions?"

"Can we try them out before we go?"

"What if mine jams?"

Ira wondered: *How will the cops know that these guns only shoot smoke*? They look real. But he didn't say it out loud. Not his problem.

Instead he walked away, feeling nervous and excited even though he was not one of the sharpshooters, nor was he one of the human shields who were getting their instructions from Nathan, over near the stage. He wasn't a transportation coordinator, either. They were already down at a lower level, at the north side of the park, making sure a fleet of motorcycles was ready for departure. He wasn't a backpack-hander-outer, or a communications crew member, making sure the walkie talkies were in working order. He wasn't assigned to one of the two-man teams that would hold up big banners. He wasn't an officially designated spokesperson. He passed that telegenic group just as they finished quizzing each other on the talking points they'd use while being interviewed on TV. They put away their packets of note cards and gathered in a tight circle, extending their arms so that their hands stacked over each other in a formation he remembered from elementary school baseball games. "Stay on MEH-sej!," they chanted. "Stay on MEH-sej! STAY ON MESSAGE! YEAHHHHH!" On the last cheer, they disengaged their hands and raised them exuberantly in the air before breaking the circle.

He almost felt envious of their solidarity. He had no real role here, but that was by choice. He intended to stand on the sidelines and watch. Be there for moral support, and to keep an eye on Oceana. So why was he feeling so jittery?

Once he saw that Oceana would be riding with Nathan, Ira accepted Zed's invitation to ride on the back of his motorcycle, even though it wasn't easy to reach his arms around Zed and hang on, because the other's backpack bulged with his video camera and equipment. Naturally Oceana would go with Nathan, Ira thought. She was his lieutenant. She had to stay close to him. But she'd kissed Ira. That meant something, didn't it?

The fluid swarm of motorcycles that was the Generation Air brigade deformed and reformed continuously as it moved west toward Sherman Oaks, grinding slowly but relentlessly between lanes of parked cars and the people who called them home, beating on like boats against the current toward their destination.

Ira had to give the governor some credit for picking the 405-101 interchange for the heli-lift. The 405, ironically, was designed to be a speedy bypass of downtown, spiriting Southern Californians down from the heights of the Sepulveda Pass, past the Getty Museum -- perched on a hillside like a white stone fortress – to descend through Westwood and Brentwood and join with Mulholland Drive before dropping to just below Ventura Boulevard. Instead of being an escape route, it became a trap. It was notorious as the freeway that *invented* the 24-hour rush hour. Even before the B.S., the 405-101 juncture was a giant, throbbing hub of frustration for anyone who had to use it, an ill-fated coupling of two major freeways in close proximity to two major thoroughfares. Rather than lightening the load by siphoning off some of the traffic, Sepulveda and Ventura Boulevards actually amped up the frenzy level of the bumper car game because they caused motorists to scramble in panic across lanes in order to get to their exits. Today, though, Ira saw that it was a giant cluster of serenity, or maybe of resignation. Cars sat motionless in its doomed lanes, one after another, like metal tombstones. Although there was evidence of habitation, the people currently living in car-partments here were nowhere in sight. Ira guessed that they'd been evacuated from the scene because of the day's big event.

Attracting no special attention, the Generation Airites parked their motorcycles off to the side of the freeway. They immediately began organizing themselves into smaller, specialized units. The sharpshooters nervously checked their weapons while looking at a large map on which were marked the locations of probable targets. Some Airites sprinted away from the group, spreading out and staring through binoculars, walkie talkies at the ready so they could give status reports when the whole thing started. More coalition members arrived, including some surly young guys with shaved heads, wearing white wife-beaters and low slung pants, with PulmoNation tattoos on their upper arms. They didn't mingle and socialize with the Generation Airites. They didn't want to be buddies; they were clearly too invested in being outsiders. Outlaws.

Ira dug a bag of chips and a bottled water from the backpack that had been given to him and joined others who were sitting cross-legged on the ground, waiting, eating, smoking. A red-haired girl next to him pushed buttons on her cell phone intently. When she finished sending her text message she looked up, unshed tears brightening her eyes.

"I sent a text to my parents," she confided to Ira, her tone heavy with emotion. "Just in case."

Ira was alarmed. What the hell had he gotten into here? A suicide cult? Were they about to be issued new tennis shoes and little purple blankets? "Just in case of what?"

"In case I get arrested," she said. "They know to call our lawyer. They thought that I was with my boyfriend. He's got a cabin at Big Bear." She shook her head sadly. "I broke up with him *two weeks ago.*" She sighed distantly and shook her head. "My Mom and Dad don't even know me."

Ira nodded sympathetically.

Some people performed elaborate stretching routines, as if they were warming up for an athletic event. Ira supposed they were, in a way, and realized that even the yoga had been purposeful. Human shields were going to have to sprint to their targets and then climb quickly on top of cars. They were ready, he conceded. Limber. An image from the distant past came back to him, of himself, crouched on an imaginary diving board high over an imaginary pool, getting his confidence pumped up for a stupid telephone call. Had that petty little man, all caught up in pointless office drama, really been him? He was above that world now. Aloft, as an artist. Fear of Sid, anxiety about hanging onto his dead-end job, concerns about other people perceiving him as a lowly office assistant when he was, in fact, A Writer – he'd shed all of those ridiculosities like a rocket lifts free of its ugly, earth-bound scaffolding as it ignites in a fiery, magnificent blast and takes to the sky. All those mundane worries that used to control him were like so much insignificant debris now, baggage from a past that existed but that no longer affected him. They were like the wild scrub brush that clumped here and there alongside the freeway, existing but hardly noticeable because people saw instead its newer, more pleasing, deliberately planted neighbors; the graceful, drooping pepper trees and fragrant eucalyptus trees.

Ira recognized TV station logos and radio station call letters amid the temporary media infrastructure assembled in front of a grandstand. Newspaper and online reporters must be represented as well, but they weren't as easy to spot as the glam TV types who were preening themselves and prepping for a live event. They couldn't afford flubs; there'd be no re-takes today. They'd arrived by helicopter, descending like gods from Mt. Olympus, and so appeared fresh and alert. Their techie counterparts, busy setting up, looked exhausted. Since they'd had to roll most of their equipment through the streets themselves, Ira guessed that many of them had been on foot since dawn. That was the advantage of the B.S., at least for the activists. The governor would probably have preferred to keep the location and time of this little shindig a secret until the last minute, to minimize interference, but he couldn't. The media – for whom this whole thing was being staged -- needed too much notice. He was amazed when he realized that there were reporters here from Japan, Australia and Great Britain. Possibly other countries as well. Could the problems of one part of one state really be of that much interest to the rest of the world?

Some reporters were already hard at work. He recognized the plastic-looking guy from the Glitz! Network, managing to talk and smile at the same time as he delivered what was no doubt an earnest yet superficial description of the story that was unfolding here. When Ira crept closer to listen, he recognized the girl in the red dress who stood next to that idiot, Wellborn or

Welldone. Something phony like that. Oh, yes: Trask Weldon. A soap opera character name if he'd ever heard one.

But his companion was Luanne Sajewski, rising star of the surprise hit, "Aunt Mom," and recent passenger on the bike-shaw of one Ira O'Riley. She looked really good in that red dress, he thought, a little surprised. Kind of hot, even though she wasn't exactly slim. And what a great smile.

Luanne was smiling as she listened to her heavily hair-sprayed co-host babble, although Ira was almost sure he detected an ironic cast to her expression.

"...almost as exciting as New Year's Eve in Times Square, waiting for the big ball to drop."

"Oh, yes," Luanne said. "I do find big balls exciting."

Weldon looked at her, aghast, choking just a little, then tried to recover. "Luanne, this is a family friendly show."

She pretended to be puzzled. "Trask, I thought we were talking about New Year's Eve. You always do such a great job of hosting the Glitz! Network's coverage of the party. Are you doing that again this year?"

Under her praise, Weldon puffed up like a pigeon preening before a potential mate. "Wouldn't miss it, Luanne. I've already signed on. And I'm told that the musical lineup will be even better than last year's."

"Really," she said, sounding enthused. "Do tell."

Ira thought: she has no idea who was in the musical lineup last year. She would never watch an imbecile like this host *anything*. As Weldon promoted his upcoming appearance in some detail, Ira moved even closer, to get a good look at Luanne's glazed – or was that dazed? – expression. How could a smart woman like her pretend to be interested in this drivel? She *must* be a really good actress. Luanne turned slightly at the movement and looked at him. Their eyes met. She recognized him, smiling in acknowledgement and giving a subtle nod, still mindful of the camera trained on her. She really did look good. Ira smiled back at her and inclined his head toward Weldon, his expression trying to communicate: *you really have to put up with an idiot here, don't you?*

It was at that moment that Zed, wielding his own camera, found him. "Dude, are you ready?" He asked loudly. Not waiting for an answer, he added, "Man, I am PUMPED! This is what it all comes down to! This is the MOMENT OF TRUTH, dude!"

An angry stare from Luanne's cameraman motivated Ira to take Zed's arm and move him away from her and Weldon. Ira was fascinated by Zed's transformation. Sleepy-eyed, deliberately mellow Zed was now in the testosterone zone. He was so amped up he seemed ready to jump out of his own skin.

Zed clapped him on the shoulder, not gently. "Ira! You don't know how lucky you are. You are here to watch HISTORY being made, dude."

They became aware of an artificially amplified voice punching through the many layers of conversation taking place around the interchange, gradually asserting its dominance.

"…and the addition of HOV lanes did not measurably alleviate the situation."

It was Governor Olmstead, standing on the hood of a BMW, working the crowd. He was flanked on both sides by *suits*. Ira recognized the mayor of Los Angeles and a few other politicians. There were probably transportation officials as well. The place was lousy with smilers. It was an effectively staged photo op, Ira realized. A dramatic picture. Olmstead's position both showed him atop a symbol of what was so terribly wrong, and also elevated him physically and authoritatively above everyone else. His fellow suits stood around him like choir members in a Baptist church who were backing up a talented lead vocalist, nodding instead of "Amen-ing" at key points he made.

"Even when traffic was moving in the Southland, it wasn't moving very well here." Olmstead smiled grimly. "Maybe that's because more than 300 THOUSAND vehicles passed through this particular cluster of freeways and roadways EVERY SINGLE DAY. It wasn't just one of the worst bottlenecks in the state. It was one of the worst bottlenecks in the NATION."

The crowed reacted, impressed. Almost proud, Ira thought.

"What did that mean for motorists who had to travel through here? In real terms?" Olmstead waited a long moment, looking around him. "It meant that those unfortunate people, collectively, wasted more than 27,000 hours a year." Olmstead allowed himself to look angry, in a controlled, gubernatorial way. "That kind of waste is UNACCEPTABLE.

"Now some have said that this traffic crisis is L.A.'s problem. Or Southern California's problem, but I reject that. It is only by working together that we will restore this portion of our magnificent state to full productivity. What we will do here today is just the first step in that process."

"You're putting a band-aid on a corpse!" someone in the crowd shouted.

"We will not allow negativity to keep us from moving toward a resolution," Olmstead said sternly, not looking in the direction of the heckler.

Olmstead's speech had distracted Ira from noticing the rather impressive number of uniformed cops who had quietly, almost unobtrusively moved into places along the perimeters of the freeways. Grasping the extent of the security that would be in place for the heli-lift, he began to entertain serious doubts about whether Generation Air was going to succeed. His mouth went dry with fear, with the growing conviction that people would get hurt today. He felt like he should leap forward, getting as close to the governor as he could, and shout out Generation Air's plans before he was inevitably tackled by cops. It would be a betrayal, but it might save the lives of his new friends.

Oh, hell. He was being overly dramatic. No one would get killed. Injured, maybe, but not killed. Not with all of this media scrutiny.

At the very least, the cops could shut down the activists' scheme in about five minutes, and the heli-lift could proceed as planned. Ira was almost hoping that it would play out that way. He hated confrontation, even when he was only participating in it vicariously.

Olmstead outlined the details of the heli-lift, with the help of a digital presentation on a giant screen set up to his right. Curving lines representing freeways lit up and smaller rectangular objects that were cars and tracks pulsed with color as he described what was about to happen.

"...calculated that the strategic removal of vehicles at key points will *eventually* allow traffic to resume moving through this interchange, albeit slowly. This will not be an instant fix, so those of you who are watching this scene and hoping to hear me say, 'Gentlemen, start your engines,' will be disappointed." He paused, presumably for a laugh. It didn't come.

"No one will be allowed to start their cars until this same procedure has been repeated at a dozen other locations in the Southland. Due to the complexity of these heli-lifts and the equipment that's involved, we anticipate that part of the process to take at least a week.

"What you WILL see is the beginning of the end -- the end of our long traffic nightmare. We are developing long-range solutions, and we'll be holding a series of town hall meetings to get your reactions to various proposals. It won't be easy, and it won't occur overnight, but we will get Southern California back to normal. And, so, my fellow Californians, I give you, OPERATION SKYWAY!"

The conclusion of his speech was met with cheers and boos, wild hoots of approval and empty soda cans thrown with derision. Olmstead pretended not to notice any of it. Instead, with a beatific smile on his face, he swept his arm upward toward the heavens, appearing to usher in the squadron of helicopters that now slid into view overhead.

CHAPTER FORTY-NINE:
THAT IS TERRORISM, SWEETHEART

"What do you people really think you're going to accomplish here today? Besides getting a lot of attention for yourselves – something you obviously thrive on."

"Good question, Cap. Our goal today is to prevent the government from returning us to business as usual, because business as usual was intolerable." Jayne Fogel was pleased to hear how unruffled she sounded.

"And the Big Stoppage isn't intolerable? You sniveling, elitist spoiled brat fanatics care more about the *environment*" -- he uttered the word snidely, as if it were something despicable – "than you do about people."

The Generation Air spokesman cringed, inwardly cursing the fact that she'd drawn the short straw – the Cap Lessing Show. She'd initially thought that not having to deal with that vitriolic, fractious blowhard face-to-face would be easier, less combative, but it wasn't. Lessing was able to project his venom quite well through the combination headphone/microphone headset his flunkie handed to Jayne, after setting up the interview. Naturally, the fat man couldn't be bothered to inconvenience himself by actually coming to this historic scene. Instead, he was broadcasting comfortably from his studio, probably while stuffing his face with glazed doughnuts.

"Cap, we are *very* mindful of the suffering caused by the B.S. We see it all around us, every day. That's why Generation Air has done so much outreach since the B.S. began, going to car communities, handing out food and supplies. We don't want this situation to go on indefinitely. But we all remember the suffering that occurred before the B.S. We can't go back to that, Cap."

"What suffering?"

"Air that made us sick, for one thing. Air we couldn't breathe."

"That's funny. I was breathing it just fine. So were a lot of other people."

Stay calm. He's just trying to get a rise out of you.

"Look, sweetheart. L.A. is no place for namby pambies. We built this city in a desert. We stole our water from the mountains. We build schools and hospitals on fault lines. The Pacific Coast Highway gets covered all the time by rockslides, but that doesn't stop anyone who can afford to do so from living in Malibu. The Hollywood Hills are a dry tinderbox, ready to burst into flames at any moment. Do you see residents moving out of the Hills? There's all kinds of crap floating in the water around the Santa Monica Pier, from bacteria to raw sewage to used condoms, but do we stop swimming in the ocean? No one and nothing is entitled to be here. Not even the palm trees – did you know that? They're imported, like everything else. Those of us who are lucky enough to live here do so because we are tougher than nature. Tougher than earthquakes and mudslides. We thrive on polluted air! It makes our lungs stronger because they have to work harder!"

"That's ridiculous, Cap. Are you even listening to yourself?" Even Jayne realized what a tepid response that was, but really, what rejoinder could she make to a statement that preposterous? He was just trying to rattle her cage. She tried to focus, but found her attention being captured by the helicopters hovering over the interchange. How many were there? A half dozen? More? Was it safe, to have airspace this crowded? What if there was a crash? She looked around for places that might provide cover. There were none.

"And those people who can't take it?" Here Cap manufactured a few theatrical coughs, and a melodramatic character voice. "Oh, I can't breathe! Help me!" More coughing, then he was back to his normal, abrasive tone. "They should move away. Or die. Natural selection. Evolution. Isn't that what you lefties are always talking about? The unproven theory you're so fond of forcing on our helpless-to-resist schoolchildren? According to your Mr. Darwin, it's good that the weak die off. Strengthens the species. Isn't that right?"

Stay on message. Don't let him steer you away from the heli-lift. "This is not a partisan issue, Cap. Everyone is affected by environmental destruction."

Lessing hooted. "But *economic* destruction is OK? That's what you're saying, because that's what we've got going on right

311

now. The air might be great, sweetie, but people can't work and they can't live the way they want to. We need to get back into our cars and get going again!"

"All Generation Air wants is for the solution to be environmentally acceptable." Jayne wondered how much longer she had to endure this torture. Why couldn't she be over there talking to CNN, instead of dealing with this idiot? It wasn't fair. She was majoring in communications at Cal State, considering a career in public relations. Now, she wasn't so sure. If this was what it was like to deal with the media…

"And you're the people who are going to determine that? What gives you the authority? You're a bunch of whiny, snively brats. Nobody voted you into office."

She wished he could see Lessing's face, then changed her mind. It would be like looking at a male Medusa, but she'd be risking madness instead of blindness. Still, an in-person interview would give her an edge because she was attractive (she had to admit to herself), and ugly men were usually intimidated by her looks. She really should have been assigned to TV, not radio. "Well, it's not that—"

"And exactly what is it that you're planning to do here today? I've got inside information that Generation Air is going to detonate bombs underneath parked cars. That is TERRORISM, sweetheart, any way that you look at it! Property damage may not mean anything to you spoiled rich kids, but what about human lives? People could be killed by these bombs. How can you possibly justify something like that?"

"That is an outrageous allegation, Cap," she sputtered. "We are not going to set off bombs—"

"But threatening to is just as bad! You'll cause a mass panic. Maybe a stampede. People could get killed!"

Jayne was so angry her cheeks felt inflamed. She struggled to maintain a calm, reasonable tone. Her screaming at him in frustration was exactly the kind of response he was hoping for. "Generation Air does not use bombs, or threats of bombs. Ever. We use only nonviolent means to make our points. We are here today precisely because we value human life so much." She congratulated herself for getting a few complete sentences out.

"Your leader, Nathan Zardoz, has a lengthy criminal record.

Do his nine arrests include any for explosives? Domestic terrorism?"

Jayne exhaled, allowing her shoulders to untense a little. She'd been braced for whatever dirt Lessing would, predictably, dig up on them. If this was the fat man's trump card, she had nothing to worry about.

"Nathan has been arrested for civil disobedience, Cap. Just like another great American, Henry David Thoreau."

"Get your facts straight, sweetheart. Thoreau was arrested for not paying his taxes."

She heard Olmstead trying to speak again, but the noise of the helicopter engines obliterated his words. The crowd cheered, reacting to the whirly birds as if they were about to see stunts in an air show. In a way, she supposed, they were.

"What's going on there?" Cap demanded.

"It looks as if the heli-lift is about to begin." It was time for her to escape this hell.

"Then we'll have to wrap this up, so you can put my K-Talk-L.A. reporter back on with me. Unless you'd care to do the honors? Give my listeners a blow-by-blow description of what's going on there?"

"No."

"Didn't think so."

Was it possible to actually *hear* someone sneer?

CHAPTER FIFTY:
A MANY-HEADED MONSTER

Once the heli-lift got underway, things happened fast. Ira watched intently from the sidelines while eating a power bar, as if he was taking in a pretty good action movie. At Zed's urging, he'd reluctantly donned the sky blue mask that'd been in his backpack, feeling as if it made him look like a gay Robin Hood. Once he had it on, though, he was pleased by the anonymity it conferred upon him. It almost made him feel invisible. He wished it was snugger, so he didn't have to keep adjusting it. It was one size fits all, which made him worry: was his head smaller than average? (*And, by extension, his brain and other body parts?*)

At a signal he couldn't see, state workers wearing bright orange vests ran to various points of the interchange. Why the high-viz? thought Ira. It wasn't like some fast-moving truck was going to knock them down. But, he concluded that costuming was an important element in spectacle. This was, after all, the home of the entertainment industry. Besides, if things got crazy and the police moved in, they'd easily be able to sort out the protestors from the people who were authorized to be there.

Some of the workers climbed onto cars and, wielding cans of spray paint, inscribed large numbers on their roofs. Ira already knew that this was so the individual helicopter pilots would know which car they were supposed to pick up. Otherwise, it would be an aerial free-for-all. Cables with large hooking mechanisms began descending from the whirly birds.

Other workers, in two-person teams, got down on the ground and pushed large slings underneath those cars, straightening up to lift the ends of the slings on either side.

Generation Air protestors in sky blue masks and their unmasked PulmoNation comrades struck like lightning, sprinting to the targeted cars and vaulting onto them. Some got into shoving matches with the spray painters and a few were knocked to the ground. They landed on their feet and sprang back up on their perches faster than Ira would have thought possible. Others were ignored. Some jumped up onto nontargeted cars and spray painted numbers on their roofs, to confuse the chopper pilots. Zed, he saw, was in the midst of it all, videotaping like mad. Ira was reassured to know that Oceana was safely on the sidelines, holding a smoke gun that she would fire if necessary.

The cables dropped lower. The end of one came close enough to its intended target for the protestor atop it to give it a hearty push out of the way. It swung in a large, potentially dangerous ellipse, causing the annoyed state worker who was trying to catch it to lean back too far and fall off the top of the car backwards, unable to brace his fall. The audience gasped, waiting. In a moment, the worker popped back up into view between the parked cars, one hand clamped onto his head but seemingly all right. He gave a brief wave to those who applauded his reappearance.

Nathan leapt dramatically onto a pickup truck that was in the center of the action. Naturally, he moved like an Olympic gymnast, thought Ira resentfully. Someone tossed a rolled-up banner to him and he unfurled it, stretching his arms above his head to hold it high. "YEARNING TO BREATHE FREE" it read. Ira had to admire the dramatic photo opp he created. Nathan turned in a circle, like Sally Field in "Norma Rae," so that people at all angles could see it. He elicited as many boos as cheers. Nonplussed, he began shouting something. Ira could barely hear it, at first, but then the protestors near him took up the chant, and it grew louder.

"WE WANT CLEAN AIR! WE WANT CLEAN AIR!"

Other spectators joined in. It spread through the crowd, to the outer edges, swelling into a loud and defiant chorus.

"WE WANT CLEAN AIR! WE WANT CLEAN AIR! WE WANT CLEAN AIR!"

The intervention of uniformed police officers just then brought the chant to a disjointed ending, as if it was a many-headed monster, silenced by degrees as each of its heads was cut off. One protestor had to stop shouting when he was physically removed from his perch by two determined cops who carried him, kicking and squirming, from the scene. Others ceased their vocal demands in order to concentrate on eluding their would-be captors by grabbing onto the hanging cables and using them to swing to the tops of other cars, like urban Tarzans. They were a nimble group, fast-moving and highly motivated, and the evasive dance they did with the frustrated cops was very entertaining.

Ira realized that it was also effective. Nothing was getting hooked up. No cars were being lifted out of the way. The helicopters buzzed overhead like frustrated wasps, cables dangling ineffectually, while the workers trying to attach the slings to them were impeded by the erratically shifting human obstacles of cops and protestors. On the large video screen that was supposed to be showing a successful Operation Skyway, Ira saw instead the furious face of Governor Jorge Olmstead. The guv seemed to be trying hard to hold it together, but the seething tension surging just beneath the handsome features was barely contained.

This might actually work, thought Ira, in amazement. This crazy scheme might actually—

And then he saw the thugs. With a horrifying sense of déjà vu, he watched as the scene's almost comic tone turned menacing in the space of a few moments. It was as if a dense storm cloud suddenly moved between the earth and the sun, casting a dark, threatening shadow over the land. They were big men, slower than the protestors but relentless and purposeful in the way they advanced on them. No, no, no, Ira protested silently. No! Now that he sort of knew these well-meaning, idealistic fools, he didn't want to see them get hurt – and it looked like a big can of whoop-ass was about to be opened on them.

The hired muscle (he was pretty sure that's what they were) split up and swarmed over the interchange, immediately demonstrating their willingness to use different tactics than the police were employing. Instead of trying to pull protestors down with minimal injury, they grabbed ankles and yanked hard, punched shins, gripped arms and swung them to the ground so they could pound fists into faces. Ribs were elbowed. Jaws punched. One protestor was beaten over the head with his own megaphone.

The thugs showed no hesitation about mixing it up with the police, who viewed this new incursion with obvious displeasure. The cops now found themselves double-tasked with getting the protestors out of the way and subduing this newer, more violent group that, oddly enough, also wanted to get the protestors out of the way. The new allies weren't appreciated, especially when cops who were trying to maintain order got attacked by them. Ira found this an especially frightening development. If the police couldn't control these guys, who could?

Chaos erupted in the car-glutted lanes of the once-mighty freeway interchange. The fighting ramped up rapidly, fueled by additional police officers that left other positions and hurried to aid their colleagues. Some bystanders panicked. They struggled to back away from the clashes, but found themselves hemmed in by the many people who pressed forward for a better view. Hundreds of cell phones were held aloft, capturing the action in photos and videos. Thousands of tweets were tweeted.

A few spectators took the opportunity to join the melee as well. Ira couldn't tell whose side they were on, if any. The fighting on the ground did enable the state workers to make progress in attaching slings to hanging cables. Generation Airites tried to return to task and make their way to those about-to-be-airborne vehicles, although they had to dodge both cops and mercenaries to do it. Still, they tried. They were tenacious. Ira wondered if he was really going to see people hanging onto cars and being lifted thousands of feet into the air, perhaps to fall to their deaths. Part of him wanted to look away.

Part of him didn't.

CHAPTER FIFTY-ONE:
LET'S NOT USE WORDS LIKE "RIOT"

Luanne saw with some disgust that her fellow reporters were thrilled that the sedate heli-lift they were sent to cover had turned into a brutal shambles. Aware that she was still performing on live TV, she was careful not to show her feelings, but the on-air types lining the location, excitedly narrating the turmoil into their cameras and microphones, seemed to her like sharks smelling blood in the water.

But she was one of them now, wasn't she? A temporary member, at least, of the media fraternity. An actress pimping herself out as a pseudo-reporter. She pretended that this was a role she was preparing for, and tried to see the horrifying turmoil through their eyes. Once she did that, she had to admit to herself: this was great TV. Raw and spontaneous. Fast-paced and full of pathos. There were heroes and villains. The line between the two had started out kind of blurry, but the appearance of the big, steroidal arm breakers had acted like a perceptual catalyst, transforming the demonstrators from annoying fanatics (she thought) to brave idealists.

She was standing close enough to Weldon, the veteran entertainment reporter, to see sweat conquering his Burnished Bronze foundation makeup and the powder that set it, giving his face an unfortunate shine. Poor guy. He was so far out of his league it was almost laughable. His professional name, he'd confided proudly to her, came from a compliment given him after his very first day of on-air reporting in a small market TV station in Nebraska, a gig he'd gotten right out of college. He'd been scared, his on-camera account of a car accident stiff and stuttery, but the station's general manager told him, "Well done." Trask decided to adapt that as his name and use it as a confidence booster while making his way through the cutthroat and competitive broadcasting industry. Whenever he ever felt stage fright, he'd think about the origin of "Weldon."

His invented moniker was failing him at this moment.

"So, um, we are watching some…um, it appears that…the

police are getting things…under control," he said uncertainly.

"It does?" She couldn't help herself. "It looks more like a riot to me. I think it's safe to say that all hell has broken loose here. I'll bet the governor wants nothing more than to lie down and cry."

Weldon, a stricken expression on his face, tried to keep it steady, but light. "Luanne, let's not use words like, 'riot.' That might alarm people. I'm sure the governor is…figuring out what to do right now. "

She looked over at where Olmstead stood, surrounded by what she presumed were advisors, because a number of them were talking at him while he stared, thunderstruck, at his unraveling career. He didn't appear to be listening to them. It reminded her of baseball umpires who don't blink when enraged managers shout at them at close range. As she watched, Olmstead took a long drink from a travel tumbler and shuddered visibly -- almost with relief.

Luanne snorted. "Yeah, right. I'm *sure* the governor is regretting ever running for governor right now." But she felt bad when she saw Trask's reaction. She shouldn't leave her co-anchor twisting in the live TV breeze. Dolt though he was, she felt that she must help him out. He was fine at chatting up celebrities on the red carpet, asking them about their upcoming movies and the after parties they planned on attending. It wasn't his fault that he was being shoved far out of his comfort zone today.

She decided to take charge. She wasn't going to try and sound like a real reporter, because she wasn't one, but she could talk all right. She knew that much. She instinctively found her character: ordinary woman talking about an extraordinary afternoon. "Well, Trask, I guess the heli-lift could still happen, although I'm sure no one expected it to spin out of control like this. There, in the bed of that silver pickup truck, we can see the Generation Air leader, Nathan Zardoz." She was glad she'd paid attention to the briefing they'd gotten. In the monitor in front of her, she noticed that one cameraman was following her cues and zooming in on Zardoz. "See him, there? In the Ford F150? He's wearing a green t-shirt and has really good hair. That cop seems to be yelling at him to come down. I'm almost glad we can't hear

319

what he's saying from here. We'd probably have to do a lot of bleeping."

Weldon smiled gratefully at her little joke.

"And Zardoz is not the only protestor on top of a car right now. Look! His buddies are also shoving the cables out of the way, again and again. They seem determined. If the protestors can keep this up for awhile, and avoid the police, they may just succeed in blocking this thing and really screwing up Olmstead's day. I mean, how long can the helicopters stay up in the air? At some point, they're going to run out of fuel, aren't they?"

Trask nodded, relieved to be rid of the burden of on-camera leadership. "Those are excellent questions, Luanne." He looked past the camera to their producer, catching her eye. "Maybe we can get a...helicopter expert to talk to us about that."

The producer, catching the cue, took on a deer-in-the-headlights look. She, too, was accustomed to working on segments about celebrities.

"There's some movement behind that 18-wheeler," Luanne said. "The one with 'McGuinn Trucking' in big white letters on the side. A blue Lexus is being lifted up, now, into the air. Seems funny to see something that big and heavy hanging from a helicopter, doesn't it? And there it goes. Up up and away."

The cameraman found it and followed it.

"Like Chitty Chitty Bang Bang," Weldon added brightly.

The spectators – who, after all, wanted to see action more than they wanted to take sides – cheered lustily at the sight of the flying car.

Luanne's attention was captured by movement on the ground. "Now we can see that some bystanders have gotten involved. There are at least a dozen large men who are mixing it up with both the protestors and the police. I don't think this is just...spontaneous. I get the feeling that they're all together."

"Wow! Did you see that guy just slug a cop?" Weldon was back on task now. Sounding confident.

A beefy man with stubby, strawberry-blond hair heaved himself up into the pickup truck holding Zardoz, whose back was to the newcomer as he concentrated on the cable that was swinging around toward him. Zardoz didn't realize the danger until he felt the beefy man's right arm clamp around him neck.

"Let's stay on that one," Luanne instructed the cameraman. "The red-headed man and Zardoz. If the leader of the protest is subdued, the whole protest might collapse." Plus we might be recording a murder in progress, she thought, horrified but also a little bit thrilled. Their footage could end up being evidence. She might have to testify.

"Subdued?" interrupted Trask excitedly, forgetting his calm, professional demeanor. "It looks like that big guy is going to kill him!"

CHAPTER FIFTY-TWO:
THE BEAUTIFUL, BRAVE AND PISSED OFF GIRL

Ira couldn't believe his eyes. The hulk who was choking the life out of Nathan was the same one – he was sure of it -- who'd slugged Ira, in that other lifetime, after Ira had called the cops on him. And that was probably him at that last Generation Air rally, too. What did this animal do? Just go around and look for opportunities to pound on people and get away with it? He and his merry band of bullies were sure having a good time doing that today. Ira watched in anguish as the big man and his big friends honed in on his new buds. The protestors were fit and quick and often evaded their pursuers, but when they did get caught or cornered they were no match for the thugs.

Nathan, his eyes bulging, struggled hard to free himself from the red-headed man's grip, even desperately flipping his body up into the air, as if he could vault away from him.

For a brief moment, Ira thought about going to his aid. The impulse died quickly. What could he do against a guy that size? Just get himself beaten to a pulp. Besides, he wasn't even officially a Generation Air member. He'd come along to watch and learn, not to get his ass kicked. Why didn't Nathan's own people help him? It was true that most of the Generation Airites who were already out there, trying to block the heli-lift, were busy fending off thug attacks themselves. Zed did run toward Nathan's car, but it was to videotape what was happening to his leader. Ira didn't blame him. That was Zed's role, after all. He'd told Ira that you couldn't trust the official, corporate-owned media to give an honest accounting of what happened here. Ira knew he was right. Zed would put this on YouTube for the whole world to see.

A few Generation Airites who'd been providing support services on the sidelines did hurry forward. Some grabbed at the red-headed man's ankles and shouting at him to stop. A few brave ones got up onto the bed of the truck. One jumped on the guy's back, clinging determinedly, his legs flopping as his opponent tried to shake him off. Another, a tall, slim woman, took a more direct approach. She got herself in front of the man and, snapping her leg back, angled around Nathan's writhing body and delivered a vicious kick to one of his assailant's shins.

No! It couldn't be! Ira grabbed some binoculars that were discarded on the ground and used them to confirm his horrified suspicion. He stared through the lens, hoping he was wrong. It was just as he'd feared. That was Oceana up there with Nathan, still gripping her smoke gun, courageously taking on the bully. He could see her face clearly. It was a composition of fury. Ira was terrified for her.

The kick got an instantaneous reaction. The bully, maddened with rage, finally shook the protestor off his back and released Nathan, who fell in a limp bundle. Although the man's attention was mostly focused on the brave, beautiful and pissed-off girl in front of him, he still took a moment to lift Nathan by the shirt collar and drop him over the side of the truck. Ira pointed the binoculars lower; Nathan lay in a heap on the pavement, his chest heaving, his hands at his throat as if they could undo the bruising effects of the throttling he'd just experienced. He would live.

The bully moved in on Oceana. She didn't back away. Not one step. She wouldn't, thought Ira admiringly. Not Oceana. In fact, she aimed another kick at her adversary, higher this time, going for his crotch. He shifted his body just in time to avoid a direct hit, but she still put some hurt on him, Ira saw. Or maybe the guy was just angry that a woman would-- Suddenly, the big man grabbed Oceana by the shirt collar and hauled her toward him, holding her a few inches off the ground. Ira felt rage overtake him like a destructive thunderstorm, roiling with lightning and fierce winds, pelting the land with hot rain. The fat bastard! He was going to hit her!

The rational function of his mind might have produced the thought that the man could be merely trying to hold Oceana immobile, to prevent her from kicking him again, but that node was temporarily disabled by adrenaline and anger.

Ira dropped the binoculars and hurried toward Oceana.

CHAPTER FIFTY-THREE:
LIKE DAVID AND GOLIATH

Luanne couldn't believe it. Although she couldn't see much of his face, because of that stupid mask, she was sure it was the bike-shaw driver -- the one she'd seen here, just a few minutes ago. She knew that hot bod. She'd stared at it throughout her entire ride. Wow. She never would have guessed he led a double life. He *had* been kind of secretive, though. Being a bike cabbie was just his day job, apparently. Something that kept him in shape for his activist adventures. She adjusted her opinion of him a little. Men who were all wrapped up in causes weren't all that appealing, romantically. She thought that fanatics were probably too preoccupied to make attentive boyfriends.

At the moment this one was zipping through the parked cars, dodging around skirmishes like a football player avoiding tackle while running for a touchdown. In mere moments he'd reached the pickup truck and bounded up into it to boldly face the red-headed, red-faced guy. The blonde girl in his clutches thrashed around ineffectually, swinging the rifle she was holding and occasionally striking him with it, to no apparent effect.

The driver said something to Red, something that made him release the girl. She dropped but stayed in the truck, scrambling to get out of the way of whatever was about to happen.

Luanne was still a newbie to show biz, but she sensed that these two parts couldn't have been cast better. The beefy, lumbering man with small, squinty eyes was the perfect villain. The other one, the unlikely hero, was the ideal underdog-who-wins-in-the-end. Or he would be, if he had spidey powers. Presumably lacking them, he was probably going to get the snot beat out of him.

"It's like David and Goliath," Luanne remarked unhappily. The bike-shaw driver was in good shape, lithe and cut, but he was dwarfed by the red-haired man, who was gorilla-like in his proportions, with an oversized upper body and abnormally long arms.

She really, really wanted a cigarette. She almost wished she hadn't quit smoking three weeks earlier, although she was still feeling the glow of that accomplishment. It would be nice, though, to be able to look forward to having a smoke when she was finally off-camera.

She would have some peanut M&Ms instead.

"Boy, the red-headed man sure looks angry," noted Weldon, as riveted to the scene as she was. "The other guy doesn't act scared, but, I think he should be."

CHAPTER FIFTY-FOUR:
STOMPED INTO A BLOODY SMEAR

The big guy swung a big fist at Ira – a fist he remembered all too well. This time, though, Ira was not trapped in the front seat of a car. This time he used his superior reflexes and agility to almost dance out of the way, like Muhammad Ali. Footwork, Ira. Footwork!

Having thrown his whole body into the punch, the man staggered off balance in its wake. Ira shocked himself by jabbing him viciously at his temporarily unprotected ribs, connecting solidly. It worked! The man grunted in pain, bending over to ward off another blow to that area. That gave Ira an idea. He clasped his hands together and brought them down hard, on the man's back, trying to drop him. It was technique he'd seen in a movie.

It didn't work. Although still bent over, the man stayed on his feet. What it did do was to really piss him off. Yeah? Well Ira was still pretty angry, too. This big heap of ugly had had his hands on Oceana. Ira punched him in the stomach, expecting to sink his fist into flab and cause pain. Instead, he encountered steel. And Ira's hand really hurt! If this guy was more muscle than fat, Ira was in big trouble.

His opponent quickly recovered his equilibrium and came at him like a locomotive, his huge fists cutting through the air, determined to hit their target.

Ira's mask was slipping. He pushed it up and returned to focusing on his footwork. Also on weaving and feinting. His adrenalin was ebbing, being replaced by raw fear. He tried to reconstitute the anger he'd felt when he saw Oceana in danger, but now that she was off to the side somewhere, he naturally became fixated on his own survival. Sure, he was in good shape these days. Much better than he'd been a year ago, certainly. That didn't mean he had a snowball's chance in hell against this guy. He must have been insane, to come up here. He didn't know the first thing about fighting. He was going to get stomped into a bloody smear. Possibly killed. On national television, no less.

Craptastic.

Feeling increasingly desperate – but trying to maintain a confident, even cocky air – Ira tried to imagine how Muldoon would handle this fight. Muldoon was a lot bigger than he was, toughened by years as a cop in a tough, tough city, but he was still just a man. Even Muldoon must find himself at a disadvantage in a fight now and then – like when James Bond went up against "Jaws" in *Moonraker*.

A punch caught Ira off guard. At the last moment, he was able to lean mostly out of its way, but even the glancing blow he absorbed rocked his world and turned his mind, momentarily, into jelly. This guy wasn't kidding. Ira had to pay closer attention! He knew he should try and hit the guy in the face, but resisted the idea. It would be like wounding – and not killing – a bear. He might inflict a little pain, but it would only make his opponent more dangerous.

CHAPTER FIFTY-FIVE:
LIKE A FEATHER CATCHING A DOWNDRAFT

"You are doing GREAT!" Luanne heard the producer say, in her headphones. "The Executive Vice President of Special Programming is THRILLED. Just keep it up."

Luanne couldn't take too much credit for the scene playing out in front of her. It was naturally compelling. She imagined that anyone who was watching a TV set at this moment would be riveted by it. It was Good v. Evil, in the form of Big and Ugly v. Cute and Lean. If the smaller guy won, he'd be a hero. If he lost, he'd be a martyr.

There was no way he was going to win.

Helicopters, dangling cables, still churned the air overhead. Another vehicle was successfully lifted, but it seemed beside the point. It almost felt like the fate of the heli-lift would be determined by the epic battle taking place in the bed of the silver pickup truck. She wondered why the cops weren't trying to break it up, then, looking around, saw that they were busy trying to separate other combatants.

Luanne saw the Generate Air leader finally getting to his feet.

"There's Zardoz," she said. "He's able to stand, but he doesn't look like he's in any shape to help out his fellow protestor."

Zardoz swayed weakly for a moment, then straightened. He moved toward the truck, holding out his arms, his mouth forming words Luanne couldn't make out.

"The blonde woman who kicked the big man is standing up now. She looks a little dazed, but not injured. Zardoz is saying something to her. It looks like he wants her to jump, but she's gesturing toward the two men who are fighting, as if she should stay. She's leaving her rifle behind her. I gotta say, Trask, I'm surprised to see the gun. I thought Generation Air was supposed to be into peaceful protests."

The blonde apparently came to a decision. She leaped gracefully into Zardoz' outstretched arms, like a feather catching a downdraft in the breeze. He turned and spirited her away from the truck.

It was almost like a fairy tale, thought Luanne.

CHAPTER FIFTY-SIX:
HIS OPPONENT, UNFORTUNATELY, DIDN'T REALIZE
THAT THE FIGHT WAS OVER

This couldn't be happening. Ira's peripheral vision registered an image that made his blood boil. It couldn't be. To confirm what his eyes refused to believe, he risked turning his ahead briefly away from the Red Hulk to look off to the side. His mask was slipping again. Annoyed, he reached up and yanked it completely off his head. To hell with anonymity.

Nathan was carrying Oceana away, as if he was the one who'd saved her. As if he was some big hero.

The end of an enormous cable, heavy with an attachment device, swung closer and grazed his temple, making him even angrier. It really hurt! He windmilled his arms like a madman, taking the Red Hulk by surprise, hitting him in the stomach, the jaw, the eye, the shoulder – any body part he could reach, raining down blows upon him so fast that he could only double over defensively, trying to protect himself.

And all the while, Ira seethed. Fumed. He'd risked his life, went up against the Red Hulk just so Nathan could take all the credit? He pummeled and kicked in a fury, intending to beat the red-headed man into submission and then make a quick exit so he could get to Oceana. He was NOT going to let Nathan ride off into the sunset with the girl. Ira socked the Red Hulk one last time, for good measure, then hopped down from the truck in satisfaction.

His opponent, unfortunately, didn't realize that the fight was over and that Ira had other things to do. The Red Hulk reached down, grabbed Ira by the back of the shirt and hauled him ungracefully back up to the auto-arena.

In disbelief, Ira resisted, kicking and thrashing, but still found himself right back where he'd been, facing the Red Hulk. Impatiently, he turned and saw Nathan holding Oceana in his arms tenderly. Nathan, comforting Oceana.

And the fight was back on.

Chapter Fifty-Seven: Like a Chubby Bird

"Boy, you may not agree with these protestors, but you have to admire the commitment you see here," said Weldon. "This guy must really care about the environment."

Luanne had to agree. "Yeah. For him to bravely take on that much larger man really shows an extraordinary dedication to his cause." She hoped the cops would stop it before the little guy got creamed, which was inevitable. At this point, he was mainly ducking and bobbing out of the way, occasionally risking a punch but mostly trying to stay out of the red-headed man's range.

The helicopters, the governor and the other official representatives of bureaucracy, the unmoving cars, the freeway interchange itself – all were forgotten right now, or at least, relegated to secondary status, like images in a photo that were deliberately blurred when the photographer focused closely on one object. Every TV camera was locked on the struggle between the big guy and the little guy. The clash felt like it was going on forever, but when she looked at her watch, Luanne saw that mere minutes had passed.

She imagined that bookies in Vegas were taking bets on it. The oddsmakers had an easy job today, unless…the bike-shaw driver managed to wear the other one down. It was true; moving targets were harder to hit. Maybe the red-headed man would get tired and quit. Maybe pulling passengers behind a bicycle all day, every day, gave the other one more endurance, Luanne thought. She considered revealing what she knew about the lean guy, but decided not to. It was only a small tidbit of information – what he did for a living – but he might not want it out there. She felt oddly protective of him. Of course, now that his mask was off, lots of people might be recognizing him.

Several police officers reached the pickup. One climbed up, but the red-haired man quickly, instinctively, shoved him off. The officer fell heavily, striking his head on the hard pavement. He lay inert.

The other cop, outraged at the assault on his partner, came

after the red-headed man with a vengeance and a flashlight. The cop swung the lethal-looking black cylinder at the red-headed man, who grabbed his arm and grappled with him. The bike-shaw driver tried to get out of their way, but Luanne saw him cringe in pain when a stray fist struck his nose. He brought his hands up to his face, too late, to protect it. Was that blood?

The cop lost his footing and fell. The bike-shaw driver seized this opportunity to give a mighty push to the back of the red-headed man, who flew out of the truck bed like a chubby bird, his arms splayed out to break his fall.

Chapter Fifty-Eight:
A Navy Blue Mass of Frustration

OMG! How could *anything* hurt this much? Was his nose broken?

Ira wanted to jump down, and stomp on both the Red Hulk and the cop, because he wasn't sure which one had hit him. He tried to wipe the blood away with his t-shirt sleeve. The pain was primitive. Soul-shattering. He would use this sensation to inform a story some day. It would be—

A hanging cable thumped him heavily in the back of the head, setting off a whole new wave of agony and completing the circle of pain, front and back. Goddamn helicopter! Through a red, throbbing haze of fury and misery, he noticed the smoke gun, lying on the hood of the car where Oceana had left it. He reached down without conscious thought and seized it, aiming it skyward almost instinctively, squeezing off a round as he'd seen the instructor do. Released into the air, the ammunition bloomed into a dense, spectacularly orange cloud that engulfed the helicopter.

"Drop it!" The cop who'd shouted this was reaching for his own gun. A real one.

Wait! Ira wanted to say. This is just a smoke gun. *And I'm not even supposed to be here. It's all a mistake. There's this girl...*

As if he were watching a movie, he saw the officer swing the gun upward and aim it resolutely at him. Hmmm. Interesting. He felt himself *not* drop the gun and concluded, with a calm and fatalistic detachment, that he was in the grip of fear induced paralysis. If he could just make his fingers open, he wouldn't die. He tried hard to unclench the stubborn digits, but they refused to function. He watched the cop adjust his hand and sight his target, which was Ira.

His life was about to end. Right here. Like this.

Craptastic.

"Drop it NOW!" snarled the cop.

Ira finally managed to let the smoke gun fall from his

hands. Above him he heard a change in sound; the helicopter was starting to move away, its pilot trying to get clear of the blinding orange cloud. The chopper's hateful cable appendage was leaving, too.

Many uniformed cops were now running toward the pickup. He knew they were coming to subdue him, not to mention pound him into a pulp.

On impulse, Ira grabbed the end of the cable hanging from the departing helicopter. The cops closest to him lunged for his legs but he bent his knees and squirmed upward, managing to just barely stay out of their reach. The helicopter rose, lifting him with it. He relaxed his legs. Fascinated, Ira watched the individual police officers blend into a navy blue mass of frustration as he got higher and further away, their faces turned upward toward their escaping prey.

Luanne was blown away. What a stunt! What a spectacular conclusion to the heli-lift! "This would make a terrific scene in a movie," she commented.

"Well, Luanne," said Weldon. "That young protestor just became a celebrity. I hope he's ready."

Chapter Fifty-Nine:
A Character with a Lot More Depth

In a high rise condo complex in Beverly Hills, Sid Kirschenbaum stared in disbelief at his high definition TV screen, which was almost as large as a Santa Monica Boulevard billboard.

In an apartment in Venice, sitting on a sofa next to her newest boyfriend, Rolf, Lupe Sevá stared in disbelief at her TV screen.

On the deck of their cabin cruiser, Mr. and Mrs. Tanner stopped sipping their Mojitos and stared in disbelief at the small screen of their battery-operated TV.

In a small, stylish West Side bungalow decorated with mid-century modern furniture, Palmer Lu stared in disbelief at his TV screen.

In a brick Colonial in a suburb of Detroit, Leia and Kevin O'Riley stared in disbelief at their TV screen.

In an undisclosed location, Blake stared in admiration at his TV screen. With heroes like that on its side, the environment just might survive, after all. He turned off the television, stood and stretched, feeling a poem coming on.

In a villa in Oahu, Cody Torrance stared at his TV screen, trying to figure out whom Sid would call to secure the rights to this story. Sid would know. It was the kind of project that would take Cody's career to the next level. Instead of an action hero, he'd be playing a character with a lot more depth: an *environmental* action hero. And it was a hot topic. People were always talking about the environment, weren't they? He wondered who should direct.

Cody thought the mask should be a deeper blue, though. That sky blue shade didn't "read" very well on camera.

CHAPTER SIXTY:
AS THEY WERE TURNING HIM INTO THEIR NEW BITCH

Relief at eluding the police soon traded places with terror. And fatigue. Ira hadn't really thought this through. Hadn't considered the altitude that helicopters could reach and how quickly they could reach it. He'd had a dim idea about dropping to the ground pretty quickly, right after he got far enough away from the police, but the helicopter got too high too fast to do that. For the time being, he was stuck at the end of the cable like a worm impaled on a fishing hook.

He stopped looking down because that scared him even more than having a handgun pointed at him had. The world he found so fascinating at ground level was incomprehensible at this height. Nothing looked as it should look. Buildings were lifeless geometrics. Neighborhoods he considered familiar, like friends, unrecognizable. People were so reduced in size as to be insignificant. Insects called the human race. It was a disturbing, alien landscape, one he hoped he wouldn't have to encounter at a high rate of speed, after he lost his grip and plunged downward.

That was a very real possibility. Hanging on to the end of the cable was exhausting. His hands cramped, the muscles in his arms spasmed from the tremendous strain they were enduring. The pilot must not realize he had a hitchhiker. A stowaway. Maybe someone on the ground would figure out which helicopter had facilitated Ira's escape, and radio the pilot so that he would land prematurely. On top of a police station, probably. At that point, Ira would either break all his bones as he slammed into the ground or get jumped on by about twenty cops, and *they* would break all his bones.

Hell, he might as well let go now, and get it over with. Death wouldn't be proud, all right.

No! He refused to die before "Her Majesty's Gangsta" was finished! If he had to, he'd complete it in prison, like that man who wrote "In the Belly of the Beast." They'd have to let Ira out to accept his award for Best Screenplay at the Oscars, wouldn't they? He pictured himself up onstage, making his acceptance speech, while a prison guard stood next to him. That would *almost* be cool! A memorable moment in the history of the Academy Awards, although "history" was a little premature, since it hadn't happened yet, and he didn't even know if prisons let people out for the evening for special occasions. The studio that produced the movie could launch a public relations campaign, appealing to the governor to intervene, getting all the audience members who loved "Her Majesty's Gangsta" to send emails. The studio would be happy to do it, since having a felon/screenwriter would generate a ton of publicity. And it wasn't as if Ira was a murderer. He was just a disturber of the peace and a resister of arrest.

But he'd probably die before that. He couldn't hold on much longer. Without warning, the helicopter descended hundreds of feet. Was the pilot getting ready to land? Had he been alerted about Ira, the criminal, hitching an unauthorized ride?

They were passing over treetops that looked, to Ira's crazed mind, like inviting green cushions. He let go of the cable and fell like a stone toward his leafy new friends. They were not as welcoming as he'd anticipated. The first branch he grabbed for eluded him. Still dropping, he knocking his head painfully against the trunk, felt his face slapped and his ribs poked by sharp branches. What a stupid idea this was! He could only hope that this bruising encounter with the tree might at least slow his descent a little.

At the last instant, his right hand closed on something firm and he stopped falling. He allowed himself a deep breath, almost afraid to believe that he was hanging in midair, and not speeding toward the ground anymore. He clamped onto the branch with his left hand as well, then managed to swing his body over and slide his leg through a crossroads of trunk so that he could let go completely and give his tortured hands a rest. He slumped there, in the crotch of the tree, resting his cheek against its rough bark, his body stretched out limply along a thick limb and his arms dangling on either side of it, as if he were embracing a lover languidly, just before sleep. He listened to the jack-hammer pounding of his heart diminish, felt his hands throbbing through the torn, bloody skin of his palms. He was very, very tired.

When he heard the sound of an approaching motor, he surrendered to peaceful resignation. He couldn't run. He had nothing left. What did that famous Indian guy whose name he couldn't remember say? He would fight no more forever. He wondered what handcuffs would feel like. What his parents would say when he called them from jail, for help with a lawyer. "Ira. You're always joking."

The motor got nearer. Would he be put in a cell with violent and diseased criminals? Maybe he and the Red Hulk would be bunkmates. Wouldn't that be nice. And Ira was sure to meet other interesting characters who might inspire his writing. He could take mental notes *as they were turning him into their new bitch.*

Maybe the cops wouldn't see him up here.

Right.

He closed his eyes and prepared to meet his fate.

"Dude! Hey, Ira! You asleep? Dude!"

It was Zed, on a motorcycle, come to rescue him.

PART THREE

CHAPTER SIXTY-ONE:
AS IF HE WERE AN ONION

The Generation Air people were doing everything possible to coddle their new, accidental hero. He had a large, harem-sized tent this time and could probably have had it filled with eager-to-please girls, but the one he wished would visit him rarely did. Too busy, Oceana said.

His tent was comfortably furnished, since his stay could be (they hoped) a long one. He felt like a bird in a gilded cage. He had an inflatable bed with a bed-in-a-bag linen set for it, a small table and chair from IKEA, a lamp, even a camping toilet -- a bucket fitted with a seat and a plastic liner designed for easy disposal -- so that he didn't have to trek downhill and wait in line at the portable toilets first thing in the morning. He had plenty to eat and drink and lots and lots of new best friends. The satellite TV in his tent, which ran off a generator, was a special luxury, and was one of the reasons he had so many new best friends. He tried not to watch it too much, because he found hearing distortions about his life intolerable, but he was irresistibly drawn to his own fame. Jesus! Couldn't they have found a better photo to use than the one from his high school yearbook? He had some pretty good pics on his Facebook page, but, no, they had to use a years-old shot of him at the height of nerdiness. Craptastic.

If it hadn't been for that picture, though, he wouldn't have recognized the Ira O'Riley that was being discussed and described on channel after channel, network and cable, news and pseudo news shows. *That* Ira O'Riley was either a dangerous zealot or a folk hero. An ecoterrorist or a visionary trying to save the world from itself. Timothy McVeigh or a "green" Jesus. He was a symbol of everything that was wrong with America. Or of everything that was right. Teenage girls thought he was hot. The blogosphere buzzed with his highly embellished legend, and his fans quickly established several adoring web sites featuring information on every aspect of his life, from height and weight to goals and ambitions. An online version of a teen magazine featured an article breathlessly titled, "Ten Things Ira O'Riley Says He's Looking For in a Girl." The accuracy level of both fansites and legitimate news sites was less than 50%. His entire background was deconstructed and analyzed, picked over like used clothing at a church garage sale. Not one expert or groupie managed to uncover the fact that he was a screenwriter. So much for the art of journalism.

He almost enjoyed hearing himself described as *menacing*.

"Well, he is from Detroit," commented one news anchor. *So naturally he's a killa, thought Ira.*

"Being of both Jewish and Irish parentage may have caused a deep psychological confusion that this young man is attempting to resolve through submersion in a cause that's larger than him," opined a psychologist guesting on a morning news/chatter/weather show in order to profile Ira for the well-coiffed hosts. "Or, he may be trying to avoid other unresolved issues, like homosexuality."

"You think he's gay?" asked the female host in an awed tone.

The psychologist shrugged. "It's a possibility."

"Watching him at that rally, he didn't really set off my gay-dar," she said seriously, as if she were pronouncing a diagnosis.

The psychologist nodded thoughtfully. "Well, your instincts might be right. You are, after all, a woman." *(Can't put anything past this guy, thought Ira.)* "We've also learned that he has a history of asthma. He may be trying to overcompensate for that. Rebelling against his limitations, so to speak."

"Interesting," the male co-host said.

"And let's not forget: he *is* from Detroit."

Both hosts nodded sagely at the psychologist's remarkable insight.

Spokespeople from environmental organizations were no better. Happy for the air time, they made the most of it, claiming Ira as one of their own, citing his deep love of the earth and all of its resources and inhabitants.

Screw this miserable planet and everybody riding on it! Ira thought in his bleakest moments. He would never recycle again.

The attention forced on his family was particularly

excruciating to him. Initially his parents were caught by the media like squirrels crossing the road when they saw a car approaching, not knowing whether to keep running or turn back. So the squirrels froze. And got flattened.

His mother was ambushed as she came out of the house and made for her car. He could tell she was going to work: she was wearing her Tuesday green suit with the silky pale gold blouse.

"My son was obviously just trying to defend himself," she huffed. "That larger man should be the one under arrest."

"He is," the reporter told her. "Mrs. O'Riley, did you know your son was involved with this group of fanatics?"

Panicked, she shook her head and pointed the keyless device at her car, pushing the button to unlock it.

"Has your son been in contact with you? If you don't tell the police where he is, you could be aiding and abetting a wanted fugitive."

"Ira is a good boy!" she said defiantly. *Couldn't she have said, 'man'? thought Ira.* "This is all a big mistake. He's a talented screenwriter!" she added, before squeezing around the cameraman and into the front seat of her car.

"The Unibomber was turned in by his own brother," the reporter called after her. "Don't you think that's the responsible thing to do, Mrs. O'Riley?"

She backed out of the driveway, refusing to acknowledge that she'd heard him.

After that, his family figured it out pretty quickly and refused to say anything to anybody. Maybe they got an advisor. They let a lawyer do their talking for them, and he refused to say much, too, just averred that negotiations were underway for Ira to turn himself in to the authorities, and that his parents were confident that this would all be sorted out and charges against Ira would be dropped. The authorities had no evidence. No case.

He'd tried to call his parents soon after his escape, but Nathan stopped him, pointing out that even using a borrowed cell phone wouldn't protect him; the police could figure out which cell tower was being used and nail down his location. Emailing anyone would similarly reveal his location. Deprived of genuine contact with the people who actually cared about him, he had to learn everything from the media.

"I've asked the…fuh…fuh…federal prosecutor to look into, uh, federal charges relating to domestic terror…terrorism," said Olmstead at a post heli-lift news conference, uncharacteristically slurring his words. "I think Homeland Security will be very…uh, very interested in Mr. O'Riley." Apparently losing his train of thought, he swayed slightly and blinked in confusion.

Ira felt a profound disconnect from reality. Domestic terrorism? Seriously? The governor looked terrible, Ira thought, feeling a little guilty about it. His eyes were bleary and his shirt appeared unfresh. Was the beard stubble deliberate? Used to show the voters how upset he was over his failed heli-lift? You almost had to feel sorry for him. He put together this big, ambitious plan and then had to stand there and watch it all go to hell. Olmstead had canceled the other planned heli-lifts until, he said, "the suspect" was in custody. When he heard that, Ira realized with a jolt that *he* was the suspect.

"Dude, he looks like a hot mess," noted Zed, sitting next to him and sharing some chips and salsa.

"Governor Olmstead, is it true that a police informant claims that O'Riley has fled to Mexico? And that you're working on an extradition arrangement with Mexican authorities right now?"

Olmstead sighed heavily. "The police have received, uh, hundreds of tips about O'Riley's whereabouts." He shook his finger at the reporters like an absentminded college professor. "There are…I mean, they are following up on…every lead. Except the crackpots."

Another reporter called out: "Governor Olmstead, the federal prosecutor's office has announced a press conference for this afternoon, and we've learned from a source that no charges will be brought against O'Riley."

Ira and Zed high-fived each other and cheered, spitting chip fragments onto the tent floor.

"Dude, for a while there, you were Osama bin O'Riley!" said Zed.

"Shhhh." Ira wanted to hear the rest of the reporter's statement.

"Councilman Alvarado says that this is an overreaction on your part. That O'Riley and his group simply staged a lawful protest that got out of hand, and you're using him as an excuse, because the heli-lift wouldn't have worked anyway."

Olmstead, his pasty face turning red, ground out an angry answer. "Alvarado doesn't know… What Generation Air did was far worse than a…a…a mere political protest. We could have…fixed this mess." He looked around him in frustration, as if his listeners didn't understand English. "It's a…crisis. CRI-sis. People, uh, wanted me to do something about it. Millions of Californians' lives…really suck right now. These protestors don't…care…about that. People are living in their cars and they're out of work and…I mean, they can't go anywhere. Look around you! But do the protestors care about any of that? No. No, they do not." He sputtered to a halt, his eyes wild, a few drops of spittle at the corner of his mouth. He rubbed his forehead, then looked up again. "They're gonna pay," he said, his tone reckless. "I swear ta God, they're gonna pay."

An aide quickly stepped between him and the reporters and waved his hands to signal an end to the press conference.

"Whoah, the guv's having' a meltdown," observed Zed. "But, dude, maybe you should turn yourself in now. I mean, they got nothing."

Ira sighed. "You really think so?"

"Yeah. Get a lawyer and get it over with. You'll be all right. Seriously." Zed set the bowl of chips down on the table. "I better stop eating these, or I won't be hungry for dinner. I gotta go do some sketches for my tile work. Some lady in Reseda wants Michael Jackson tiled in her shower enclosure. Sick, huh?"

After he left, Ira considered what Zed had suggested. Should he turn himself in? He couldn't, seriously, be in that much trouble, could he? Innocent people had been railroaded before. Look at that poor schlub arrested for bombing the Atlanta Olympics. Did that guy ever get his life back, even after being exonerated?

He was almost more afraid of the media than of the law. He would be hounded if he came out of hiding. He was sure of it. Maybe he *should* flee to Mexico. It would be better than waiting around here for capture, or cameras, although that was unlikely. Nathan kept lookouts posted at crucial vantage points. High elevations, mostly. If the police or the media did figure out where Generation Air's camp was, the lookouts would see them coming and notify Nathan, who had carefully worked out escape routes for his people to use. All the law would find would be empty tents and full portable toilets. The Generation Airites could hide indefinitely in the thousands of wilderness areas of the park.

The media continued to peel back layers of his life as if he were an onion.

Ira couldn't believe it when Kim Lefertowski, the girl he'd schtupped in junior year, stepped forward to appropriate her fifteen minutes of fame. WTF. Identified as "Kim Wiggins, Former Girlfriend," she didn't have much to offer her interviewer. "He was a real sweet guy," she said. "I never thought he'd get mixed up in anything like this."

"And you two dated throughout high school?" the female reporter asked chummily, as if she was chatting with a girl friend.

"Yeah," Kim said vaguely. "And then we just grew apart."

Grew apart. Right. *You dumped me when you were able to upgrade to a better class of boyfriend.* He was pleased to see that Kim had gotten plump again. Time to go back to fat camp, Kim. Her husband, whoever he was, could have her.

Even Sid got into the act. "Yeah, he worked here. He was good with the clients, I have to say, but I hadda let him go. It was clear that his mind was elsewhere. Now I know where."

You know nothing about me, Sid. You never did.

Mrs. Tanner got her time on camera when the police showed up to execute a search warrant on Ira's car-partment.

"Ira's a great guy," she insisted loyally. "People shouldn't believe the things they're hearing about him."

"Dude! You didn't tell me you were getting it on with a cougar." Zed was lounging in his tent, watching TV with him when Mrs. Tanner came on. "She is one hot mamacita."

At any other time, Ira would be looking at the tanned cleavage presented by the fuchsia bikini top Mrs. Tanner was wearing, along with a more modest pair of shorts. Instead, he was focused on the police officers behind her, swarming over his little car like ants over leftover picnic food. *No, not the trunk,* he prayed. They popped the trunk open and started removing his belongings. *Not the laptop. Please, dear God, don't let them take the laptop.* A stout, no-nonsense female cop lifted up his laptop and carried it away. *Maybe they won't see the external hard drive. The backup disks.* He'd been smart this time, making sure he had redundancies in place, so that his screenplay would never again—

They took it all. He watched the navy blue zippered nylon case holding his external hard drive and the backup disks and the briefcase with inner pockets containing his zip drives, all being spirited away. He couldn't do it again. He could not rewrite "Her Majesty's Gangsta" again.

It was gone. Again. This time for good.

It wasn't destroyed, though. It wasn't in the hands of some anonymous thief, like last time. He had a chance of getting it back from the police. Someday. He felt miserable. He imagined some cop reading "Her Majesty's Gangsta" for clues, or simply out of curiosity. It was almost finished now. What if some corrupt cop stole it and took it to a producer himself, pretending that he'd written it? Oh, God. Ira would kill himself if that happened.

His melancholy deepened. He felt as if he were falling in slow motion down a well, descending into darkness as the light shrank to a pinpoint.

Muldoon and Stowaring are imprisoned in a small, dank room. Both are tied to chairs. Both show signs of having been beaten and tortured.

CLOSE SHOT: A RAT scurries along a wall.

Muldoon, disgusted, stomps on the floor to try and frighten it.

CLOSE SHOT: The rat looks at him quizzically, unafraid.

MULDOON
No one's coming for us.

Stowaring says nothing.

MULDOON
(CONT.)
Not even going to argue with me? (he sighs theatrically) Baby, where did our love go?

STOWARING
Will you stuff it? I'm trying to think.

MULDOON
Know what I think? I think no one's coming for us. They can't find us. Or maybe they just can't get to us.
(pause)
I wonder what they're doin' to Sabrina. Why are they keepin' her separate?
(frustrated)
We gotta get to her!

STOWARING
Maybe the transponder will...
(without enthusiasm)
alert someone.

MULDOON
Oh, yeah. That gadget in your ring.
(sarcastically)
The one Q gave you.

STOWARING
(quietly furious)
Don't you dare make remarks about James Bond.

MULDOON

*Maybe if James Bond was here,
he could get the damn thing
working.*

STOWARING
Maybe the signal is blocked.

MULDOON
*The point is: we're on our own.
If we're going to get out of
here—*

STOWARING
*Do you have a plan? Or are you
just babbling? As usual.*

MULDOON
*Oh, I got a plan. I'm gonna be
home by the day after
tomorrow.*

STOWARING
*You're that eager to return to…
          (a snide tone)
Detroit?*

MULDOON
*It ain't so bad.
          (he sighs heavily)
I miss Buddy's Pizza.*

STOWARING
          *(sharply)
I told you: DON'T talk about
food.*
SFX: GUNSHOTS

Both men turn in the direction of the sound, tensed for action.

SFX: MEN'S SHOUTS, SCUFFLING, MORE GUNSHOTS

Sabrina bursts into the room, holding a gun. She has a bruise under one eye, but otherwise appears unharmed. She hurries to Muldoon, stuffs the gun in her belt, takes out a knife and cuts him loose.

> MULDOON
> *Where'd you get that?*

> SABRINA
> *Off one of those guys back there.*

She cuts Stowaring loose. He rubs his wrists.

> MULDOON
> *You overpowered 'em?*
> *(admiringly)*
> *What a woman!*

> SABRINA
> *(modestly)*
> *Ah, they were pussies.*

> STOWARING
> *(in a snide tone)*
> *Charming. Can we go now?*

Sabrina rode to the rescue of not only Muldoon and Stowaring, but also of Ira. She inspired him to write a few scenes on a borrowed laptop, but his enthusiasm was like an engine leaking oil. Sabrina brought in some new, badly needed lubrication, but it didn't last long, and the pistons and rods of his writing mind were in danger of seizing up and destroying his engine. Without the bulk of the script, he felt disconnected. What if these fragments were all he ended up with? The beating heart

348

of the screenplay was on his own computer, which was in police custody. He felt like he was on life support, kept nominally alive but missing a vital organ. Soon, he stopped writing altogether.

Ira's worsening depression was exacerbated by what he came to recognize was homesickness. He was too old for that, wasn't he? Nonetheless, he missed his mom and dad and his room back home. He missed Buddy's Pizza himself. And the Tigers. He even missed snow, but only when it was freshly fallen and sparkling like diamonds under the streetlights, not when it was days old and pushed to the curb in dirty grey mounds.

He'd struggled so hard to succeed – or at least to *survive* – in Los Angeles, the brave new world that had such creatures in it, both before the B.S. and after the B.S. Both times, he'd navigated challenging circumstances and managed to figure out how to supply himself with the necessities of life while continuing to write, write, write. Now, his existence had been dismantled a second time, and, like Humpty Dumpty, he didn't think he could put himself together again.

A woman could make a difference. Was the voice in the back of his head deliberately taunting him? Getting a girlfriend seemed as remote a possibility as getting "Her Majesty's Gangsta" produced.

Oceana was always friendly to him, but that was all. As with a lot of the Generation Airites, he perceived a certain admiration for him in her manner since the heli-lift. Ira, through no fault of his own, had made them all look good -- to most Americans, anyway. The name "Generation Air" was now a household phrase, its members thought to be people who bravely stood up for what they believed in.

"I was just trying to help you," Ira had protested to Oceana. "That's the only reason I got up on that car."

"You helped a lot of people that day," she'd said beatifically, frustrating the hell out of him.

He grew morose, spent more and more time alone in his tent, shunning most visitors. Zed – easy-going, non-hero-worshipping Zed – was always welcome, but Zed got busy with new mosaic commissions, so Ira saw less and less of him.

He spent too much time inside his own mind, which these days configured itself as a maze with no exit, no escape. Every mental route he tried brought him up hard against a brick wall. The only chance he had of ever seeing his screenplay again meant turning himself in and becoming (possibly) a convicted criminal and (definitely) a media freak. He knew he would have to do it soon. Doing nothing was becoming more and more intolerable, even for a coward like himself. What was that expression his father liked so much? Time to shit or get off the pot.

"Things can't get any worse," he said one afternoon, then thought: *And now I'm talking out loud to myself.*

A moment later, he heard Oceana's voice call out, "Ira? Are you in there?"

A prayer answered?

"Come on in."

She did, looking so pretty, so ethereal in her white, filmy dress that it almost hurt to gaze at her.

"Ira, come and join us by the stage. Something very nice is about to take place."

Very nice? She was beside herself with excitement. Nothing to do with him, he thought churlishly. "I'm kind of busy. What's going on?"

"Oh, Ira," she scolded. "You can make a little time for this. Everybody else is going to. It's important. A wedding ceremony.

"Nathan and I are getting married. We'd like you to be there."

Chapter Sixty-Two:
Her Bouquet of Deadly Blossoms

Why did Zed look so troubled? Or was he misreading the expression on his friend's tanned face? Maybe he was just preoccupied. Ira watched Zed fidget absentmindedly with his hemp bracelet, frowning, as if he was trying to come to a decision. Like everyone else gathered here, he was dressed casually, in his usual long, baggy, shorts – faded beyond any recognizable color – a yellow tank top and blue flip flops. Ira wondered if Zed was in love with Oceana, too. Maybe most of the men here were in love with her. How could they not be?

He felt suffocated by a sickening sense of inevitability. Of course Oceana was going to end up with Nathan. They were like two arrows somehow shot together from a single bow, going in the same direction, at the same speed. Ira was a fool to have thought he could change their trajectories in midair and separate them.

Oceana couldn't stop smiling. She held a simple bouquet of Oleander blooms as she gazed adoringly into her bridegroom's face. Ira was standing close enough to smell the fragrance of the pink flowers. He reflected bitterly on their inappropriateness for a wedding. They were beautiful and smelled candy-sweet, but they were poisonous as hell.

They were a lot like Southern California, he thought. He barely listened to the ceremony, which was being conducted by some nondenominational minister, brought to Griffith Park on motorcycle for the service and sworn to secrecy. The balding and sincere young man stuck to a fairly ordinary script, leaving gaps that were filled in by the bride and groom.

"If you live to be a hundred," Oceana said, "I want to live to be a hundred minus one day, so I never have to live without you."

Nathan responded: "I have nothing more to give you than my heart."

How terribly sweet, thought Ira. If Muldoon were here, listening to this tripe, he'd look over at Ira and mime sticking his

351

index finger down his throat, as if he were forcing himself to vomit. Thinking about Muldoon cheered Ira up a little. He welcomed the distraction, because it kept him from paying close attention to the wedding taking place on the stage just a few feet away from him. When he focused in again, it was, mercifully, almost over.

"If anyone here knows of any reason why these two should not be wed, let him speak now or forever hold his peace." The minister, having uttered this standard phrase in a sedate monotone, proceeded without pause to the ceremony's conclusion. "I now pro—"

"Wait!"

Ira was astounded by Zed's interruption, but it was what came next that really stunned everyone assembled there.

"He took bribes, Oceana. Nathan has been taking bribes."

The minister staggered a little, perplexed. He'd clearly never had this happen before, and was at a loss.

Oceana looked at Zed in confusion. "What do you mean? Is this a joke? Zed, we're getting married here."

Nathan, Ira noticed, said nothing, but looked thunderstruck.

Zed sighed heavily, shedding his laid back surfer dude self like a snake's skin, to reveal a serious young man underneath. "He's been taking money from a consortium. A group of corporations that *wanted* traffic to stay bad so they could pressure the state government to build double decker freeways." He ticked names off on his fingers. "Sperling Engineering. Canali Construction. Some others. Big players in the industry. They wanted to screw up the heli-lift and back Olmstead into a corner, so he'd be forced to go with their proposal, and pay the jacked-up price they're asking. They're sprinkling other bribes around so that it ends up being a no-bid project. Investing a few million under the table will bring them billions in profits. It'll be a huge project, after all. Nathan is in on it, Oceana. He's dirty."

She gasped and turned toward Nathan, waiting. Still loving, but now doubting.

Nathan shook his head and reached out, taking her hand in his. "You have to understand, Oceana. We all had the same objective: to prevent things from returning to the status quo." He glanced down at his wedding guests. "Of course I don't support

352

their ultimate goal, but short-term, we were all after the same thing, weren't we? So, yes, I took their money."

Some of the Generation Airites looked as if they were in shock. Others actually started crying. Ira felt a little bit sorry for them. But what did he himself feel? Satisfaction? Glee? Not when he looked at Oceana's face. She was devastated but fighting it, trying to reason through what Nathan was saying.

"But...just building double deckers will keep the air polluted. Won't it?" She was almost pleading. "Help me to understand, Nathan. Won't that just make things bad again, because it will make room for the cars?"

"It'll make room for even more cars!" someone shouted angrily.

"How much of that money went into your own pocket, Nathan?" demanded a stocky young man.

"None!" he protested. "This wasn't to enrich myself!"

"He put a down payment on a Corvette," said Zed quietly.

Oceana gasped in horror. "A gas guzzler? OMG, a GAS GUZZLER, Nathan?"

Nathan glared at Zed. "How do you--?" Then to the others: "That was just...for transportation. Until Los Angeles gets a comprehensive mass transit system." In frustration: "I'm going to need *some* way to get around. The money I took was...mainly...to keep all of this going." He flung his arms wide open. "How do you think we pay for all this?"

"I thought...from donations," Oceana murmured tearfully. "I know I've given a lot."

"You people don't understand," Nathan insisted defiantly. He jumped down from the stage to be closer to his followers, but many of them backed away from him. "Yes, I made a deal with the devil, but it was done for the greater good. Sometimes we have to make difficult choices. Make sacrifices in order to achieve a larger goal." He softened his voice and looked up at Oceana. "Don't you, at least, believe in me, Oceana? You know me better than anyone. You know what's in my heart."

Oceana was awash in tears, crying for the death of innocence. "I thought you stood for something. Something important. You bought a car *that isn't even a hybrid*? I don't even know you!" She flung her bouquet of deadly blossoms to the ground and ran. Nathan stood still for a moment, stunned, and then followed her.

Good luck with that, Ira thought. *She is so over you.*

"Damn, I hated to do that." Zed was standing next to him, watching two lovers, their stars no longer crossed, recede into the distance. "Dude, I just couldn't let her go through with it without knowing what she was marrying. I mean, she hero worships him." He sighed again. "She's such a sweet, naive kid."

"Well it's a hell of a surprise," Ira said. "Zed, how did you know all this stuff about Nathan?"

Zed smiled ruefully, the metallic robot eyes in his earlobes glinting in the afternoon sun. "Dude, I'm a cop. Working undercover."

PART FOUR

CHAPTER SIXTY-THREE:
HARSHING MY MELLOW

And so, in the end, Ira let go. He pictured himself as having been in a rubber raft, paddling desperately against a strong current so that he would not be swept into the rapids ahead. He'd fought the inevitable for such a long, long time.

Then he simply let go. It was time. But instead of curling up helplessly in a wet, miserable human ball (like the old Ira would have done), waiting for his raft to puncture on a rock and deflate, or flip over and eject him into deadly waters in which he would drown, the new Ira sat up straight and steered through all those hazards that his little raft encountered at high speed.

The Generation Air people, despondent at losing their hero Nathan, were grief-stricken when they realized that their hero Ira was about to leave their ranks. Ira ignored them. Their attempts to persuade him to stay with the movement were half-hearted, because they were despondent over recent developments. With the failure of the heli-lift, politicians and the business community decided that the B.S. would be resolved with the construction of double-decker freeways and secondary streets. It was to be an incredible undertaking. The logistics of plotting the roads and directing traffic to the appropriate levels was already in progress. Environmentalists mourned. There would soon be more room on the roads for fossil fuel burners, which would allow them to multiply. The return of smog was inevitable.

Upon Zed's advice, and with a lawyer hired by his parents at his side, Ira turned himself in. Desirous of capitalizing on Ira's fame -- however fleeting it might be – the district attorney made some noise about an assault and battery charge. When Ira's attorney reminded her that the entire country (and a good part of the world) had watched the video of Ira taking on a much larger opponent in order to save a woman from the bully, the D.A. relented. The David v. Goliath-like altercation was well documented, and juries loved underdogs. Ira's property was returned to him. The only thing he really cared about was his laptop. He charged it and fired it up as soon as he could, relieved to find "Her Majesty's Gangsta" intact. Thank God! He set about integrating the newly written scenes into the rest of the screenplay, a little sad that he was nearly finished with it. There would be a grieving process when it was all done, he was sure. Writing that final "FADE OUT" would be bittersweet.

But he'd get over it.

Ira moved into a new car-partment, because paparazzi and media types were staking out his old one. Having navigated the first danger – the law -- in his new and turbulent waters, Ira moved on to confront the next one. He did a brief, disconcerting and probably ill-advised interview with a reporter from a local news show who ambushed him when he left the police station. Yes, he was glad that he was not going to be charged with anything. He would rather not say where he'd been all this time. No, that beautiful blonde girl was not his girlfriend. Belatedly, he realized that he had to take control of the situation. Grip his oar firmly and make himself go where he wanted to go.

"I just want to put this whole thing behind me," he declared, looking resolutely into the camera. "I'm a screenwriter, and I've got to get back to my work."

His lawyer, emerging from the building behind him, hurried toward him and ended the interview, but Ira had succeeded in determining his new direction. He had an agent soon after the interview aired on the evening news, choosing one from among the dozen offers that came his way, channeled through his lawyer.

Ira tried to get back to the bike-shaw business for awhile, but his fame made people more interested in stopping him for autographs and pictures than for rides. It turned out not to matter. His agent soon arranged a lucrative schedule of appearances that effectively ended Ira's life as a cabbie. He took in more money than he'd dreamed possible, doing interviews about his experience with Generation Air. He made the rounds in L.A., and then was taken by helicopter to L.A.X. and from there, flown to New York for more interviews and appearances. In each, he managed to mention his screenplay, although that part was sometimes edited out. He tried not to get frustrated about that. The time it stole from his writing schedule bothered him more, but he knew this phase of his celebrity wouldn't last. It couldn't, could it? How could people stay so interested in the (brief) time he'd spent as an environmental activist, and the (longer) time he'd spent hiding out? It was absurd, really. How much longer would he be treated as a folk hero? And wouldn't there eventually be a backlash, when people got tired of hearing about him? When they realized that the emperor had no clothes?

He revealed the Griffith Park location, since the Generation Airites packed up and left soon after Nathan's cashiering. It was funny: the police had known about the encampment all along, through Zed. They'd known where to find Ira. He was a little miffed to learn that he was not quite the hunted desperado that he'd imagined he was. Governor Olmstead had fixated on him as a symbol of the failed heli-lift and pressured the cops to go after him, but after a cursory investigation, the police lost interest in him. Olmstead wasn't making much noise these days – about Ira or anything else. The governor was keeping a curiously low profile lately. There were whispers about a health problem. Ira hoped that he hadn't been responsible for causing Olmstead to have a nervous breakdown or anything. He kind of liked the guy.

Ira visited with Matt and Meredith, cooked with Rachel, joked with Ellen, chatted with Larry, answered serious questions from Cooper and spent an intense morning with Oprah for her Super Soul Sunday show, veering between hilarity and something close to tears. She was *so understanding*! Cap Lessing kept hammering Ira's agent to book him on *his* show, but the agent wisely resisted.

The exhausting round of promotional activities paid off. His fifteen minutes of fame stretched to thirty, and his agent got him a 1.2 million dollar advance for his autobiography. Sweet! He would have to start writing it soon, though, so he pressured himself to finish "Her Majesty's Gangsta" as quickly as he could. He wasn't enthused about writing his own story. There was no imaginative rush in it for him, no way to leave his dull grounding in reality and climb into the roller coaster cart of make believe that took him high and dropped him heart-jarringly low as there was when he was working on a screenplay about fictional characters. It was a thrill ride that whipped around corners in his mind and threatened to fly off the tracks completely at times. For 1.2 million, though, he'd nut up and get the other thing written. His agent promised to hire a ghostwriter to help him with it.

He did his best to work out the final few scenes and polish his screenplay in green rooms and on airplanes. The day he finally typed, "FADE OUT" on his keyboard to bring the saga of Muldoon and Stowaring to an end was a day of jubilation! He couldn't wait to hear his agent's reaction. The man would finally see what Ira was *really* about. Getting so much attention and money for being in the wrong place at the wrong time, and maybe doing the wrong thing felt fraudulent. That wouldn't, of course, keep Ira from cashing those checks. He wasn't an idiot. But he felt an increasingly urgent need to finally step into his real life. To assume his real identity. He was a writer. When all this silly hullabaloo over his accidental activism was over, he would still be a writer. Impulsively, he also emailed the screenplay to Sid, just to let Sid see how he'd underestimated Ira. Ira was no desk jockey! He was an Artist. Maybe that bastard Palmer would read it, too. If he even *could* read.

To stop himself from obsessing on how quickly his agent would get to "His Majesty's Gangsta," Ira called Zed and arranged to meet him at a coffee shop, to celebrate with more caffeine than the human nervous system should ever have to tolerate.

"Dude! Awesome. That's great that you're done." Zed raised his cup of Mochamonica and tapped it gently against Ira's Cappuccino Fredo. "I want to read it. I want to see it on the big screen. I want to stream it but still buy it on dvd, just so I can say, dude, I know the guy that wrote this."

Ira savored the moment. He looked around at the other coffee shop customers. They sat in twos, talking quietly, or alone, reading or working on laptops. Not one of them had any idea that the taller of the two men sitting at the table closest to the herbal tea counter was about to have his destiny drastically fulfilled. He wondered how many of these strangers had something to do with the entertainment industry. In L.A., every bagel shop and dentist's waiting room yielded up at least a few people employed in the biz. He fast-forwarded to two years ahead, to when his movie would be in theatres nationwide – no, beyond that – to when it was nominated for a Best Screenplay award. He imagined that the two girls at the table near the window worked in post production. The guy in the t-shirt and jeans? A key grip. A couple he'd heard ordering vegan low-fat banana-nut muffins had that actory look: anorexically chic, both with the kind of bone structure in their faces that was almost too sharply sculptured for real life, but would look good on camera. This was probably the first solid food they'd eaten in days. They'd *all* be pretty impressed, he thought, if this were a year from today and they realized that a Famous Screenwriter was sitting in their midst, just like an ordinary person. As it was, a few people had recognized him when he'd come in – he could tell by the double takes, the slight shifting of expression that registered a sighting. No one bothered him, though. Not here, in a town where The Famous Walked Among Us all the time, like ordinary mortals. He himself had once seen Diane Keaton in a bookstore.

No, Ira's celebrity was greatest in flyover country.

He still had trouble wrapping his head around Zed's double life. "So why stay with Generation Air after the heli-lift?"

"Dude, I had to follow the money. Find out more about what Nathan was up to. The feds got interested, too. Some corporate types are probably going to prison for bribing politicians."

"Like Olmstead?"

"No, dude. They probably didn't try him because he's already rich. Doesn't need bribes." He chuckled. "It's awesome."

"So, let me get this straight. These companies you're talking about: they're the ones that are already building the double deckers, aren't they? People are already driving on them in some places. I mean, what are they gonna do? Make the dishonest companies dismantle the on-ramps to the second levels that they've put in place? Get the cranes back to lift away the big chunks of elevated roads that they've installed, so that they can go over budget by hiring new, not-yet-corrupt companies?"

"No, dude. That ship has sailed. Even if a few guys do some time over it and a few companies pay million dollar fines, it's worth it to them. They made billions."

Ira sighed. It was much too complicated and labyrinthine. He preferred a fictional world, one in which he keep the plot twists manageable. Like Muldoon, he was a simple guy.

But he had to know: "Will Nathan go to prison?"

Zed shrugged. "Don't know. That's not up to me. Did he actually commit a crime, or is he just a hypocritical sleazeball? And if he did do the crime, will he do the time? Or make a deal and throw his corporate pals under the bus. Ya got me, dude. All I know is, my part's done."

"What's next for you?"

Zed grinned, squeezed the tips of his right thumb and forefinger together and drew them across his closed mouth. "Loose lips sink ships, man."

"Well at least tell me this: do you even surf?"

Zed looked wounded. "Dude, I *live* to surf. I surf, like, every chance I get. It's my life. I was real serious with this girl awhile back. Stacey. And we were supposed to go to her sister's wedding. But there was this storm and my buddy called and said, 'Dude, you have to come to Newport Beach *right now*. The waves are awesome.' So, you know, I had to go. And he was right. We had an amazing day. I mean, do I want to put on a shirt and pants and *shoes* and go talk to a bunch of people, or do I want to get in the water and ride some gnarly nine foot waves? You tell me."

"You skipped her sister's wedding?"

"You never know when another storm like that's gonna come along. Of course, Stacey dumped me and ended up dating some guy she met at the wedding. I really miss her sometimes. She was great. But I gotta find a woman who surfs. Or at least, gets it. That's all there is to it."

"Are you really a mosaic artist?"

"Sure. I do that on the side. Dude, the way to make people think you're something you're not is to have just enough reality in the mix so you can sell it."

"The devil mixes the truth with his lies."

Zed looked wounded. "Dude, I'm on the side of good, remember?"

Did you really think Generation Air was some big menace to society?"

Zed shrugged. "Somebody did. Some groups destroy property and endanger lives. Doesn't matter what their cause is.

If they're blowing up multimillion dollar ski lodges, that's not cool. Or, sometimes the group is mainly cool, but a few of its peeps are lunatics. You know, they get all worked up and go off the reservation. If we didn't have a guy on the inside, and Generation Air turned out to be, you know, crazy violent, the public would howl: 'Why didn't the police know about these people?' So, we try to get in front of that. You know. Protect and serve."

"And you do that by spying on people."

Zed looked wounded again. "Ira, you are harshing my mellow. I *infiltrated*, sure, but I also helped out. I mean, dude, I care about the environment. I gotta live here too, you know. I videotaped stuff. Pitched tents. Helped stuff backpacks. Took my turn cooking. Got your ass out of that tree."

Ira smiled. "Yeah you did. Thanks, by the way."

Zed laughed out loud. "I couldn't believe it when you grabbed that hook and just…flew away. Who did you think you were? Peter freakin' Pan? I thought you were gonna fall and break your neck."

"Dude, so did I!"

They both laughed at that. They sipped in silence for a moment.

"Any idea where Oceana went? Or what she's up to these days?"

"What you really want to know is: did she hook back up with Nathan?" Zed shook his head thoughtfully. "No idea. Maybe she forgave him. He's a persuasive guy. Maybe he convinced her that he was just doing it for the cause. She is so gullible. Not the brightest girl, but sweet. I feel kind of sorry for her. She may be with him right now."

"He's not in jail?"

"Nope. I'm not sure he committed any crimes. What he did was just sleazy. Generation Air is – or was – a legitimate not-for-profit. Nathan accepted contributions from the enemy, that's all. The elected officials who took bribes – now that's a different matter."

"Yeah."

"Ira, forget about her. She was never for you. She's like a pretty picture you hang on your wall. You enjoy looking at it, but that's all. She's not even close to being your type."

"Really. And what's my type?"

Zed sipped his Mochamonica and squinted pensively, fingering his puka shell necklace. "What you need is a woman who'll give you shit."

Ira reflected on this, on Kim and Lupe and the many other females who'd managed to resist him. "Don't they all?"

CHAPTER SIXTY-FOUR:
IN GOD'S POCKET

Ira ignored Zed's advice. He did not forget about Oceana. In fact, he thought about her a great deal, although when he summoned up her image and tried to concentrate on that beautiful, sculpted face – and recreate the brief, moonlit kiss they'd had -- the picture kept turning into Oceana jumping ungratefully into Nathan's arms at the heli-lift, leaving Ira to possibly get beaten up on her behalf. He also flashed a lot on Oceana holding a wedding bouquet while standing blissfully next to Nathan, giving not one thought to the feelings of Ira, not even noticing his wounded but also smoldering-with-anger expression as he stood nearby, watching.

Ira kept rewinding and pushing "play" in his memory, again and again, trying to get a more satisfying outcome, but he couldn't make the process work to his satisfaction.

He needed to fish or cut bait. To either get this woman into his life or out of his mind forever, because as it stood now she was like an earwig. That episode of "The Twilight Zone" had scared the crap out of him. For weeks after he saw it on a cable station in the middle of a sleepless night, he'd slept with folded up washcloths pressed against his ears, taped uncomfortably to his head. In that episode the earwig crawled into a man's ear and chomped painfully and slowly through his brain. He screamed in agony ... but miraculously survived! Then came the bad news from the doctor: the earwig was a female, and she'd laid eggs in his brain!

It didn't matter that later, Ira had taken the trouble to look up "earwigs" and discovered that not only could they not chomp their way through human heads, they were vegetarians, not brain eaters. The allegory still worked, though. Oceana -- the *fantasy* of Oceana -- was burrowing into Ira's brain just like an earwig, causing him considerable pain. He needed to get her out of there, preferably by making her materialize as a real-life girlfriend who would replace the image.

The opportunity to do that came when he was invited to

visit the set of "Sky Soldiers," the movie that was being made about his life. Had she changed her cell phone number since the last time he'd seen her (the wedding that didn't happen)?

She answered on the third ring. "Ira! It's so good to hear from you."

That was a promising start. "How've you been, Oceana?" Such an inadequate question. What he really wanted to ask was, *"What happened after you ran away from your would-be wedding ceremony? Did Nathan convince you to get back together with him? If not, do you have a new boyfriend already? Where are you living now? What are you doing with your days? Do you still look hot?"*

Instead, he said: "I was worried about you. After...what happened."

"Oh, you're so sweet to think about me. That's so like you, Ira. I was upset for a little while, but now I'm just fine."

Are you with Nathan? Still? Again? But he couldn't bring himself to say the words out loud.

"I'm keeping busy," she said, vaguely. "And you are too, I see. Quite the celebrity, aren't you?"

He seized the opening. "Yes, it's pretty silly, but what can you do? The powers that be decided that there should be a movie about me, and a book, and so I went along with the program. Resistance is futile, and all that. But that's kind of why I'm calling." Ira gulped, hoping that she couldn't hear the sharp intake of air or if she did, that she wouldn't interpret it as nervousness on his part. This was ridiculous. Why was he still so anxious around this woman? He stumbled on. "I'm going to the set of 'Sky Soldiers' tomorrow. Have you heard about it? The movie they're making about our little adventure?"

"Oh, sure," she said. "There's quite a buzz about it."

"They're shooting the heli-lift scenes now, before traffic gets moving again at the 405 and 101. Anyway, it occurred to me that you might want to go with me. You could meet Cody Torrance, and Wendy Nash – she's playing you, you know."

There was a brief silence on her end. A brief, *strained* silence? He'd probably overplayed his hand. Oceana had grown up around famous people. Meeting a couple more wouldn't be any big deal for her. Also, he'd made it sound like a date. He *wanted* it to be like a date, but he'd have to finesse her into it.

"I'd just like to get your take on it, you know, since you were there, and all," he said, a little too quickly, jumbling some of his words together. Could she tell he was bullshitting? "I know the movie won't be entirely accurate. I mean, they never are, are they? But…we were trying to do something important. Something big. It may not have worked out exactly as we planned, but we still had our moment in history. And Oceana, you were much more important in Generation Air than I was. I'm surprised that you don't resent me, for all this attention that I'm getting."

"You were magnificent that day, Ira," she said, quietly insistent. "You inspired all of us."

Her sincerity threw him momentarily off balance. "Well, I'd like to…hear your reaction. To the movie. In case I get to have any input." He paused, wondering how to close the deal. "I'm not sure that I will," he concluded lamely.

"How will we get there?"

She was considering it! Or was she just looking for a way out? It was still impossible to get around most of L.A. in a car.

"I've got a motorcycle now," he said. "Even took a course in how to ride it. You'll be as safe as if you were in God's pocket." *Jesus, Ira. Could you sound like more of a nerd?* Why on earth one of *his father's* favorite expressions had slipped out of his mouth at this moment was a question he couldn't answer.

Nerdiness apparently had its appeal.

Oceana laughed. "Well, when you put it like that… Sure, Ira. Why not?"

CHAPTER SIXTY-FIVE:
WHAT A MISMATCH THAT WOULD BE

Cody loved this part. He'd watched very carefully as the stunt coordinator had demonstrated the moves and he knew he was executing them perfectly. He was happy to leave the truly difficult maneuvers – like falling out of the pickup, or being airlifted by a helicopter – to the professionals, but when it came to a fake martial arts battle, he was in his element. He was not an actual black belt or anything, but thanks to the intensive work he'd done with a trainer once he'd signed on to this movie, he felt terrifically limber. He grabbed his opponent's arm and, turning, bent over. The man flung himself over Cody's shoulder and made it look like Cody flipped him and slammed him into the ground. He jumped to his feet quickly, though, and the two traded blows and elaborate high kicks for several intense minutes.

What really sold a fight scene, Cody knew, was good acting: the expressions and reactions. Plus the sound effects that were added later. He made sure that Ira – *his* Ira – looked genuinely apprehensive when the other actor's fist was sailing toward his jaw (even though he knew it would only *appear* to hit him), and he transformed his face into a kinetic mask of triumphant fury when he appeared to be delivering the series of furious punches and kicks that would, finally, end the fight and leave his opponent semi-unconscious. Of course, it was actually a stunt man who would fall off the truck, executing a spectacular mid-air flip (because "Ira" hit him so hard), landing on thick pads on the pavement below.

Cody relished the challenge of playing a character who *really cared* about an important issue. He'd never before mined the ideological part of himself for a role. It was invigorating, getting in touch with his previously inert idealism. When he was done shooting this movie, he was going to find a meaningful way to help out the environmental movement. Or some other movement. He'd ask his manager what would be the best fit for him. He didn't want a disease, though. Those public service announcements were always such downers, even though they were well-intended. Maybe an endangered species?

The take ended. Cody accepted a bottle of water from an assistant. He saw someone talking with the director and realized that it was Ira O'Riley in the flesh. He'd only met him once in person – during contract negotiations. A nice enough fellow, although sort of nervous, which made Cody nervous. He supposed he should go over and say hello to Ira, since he was, after all, *playing him.* Cody noticed the girl standing next to Ira: a long-legged, short-haired blonde. Even from here Cody could see that she was quite beautiful. There was a dreamy quality to her. Her figure was graceful, proportional, which probably meant that her breasts were real. Real breasts! He was intrigued. Who was she? Obviously not O'Riley's girlfriend. What a mismatch that would be. He decided to walk over and speak with Ira. Find out who that girl was.

After all, he'd been a little bit lonely lately. And things almost always worked out for him.

CHAPTER SIXTY-SIX: WOMAN SECURITY

Vilma was hollering again, something about his leaving his dirty clothes on the bedroom floor. She yelled almost as much as Bernice, but a lot of it was in Spanish – or at least, in a real thick accent – so she didn't sound as sharp-tongued as Bernice had.

"I clean for other people all day!" she complained, at full volume. "Every day I clean! Then I come home and clean? If I gonna clean up after you, you gonna pay me!" She was beautiful when she was angry, he thought, even when she was a little sweaty from work and had her thick black hair tied back in a pony tail, like it was now.

"Lo siento," Lester said. "Mira. Look." He picked up his dirty boxer shorts and took them into the bathroom, making a big show of dropping them cooperatively in the hamper she stood next to, her arms crossed angrily in front of her.

"Y los otros, tambien," she insisted.

"What others?" Lester knew what she was talking about, but he enjoyed baiting her. She enjoyed it too, he thought.

"What others? What others, you ask me?" Vilma marched into the bedroom, pointing at objects on the floor. "Your sock. And...your sock. And shirt." She turned on him. "You see my socks on that floor? My shirt? No! If I gonna be your maid, you gonna pay me a hundred dollars a day. No! Two hundred dollars a day. As it is, I'm your cook and you don't pay me for that."

That reminded him: he was hoping she'd make wet burritos tonight. She usually did, on Thursday nights. But maybe she was really mad this time. For a short woman, Lester thought, she sure could be bossy. He could handle it. If he couldn't, he wouldn't have told her that they should get married, as soon as his divorce from Bernice was final. Vilma didn't say yes, but she didn't say no, either. This woman had him by the short hairs and she knew it.

"This gonna change or I leave you," she said, with not even a hint of a smile.

That got him moving. Lester scurried around the small bedroom, collecting soiled articles of clothing and even pulling

on the bedspread a little to straighten it. Since Vilma got up
before him every morning he was the one who was supposed to
make the bed, but he rarely did. He jammed the dirty clothing
into the hamper.

He met Vilma soon after getting out of jail, through one of
his buddies from the box city. They hit it off right away, and she
didn't even mind that he'd been in a little trouble. Not as much
as he could have been, considering he'd hit a cop. His lawyer
managed to make a good argument that he'd struck out blindly,
in the heat of the moment, not even realizing he was assaulting
and battering a cop. Lester never told her that he'd been *hired* to
be there that day, busting heads. He just told her he was
watching the heli-lift and got upset about what those
demonstrators were doing. He couldn't have given them the
name of the guy who hired him to cause trouble, anyway, or
where to find him so what would have been the point of bringing
it up?

Besides, he no longer did those kinds of jobs. He didn't
have to. He was working steadily on one of the many double-
decker freeway projects underway in the Southland. Some were
already finished. Traffic was starting to roll again, at least in a
few places. People were moving out of boxes and cars and into
real apartments and homes, but just a few so far: that's why he
and Vilma got this apartment real cheap. He felt pretty good
about signing a lease. Lester knew his foreman thought he was a
hard worker – because he was. Lester was sure that when the
segment he was working on was done, he'd get work on a new
part of the massive project. For the first time in a long time, he
felt as if he had some job security.

And woman security. He hoped so, anyway. He was crazy
about Vilma, bad temper and all. He kind of liked it when her
dark eyes flashed in anger. She was a firecracker, that mujer!

"Tell you what, baby, I'll do the laundry tomorrow. In fact,
I'm gonna do the laundry all the time. That'll by my job from
now on."

She stared at him, deeply suspicious. "You mean it?"

"Yeah." He pulled her toward him, putting his arms
tentatively around her, trying to judge whether she was ready to
make up.

Her body stayed rigid, but the beginnings of a smile tugged at the corners of her mouth. "You gonna stick to your word this time?"

"Si, claro," he assured her. "Of course. I know you work hard. I don't mean to make you work when you get home. I just…have some bad habits. I can change them. Don't be mad anymore, baby. I hate it when you're mad at me. C'mon. Te amo, baby. Te amo mucho."

She softened and let him kiss her. It was gonna be a good night.

CHAPTER SIXTY-SEVEN:
NO ONE WILL EXPECT HIM TO GET THE BALL

Ira had been riding for a terrible fall and he never even saw it coming.

"It's just...not good enough, Ira."

"I'll tweak it some more. Do some rewrites."

"You don't want to spend your time on that. You're supposed to be working on your biography, remember? That deadline is going to hit you like a freight train if you don't watch out."

"I can do both." Yes, he could. He had plenty of free time, especially since he wasn't going to be going out with Oceana. She was too busy dating Cody Torrance, according to the tabloids. The fact that Ira had been the one who introduced the two of them still left a bitter taste in his mouth. He was trying hard to be glad that the Oceana Question was finally resolved: she would never, ever, *ever* find him attractive.

The pause that followed was so long that Ira wondered if his cell phone signal had cut out.

"Hello?"

"Ira, you got enough money from other things. Maybe you're just not cut out to be a screenwriter. Listen, how many tickets you want for the premiere of "Sky Soldiers"? Cody Torrance said on Access Hollywood that it's going to be a big, big movie, Ira. Boy, the folks back home in Minnesota will be impressed when they see Cody Torrance playing their boy Ira, won't they?"

"Michigan."

"Michigan, Minnesota, whatever. They'll be impressed all over the country."

His agent Max, like every third person in Los Angeles, was originally from New York. He was still talking, in what Ira had come to realize was a grating and irritating accent.

"So forget about 'His Majesty's Gangster,' Ira. I showed it to a few people and they think the time just isn't right for this kind of project."

Ira snorted. "So which is it, Max? It's not good enough or the timing is wrong? I thought you were going to package it with "Sky Soldiers" – give the studio permission to do a movie about me if they greenlighted my screenplay, found a director for it. I wasn't expecting a huge budget or anything," he sniffed.

"The studio wouldn't have gone for it, Ira. You're not known. There's too much money at stake. And I'm doing you a favor by not even bringing it up to them. Even if they agree to the project, they'd just hire a more experienced screenwriter to rewrite it, and that'd hurt your feelings."

"But if they could just read the screenplay they'd see—"

"Ira, I hate to be so blunt, but I'm your agent and I got to be honest with you. 'Her Majesty's Gangster'—"

"Gangsta."

"Gang*sta* is crap. It's predictable. Formulaic. The characters just don't...come alive. Believe me, I've read hundreds of screenplays, and I know what sells. Yours won't sell, not even with rewrites. The best thing for you to do is to put it in a drawer and work on your autobiography. Consider it a learning experience. Maybe you could write another one down the line." He didn't sound particularly encouraging.

Ira hadn't played any organized sports when he was growing up. The asthma made that impossible. He vividly remembered, though, one golden autumn afternoon when the kids in the neighborhood were playing football in an empty field. "C'mon, Ira! You can play. C'mon." His friend Bennie urged him to join in. He did, feeling pretty excited, hoping that his mother wouldn't find out.

The quarterback, a loudmouth kid he knew as Woody, decided to use Ira to his advantage.

"No one'll expect *him* to get the ball," Woody said, jerking his thumb in Ira's direction. Then, to Ira: "Can you catch?"

Ira stuttered. "Uh, not really."

Woody decided to fade back and make it look like he was going to throw the ball to one of several guys who went long, but then hand it off to Ira, who would run like hell while everybody was looking the other way.

It almost worked. Ira did manage to stumble a few yards in the right direction, but not everybody was looking the other way.

He got tackled by a fat kid named Ralph. Ira hit the ground hard with Ralph on top of him and several others piling on top of Ralph. He felt the air leave his lungs all at once, in a sickening whoosh. That panicky sensation of not being able to breathe at all, all at once, was worse than any asthma attack he'd ever had.

That sensation was similar to what he was feeling at that moment.

CHAPTER SIXTY-EIGHT:
A NEW RIDE AT DISNEYLAND

Thank God for Sara Palin. She'd courageously blazed a trail for him. Resigning as governor before his term was up would not be nearly as newsworthy as it would have been if she hadn't done it first.

Jorge Olmstead looked over the notes he'd made on the statement his speechwriters had prepared for him, not entirely satisfied with the tone. His last appearance as a public official should represent a carefully crafted exit strategy. He was certainly *not* laying the groundwork for any future forays into politics. He'd had enough of that arena of insanity, where he'd felt at all times like a Christian being fed to hungry lions. No, no. He was glad he'd tried it, glad that he had a little place in history, as governor – for part of a term – of the most populous, arguably most powerful state in the Union. He was so over it now. The citizens of California did not appreciate him and the citizens of California could kiss his ass.

He did need to leave the door open for whatever he decided to do in the private sector. He did need to present a dignified, rational explanation for why he was stepping down, making a note to do better with that than Palin had, in her incoherent parting remarks. Should he refer to the fact that he'd been away for awhile? His advisors were in disagreement over that, as well as over whether or not he should disclose the fact that it was due to a relapse. Olmstead was inclined to be open. It had always worked in the past, but would the public forgive him yet again?

Had he been to that well one too many times?

Why should he give a damn what the public thought? Anger flared in his chest and up his throat like acid reflux. Traffic was starting to move again, but was he getting any credit for it? Of course not. He and the legislature ended up going with the double decker idea, for freeways and even some secondary streets. They really had little choice; the situation was desperate. Planning how the upper levels of the freeways would be joined to the existing roadways was a logistical quicksand pit, but several top engineering firms were keeping their top engineering minds busy figuring out how to climb out of it. Olmstead had tried to emphasize the upside of the project: not only would L.A.'s traffic flow be better and faster than it was before, lots of workers were needed for the project. And it wasn't like motorists were being inconvenienced by roadwork, because traffic wasn't moving anyway. He should have been hailed as a visionary. Already, representatives from other metropolitan areas were asking for information on the project. As usual, California would lead the way.

Naturally, some locals screamed about how unsightly the retooled freeways would look. Olmstead responded by directing the engineering firms to hire theme park designers as consultants on the project, so that southern California roadways would resemble a new ride at Disneyland. That didn't satisfy the negativos, though. They complained that the upper levels rising skyward were spoiling the view, blocking the mountains. Then there were the inevitable earthquake alarmists, predicting disaster, even though the new roadways would be built to earthquake-resistant code. And of course, some whiners had to point out that those pesky air quality problems would return. There was just no pleasing people. Years from now, when traffic was running smoothly on the double decker freeways and everyone was used to them, he'd be appreciated. He'd go down in history as the man – the *visionary* who'd solved California's traffic crisis and made it possible for even more people to move to the state.

He was enjoying rehab. It was quiet. Serene. No one here bothered him for decisions, or expected him to go to meetings, show up at important events and answer questions from reporters. This luxurious oceanside retreat was like a safe, pleasant cocoon. The other *guests* were high-profile types, too, which enhanced his comfort level. He wished he could stay here forever. Sometimes he felt a little lonely, especially at night, but soon he'd be allowed visitors. Misty could come and see him.

He had to finish his edits and get the speech to the front desk. A messenger would pick it up in a few hours and take it back to his staff, where it would be reworked and refined. He was happy that his final act as a public official would take place soon. He was more than ready to move on.

Chapter Sixty-Nine:
Has Been Island

He never knew he could have this much money yet be so miserable.

His dream was like a sweet-smelling summer campfire that burned steadily as long as it was fed more pine logs, flaring brightly and even beautifully at times, spitting sparks and crackling, giving pleasure and comfort and hope in the night, until it was suddenly, tragically extinguished by an unexpected storm. His dream was a heap of soggy, half-charred logs lying in a sand pit. He couldn't get it lit again, no matter how hard he tried.

Ira held up his empty beer bottle, catching the eye of his server. Why not? He loved this restaurant, appreciated the way the manager looked out for him. On his first visit post heli-lift, Ira was bothered by autograph-seeking fans who migrated over from another table in his section while he was trying to enjoy his salad. Since then, the manager and staff kept a watchful eye on him and diplomatically steered the groupies away.

They *should* take care of him: he spent lots of money here and tipped well. It was no problem for him to do so now, since the Benjamins kept rolling in. Ira discovered a secret: money attracted money. He'd been paid ridiculous sums for authorizing the screenplay about himself and for writing his autobiography (which was, in fact, being written by a ghostwriter who periodically did interviews with Ira, then went away and made up wildly exaggerated versions of the accounts Ira gave him). Those ridiculous sums, in turn, attracted other ridiculous sums, for equally ridiculous things. He got endorsement deals and spokesperson offers. People paid him to show up at events, make a few remarks and sign some autographs. His picture was used on company web sites. He was hired to do a TV commercial for a manufacturer of elaborate backyard jungle gyms. The script called for him to say: "You can be an environmental hero like me" while standing atop a combination geodesic dome, swing set and slide that was made to look like a pirate ship. After delivering his line, he had to slide down the tunnel-enclosed slide. When he emerged at the bottom, he was required to say: "The Archdale Company brings the fun right to your backyard. And because everything we make is from recycled materials, you're helping your kids have a better future."

His server put a fresh beer in front of him. Ira drank it, cringing at the memory of the inane dialogue he'd had to repeat, in take after take, until the director was satisfied. An environmental hero! He'd stopped protesting that he was not the guy everyone thought he was because no one listened. Or cared. He was the guy everyone *wanted* to think he was, which produced in him a feeling of detachment from himself, as if he were astrally projecting (an experience promised by any number of spirit channeling-and-aura reading types who'd hung out their shingles in the Southland), looking down at himself and what he was doing and feeling very little emotional connectedness to it.

That was probably a good thing since in his new incarnation as a set of powerful symbols, he had as many detractors as admirers. Environmentalists had been the first to claim him as one of their own. That caused an equal and opposite reaction among their counterparts: the climate change deniers, who quickly printed up thousands of bumper stickers decorated with a bull's eye imprinted over Ira's face, next to the slogan: "Be on the lookout for HOMEGROWN terrorists, too." The women who paid for French cut t-shirts that read: "I ♥ Ira O'Riley" and joined fan clubs devoted to him and read advertisement-filled blogs that were purportedly written by him (but were not, in fact) didn't care about his alleged environmentalism or terrorism. They thought he was hot. So did the celebrity fitness guru who released a new DVD based on "the workout that keeps Ira O'Riley in fighting form." An airline used the video clip of him clinging to the hook, flying perilously away from the heli-lift, in an ad that became hugely popular. "That great deal on airfare might not be such a great deal after all," went the voiceover, as the camera zoomed in on Ira's terrified face. His close-up was replaced by a shot of a luxurious-looking airplane interior. "Fly in comfort with Rodan Airlines." Politicians mentioned him in speeches. Late night talk show hosts used him in their monologues. A chain of bicycle stores advertised the "Ira Special" – the same brand of bike used by Ira when he had his bike-shaw service. Battered women advocacy groups invited him to appear at fundraisers, to discuss his abhorrence of violence against women, and recount the thrilling tale of how he'd taken on that much larger man who'd obviously been clearly threatening the tall blonde woman. Ira *did* abhor violence against women, but he declined to be a designated hero.

He did, however, say yes to any number of commercial propositions, reasoning that, since so many people were profiting from his persona, he should do the same. He tried to make that ease the ongoing sting of being overlooked for the one thing he *wanted* to be known for. Of all the identities being superimposed on him by people he didn't even know, none was that of "writer." Not one of the pundits, experts, bloggers, comedians, tabloid reporters, TV anchors, radio talk show hosts, not-for-profits, strictly-for-profits, city council members or state legislators who invoked his name in this context or that, to make a point or a punch line, bothered to mention the fact that he was a screenwriter.

Well maybe he wasn't. If no one would agree to produce "Her Majesty's Gangsta," could he really call himself a screenwriter? If a tree fell in a forest and no one is around to hear it…?

He tried not to think about that. Instead, he focused on the incredible amount of money that was coming his way. It was intoxicating to him at first. Once the buzz wore off, however, the inevitable hangover set in.

The money freed him in a way that was so alien to the Midwestern work ethic burned into his core that he couldn't grok it, much less enjoy it. For the first time since he was 16 – when he'd put on a paper hat and gone to work dropping wire baskets of French fries into vats of superheated oil – he didn't have to get up every day and go to work at some job that had nothing to do with who he was. He was no longer a wage slave. He didn't have to set an alarm, wear clothes he didn't particularly want to wear, punch a clock, do boring menial tasks or put up with co-workers he didn't particularly like. He did not have to take shit from an overbearing boss like Sid, and as long as he didn't go crazy and spend his newfound wealth like some of those trailer park lottery winners who burned through their millions and had to go back to their chicken plucking jobs in about six months, he'd never have to take shit from an overbearing boss again.

His going broke wasn't likely, and not because he was a financial guru (although he did hire an advisor). No, he wasn't going to run through his money because he wasn't spending it. Not very much of it. Now that he had money, felt security for the first time, knew it was there and could be counted on if he *did* want to buy something, he felt no burning need to buy anything. He was rich. Maybe not by Southern California standards, but definitely by Michigan standards. But it was almost as if having so much money neutralized it, emotionally, as an object of desire and passion.

WTF. *Nothing in life worked out the way you thought it was going to, apparently.*

"Why is this man even famous?" Cap Lessing had raged about him on a recent show. "Why do we keep hearing the name, Ira O'Riley? Enough, already. He's had MORE than his fifteen minutes of fame." Ira thought the abrasive talk show host was probably right.

He dabbed at his nose with a Kleenex. Now that traffic was moving, at least in some places, the air was, once again, becoming unbreatheable. Soon, he would start to wheeze. He could tell that day was coming, could feel his lungs working just a little bit harder than they'd had to during his halcyon bike-shaw riding days. He should get the hell out of Dodge. Take his money and move to greener pastures – or at least, cleaner air. The entertainment industry obviously didn't appreciate his talent. His mother kept hinting that he should move back to Michigan. Maybe he should. He'd certainly, finally, get some respect from his friends and relations, since he was such a celebrity.

For all the wrong reasons.

One of the first things he'd done with his money was to buy his parents a flat screen TV as big as a Santa Monica Boulevard billboard. He had it delivered and installed as a surprise. They were excited about it ("Ira, the neighbors saw the delivery truck and they've all been over to see it. It's the biggest TV in the subdivision!"), but also, he could tell, uncomfortable with it. By giving them a gift that large, Ira had reversed a basic law of nature as they understood it. Parents gave to their children. Children did not give to their parents. His Mom and Dad had no idea how to accept something that expensive from their son.

Ira was pretty sure his Dad would still use it to watch the Lions lose every Sunday during football season, though.

INT. RESTAURANT – DAY

IRA O'RILEY looks up at LUANNE SAJEWSKI, who is standing next to his table. She's attractive in a girl-next-door way, with a broad, genuine smile and easy-going manner.

> LUANNE
> *Excuse me. I hope you don't*
> *mind. I'm Luanne Sajewski.*
> *(pause; awkwardly)*
> *Your agent told me you hang*
> *out here a lot, and so I've been*
> *dropping in, hoping to meet you.*

Ira stares at her, perplexed.

> IRA
> *My agent is telling people where*
> *to find me?*

> YOUNG WOMAN
> *Well, my agent called him for*
> *me. As a favor.*
> *(awkwardly)*
> *Oh, you do mind?*

> IRA
> *I just…don't understand.*

> LUANNE
> *Well, I wanted to talk to you.*

*We've...actually met before. I
don't know if you remember.*

IRA
*(being charming)
I never forget a good tipper! Do
you want to...sit down!*

She sits at his table.

LUANNE
*I'm not a stalker. I just had to
tell You how much I love "Her
Majesty's Gangsta." It's
amazing. My agent, Sid, had it
sitting on his desk and I asked if
I could read it. Ira, I am
desperate to play Sabrina. She
is such a terrific character. I
mean, you really know women,
don't you? I just love her. Ira, I
get her.*

IRA
But I don't—

LUANNE
*You'll have some input into
casting. You could talk to the
director.
    (talking fast)
And I know I haven't done any
feature films yet, but I am more
than ready. I have an extensive
background in theatre, Ira. I
can do a lot more than just
sitcoms. And...I'm willing to
read for the part.*

382

Wait a minute. Wait a minute. Ira felt an uncomfortable jolt, as his brain tried to sort out reality from fantasy. This wasn't one of the scenes that wrote themselves more or less continuously in his head. This was really happening.

Luanne Sajewski, famous actor, was begging him, Ira O'Riley, for a part in his screenplay. Luanne Sajewski loved "Her Majesty's Gangsta." Luanne Sajewski was treating Ira as if he were a powerful Hollywood Player. He stared at her, transfixed and troubled. She looked even better than she had the day of the heli-lift, when she wore that red dress. She was wearing jeans and a simple top today, but the fit was very flattering. Had she lost weight? Or was it just that she inhabited her body with such confidence? And what a smile she had. It felt like a spotlight shining over him.

"Um, Ms. Sajewski, could we have your autograph, please? We love your show. We never miss it." The middle-aged woman who'd interrupted them looked to her stocky husband for agreement.

"You just crack me up," the man said. "When you do that thing? You know? That thing you do when your nephew comes in the door? How did you ever think of that?"

"Oh, it just popped into my head one day, so I tried it," Luanne said warmly. She looked over at Ira with a "just wait a minute" expression, while signing the pieces of paper the couple put in front of her. "The director liked it, so it stayed in the show."

"Well you are a riot," the man said. "A real riot. Can we take a picture? If we don't, nobody will believe we met you." He handed a digital camera to Ira. "Would you mind?"

Ira snapped off a photo of Luanne with her two fans bookending her, then handed it back, impatient to get on with their conversation. He was relieved when he saw the restaurant manager smoothly usher the man and woman back to their table.

"Sorry about that," Luanne said to Ira. "Could I get a margarita, please?" she called to the retreating back of the manager.

A famous star was apologizing to him, Ira O'Riley. He grinned at the irony.

"So, anyway," she said, pulling a DVD from her purse. "I brought you my demo tape. It's got clips from some of my stage roles. It'll give you a better idea of my range."

Ira didn't take the DVD. "Luanne, 'Her Majesty's Gangsta' isn't going to get made. I'm really flattered that you're interested, but…you're wasting your time."

"What?"

"It's been turned down. By everybody. I'm told it sucks."

"No it doesn't."

"My agent won't even shop it around anymore."

"So get another agent."

"I tried. No takers. Not for screenwriting, anyway. There are plenty of agents who want to represent Ira O'Riley, Incorporated. Environmental folk hero."

Luanne slumped in her chair, looking deflated. "I don't believe that. It's too good."

"What did Sid think about it? He must not have liked it. If he had, I'd have heard from him."

She grimaced. "Uh…Sid…didn't read it. I just saw it sitting there, in a pile of scripts on his desk. That shouldn't bother you. You used to work for him, didn't you? You know he doesn't read most of those screenplays."

Oh, yes. Ira remembered the pile of scripts on Sid's desk, gathering dust. He'd foolishly thought that "Her Majesty's Gangsta" would be different.

"Don't worry about Sid. He's good for making deals, but I don't know if he'd even recognize a good screenplay if it jumped up and bit him in the ass."

"Why did he even bother printing it up?"

"Oh, I think Palmer did that. Because it was from you, he thought that Sid might—" She couldn't figure out how to finish the sentence.

"Did Palmer read it?"

Luanne nodded at the server who set her drink down in front of her. "I don't think so. Who cares? He was probably too busy touching up his roots." She grinned at him. "Or practicing his British accent."

Ira snorted. "Isn't that the phoniest thing you've ever heard?"

384

"I think he's probably from someplace like Youngstown, Ohio or Butte, Montana. What a poser. You run into a lot of that here, don't you?"

He was surprised at how relaxed he felt around her. That was good, because he had to dab at his nose again with a tissue. It was not exactly a suave gesture.

"Seasonal allergies?" she asked sympathetically.

"Asthma. It was OK for awhile, but now that traffic is improving…"

"Oh, that sucks."

"I've been thinking about moving to Malibu," he said, surprising himself. In the back of his mind, he *must* have been thinking about it. It made sense. He'd be able to breathe in Malibu. And, unlike during his peon assistant days, he could now afford to live there.

"I'm renting a beach house there," she said. "Production of 'Aunt Mom' is going to move back here soon, from Las Vegas. So, let's talk some more about 'Her Majesty's Gangsta.' I love that title, BTW."

"You're relentless, aren't you?"

"Yep."

"Luanne, I told you. It's dead in the water. I wish it wasn't, but it's a non-starter."

She flung her arms out and moved her head from side to side – an exaggerated comic gesture he'd seen her do on her show. "Oh, so that's it. You're just going to give up. What happened to the guy standing on top of a car, challenging a dangerous thug twice his size?"

"That wasn't even…me. I don't know who the hell it was." He stopped himself. "Look, I've tried and tried to get someone interested in it. Maybe we're both wrong and it really does suck."

"Well now there'll be two of us trying. I must have some clout." She smirked. "I'm pretty famous, you know. At least for the moment."

"Yeah. I'm happy for you. The thing about 'Her Majesty's Gangsta' is: I'm over it. I'm done being rejected. That screenplay has been retired to the bottom drawer of my file cabinet. I'm not going to shop it around anymore. I just don't have it in me."

"You can't give up now, Ira!" Luanne's raised voice drew some curious stares. "Think of it like, like it's your baby. You gave birth to it. That couldn't have been easy. I'm sure it was a long, difficult, painful delivery."

"You got that right."

"So you squeeze it out, and then you just walk away from it? Abandon it? If that was a real baby, you'd be under arrest right now. I'd be calling the authorities on you."

He felt under attack. "Why are you giving me shit?"

"Because I want that role, Ira. I'm not kidding. And I am relentless. Sabrina is a—"

Their table suddenly rocked. The floor lurched. Light fixtures hanging from the ceiling swung back and forth drunkenly on their chains. From outside came the shrill warnings of car alarms.

Luanne's face went pale. She rose unsteadily, her hands splayed on the table for support, although it, too, was still moving. "Oh my God," she muttered. "What? Are we...? What do we...?"

Ira was surprised to see her so transformed, and so quickly. She went from brash to frightened in an instant. He stood quickly, instinctively, and embraced her. He could feel her trembling.

"It's OK," he told her. "It's not even a big one. See? It's already over."

"An earthquake?" She stared at him. "Dear God. A real earthquake?"

He nodded.

"I...I...I've been through my first earthquake." She tried to smile, but couldn't manage it.

Ira understood. When you've spent years living in a geologically tame part of the country, feeling the earth move under your feet was a profoundly disturbing experience. It was a confirmation of what you'd always suspected, in some carefully suppressed layer of your brain that held the scariest truths: that the bottom could drop out of your life at any second. Existence could end in a heartbeat. Nothing could be counted on – not even the ground you walked on. This, of course, was true everywhere, but in earthquake country, you were forced to confront the truth with every shake, rattle and roll. An earthquake rocked more than the landscape: it shook your very psyche, reducing it to the consistency of jello left out of the fridge for several hours, so that it could no longer comfort you when you were troubled by the Big Questions.

Minor earthquakes were actually worse than big ones, because they prompted you to imagine what *might* have happened.

Luanne moved her shoulders slightly, indicating that it was time for him to release her.

Ira let go of her and stepped back, feeling suddenly awkward. He'd been holding her as if they were lovers when they barely knew each other. He saw her looking around, trying to reassemble her reality. Ira thought: *she doesn't realize that it's gone for good.*

"My first earthquake," she said, but the tremulous smile she summoned up was not authentic. It was a brave version of that famous TV grin of hers. "Wait'll my friends in Altoona hear about this."

The other people in the room were settling back into their restaurant experience, recounting the earthquake, trying out the details of the stories they would tell about it. A few were still processing their surprise. It was easy to tell the longtime residents from newcomers and visitors.

"Why don't you sit back down, Luanne. You O.K. now?"

"Yeah, sure." She sat, but she still looked dazed. "I don't know why an earthquake should bother me. I mean, this is L.A. I should have been expecting one." She picked up her glass and tried to drink from it, but her hand trembled violently.

Ira reached over and put his hand around hers, bringing the glass safely back down to the tabletop. She didn't seem to notice.

"It just felt so...strange. As if my whole life...*changed* somehow. In an instant. Like when the earth shifted, my life did, too. And I wasn't ready for it. You know?" She finally collected herself and focused her gaze on him. "God, I must sound crazy."

"No. Not at all. It's unsettling."

She nodded, but her expression looked unconvinced. "You're just being nice. You must think I'm pretty silly."

"Luanne, I'm not that nice. Not anymore. I was pretty freaked out, my first tremor. You live here long enough, you get used to them."

"Really?" She sighed, deeply. "I don't think I ever will." She held her hand in midair, parallel to the table, as if she were trying to levitate it. "Look. I'm still shaking. Silly. I'm not usually one of those silly girls. I guess I just…conveniently forgot about the whole earthquake thing. I mean, you hear about them, but I didn't think it would feel that…*strange*." She slumped a little in her chair. "It almost makes you want to get the hell out of California, doesn't it?"

Ira put his hand over hers. Just to comfort her. Somehow, it felt right.

"Nah," he said. "I could never leave this weather."

"So. Back to business. And you know, Ira, if we can't get someone to make "Her Majesty's Gangsta," we could finance it ourselves. I've got money now. You've got money. We could at least afford to make a low-budget version and use it to interest a big studio, so that they'd realize its potential and agree to make it on a grand scale."

He felt dizzy. "That sounds way too risky. Even a low budget movie can cost a lot, especially if we're going to include any of the action scenes--"

"We've *got* to include the action scenes," she said firmly. "Otherwise, they won't see how *magnificent* the story is!"

"Jeez. I don't know."

"C'mon, Ira," she prodded, as if they'd known each other forever. "I know some people in the industry now. I've got connections. We're both smart people. We can figure out how to make this happen."

Ira felt that old excitement returning like a long-lost friend. "You're right. What do we have to lose?"

EXT. TRAILER PARK – DAY

CAMERA FOLLOWS TWO YOUNG BOYS RIDING BICYCLES, WITH A SMALLER BOY RUNNING BEHIND THEM, TRYING TO CATCH UP. THEY PASS-

EXT. TRAILER -- DAY

A wooden sign hanging crookedly on the front of the trailer reads, "Welcome!"

INT. TRAILER -- DAY

Ira sits at a built-in table in the kitchen area, typing on a laptop. The trailer is cramped, its furnishings worn. A copy of "Variety" lies on the table next to his computer.

                    IRA
          No, he didn't say anything more
          about the lawsuit.

He stops typing.

                    IRA
                  (CONT.)
          We're never going to see that
          money again, Luanne.
                  (brightening)
          Oh, I almost forgot. Your agent
          called. You made callbacks for
          "Has Been Island."

                    LUANNE
                  (V.O.)
          Why didn't you tell me right
          away? That is great news.

Luanne comes through a curtain covering a doorway and enters the kitchen. She is heavier than the last time we saw her, with a stomach roll visible underneath her polyester waitress uniform.

                    IRA
                  (frowning)
          Is it really?

LUANNE
Well, that "Aunt Mom" reunion
special looks dead in the water.

IRA
*It was a dumb idea to begin
with. A reunion show for a
sitcom that ran for only a
season and a half?*

Luanne, looking in a mirror, combs her hair.

LUANNE
*"Star Trek" ran for only two
seasons, and look what it turned
into. A franchise.*

IRA
*"Star Trek" didn't have a lead
actor arrested for having a
massive kiddie porn collection.*

LUANNE
*That son of a bitch Peter
Walker. And I thought he was so
nice.*
          (shaking her head)
*He ruined everthing. We can't
even get syndicated.*

Luanne applies lipstick.

IRA
*But do you really want to do
"Has Been Island"?*

LUANNE
*It'd get me back in the public
eye. Maybe get my career jump-
started again.*

She leans over and kisses him.

LUANNE
(CONT.)
*I'm working a double today, so
don't wait on me for dinner.*

*She leaves the trailer, closing the door behind her. Ira watches
her go, then stares off into space for a long moment. Then he
looks back down at his laptop and resumes typing.*

CHAPTER SEVENTY:
KEEPING IT REAL

Luanne closed the document thoughtfully and put the laptop in "sleep" mode, wondering what she was going to say to Ira. She *knew* he'd be waiting for her reaction, and she knew just where he'd be waiting for it, too.

She walked through the great room, which was lit dramatically by the dying rays of the late afternoon sun. It was her favorite room in the house. *Their* favorite room, which was saying something, because it was a magnificent house. But in spite of his success, Ira was still so sensitive about his writing, especially when he'd *just* finished something and it was still fresh. She'd have to word this carefully.

He was in his favorite place; on the balcony overlooking the beach. He never missed a Malibu sunset, not if he could help it. It drew him, dusk after dusk, like a powerful drug. A glass of wine rested on the glass-topped, wrought iron table next to his wicker love seat, forgotten for the moment, while he gazed westward, at the brilliant orange and pink streaks fanning out over the sea like translucent wings.

He came back to earth when she sat down next to him. She could read him so well: he was anxious for her reaction, but determined to play it cool.

"I was thinking we should go to Hyacinth House this weekend," he remarked. "Get away from it all for a few days."

"Yeah, I'm glad we bought the place. Feels good sometimes to be tucked away in the canyon, where no one can find us." She sensed that he was dying to ask, and decided to put him out of his misery. "Babe, I love it. It's brilliant."

The naked need on his face moved her deeply. "Really? You mean it?"

"It's the best writing you've ever done. You've taken it to a whole new level. You really went deep on this one. These characters – what happens to them – it's so *intense*. The twists and turns…there's not a predictable moment in the entire screenplay."

He exhaled, visibly relieved. She was touched that her opinion meant so much to him.

She moved closer to him. His arm went around her obligingly, and he rested his cheek against the top of her head.

"You *are* going to change their names, aren't you?"

"Oh, yeah, of course. That was just... I don't know. Part of the process. Now that the characters have lives of their own, I'll give them names of their own."

She punched him playfully. "And what's this about *Luanne* having a belly roll? What are you trying to say? That I'm fat?"

He pretended to be wounded by the punch. "It's fiction! I was keeping it real. No! I mean, I was keeping the *character* real by making her flawed, when in fact, the *real* Luanne is almost perfect, so I needed to change her. For the sake of the story." He paused. "Have I dug myself out of the hole, yet?"

"Yeah, but keep that shovel handy, mister. You never know." She wished she didn't have to say what she was about to say. Even a small critique at this moment – when he'd just finished a project – was a delicate matter. "There's just one thing," she said tentatively."

"I KNEW it!" he said, stiffening. "I knew there was a big 'but' coming. You *hate* it. You just didn't want to hurt my feelings."

Luanne laughed out loud. She couldn't help herself. "You realize you go through this every time you finish a screenplay, don't you? Do you *enjoy* putting yourself through agony?"

"What is the 'but'?"

He was not to be mollified, she saw. She took a deep breath and spoke slowly, carefully, as if to a child. "I love it. I mean that. And that's really the reason why... It's just that you get to know these people so well. To *care* about what happens to them. That's why that ending *killed* me. Yes, it was beautifully written. The specificity, the nuances of the relationship. But...do you have to end it that way? We've been pulling for that main character throughout the whole story, going through all these struggles with him, and then he finally finds the love of his life and they're both on the verge of realizing their dreams, and you just...squash them like bugs. Leave them with this miserable existence. The ending just ripped my heart out."

"You really do love everything but the ending? You're not bullshitting me?"

"I adore this screenplay. I am not bullshitting you."

Long moments passed before he spoke again. "I'll have to think about it, I guess. If you feel that strongly about it. But you know this is a whole different kind of screenplay for me. If this gets made, it's not going to be a popcorn movie. It's….intimate. A character study. A story that moves people, *resonates* with them." He stroked her hair. "I was serious when I said that I wanted to keep it real. And happy endings just aren't real."

Luanne didn't answer. It was his screenplay, his decision to make.

They sat on the balcony for a long time, content to hold each other close, listening to the waves lapping gently at the shore, watching the spectacular light show peak and then drain from the sky, leaving the sands and waters below bathed in serene darkness.